the
burden
of trust

The Price No One Expected to Pay

Tabitha Young

LADERO FICTION is published by
Ladero Press LLC
229 Kettering Road
Deltona, Florida 32725

First Ladero Press Printing, September 2018

ISBN: 978-1-946981-20-2 Paperback / 978-1-946981-21-9 Epub / 978-1-946981-22-6 Mobi

Printed in the United States of America
Set in Palatino Linotype
Cover Designed by oliviaprodesign

All Ladero Press publications are available at bulk discounts. For details, contact Sales at sales@laderopress.com or write: Ladero Press Sales, 229 Kettering Road, Deltona, Florida 32725.

This is a work of fiction. Names, characters, places, and incidents are either the product of the author's imagination or are used fictitiously, and any resemblance to actual persons, living or dead, business establishments, events, or locales is entirely coincidental.

www.laderopress.com
www.tabithayoung.com
Printed in U.S.A.

Dedication

Throughout the journey there have been many teachers. Some came along and taught only one course, while others continued to develop my skills beyond the semester. To each of those teachers, I'm grateful for the bits of knowledge they have provided, because without each of them I would have never made it to this place.

"Shhh…my darling. It's almost over. We're basically there." The small child continued to cry in agony as the turbulence and pressure tortured her ears. Wrapped in a powder pink soft blanket, one of her favorites, Kate continued to soothingly rock the baby to try to temper the cries. While her heart ached for the baby's tears, she still loved these moments, where her baby was safe in her arms. The stewardess came on the intercom and announced it would be fifteen minutes before arrival. Exhausted, Kate closed her eyes only for a moment, still mindlessly rocking the child when the ding appeared.

Ding.

Ding.

DING!

Her arms were empty. It was the same dream as before. No matter how many times she had it, the result was still the same. She'd wake up full of guilt and anxious about a decision that she couldn't change. If she had the power, she would go back in time and make the right choice; instead, she would suffer every moment afterwards. This particular dream was interrupted by the annoying sound of a monotone pilot announcing their descent into JFK.

The flight landed at one o'clock in the afternoon.

As the 747 taxied down the runway, the palpable pressure increased, causing Kate's stomach to float momentarily until it rumbled to a gradual stop. Anxiously, she fidgeted with a fistful of rattling keys in anticipation of getting off the plane. All she could think about was her "baby," Aika, an overweight, slobbery bullmastiff. Her shiny coat and golden color made touching her fur almost irresistible. Most people were daunted by the idea of approaching her because of her size and breed, but she was the most loyal dog Kate had ever had—well, she was the only dog Kate had ever had. *I have to call the kennel as soon as I'm out of the airport,* she thought, her left leg twitching.

She gathered her belongings and waited her turn to shuffle into the line of passengers stacked up like a deck of cards waiting to deplane. Finally, she reached the exit hatch and stepped down the stairs. A swift, damp breeze hit her face as she reached the bottom step, and a chill shot through her entire body. Sunny with a slight breeze, and 65 degrees was heaven to a New Yorker, but to a Floridian it was winter weather! Quickly, she scrambled to pull a light windbreaker out of her purse and continued to follow the herd of weary travelers toward the terminal doors. The warmth of the terminal greeted her as she headed toward the baggage claim, and the feeling started to return to her cheeks, but her heart wouldn't stop racing. Searching the hordes of bustling people, Kate was anxious to find her childhood friend, Alexa.

From her peak view on the escalator going down to the baggage claim, Kate finally spotted Alexa all the way in the back, standing far away from the motley, chattering mob of people. Unable to contain her excitement, Kate started to yell at her friend, her voice echoing in the large hall. Immediately, both grinning, they began to zigzag carefully toward each other, deftly dodging people and their bulky luggage. Once they were in each other's arms, Kate exhaled her anxiety away.

"Oh my God! You look amazing! New York has been good to you." Kate admired Alexa's retro look as she stepped back, holding Alexa at arm's length with her hands firmly on her shoulders.

Alexa was slim and pale as chalk. Her long hair was bleached blonde with black undertones. A long, loose, navy vest was draped over her baggy cream T-shirt, which had the words "Enfant Terrible" emblazoned across it in red. She wore a dark, frayed denim skirt over black stockings printed with small white skulls. Suddenly, Kate felt ordinary in her six-year-old, worn-out, black converse tennis shoes; plain, dark-green T-shirt, with no logo, that had been picked fresh from the hamper; and long, messy brown hair pulled into a ponytail.

Envious of Kate's effortless, perfect complexion, Alexa smiled, "I love your tan; as you can see, there's not much sun up here." Even though Alexa grew up in Florida, she was always as pale as a marshmallow. Whenever she went into the sun, she would burn as red as a cooked lobster, and then peel back to a creamy alabaster. That was why she fit in so well in New York—that, and her outrageous sense of fashion.

"I'm so excited that you're staying for two whole weeks—this is going to be so much fun!" Alexa said as she grabbed Kate's hand and led the way to the baggage carousel. Trivial chatter filled the forty-five minute wait for the flashing red light and the conveyor belt to finally start lurching into motion. Then the bags popped out of the mouth of the carousel: one, two, and three.

Ten minutes later, Kate spotted her worn purple suitcases, and after she dragged them off the carousel, Kate shouted to Alexa, "That one's mine, too." Alexa's eyes narrowed in confusion but followed instructions as she lifted the too-light suitcase off the carousel. "What is this for?"

"My mother is expecting *several* souvenirs," Kate disgruntledly mumbled.

Alexa gave Kate a meek smile. She knew that at times Kate's mother could be difficult to bear.

As they stepped outside the airport, Kate was taken aback by the turbulent mass of rushing people. Unexpectedly, someone bumped into her from behind, his face buried in his phone, fingers scrambling across the keys; a half-hearted apology mumbled as he peevishly stepped around her. Unfazed, Alexa assertively grabbed Kate by the arm and yanked her and the heavy luggage along to an opening in the crowd that Kate's untrained eyes had missed. Once Alexa reached the curb, she let out a loud whistle, and a taxicab stopped right in front of them. The whistle faded into an annoying ring, which began to rattle Kate's eardrum. In an attempt to get rid of it, she began to rub her ear furiously.

The cab driver, who looked like he was on his third straight shift, sluggishly got out of the driver's seat to load the suitcases into the trunk. Once back in the car, he yelled toward the backseat, "Where to?"

Without missing a beat, Alexa rattled off, "Take I-678 to I-495W to Thirty-fourth and Madison, then left on East Eighty-fifth."

"You got it, lady." The tires squealed, and the taxi sped off into traffic. The musky smell of the cab was bothersome to Kate's sensitive nose. The old, cracked, gray vinyl siding had long ago been masked with duct tape. Kate couldn't understand how Alexa was comfortable with placing her three-hundred-dollar purse on the germ-infested seat with who-knew-what embedded in the cracks.

It wasn't ten minutes before Alexa began to divulge all the unnecessary details of her current love interest. One of many. Alexa had mastered the talent of love'em and leave'em early, which was beneficial since they were all jerks.

"I swear it shouldn't be this difficult to find someone. I live in New York for Pete's sake!" Alexa complained.

"What happened to the last guy?"

"He turned out to be married. Typical, they're either gay or married."

"That does create a problem," Kate slightly smirked.

"What about you? Have you started dating?"

Kate's eyes flickered out towards the busy streets trying to avoid this conversation.

Alexa pressed on, "Kate, it's been…"

"I know how long it's been," softly Kate whispered.

Alexa slumped her elbow on the broken armrest and mumbled, "I guess some things never change."

Making light of the situation, Kate laughed. "Like me having to listen to you whine about boys for hours on end."

Mischievous eyes glared at Kate when Alexa replied, "I guess that's why you always liked…"

The sudden jerk from the cab driver slamming on his brake caused Kate to almost break her nose on the driver's side headrest; Alexa barely budged. Parking in front of Alexa's building, the cab driver yelled from the front seat, "That will be forty-two seventy-seven!"

After Alexa handed him cash, the cabbie almost flung the suitcases onto the sidewalk, then scurried off to find his next customer. Today, especially today, Alexa prayed that the elevator would be working. On Kate's last trip, they had to lug the suitcase up twenty-six flights of stairs, alternating between floors.

A quick call had to be made to the kennel to check on Aika. Just as Kate expected, there were no issues as Aika was beloved by all the techs. The girls then dragged Kate's suitcases up seven brick stairs to the front of the apartment complex. Upon entering the building, Alexa saw the light at the end of the tunnel as the elevator light blinked, then dinged, and a fat, middle-aged Italian-looking man stepped out. Both girls smiled.

The apartment was small and expensive, but that didn't matter; all Alexa cared about was living in Manhattan. The building was old, with cracks in the walls and outdated appliances. No matter, since Alexa didn't cook.

The few days that Alexa had to work, Kate ventured off into the big city for some sightseeing. On Fifth Avenue, the large gold letters of FAO Schwarz made her stomach flip. She knew that she had to go in; she had promised her niece Elizabeth. The thought of being surrounded by all the children and their loving parents tore her heart to pieces. Then, the vision of a disappointed niece appeared and Kate no longer had a choice.

Slowly walking on the outskirts, trying to stay away from the crowd, Kate found a few items that would bring a bright smile to Elizabeth's cheeks. Oh, how Kate imagined Elizabeth's brown curls would bounce in excitement while her blue eyes sparkled when she opened the gift! The sound of a child giggling caught Kate's attention. Unable to pry her eyes from the scene before her, Kate's heart shattered into a million pieces as she watched a loving mother and young daughter pick out a doll together. Tears began to form and more than anything Kate wanted to reach out. She wanted that feeling; it should have been hers, not this emptiness she was left with.

Before leaving, Kate spotted a teddy bear for Elizabeth and checked out with nice a silvered hair woman, who happened to enjoy her job a bit too much. Happily, Kate walked down the streets of New York carrying a large teddy bear under her arm.

Later that evening, Kate finally made her way to the apartment on the 26th floor. Today, the elevator was not working. Huffing and gasping for air, Kate busted through the door and collapsed on the couch.

"Goodness. What's the matter?" Alexa asked, still dressed in her black empire waist skirt for work.

"The…the…the…"

"The?"

"The…elevator…wasn't…working." Wheezing, Kate's chest rose vigorously.

"I know."

"You're not even breaking a sweat."

"It's only 26 flights."

"Only 26 flights," Kate chirped getting water from the fridge. "Says the health nut!"

"Speaking of nuts, are you hungry? I'm starved."

"Me, too! I could go for a big greasy burger after all those stairs."

Alexa knew exactly the place to go. She dragged Kate down the 26 flights of stairs and hailed a cab over to Houseman on Greenwich Street, where they had some of the best burgers in the city. The fresh smell of hot grease welcomed them when they entered, and quickly, they grabbed two bar stools by the window. Alexa came back with two Houseman burgers: double-deckers dripping with juices and covered with cheese and caramelized onions. Their taste buds were not disappointed.

"Mhmmm…This is delicious," Kate complemented while a drop of grease dribbled down her chin. Quickly, she tried to catch it with her napkin.

"This is my splurge place. It's perfect, especially after a night of drinking."

"I can see that. Wish we had a place like this in Florida."

"You should move to New York, for the food alone."

"Nah. Big cities aren't really my thing."

"You never know, you could always meet someone," Alexa mumbled with a mouthful.

"How's work going?"

"Dreadful. No one should be forced to spend all their time in a cubicle."

"I'm sorry, sweetie. Things will get better."

"I did get a promotion a few months back."

"That's great! Congrats! What are you doing now?"

"I'm an Account Manager for some of the smaller clients at the Ad agency."

"Why didn't you tell me sooner? I'm so excited for you!" Enthusiastically Kate hugged Alexa, trying not to get grease on her.

"Thanks."

"How's the acting coming along?"

"That's dwindling down to nonexistent. Besides fashion seems to be my focus these days."

"Sounds right up your alley, knowing how much you love to shop."

"Maybe one day I'll be a personal shopper for someone famous."

Kate smiled at her best friend, wishing her nothing but the best.

Two days later, Alexa came home exhausted not only from work, but also from the horrid flight of stairs. She cursed the maintenance man under her breath for not fixing the elevator. Carelessly, she threw her keys and Coach purse onto the already cluttered counter, kicked off her nude, three-inch platform Jimmy Choo heels, and let out a gigantic sigh of relief, as she did every day when she came home from work.

Not five seconds after Alexa had made herself comfortable on the couch, she shot up and squealed with excitement.

"So the greatest thing happened at work today! The Vice President of my company got tickets to this national children's fund-raising charity event; however his daughter just came down with chicken pox. Ironic, isn't it? So anyways, he offered the tickets to my boss, but she had a prior engagement and gave them to me!" Completely enthralled with her news, Alexa had all but jumped off the couch and into Kate's lap, who had been quietly reading a book.

Desperate, Alexa tried to get Kate's attention. "It's one of the biggest parties of the year; anyone who is anyone is going to be there."

Smiling to herself, but keeping her eyes firmly intact on the small black printed words of *Jane Eyre*, Kate asked, "Where is it being held?" While Alexa's enthusiasm humored Kate, the idea of spending her evening in a formal ballroom, dressed in an uncomfortable gown while people blabbered about themselves, was not on her vacation to-do list.

Luckily, Alexa knew Kate's weakness – historical buildings, and with a sly look Alexa exploited Kate by proclaiming, "The original City Hall."

Before the words could get out, the beloved *Jane Eyre* was quickly tossed to the side, "I've always wanted to see it!" In a rampant burst of excitement, Kate flung herself into Alexa's arms, hugging so tight that Alexa's pale cheeks began to turn bright red.

When her adrenaline began to slowly wind down, Alexa immediately focused her attention on the next issue—dresses. Not having expected to attend a formal event, Kate was not equipped with the proper attire for such an occasion, but luckily Alexa had dresses to spare.

The National Children's fundraising event was one of the biggest events of the year, full of potential clients for Alexa. If able to land a large account, she would be guaranteed that promotion she'd been dreaming about for the past six months. On this extremely important night for her career, Alexa wore a dark purple gown with a focal point of an extravagant, eggshell-color flower trimmed in gold. For hours, she struggled to make every detail perfect. While waiting for Kate, Alexa practiced different industry phrases for potential clients.

The bathroom door slowly opened and a nervous Kate appeared. Alexa's mouth dropped in awe. Despite her trembling fingers, Kate was flawlessly stunning in the black, elegant, floor-length dress with a stunning empire waist. In all the years of their friendship, Alexa had never pictured Kate like this. Of course, Kate was beautiful, but it had always been a natural look. Now, add in the make-up, heels, and a dress, and Alexa was standing in front of someone completely different.

"Wow! You're going to get *a lot* of attention tonight." Alexa gazed at the perfect combination of elegance and beauty that stood before her.

"Hopefully not too much." Meekly, Kate tugged at the silky material clinging against her skin.

"This feels like prom again."

"I didn't go to prom, remember, no one asked me." There was silence as Alexa remembered how hard Kate had it in high school. All the boys teased her, and the girls ignored her, all because she had her nose in a book.

The mere idea of being surrounded by gawking men sent Kate's nerves into a frenzy. She couldn't do this. She wasn't strong enough. *Maybe I shouldn't go. This was a bad idea.* Immediately, her trembling fingers reached for her collarbone and grasped the smooth, sterling silver rings that hung from a dull chain. In the past four years, the only items that could provide Kate any comfort were her wedding rings.

Canceling was not an option. Recently, Alexa had gone above and beyond the call of a best friend, and Kate couldn't let her down, especially tonight.

The invitation, printed in gold script, dictated that the event would start promptly at nine o'clock in the evening. While the trip across Manhattan on the FDR would only take roughly 30 minutes by cab, the act of flagging down a cab could sometimes prove to be difficult. At 8 p.m., Alexa led them both to the curb and hailed for a cab.

"Don't you just love the city?" Alexa complimented with her arm extended out.

At first, all Kate could see was the trash mixed in with wet leaves, mud in the curbs of the street, and not to mention the foul smell rising up from the underground sewer.

It didn't take long for the city to wind down into a dim dusk where Kate could no longer see the imperfections that once irritated her senses. Beautifully lit trees and warm yellow hues from neighboring townhouses reminded Kate of a play on Broadway. The sewer smell had disappeared into the cool, fresh night breeze that whipped against her cheeks.

"It's quite remarkable." The girls smiled at each other.

"Yes. Finally a cab." Alexa sighed with relief from her tired arm. "Let's go." Once in the car she rattled out a bunch of numbers that didn't make any sense to Kate, and the cab driver immediately sped off, joining the traffic on the busy streets of New York.

When the rusty yellow cab pulled up in front of City Hall, both girls gazed through the fingerprint-smudged windows and stared in amazement.

"Are you ready?" Alexa asked out loud, more to herself than anything else.

"About as ready as I'm going to be." The sight of the guests dressed in designer labels made Kate nauseous. *The things I do for Alexa*, Kate thought silently to herself.

After making it through the check-in process, Kate and Alexa entered the rotunda. Almost immediately, Kate was awestruck by the soaring space accented by a grand double stairway. Sadly, guests were not permitted access. A burgundy velvet rope at the base of the staircase held a sign: *Employees Only*. Before Kate could capture the room's beauty, Alexa pulled her away.

The ballroom was long and narrow, with white marble borders that accented a hundred-year-old crystal chandelier. While most guests barely noticed the palatial jewel dancing above their heads, Kate became enthralled.

"Hello, do you want a drink or not?" Alexa's obtuse comment snapped Kate back into reality.

"Yes. Yes of course." Kate smiled feeling silly.

Hand-in-hand, Alexa led Kate through the crowd toward the bar. Kate's eyes nervously scanned the room as every man she passed turned their heads in admiration. This made Kate uncomfortable. Very uncomfortable.

In a soft whisper, Alexa leaned into Kate and said, "Do you realize how many influential people are here?"

Kate glanced around the room, but she didn't recognize anyone. "Nope." She smiled at Alexa.

"That woman standing there to your left, that is Anna Wintour."

"Who?"

Alexa's jaw dropped.

"She is the Editor-in-Chief at Vogue. Only the most important person in fashion."

"Cool. She has cute shoes." Kate giggled.

"Her shoes are not *cute*, they are extravagant. Anna Wintour doesn't wear anything cute." Alexa had to remind herself that Kate lived in a small town in Florida and was not aware of the fashion world.

Shortly after the drinks were served, a cute attorney approached Alexa and within a few minutes of flirty chitchat, he invited his friends over, another lawyer and an editor for a small fashion magazine. Happy that Alexa had found a group of admirers, politely Kate excused herself to enjoy the eighteenth-century architecture.

"Excuse me, ma'am?" A gentle, deep voice whispered behind Kate. Slowly and mildly confused, Kate turned and found herself greeted by a handsome man, six feet tall, who held a glass of champagne in one hand while the other was casually tucked into his black tuxedo pocket.

The fact that his dark, piercing eyes were focused solely on her confused Kate, "Excuse me?"

An intrigued smirk appeared while his limp hand smoothly broke from the tuxedo pocket and gently, almost seductively, landed on Kate's bare shoulder. "Are you OK?"

This was exactly the type of attention that Kate wanted to avoid. Kate flung his unwanted hand and demanded, "What?"

"Did it hurt when you fell from heaven? Only an angel could be as beautiful as you." Instead of reading her unimpressed look correctly, he took a confident step forward, almost as if he expected Kate to blush. However, she quickly took a step away from him.

Insulted, Kate condescendingly questioned, "Do those cheesy pickup lines really work?" Before he could muster up an answer, Kate walked away, shaking her head.

It wasn't long before Kate found herself passing through the elaborate French doors and alone on the veranda. The chilliness of the night breeze provided goose bumps on her bare shoulders. She didn't mind; the fresh air was invigorating compared to the stuffy vibe inside.

A bright full moon's reflection in the still fountain's water enticed Kate's wandering eyes from the historically landscaped garden. It took only a matter of seconds for the pointless chatter from inside to fade into a barely muffled tune. This unexpected, yet appreciated, quietness allowed Kate to reminisce on a happier time in her life.

Kate's eyes opened, after being instructed very suggestively to keep them closed. When the whisper said, "Now," Kate found a romantic beach picnic lit by the warm hue of the full moon. Kate's heart fluttered and melted in happiness at the same time. She had never felt such love, not until now.

A roaring laugh from inside broke Kate's concentration. She lifted the glass to her colored lips and found that only a small droplet of wine remained. Slightly disappointed that she would have to return to the arrogant crowd inside for a refill, Kate huffed quietly to herself.

The room buzzed about gossip and greed. When the main topics of scandal dwindled to nothing, the conversation inevitably switched to money.

Politely, Kate maneuvered through the crowded ballroom, smiling and nodding as she passed. Steps away from the bar, a woman surprisingly introduced herself to Kate. The warmth of her smile appeared to be genuine, and Kate allowed her ridged shoulders to relax.

"I'm sorry for the intrusion, but that dress is exquisite. The best I've seen all night," the woman said in a friendly tone as she placed her well-pampered hands on Kate's wrist. Blushing from the sincere attention, Kate smiled back, swooshing her dress like a little girl.

"Oh. Thank you. I borrowed it from my friend. It is pretty, isn't it?" For the moment, Kate continued to smile, relishing the compliment. That is, until a few unfriendly heads turned toward her. While the curl on the woman's smile remained intact, the warmth instantly disappeared. Her posture became ridged and her tone more formal, "For a hand-me-down, it is lovely." A smile did not follow.

"Thank you for your kind words." Kate turned away from the women who now snubbed her. From behind, Kate could hear them cackle about her used dress. The understaffed bar took forever to pour Kate's glass of merlot, and while she waited a faint conversation caught her attention.

"John, I don't care how much you like this girl, you know what it means when a girl is from Kansas—dirt poor. Cut your losses and move on. Hope you had fun slumming."

"Dude, I know you're right, but she was so hot."

This was more than Kate could handle. Agitated by her surroundings, the looks, insolent comments, and sloppy attempts at flirting, Kate could feel her anxieties kicking in. *I don't belong among these types of people. They don't want me here...and I don't want to be here either! I'm so tired of their elitist attitudes.*

With each passing second the frustration grew while Kate remained waiting for her drink. After the bartender despondently poured her drink, he wiggled his way back to the lonely drunk blonde who flashed her diamonds like candy.

With a full glass of merlot above her shoulder, Kate shuffled through the crowd trying to balance the wine in one hand and maneuver people out of the way with the other. Eyeing a clear spot ahead, Kate sought her opportunity for a smidgen of personal space. It became clear very quickly to Kate why there was so much room. Right as she exhaled the claustrophobic feeling away, four sets of extremely intrigued eyes zoned in on every inch of her. The fifth set of eyes, a famous actor, was not so amused by her presence.

He drunkenly commanded his friends to listen, "Look away, fellas. Anything that bleeds for five days straight without dying can't be trusted." The boys' roaring laughter echoed in Kate's ears. Embarrassed, Kate took two steps forward and stopped. Slowly and very meticulously, Kate turned her head toward the group that still condemned her. It didn't take long, but the four that noticed her angry glare immediately stopped laughing, and started to cough under their breath. The actor, who had turned his back to Kate in a dismissive manner, continued to laugh until he realized he was the only one. When he turned, infuriated eyes confronted him.

"We can't be trusted?" Kate spoke calmly to make sure she had their attention. "We can't be trusted! Who's going to trust your tiny dick that's only good for two pumps and a dump before you're watching sports center." Kate's angry eyes flickered across their faces—leaving them speechless, not a peep from any one of them. Quickly, her daggered eyes returned to the flabbergasted actor and narrowed even further at him as she continued. "And *we* can't be trusted. Pathetic!" Without another word, she walked away. From behind, she could hear the guys harassing the actor for being scolded by a woman.

Completely humiliated by what this woman had said, the actor quickly called out and demanded of her, "Excuse me? Do you know who I am?"

Kate yelled out loudly, "Yeah. You're the little dick guy." The men in the group laughed again that this woman was strong enough and smart enough to put him in his place -- not once, but twice.

"I'm Chris Cody!" By Hollywood's standards, he was nothing short of gorgeous. He had it all: the perfect rock-hard body, a charming smile, and the most captivating amber eyes. Girls everywhere gushed for him, so when he flashed his million-dollar smile, he expected nothing less than for Kate to do the same.

"Who cares?"

Ready for the night to end, Kate found a table on which to place her drink and began to search for Alexa. As she disappeared into the crowd, Chris felt compelled to chase after her. His intentions were only to gently brush her arm, refocusing her attention, but when he approached, he accidently grabbed Kate's thin arm harder than expected.

The grip around Kate's skin shocked her. Kate glared at his fingers, then slowly lifted her face and narrowed her facial expression, "Have you lost your mind?" Apologetically, Chris quickly dropped his hand, realizing that he crossed a line.

Intrigued by her, he was also impressed with her bravery, since no one had ever stood up to him before. "Sassy, aren't we?"

"Sassy? Are you a moron? I'm insulted, why would you treat people like that?"

Chris was completely stunned—it had been a decade and a half since the last time someone had spoken to him like that.

There was nothing Chris could say. For the first time in a long time, someone had rendered him speechless. Disappointed by his lack of competence, Kate huffed and yet again walked away. It wasn't three steps before Chris yelled out, "Wait!"

Irritated, Kate slammed her heel into the floor and yelled, "What? What do you want?" The sound of her voice echoed in the hall, causing close-ranged bystanders to hush and scowl. Some glared nastily at Kate, while others were curious to hear Chris.

Nervously, he stuttered, "What's your name?" In a room full of his peers, who idolized him, he knew that he must have looked ridiculous, desperately pleading for this unknown woman's acknowledgment. Even with a reputation of being the most sought-after bachelor, he didn't care how pathetic he looked as he tried to get Kate's attention—there was something special about her, and Chris wouldn't stop until he found out what it was.

"Why do you want to know?" Unable to lose him in the crowd, Kate appeased him for a moment while her eyes continuously flicked past him in search of Alexa.

He was powerless to capture her full interest, "Are you always this difficult?" He hoped that Kate wasn't in search of her boyfriend, since he'd just spent the last few minutes making a fool of himself.

Her eyes immediately snapped back from the faceless crowd to him to declare, "Yes! Are you always so shallow and mindless?"

"I'm sorry if I offended you back there. I'm just playing the part. I didn't really mean what I said." Attempting to make light of the situation, Chris shrugged his broad shoulders and flashed Kate his million-dollar smile.

With her arms folded and foot tapping rapidly against the wooden floor, she responded, "That was the crappiest apology I've ever heard."

It was an extremely rare moment when Chris would have to apologize for something. Normally, even if he was wrong, somehow people ended up apologizing to him. Strange how that worked, but he just accepted that it was part of life.

"Typical actor, always in character. Do you even know the real you?" Finally, Kate spotted Alexa across the room being admired by a different group of men from earlier. Not allowing him the opportunity to answer, she walked away. Like a lost puppy dog, Chris quickly followed along beside her.

"Of course, I know who I am! Geez, can you slow down?" Dodging around people as if they were orange traffic cones, Chris tried to keep up.

It didn't take long for Alexa to notice Kate and how upset she was. Politely, Alexa excused herself.

"What's going on?" While Alexa knew that Kate wasn't going to have the greatest of times, she also didn't expect her to be so angry.

"I'm ready to leave." With her pink cherry cheeks flushed, she continued to ignore Chris, who confidently stood his ground.

With a flirty smile, Alexa inquired, "Who is your friend?"

"NO ONE! He is *not* my friend. LET'S GO!"

"OK." In agreement, Alexa nodded her head, put her arm around Kate, and led her toward the door.

"Wait, when can I see you again? I don't even know your name!" Chris yelled, exasperated, which caused every head in the room to turn and stare. Kate stopped Alexa and turned to face him.

Quietly and calmly Kate said, "You're the big shot, figure it out." Silently, both girls walked out of the ballroom leaving Chris alone with hundreds of gawking eyes.

Chapter Two

While Kate loved visiting Alexa in New York, she was eager to return home to Florida. She missed the smell of the salty ocean, the warm sun against her cheeks, and the comfort of her soft sheets, but mostly she missed her baby—Aika.

At the kennel, she arrived to find an excited dog sitting next to the vet tech impatiently wagging her tail, ready to go home.

Instantly, she knelt down and gave Aika a big hug as she said in a baby talk voice, "Hey girl, did you miss me?" With her large tongue, Aika gave her a slobbery wet kiss. "I'll take that as a "yes."" Kate signed all the paperwork and took her baby home.

Her split-level floor plan, cottage-style home faced inland, with the ocean knocking at her back door. The white trim was slightly weathered and the blue paint somewhat faded, but it was home. Surfboards were always ready by the back door, as they waited for their next chance to ride the waves. When the mood struck her to go surfing, which was quite often, all she had to do was grab her pre-waxed board, open her white aluminum screen-porch door, and walk down a few old rickety wooden steps, until she felt the soft sand between her toes.

Every morning, without fail, she opened all the windows and filled her home with the fresh, salty smell of the ocean. There was no doubt about it; living on the beach had its perks. The three-bedroom, two-bath pool home had vaulted ceilings, tile floors, and plenty of windows that gave the home a feeling of openness and comfort. This house was everything she had ever wanted.

From the outside, it would appear that Kate, at the ripe young age of twenty-nine, had the perfect life. Four years ago, after the tragedy, Alexa had been there with her day and night. Slowly, she had taken the baby steps needed to put her life back together, and her friends had been the support system she needed.

The depression that followed was unbearable, causing her to reduce her work hours. The days were long, but the nights were even longer. The guilt laid a heavy burden on Kate's heart. It was not only the loss she suffered, but also the decision she had been forced to make. While it gave her financial freedom, it also caused her eternal guilt. Every night she would wake up screaming out for her lost loved one, wishing she could undo the devastating life decision she made four years ago. If only she had made the right decision, maybe her life wouldn't feel so empty.

Kate's family was extremely traditional, with a stay-at-home mother and a hard-working father. High school sweethearts, Emily and Mike had married shortly after graduation and raised two beautiful girls. After thirty-five years of marriage, they still lived in the house they had bought in their early twenties.

While Kate had stayed on a straight path, her sister, Sandra, was a rebellious teen and at the age of 37, she still hadn't grown out of it. Irresponsible, Sandra could barely keep a job, much less a steady boyfriend. Even with an unexpected pregnancy and a beautiful baby girl, Elizabeth, she still couldn't change her wild uncaring ways.

Saturday morning, two days after Kate returned from New York, she sat outside on her patio enjoying the cool, refreshing breeze that rolled off the ocean. Still in her mismatched night outfit, she read the paper and sipped on her tea, while Aika lay in her normal spot, directly on top of her feet. Out of the blue, there was a knock at the front door, and Aika's head popped up from its resting spot and let out a loud bark. The unexpected sound of the knock made her jump in her seat. Now with suddenly jittery hands, she almost dropped the hot tea on herself.

Placing the half empty red coffee mug on the glass patio table, she lightly kicked Aika out of the way and mumbled, "Oh, Aika! Come on, move."

Not one to like surprises, Kate took her time walking through the house as she tried to figure out who was on her doorstep. Naturally, Aika trotted behind her, grunting the whole time. There was another knock, this time a bit louder than the one before. Cautiously, she looked through the peephole, but the person's back was turned, preventing Kate from identifying her visitor.

On the arm of the couch laid an off-white cotton housecoat. Before Kate opened the door, she tightly wrapped the robe around herself and commanded to Aika, "Sit. Stay." Slowly she opened the front door, the bright sun causing her eyes to squint. The man turned around flashing that charming smile that had annoyed her less than a week ago—today would be no different.

Her mouth dropped open in shock—she was unable to believe who stood on her doorstep. Pleased with himself, Chris leaned into the doorway, his medium-length, light golden-brown hair sparkling in the sun. His amber eyes were warm like a cup of coffee, his mouth framed the perfect radiant smile, and his body appeared to have been chiseled out of marble by Michelangelo. Once she realized that her mouth was still open and dry, she quickly closed it and took a small step back, unable to believe that Chris Cody was at her front door.

With a smug look, he showed his satisfaction at proving her wrong. He gazed upon her proudly and said, "Good Morning, Miss Katherine Woods." Rendered speechless, she couldn't grasp the idea that this man, whom she had publicly humiliated, had taken the time and effort to seek her out.

Uncharacteristically, her mind went blank, and all she could mumble was, "What are you doing here?"

"You told me that I would find you if I wanted to see you again. Well, here I am."

"No, I told you to figure it out, I didn't mean for you to show up at my doorstep."

"Well, I did, and I'm here."

Slightly smitten with his efforts, Kate still held back a smile. The man she remembered from the fundraiser was arrogant and rude; and even though this didn't seem to be the same person, she would not give him the benefit of the doubt.

"Are we going to stand here forever, or are you going to invite me inside?"

She could see that the sun's hot rays were beating down on his head, and the sweat beads were starting to develop on his forehead. But she didn't budge. Aika let out a loud, defensive bark and prepared to attack. In a motherly tone, Kate turned around and commanded with her index finger extended, "No. Down." Reluctantly, the bullmastiff laid down on the cool marble tile and growled, not taking her eyes off the strange man who stood in the doorway.

Insulted by his presumption, she responded, "I'm not letting some stranger in my house; I don't care how famous you are."

Given his publicity, Chris had assumed that he didn't need an introduction. Shocked by her reaction, he stood up straight, with his right hand placed on his chest, and in an actor's tone replied, "Pardon me, where are my manners?" Another charming smile flashed as he continued. "My name is Chris Cody."

"If you are who you say you are, then where are all of your fans and paparazzi?" She knew it was Chris and that she was going to let him in; she just wanted to watch him sweat for a minute.

"I didn't tell anyone that I came here." As he began to sweat profusely, he was desperate to get inside, protected from the sun in the cool air conditioning. Unaccustomed to the blazing heat, he prayed that his extra-strength deodorant worked.

Thankfully, it didn't take Kate long to let up on her interrogation; once she felt he had suffered enough, she stood back and held the door open for him. They smiled at each other awkwardly as he sluggishly walked past her into the house, exhausted from the heat. In the small entranceway, she could smell his designer cologne mixed in with his fresh spring deodorant and, surprisingly, the aroma was pleasing to her senses. It reminded her of someone who had worn similar cologne, and her heart quickened at the memories.

The moment he walked through the door, Aika began to bark uncontrollably, and Chris timidly backed himself against the now-closed screen door as it clicked against his heels. Crowded next to Kate, so close that he could smell the scent of sweet melon shampoo in her hair, he pathetically looked to her for protection.

"Aika!" Embarrassed and slightly aroused from the cologne scent that lingered in the air, Kate scolded the protective dog. "She's normally very friendly, but she doesn't like strangers."

"Aika?"

"Yep. It means little love in Japanese." She smiled.

"It's OK girl." Kate comforted the happy puppy before she snorted and strutted across the room. After she chased her tail three times, she finally laid down in her large, green, hair-covered bed. She nosed a squeaky toy that used to resemble a soft pink pig to the side and glared at Chris from across the room.

When Kate stood up, her ankles popped as she extended her legs, and when she faced him, there was a serious expression upon her face. "So you didn't answer my question—what are you doing here?"

Cautiously, he moved away from the door as he explained the situation. "After our encounter, I thought about the things you said to me and realized that its been a long time since anyone has spoken to me that way. Believe it or not, I wasn't always this way."

"An ass!"

It took a moment for him to gather his words together after being taken off guard by Kate. "Yea. I guess. I need to get my priorities straight. That night, there was just something about you that was so different. So much honesty."

With curious eyes, she wondered, "That's great. But again, I don't understand what that has to do with me?"

"I want you to help me."

After the charity function, Chris had pondered why Kate had rejected him. In his black stretch Escalade limo, with twenty of his closest friends, he had sat back and watched and really listened to them. Not a single person was interested in him; the guys tried to casually talk up movie deals, and the women threw themselves at him for bragging rights. Suddenly, all the pointless chatter became a loud static noise that gave him a headache. Then something unusual happened. He felt repulsed by himself and the leeches in his limo. No longer able to handle the pretentiousness that surrounded him, he had kicked everyone out. For the first time on a Saturday night, he had sat alone in silence and thought, *This is what I wanted, right? If I've gotten everything I wanted, then why am I so unhappy?*

Abruptly interrupting his idea that Kate would help him on his path of self-discovery, she protested, "Oh no, no, no, no . . . I can't help you! I don't have the time to help you through a mid-life crisis." Flamboyantly, her crossed arms flew in the air as she continued. "Isn't that what therapy is for? Go see a shrink."

Over the last couple of years, she had worked extremely hard to get her life back to some kind of normalcy. The last thing she could handle was some insecure actor who probably expected her to fulfill his needs. At this point, she couldn't afford another setback, and Chris would be exactly that.

"Kate, there is no one else. I don't trust anyone else to not lie to me."

With nowhere else to turn, he stood awkwardly in Kate's living room, silently awaiting her answer. Internally, she debated if she should give him what he wanted. She was scared it would come at a great cost to her. Deep down she could sense that there was a connection building between them and began to feel sorry for him. "You're not going to let me get out of this, are you?"

"Nope." Excitedly, like a five-year-old boy, he shook his head back and forth and smiled.

"Fine! But all I can offer is someone to talk to. I go by Kate, not Katherine." Not pleased about the situation, she stomped past Chris as she walked out onto her patio, back to her paper and now cold tea. *What in the world do I have to offer someone who has everything? I need to figure out how to talk myself out of this.*

The moment he opened his mouth, a flood of personal information came pouring out. Spending a majority of the day out on the porch, she learned a lot about Chris Cody.

She was flabbergasted to hear Chris tell her that he had grown up in the slums of San Francisco with his mother and no father to speak of. What he had called home was a small, cramped two-bedroom apartment on the third floor of a rundown complex. The paint on the walls had peeled, and it wasn't uncommon for the lights to flicker on and off—then off completely, until his mother, Julia, could scrounge up enough money to have the electricity turned back on. During the day, his mother worked at a small diner a couple of blocks from the apartment, and at nights, after she put Chris to bed, she snuck out to dance at a gentlemen's club. Unable to sit back and watch his mother struggle, he did the best he could to help out. At the young age of ten, he offered to carry bags home for elderly ladies. For his good deeds, the sweet seniors would give him a few dollars. Every cent he made went to his mother.

As a child, he found pleasure in mimicking other people, and he was pretty good at it. Since there weren't that many kids in his neighborhood, he found himself, almost daily, entertaining the older men who gathered around the red brick building to play poker.

One day, while Chris sat idly outside the local grocery store waiting for someone to come out to take him up on his services, a man in a sleek, expensive suit walked into the store. Through the window, he watched him put a flyer on the bulletin board. When the automatic door flung open, the mysterious man stepped outside, putting his black-with-white trim hat back on. He gave an encouraging smile as he looked down at Chris with his scraped knees, and then, ever so casually he glanced back at the board. This piqued his curiosity, and the moment the man disappeared into the parking lot, the boy ran into the grocery store and read the flyer:

Young Talent needed for local commercial.
Auditions Thursday November 15 at 2 p.m. at Folders Studio.
If selected, pay is $200.

Deep in the pit of his stomach, Chris knew that he had to attend this audition; it was the chance of a lifetime. In order to make it to the audition he would have to skip school, but luckily the teachers rarely paid him any attention.

Intrigued by the flyer, he lost himself in a fantasy world, a place where he was the recipient of stardom, fame, and fortune. On stage, he could hear fans screaming out his name . . . but then reality clicked back when he realized that it was Eleanor, a regular client, requesting that Chris carry her heavy grocery bags. While he heaved the large sack of potatoes on his shoulder and slowed his pace to match hers, he continued to dream of being a star.

The next week at the audition, hundreds of kids sat impatiently and waited with their agitated parents as they read the script over and over again. At the end of a long hallway, which had the kids and their parents seated in black folding chairs on either side of the wall, a young lady sat behind a flimsy desk on wheels, registering the actors auditioning and providing them with the material.

The young woman, who couldn't have been older than twenty, with metal braces on her teeth, greeted Chris enthusiastically as she handed him a small pamphlet. "Have this memorized by the time they call your name. Please sign your name here." Nervously, his fingers shook with the pen in his hand as he timidly scribbled his name. Ever so quickly, he took the pamphlet and found a seat all the way at the end of the hallway. While he quietly read the lines again, he observed the room and noticed that he didn't sound like the other children; they were confident and secure in their abilities.

Eventually, almost all the children had left, while he and a few others continued to patiently wait their turn. Bored, he sat in his folding chair, swinging his short legs back and forth until his name was called. When his own name rung in his ears, his feet stopped swinging, and he gulped nervously.

On the other side of the large, wooden double doors that so many children had already passed through, he found two men dressed in polo shirts and khakis, sitting on one side of a large, laminated table with a stack of paper piled in front of them.

Already aggravated from a long day, the man in a solid black polo yelled, without even glancing up at Chris, "Come on kid, we don't have all day!" Intimidated, he jumped and hurried into the center of the room. Unsure of himself, he nervously stood before them with his sweaty palms intertwined. Instantly, he recognized the other man from the grocery store, who now wore a blue polo. Without a word, he nicely pointed behind Chris toward an empty, light green stool.

Chris pulled himself up onto the stool as the man asked, "Did you memorize the lines?" Too scared to speak, Chris nodded in agreement, and with an encouraging voice the man continued. "OK then, when you're ready, go ahead and start." With a perplexed look, he froze, unsure of what to do.

The man calmly asked as he rubbed his forehead, "Son, do you know what the audition is for?" Nervous that he had blown his chance, he just held onto his pamphlet so tight that the pages got crumpled and damp from his sweaty palms.

"No." When he spoke, his voice jumped up an octave like a teenage boy going through puberty.

Irritated, the other man grumbled, "Good grief, let's get on with it, kid."

The man from the grocery store snapped at his partner, "Give him a minute." Wisely, he came around from behind the table and slowly approached Chris. He placed his wrinkly, olive-toned right hand gently on Chris's shoulder and asked, "Son, you have read the lines, right? This is for a cereal commercial, so I want you to read those lines so every kid in America will want to eat the cereal. Can you do that?"

A light bulb went off as it became clear what he was supposed to do. For clarification he asked, "What kind of cereal?"

"Does it matter?"

"Of course! If it's that yucky healthy stuff my mom tries to make me eat, how am I supposed to convince all kids to eat it?"

Amused at the boy's cleverness, the man chuckled out loud. "All you have to do is pretend that this cereal is your favorite cereal in the whole world."

Still a shy ten-year-old kid, it took him a few minutes to get comfortable, but after that, he confidently and articulately mimicked multiple characters—and both men were impressed. This was just the beginning of his career.

The man from the grocery store who had been so kind to Chris turned out to be a talent agent, Henry Stewart, who eventually became his first positive male role model—or so he thought. During the next several years, not only did Henry become a major part of Chris's life, but he also booked Chris nonstop with acting gigs and acting lessons with professional coaches. With his first big paycheck, he moved his family to a nicer home. In six short years, he had made more money than he knew what to do with.

Everything was perfect; now that he could afford to take care of his mother, she no longer had to dance at that filthy club and could spend her time being a full-time mom. For a brief period, he was proud of his mother; she appeared to be like all the other moms at school.

But then in the blink of an eye, everything changed. Chris came home early one day from rehearsal to find Henry assaulting his mother. Backed into a corner, scared for her life with her arms lifted, protecting her face, Julia cried and begged for Henry to stop.

When Chris walked in he heard Henry scream, "If it wasn't for me, that runt wouldn't have anything! I didn't have to put the flyer up in THAT grocery store! So you'll continue to put out as long as I want!"

There was an earth-shattering sound in his ears when he heard those words. Everything had been a lie—all the hard work, everything he thought he had accomplished, had been given to him, not because of his talent, but because his mother was sleeping with his agent.

When his mother saw him, her oxygen-deprived lungs screamed, "Chris, get out of here. GO!" Full of panic, her biggest fear was that Henry would take his anger out on her son. Henry looked above his shoulder to see Chris, but he didn't release his grip.

Angrily, Chris stepped forward, demanding, "Get your goddamn hands off her!" Intrigued by the challenge, Henry threw Julia back against the wall like a limp rag doll and turned his broad stance toward the boy. At sixteen, he was about to have his first man-to-man fight.

Like an angry linebacker, he charged toward Henry and tackled him into the wall, barely missing his mother, who scampered to the safety of another corner. Henry took his balled-up fist and sucker-punched Chris in the gut; with his untrained eye, he never saw it coming.

Bowed over in pain, it took him a second to get the strength to stagger to his feet. As they circled around each other, both with their guards up, Henry made a fatal move as he threw his fist head on toward Chris, who easily blocked the punch, grabbed Henry's arm, and twisted it behind his back. Henry struggled to break free, but he had full control as he dragged him out of the house.

Red in his face, blue veins popping in his neck, Henry screamed as he tried to fight his way back into the house. "I made you! I created you and I can destroy you!"

"You're pathetic. Don't ever come around here again." Furiously, he slammed the door in Henry's face.

After taking a large breath to try to allow the anger to subside, he immediately went in search for his mother. Curled up in a corner in the hallway, she sobbed as she held her head tight in the safety of her arms. Blood from her cuts dripping down on the ripped green shirt that had left her exposed, she was ashamed that her little boy had to step in and save her. This was not how she wanted him to become a man.

He rushed to her side and knelt down beside her, but she refused to look up. "Mom, it's OK, he's gone."

She just sobbed harder.

In a sympathetic voice he continued, "Don't cry. I'm not going to let anyone hurt you." He wrapped his arms around her and pulled her into his protective embrace as he slowly rocked her like a small child and whispered, "Let's get you into bed." Timidly, she looked up at Chris and much to her surprise, there wasn't any judgment in his eyes. Ashamed, she patted her cheeks dry of the black mascara tears and allowed him to nurse her back to health.

From then on, Julia continued to live with Chris until the day she died; he was twenty-nine. The year before, the doctor had said it was just a small lump and probably benign—nothing to worry about. Two weeks later she had undergone a double mastectomy and started intensive chemotherapy. He made sure she had the best doctors, but even then, with the newest medication, it didn't make a difference. Three months after being diagnosed with breast cancer, the doctors said there was no hope. They told Chris to make her as comfortable as possible and to cherish the remaining time. A month later, she was gone.

After that, and with the increase of fame and fortune, he easily lost his way. When he became a multi-million-dollar corporation, Chris was constantly torn in several different directions. Through experience, he began to notice that the meaner he was to people, the more they did for him. It was never his intention to get anyone fired—not in the beginning, at least. The more the industry pulled him, the less patience he had. Even if everything was perfect to his specifications, he would find something to complain about. Eventually, this just turned into a habit—a bad one. These same rules applied to his personal life as well. The more he ignored a girl, the harder she would try, and when he was tired of her, he shooed her along. This, too, eventually became a habit.

In the six years since he'd lost his mother, Chris was no longer the sweet boy who protected her; at the age of thirty-five, he had turned into someone that his mother wouldn't even recognize. All of his dreams had come true—but at a steep price.

Most people, including Kate, assumed that Chris came from a well-off, loving family, and his only life experiences were the ones he played on the big screen. By the end of their conversation, Kate sympathized with his pain. Kate knew all too well what it felt like to have one's world turned upside down in an instant. The guilt she felt after the tragedy consumed her and every aspect of her life. It took over a year before there was a day that her emotions didn't cripple her. That one decision. The one she wished she could reverse. One single life altering decision changed everything.

As the day wore on and Chris's therapy session began to die down, Kate's stomach started to grumble. Slightly embarrassed by the fluid noises that erupted from her body, she wrapped her arms around her stomach, "Oh my, I'm starving! Are you hungry?"

Enthralled by his own story, Chris hadn't realized he was hungry until she mentioned it. "I am. What's good to eat around here?"

With a sneaky smile she asked, "Do you like seafood?"

Nonchalantly, he nodded his head in agreement.

Still comfortable in her nightclothes, even though the robe had been flung across the back of her chair, she said, "Well I know this great little place . . . Let me get ready and we'll go."

Kate accidently slammed the bedroom door a little too loudly as she quickly scrambled into a pair of light blue baggy jeans. Tangled in the jeans, she practically fell into the closet as she tried to walk before the jeans were completely on. A bundle of nerves, she grabbed the first random T-shirt from her closet.

Almost silently, she came around the corner, pulling her soft green T-shirt down, to find Chris patiently waiting for her. With his hands folded behind his back, he was leaning forward to get a better view of the family photos on the dark cherry wood bookshelf. Even though he wasn't touching anything, it still rattled her nerves; the idea of Chris Cody snooping through her things. Immediately, she interrupted him, "Are you ready?"

Surprised by her abruptness, he staggered back away from the bookshelf. "That was quick." He was unable to believe that it only took a woman five minutes to get ready, but when he looked at her, he realized why it didn't take so long. "You're not wearing that, are you?"

Kate lifted her eyebrows and asked, "Why? What's wrong with what I'm wearing?"

"Your jeans are torn and that shirt is not flattering at all." He couldn't take his eyes off the dirty, ratty frays at the end of her jeans and the wrinkles that were so creased it looked as if they were ironed on.

"Good thing I'm not trying to impress you." Annoyed with his preppy attitude, she rolled her eyes and suggested, "Let's go."

In the pitch black of the garage, her hand searched the wall for the large button to open the door. As the light began to fill the dark space, she saw his car, which was blocking the driveway. More than likely it was borrowed from the dealership, but it was obviously brand new and expensive—too expensive for Kate's taste.

When the sun reflected off the aquamarine paint, the two-door sports car sparkled like the Hope Diamond. As soon as her eyes had refocused from the blinding light, she asked, "We are not taking that, are we?"

"What? It's a Porsche Carrera GT!" Offended, Chris couldn't figure out why she was so repulsed—grown men went weak in the knees for it.

"It's too flamboyant for where we are going. Let's take my car." He started to protest, but she stopped him short as she raised her palm facing toward him. "There is nothing glamorous about me. If you want to hang out, you better get used to doing things like average Americans."

She grabbed her keys out of her black, over-the-shoulder purse and double-clicked the remote. The 2011 blue Honda Civic beeped as the orange turn signal blinked in unison. Proud of herself, she turned toward Chris and smirked, "Now, this is practical."

Chapter Three

The restaurant of Kate's choice was a small hole-in-the-wall raw bar. SeaPort Raw Bar had the best oysters in town. The parking lot was nothing more than a mound of dirt, and the building looked like an abandoned shack that managed to avoid the inspectors 'condemned' sign years ago.

The inside of the restaurant wasn't much of an improvement. As Chris opened the heavy wooden door, which held a small brass porthole-like window, the aroma of fresh fish assaulted him, and immediately his face twisted up in disgust. While they stood in the waiting area, he tried his hardest to remove the stench from his senses. No matter which way he turned or how many times he breathed out of his nose, he couldn't escape the smell. The hostess greeted them with a warm smile. "Welcome to SeaPort. Two?"

"Yes, can we sit on the deck? Before he loses it." Kate giggled as she extended her thumb toward Chris.

An unimpressed, thin-lipped smile appeared as her eyes scrutinized every little detail of Chris. It was apparent she wanted to ask something, but instead she silently led them to the small outdoor deck with a view of the ocean. Once through the restaurant doors and on the deck, he took a deep breath of fresh air that infiltrated his lungs with relief. After they sat at their table, which was solid wood, firm and heavy with several dents from bar fights and drunken carvings, the hostess politely handed them a front-and-back menu card, which was only laminated in the sense that it had once been covered when SeaPort originally opened ten years ago.

The waitress, who was barely a day over twenty-one, wore cut-off jean short-shorts and a bright pink tank top with the SeaPort's logo on it. Just like every other beach bunny in this small town, she had her long, blonde hair pulled back into a pony tail, her skin was kissed by the golden sun, and she shamelessly flashed her baby blues at Chris.

Kate interrupted the waitress's flirting as she coldly ordered, "I'll have a Bud Light bottle." Chris quickly turned his attention to Kate and ordered himself a Heineken. Like a scolded puppy, the waitress sulked back to the kitchen.

Chris silently fidgeted with the menu as he continued to flip it back and forth, undecided on what to order. When she had mentioned seafood, this wasn't exactly what he'd imagined. Accustomed to a different lifestyle, he assumed she meant at least a three-star restaurant. This rundown local establishment and the young, hardworking waitress reminded him of his life before fame, with his loving mother.

In need of guidance around the menu he asked, "What's good here?"

With a smile, she looked up from the menu she had pretended to look at. "Pretty much everything's good. I like the raw oysters on the half shell." There was no need for her to review the menu—she always ordered the same thing.

The waitress brought out the drinks. She was now extremely nervous and simultaneously excited—as if someone had whispered a secret to her in the kitchen—and stood ready to take their order, with her pen and pad in hand. Chris motioned toward Kate; who ordered her usual dish. After contemplating the grouper, he backed out at the last second and decided on the burger.

When Kate glanced up from her brown bottle, she discovered an intense stare and charming smile, and immediately butterflies began to shuffle in her stomach. Her nervous eyes wandered in every direction except toward Chris.

Captivated by the cloudless, pale blue sky, her nose tickled with the sea-salt smell in the air while she watched the white waves crash into the wet seashell-strewn sand. In silence, she waited for the moment when someone would recognize them—well, not her, but Chris, which would ruin everything. The last thing she needed were reporters who would pry into her life—well, it wasn't her current life she was worried about, but if they found out what she'd done, the result would be devastating.

In an attempt to get her attention, he gently put his hand on hers and whispered across the table, "What's the matter?"

For a moment, she stared at him confused, and then automatically jerked her hand from under his. "I'm just curious."

Intrigued by her comment, he placed his hand on his lap, and asked, "About?"

She began to nervously twist the ends of her light brown hair. Kate tried to be inconspicuous as she leaned over the table and whispered, "Why hasn't anyone recognized you?"

Humored by her worries, he couldn't help but chuckle, "Ahhh . . . jealous of the fans stealing me away." Before she could respond, the waitress, with the same love-stricken smile, brought out their food and a second round of drinks they'd ordered earlier. Kate quickly leaned back to allow the waitress to put the plates down.

When they were alone again, Kate rolled her eyes as she unwrapped her plastic silverware from the napkin. "Not quite."

"People have noticed. In this restaurant alone, several people have done double takes and whispered amongst themselves."

Pleased with himself, Chris leaned back with his hands folded behind his head, and gloated, "But don't worry, people think I'm in Tahiti."

It didn't help her concentration that his muscles flexed like a damn neon light. Shaking her head clear of the distraction, she placed her forehead in the palm of her hand and said, "What? But you're not in Tahiti, you're sitting right here!"

"I know that, you know that, but a rumor was leaked to the press that I was going to Tahiti, so I hired a double to go in my place. Lucky bastard!" He dropped his hands and directed his attention toward the gigantic burger.

"Why is he a lucky bastard?"

"Because he's lying on a beach, drinking, and looking at beautiful women, and I'm paying for it."

Slightly insulted, Kate readjusted herself and boldly suggested, "Well you can always go and join him."

When he looked up from his plate there was a twinkle in his eye as he whispered, "I'm exactly where I want to be." Kate held back a blushing smile.

Relaxed and with a belly full of good food and beer, Chris rubbed his stomach as he unexpectedly smiled. "I can't believe that you ate all that food—impressive."

"Why is that? Don't the women you date eat?"

"Not like you do."

With the third and final round of beers, the waitress brought the check and placed it in the middle of the table. The moment she turned her back, both Kate and Chris reached for the black vinyl binder. Even though she was much quicker than Chris, he managed to grab a small corner and maintain his grip.

Taken off guard by her dominant behavior, he flashed the Prince Charming smile. "I got it."

"No. I got it." Stubborn like a mule, she refused to let go. They were both not accustomed to someone else paying for them.

His patience began to wear thin, as he replied firmly, "Now, stop. It's not a big deal, let me have the check."

With both of their hands still gripping the binder as it floated above the tabletop, she asked angrily, "Why are you being so difficult?" Annoyed, she pulled the check harder and snapped at him, "Why don't you let me pay for the damn check? Are you so insecure about a woman paying?"

"No! I was raised to be a gentleman, and that's what I'm trying to be!" Forcefully, Chris yanked the check out of her hand to prevent the fight from continuing in never-ending circles. Aggravated, Kate fell back into her white plastic chair, folded her arms across her chest, and huffed.

With a satisfied smile, he asked, "Are you always so stubborn?" He liked it when Kate pouted; it wasn't bothersome with her, the way it was when other women did it. For some reason, it was cute when she did it.

Annoyed with his buoyancy, she argued back, "Are you always so arrogant?"

Aside from the three hours they spent together at dinner, he wasn't ready for the evening to end. Casually, he suggested a short walk on the beach after he signed the check. When he stood from the table, he gently offered his hand and with a head nod said, "Come on." The thought of taking his hand glimpsed through her mind, but she resisted and stood on her own.

On the beach, the fire red sunset glowed in the soft, pale blue sky, and the transcendent clouds surrounding the sun had a purple hue. The intoxication from the beers began to take effect as she carelessly rolled her blue jeans up to her knees, threw off her flip-flops, and started to splash around in the salt water.

In mid-swing of a kick, she noticed Chris who stood on the shore watching her intently. Immediately, shyness overcame her, and almost childlike, she clasped her hands behind her back and joined Chris on the dry sand, self-conscious. An arm's distance away, Kate tripped on an unseen rock and almost landed face first. Automatically, he caught her in his protective embrace. Foggy from the three beers, she allowed herself to be secured by him as she stared into his eyes. A connection sparked between them, and naturally, Chris reduced the lingering distance as he leaned in for a passionate kiss. With a knee-jerk reaction, she jumped back; she was shocked at the position she had gotten herself into. *No, this isn't happening to me.*

Confused at what had just transpired, they stood a few feet away from each other in silence. The awkward tension between them became too much, and she whispered, "I'm gay!!!"

Not what he expected to hear, Chris tilted his head and asked, "What?"

I'm married, I have a boyfriend, I just can't do this; these were the responses that Chris was prepared for—but not *I'm gay*.

"I'm sorry. I don't go that way. I'm gay." His speechlessness left Kate feeling unsure and humiliated. To avoid further embarrassment, Kate walked away and sat down on the sand dunes.

He had never endured such an elaborate display of sensitivity, especially regarding something that seemed so trivial. Attempting to provide some comfort, he cautiously sat next to her, but before he could say anything, Kate blurted, "Look, I understand if you don't want to be friends, I just want to be clear that there isn't anything between us."

Kate lied.

The moment he embraced her, something unusual and unexpected happened, she felt a spark, a connection, something that she hadn't felt in years. Still mortified by her reaction, she hid her face in between her knees while her long brown hair flowed in all directions toward the sand.

"Why would you think there's something between us?"

"You sought me out, paid for lunch, and of course...what just happened over there." Without lifting her head, she pointed her index finger toward the spot where she'd fallen.

Amused, Chris chuckled quietly to himself as he explained, "You left me with quite the impression, and I wanted to spend some time with you. We had lunch because we were hungry and that over there, well, you fell, and I caught you. Doesn't mean I want to marry you."

Surprised by his lightheartedness, she mumbled under her arm, "Mmhmm amont me mhming mhmy abobahm mrm goo?"

"What? Kate I can't understand you when your heads' buried in your arms."

She reluctantly raised her head slightly and tried again, "I SAID, what about me being gay? Isn't that a problem for you?" Kate had expected to see Chris walk away, but when she peeked from under her thick hair, much to her surprise, Chris was still next to her.

It was her sophomore year in college, when her then-girlfriend strongly suggested that Kate reveal her identity. This caused more heartache than expected. Kate knew that her mother would have a hard time, but she couldn't have predicted that friends she had had since childhood would turn their backs on her. Small towns were unforgiving for indiscretions, which Kate learned firsthand. It took time, but the whispers and glares slowly began to disappear as the locals ignored that particular item.

Has this girl been living in a bubble for the past ten years? Chris thought.

As a peace offering, Chris held out his open hand. "Kate, relax—I work in entertainment, everyone is gay. Stop freaking out. Do you think you can handle being friends?"

"Friends?" Almost cautiously, Kate offered him her right hand, feeling his rough callous rub against her skin. The ocean breeze blew long strands across Kate's eyes and without letting go, she scooped them to the side.

With a bright smile, Chris pulled Kate into a friendly hug whispering into her ear, "We better get going before someone else finds out you're gay."

Kate playfully smacked him on the back, screeching into his ear, "Jackass!" Once he'd stood up and dusted the sand from his beige shorts, Chris happily helped Kate up and staggered back to the car with his arm slung around her shoulder.

The next morning, Kate woke up with a pounding headache. A lightweight, three beers were enough to make her tipsy, but left her with a hangover the next morning. She rolled around and found herself face-to-face with Aika's gigantic smile.

"Whew! Your morning breath reeks." Immediately, she fanned the hot air out of the slobbery beast's mouth as she leaned back. The puppy licked her nose and gave Kate an insulted look.

"Fine, let's get some breakfast." The moment the word *breakfast* escaped her lips, Aika excitedly jumped off the bed bumping Kate's stomach in the process. Still groggy, she crawled out of bed and on the way to the kitchen she pondered, *Did Chris Cody actually show up at my door? Oh my, I can't believe I freaked out when I told him I was gay! How embarrassing. Good thing I don't have to face him ever again.*

She popped a couple of aspirins in an attempt to stop the headache from hell, fed Aika, made her tea, and grabbed the open book lying spine-up on the counter. On her way to the patio, with her hands full, she heard a knock on her door.

In disbelief, she almost dropped her coffee mug, shook her head, and mumbled, "Oh, no. This can't be happening twice!" After she put her tea and book back down on the counter, she quickly grabbed her robe, which hung on the back of the bathroom door.

While she wrapped the soft cotton around her bare skin, she peeked through the peephole and saw Chris's smiling face. She stomped her foot angrily and cursed under her breath. With a confused look, the large pooch just stared at her with a tilted head. Before she opened the door, she quickly ran her fingers through her tangled morning hair.

"Good morning, sunshine!" Chris greeted her energetically as the front door swung open.

She left the door open, mumbling as she walked away, "It's too early to be so peppy." A cheery smile appeared on his face with satisfaction in his ability to get under her skin. Under his ripped biceps, he carried two large, brown paper bags.

"What's all of this?"

"I wasn't sure what you liked, so I got coffee, bagels, doughnuts, tea, and croissants." Still half asleep, she just stood there in her pajamas and watched him comfortably unpack the items on her dining room table, as if they were lifelong friends. Wanting her fair share, the eager pup got Chris's attention with a soft bark.

"Don't worry girl, I didn't forget about you." Immediately, he pulled a large thick rawhide out from a separate bag and offered it to the dog. Salivating, she waited for her mom's approval and, once Kate nodded her head, Aika slowly took the treat from Chris's hand and trotted off.

While Kate stood there and continued to watch Chris, she noticed something was different. Then it hit her; his long hair wasn't tucked behind his ears. It was short, really short, in a crew cut with a tight fade on the sides.

"You cut your hair?"

"Nope. Yesterday I was wearing a wig." Relieved to be itch free, he rubbed the semi-bald portion of the back on his head with his free hand.

Completely ignoring the fact that he just said he wore a wig, she yawned and mumbled, "How long have you been up?"

"Six thirty. I went for a run, did some work, and the rest of my day is free to spend with you," he answered casually while continuing to fill her table with breakfast pastries.

"Ugh. I don't know how you do it. I can't get started until I have my morning tea." Sluggishly, she slowly dragged her feet into the kitchen to get plates.

Two muffins in hand, Chris commented, "Good to know." A low grumble hummed in her vocal cords as she reached for the porcelain plates in the cabinet next to the microwave.

"Wait! What? Spend the rest of the day with me?" In mid-motion, her hand froze on the handle of the half-opened cabinet. "I figured after yesterday, you would've been running back to Hollywood." Now, Kate was awake.

"I don't scare that easily. I thought that since on yesterday we spent so much time talking about me, today we can talk about you, since you seem to be so forthcoming and honest with your opinions." For a smug reminder, he placed a purposeful emphasis on the word *honest*.

Kate huffed as she opened the cabinet entirely and got the saucers down. "OK, but you have to promise never to mention what happened yesterday to another living soul, got it?"

"Got it." Jokingly, Chris saluted her with his left hand raised to his eyebrow and stood at attention.

Not amused by his gestures, she shook the plates in her hand at him and demanded, "You need to promise!"

When he came around the kitchen corner, Chris leaned into her so close that she could smell the peppermint gum on his sweet breath as he whispered, "I promise never to bring it up again." Frozen in place, she stared into his eyes; ever so smoothly, he gently took the plates out of her hands and turned away.

With his hands full of the breakfast pastries, he headed toward the patio as he smirked, "Do you mind if we eat on the lanai? It's a beautiful morning."

Did he just charm me? It almost worked. Frustrated by her own answer, she stomped to the patio, where Chris had breakfast waiting.

Kate sulked as she walked through the sliding glass door. "OK, so what do you want to know?"

As the feeling of déjà vu began to creep upon her, Kate was not particularly thrilled about the idea of this guy bombarding her with personal questions.

"Tell me about your parents?" he inquired as he sipped on his coffee. "Do you have siblings?"

"My mom stayed home, and Dad retired from the police force." A proud smile appeared on her thin lips as she thought about her dad dressed in his navy blue police uniform. "I have an older sister, Sandra; we don't see eye to eye on things."

"Oooh. Sister rivalry—spill the dirt."

"Not really anything to spill; she and I are complete opposites." There was a moment of hesitation before she described her sister. "Sandra always had a hard time keeping herself out of trouble. She always acted like an angry teenager, even as an adult. The only good thing she produced is my three-year-old niece, Elizabeth. I love that baby to pieces."

After he swallowed his sip of mildly warm coffee, he said, "Wow. Guess every family has issues."

She nodded her head silently in agreement.

"When did you know that you were gay?" Kate heard this question several times in her lifetime, but normally from people who had known her for a while. Unprepared for his bluntness, the warm sweet tea choked on the back of her throat. When she regained her composure, she gave him the standard answer, "I guess I've known it all my life, but I didn't come out until college."

"Why did you wait so long?"

Not a fan of this particular question, she shoved a large bite of blueberry muffin into her mouth as a stall tactic and ungracefully mumbled, "It's complicated. My family is very traditional, and I was extremely worried about their reaction." This answer always caused the recipient's facial expression to reflect a small amount of judgment toward her family for not being fully accepting. For Chris, this was not the case. In his warm eyes, there was sympathy, not an ounce of judgment. The corner of Kate's lips curled up, surprisingly happy.

"What happened?"

"It wasn't easy. My mom was disappointed; to her, I turned my back on what was natural. She and I fought about it for years; even today she still can't accept it 100 percent. My sister was happy that our mother now had someone else to harp on besides her."

"That's horrible. How can your mother think that being gay is unnatural?"

"My mother is who she is and will never change. But now, my dad, he is truly amazing."

A supportive smile appeared as he leaned his body weight into the chair's armrest and asked, "Why is that?"

"At family dinner, when I came out to everyone, he was extremely quiet, but later that night he pulled me aside and told me that he has known for years, and no matter who I love, I'll always be his baby. He also told me how proud he was of me, and that it took a lot of courage to do what I did." Tears started to well up in her eyes as she remembered how safe he had made her feel when he hugged her and whispered that everything would be all right.

They were both silent for a moment.

Chris slowly leaned forward in his chair and softly put his hands on her knee, "Your dad sounds like an extraordinary man. I never realized how difficult it must be, coming out."

To keep her tears from erupting, she quickly swallowed, and stuttered, "It's not easy, but trust me when I say that I had it easy compared to a lot of people. There're parents out there that have rejected their children. I know people whose parents are so homophobic that they were kicked out of their house as their parent's proclaimed they were dead to them."

Sympathetically, he lightly gripped his fingers around her knee as he tried to give her the best encouraging smile he could. "How could anyone do that?" he whispered softly.

Kate simply answered sadly, "That's the world we live in."

Out of the blue, a loud knock interrupted their conversation. As they turned their heads toward the thumping, Aika, who was napping comfortably on the warm concrete, began her protective bark as she slothfully made her way to the front door. When Kate's eye caught a glimpse of the clock on the beige stucco patio wall, she yelled out in a panic, "Shit! I totally forgot. I can't believe its two o'clock already!"

Surprised and concerned by her rash reaction, Chris asked, "Forgot what?"

Slightly embarrassed as she stood in her pajamas in the middle of the open sliding glass door, she gave an apologetic smile and said, "I completely forgot that my parents were coming here today!" Without another word, she dashed into the house and slammed the bedroom door behind her as she searched through her closet for something to wear. There was another knock. In the middle of the living room, Chris stood frozen and watched Aika bark furiously. He could hear Kate cursing through the bedroom wall, and was unsure if he should wait for her or just answer the door. When he heard a loud thud and an even louder "Shit" emitted from the room, he decided it would be best not to interfere.

When Kate came out of the bedroom in an old pair of jeans and a wrinkled, faded blue tank top, with her hair in a messy bun, she found Chris frozen with a perplexed look on his face.

"Look, I'm apologizing in advance for anything that may or may not happen. My family, well, mainly my mother, can be a little unorthodox," she warned.

Thinking she'd lost her mind, the strangest expression appeared on his face as he responded, "It's just your parents; how bad can they be?" The knocking had stopped, and the doorbell began to ring impatiently as he continued. "You might want to let them in before they break down the door."

Prepping him for the inevitable, she put her hands on his shoulders and forewarned, "You asked for it!"

When she opened the door, she heard her mother's nagging voice say, "Well, someone has to be home. There's a car in the driveway, for goodness' sake."

Slightly nervous about her mother's reaction to Chris, Kate choked, "Hi, Mom."

Before Emily could even make it through the door, her imperious floral perfume aggravated Kate's sinuses. When she was able to escape from her mother's lung-crushing hug, she casually wiped the thin layer of tan foundation off her cheek—Emily always wore too much makeup.

While Emily was distracted, Mike, Kate's dad, snuck into the kitchen to put the beer in the fridge. With the best of intentions, Chris maneuvered around the preoccupied women, made his way into the kitchen, and politely introduced himself. The uncomfortable tension between them was not only instantaneous, but it clouded the room; so thick, a knife could cut it.

Chris nervously held out his shaky hand to Kate's father and stuttered, "Hello, sir." With no reaction, Mike stared at Chris with prying eyes and analyzed every detail of him. He was not pleased with the idea of a strange man alone with his little girl.

Unaware of the awkwardness between Chris and her father, Kate threw herself into her dad's burly arms as she inhaled the familiar scent of his Old Spice aftershave. "Daddy!"

With an enormous smile, Emily reached out her hand and introduced herself. "It's nice to meet you. I'm Emily." There was no hesitation as Chris took her hand, kissed it, and flashed his pearly whites. "I'm Chris Cody, and the pleasure is all mine."

Flustered by his charm, Emily blushed and stumbled through Mike's introduction. "This is my husband, Mike."

"It's nice to meet you, sir." Chris responded firmly. Forced by the gazing eyes of the girls, he reluctantly shook Chris's hand and muttered, "Chris Cody? Like the actor?"

"That's correct, sir."

An awkward silence occupied the room: no one knew what to say. To break up the tension, Kate grabbed some beers from the fridge and blurted, "Let's go outside."

Unfortunately, moving from one room to another didn't ease the pressure. Once outside, everyone sat on the edge of their seats as they sipped on their beers. It didn't take long for Emily to begin the conversation, and once that happened it was a constant stream of personal questions for Chris. Kate tried to deflect the attention away from him, but when he accidentally mentioned the things Kate said the first night they met, the tone of the conversation quickly changed. Still believing that Kate was a child, Emily tried to reprimand her for her actions. *This is not how ladies behave. Why must you be so crude? This is not how I raised you.* This did not work out very well, instead of gracefully ignoring the scold, she just lashed back at her mother. It was always like this, Emily couldn't stand Kate's strong personality, and Kate refused to be punished for it.

More than eager to leave the room, she picked a few of the empty bottles up off the table. "Dad, are you ready for another beer?"

"Sure," he said, and even though his bottle was still half full, he let his daughter have the escape she needed.

For a few seconds, Chris, Emily, and Mike awkwardly just stared at each other. "I'm going to see if she needs any help," Chris said politely as he pushed back the chair that rattled against the concrete, and took the remaining bottles. "Excuse me."

The bottles slipped out of Kate's hand, crashing into the sink when she realized Chris was right behind her. When she turned around, his arms were almost wrapped around her as he carefully leaned in closer, briefly brushing up against her to put the other bottles in the sink. Taken off guard by his closeness, she held her breath until he pulled away, which he did ever so slowly.

The penetrating electricity between them caused her heart to beat irrepressibly as she stuttered, "You keep sneaking up on me."

With a crook in his seductive smile, he whispered delicately, "I'm sorry, I didn't mean to scare you." There was passion in his intense eyes that suggested something different.

"You didn't scare me." Despite the unexpected squeak in her voice, she maintained her firmness, or at least she tried to. "Sorry about all the questions . . . my mother likes to talk a lot."

"Your mother is great. No need to apologize. I'm having a good time, so stop worrying." Lightly, he kissed her cheek, and then as if nothing had happened, he turned around, opened the fridge, and grabbed four more beers.

Kate could hear her dad saying, "Emily, let her be" in that familiar tone, the one where he had to pull the reins in. Small moments like that were why she loved her dad so much.

With the sun starting to set and a nip in the breeze, Emily and Mike decided to call it a night.

"It was very nice meeting you." With a drunken smile from ear to ear, Emily hugged Chris.

"The pleasure was mine."

Sleepily, Emily patted his shoulder as she balanced herself and slurred, "Now, don't be a stranger." Chris nodded his head in agreement. "Yes, ma'am."

"Hope you are not planning on staying too late?" The tone of Mike's voice was not threatening, but promised that if Chris crossed his boundaries, there would be a price to pay.

Eager to get her parents out of the house, Kate cut the conversation short. "OK, it's time to go!" Positioning herself in between her parents and with her hands on their backs, she helpfully steered them to the door.

"Love you, Dad." With his little girl in his arms, he smiled as he gave her a big bear hug.

Kate wrapped her arms around her mother, kissed her on the cheek, and said, "Love you, Mom."

"Love you too, sweetie. Be good to that one." Sloppily, she pointed with her curved index finger toward Chris and implied her usual message.

Exhausted, Kate mumbled, "What are you talking about?"

"I just have a good feeling about him."

"OK, Mom. You have a feeling about all men."

She hated it when her mother tried to set her up. Even though Emily claimed to accept her sexuality, she still felt the need to introduce her to men, despite Kate having been out of the closet for ten years. Fortunately, for her, Mike didn't try to change his daughter.

"Come on, Emily, let's leave the kids be." A loud yawn escaped his mouth as he covered it with his fist and gently pulled his wife by the wrist out the door.

In the comfortable stillness of her home, Kate allowed herself to lean against the wall letting out a sigh of relief. She rubbed her fingers across her temples attempting to remove the throbbing headache. After forcing herself away from the supportive wall, she was pleasantly surprised to find the patio lights turned off and Chris juggling empty bottles while closing the sliding glass door with his left foot. In disbelief, she stood frozen and watched him, with her mouth slightly ajar.

"Where do you want these?"

"What?"

"The bottles, Kate. Where do you put glass bottles?" he dangled an empty bottle in front of her to get her attention.

"Oh. There's a recycling bin in the garage." She glanced at Aika, who was staring back with the same questioning look: *What in the world is he doing?*

A few seconds after he found the recycling bin, he noticed that the garage was organized. Too organized. Everything was neatly in order and in a specific place. After he clicked off the light, he went directly to the kitchen, wiped off the counters, and poured Kate a glass of ice water.

Kate softly rubbed the dog's belly, almost comatose, stretched across the leather and her lap. Disturbed by the rattling noise when Chris put the glass down on the coffee table, Aika let out an annoyed low growl. Kate snapped her fingers, and then pointed her index finger drowsily in the general direction of Aika's bed. The large brindle pup reluctantly lugged herself off the couch.

Once the spot next to Kate was free, he joined her and laughed. "You have a way with words, don't you?"

Barely able to keep her eyes open, she mumbled, "Why are you here?"

"I like spending time with you; I've never met anyone like you before."

"You're telling me, of all the places you've been, and all the people you've met, you never met a lesbian?"

With his body turned sideways toward her, his elbow sunk into the back of the couch, and his head rested in his open palm, he sweetly smiled and said, "What are you doing tomorrow?"

The moment she opened her mouth, a yawn escaped as she mumbled, "I have to work."

"Where do you work?"

"I'm work freelance as a graphic designer." With heavy, tired eyes, she glanced up at Chris from under her fallen eyelashes.

"Freelance? How can you afford this large house doing that?" Instantly insulted, she lashed out, "Excuse me. That is none of your business!"

"I'm sorry. I didn't mean to offend you. My friends and I talk about this stuff all the time." Immediately, he leaned away from Kate, who looked like she was about to blow a gasket.

"I'm not one of those people at the fundraiser you call your friends, who gawked at me. I don't understand how you can even call those people your friends." Defensively, she crossed her arms while the flushed pink of her cheeks intensified. Friendship to Kate was an extremely important concept of her life, and for Chris to take the term so lightly made her mad.

Silent for a moment, he began to ponder back to a time when true friendship surrounded him. Before his career, before his fame, he had three friends that were more like family.

"I don't have friends like you do. Other than you, the people that surround me only need one thing from me." She already knew what people wanted from him, and it wasn't his charming personality.

"Don't you have friends from your childhood?"

He stared out of the sliding glass door into the silver moonlit night and sadly whispered, "I used to."

"Used to? What happened?" The sadness in his voice caused her eyes to curiously open.

"My three best friends were Sam, Eric, and James. We were extremely close. For years, I could turn to them for anything -- that is, until I thought I stopped needing them. When the fame took over, I tried ordering them around like my staff and that didn't work out so well. We haven't spoken in years. I'm starting to think I might need to apologize."

"Good for them!"

Chris automatically and wholeheartedly expected Kate to be on his side and when she wasn't, his mouth dropped in shock, "What?"

"I'm not going to sit here and feel sorry for you! Nor am I going to sugarcoat anything—that's why you're here, right? Chris, you act like a dick and wonder why you don't have any friends. News flash: People have feelings!" In midair his mouth continued to hang open, drying out his tongue, until she placed the tip of her index finger under his chiseled jaw and closed his mouth.

"Kate!"

She pointed her finger sternly at him. "And don't go around asking people how much money they make. It's rude. I don't ask you how much money you make."

"You can always Google it," he joked.

"I don't care about your money. Don't you get it? I don't care about money the way you do. To me, people are more important than the dollar sign." Considering this argument finished, she let out a loud yawn and muffled, "How long are you staying in town for?"

"I'm not really sure yet. I rented a small beach house for a while, but I might have to go back to California for business." With his elbows resting on his knees, he placed his head in his hands as he massaged his forehead.

Barely able to keep her eyes open, she nodded and mumbled something that sounded like, "That's nice."

"Come on, Kate, you have to go to bed." He woke her with a sweet nudge that was just enough to get her off the couch.

Trying to fight the weight of her heavy eyelids, Kate mumbled, "OK. OK."

At the front door, Chris gazed at a sleepy Kate and said, "I had a really good time. This is the most fun I've had in a long time." Like they had been life long friends, he comfortably hugged and kissed her forehead.

The next morning, Kate stumbled out of bed to the annoying beeping of her alarm clock at 6:45 a.m. After she scrambled through the sheets and hit the clock several times, the buzzing finally stopped. Her giant baby whined at the door, patiently waiting to empty her bladder. She got out of bed, threw on her robe, and opened the back door. Aika almost knocked her over bolting outside.

"Stay out of the neighbor's yard."

Her tea was prepared, and Kate turned on the Mac desktop that was surrounded by messy piles of papers. The email dinged, reminding her that she had a project due by the end of the day. The tea mug was placed in its normal spot that was marked by a brownish ring on a stack of papers that never moved. Fifteen minutes later she remembered Aika was outside and hurried to call her back in.

Aika went right to her bed and Kate back to her desk, where they both worked diligently for the next couple of hours.

The good and bad thing about living in a small town: everyone knows what's going on with everyone else. Through the gossip chains of old biddies in hair salons and bored housewives, anyone who lived in Rockledge at that time knew what had happened. She was that *poor Kate*, the woman who had lost everything, and then to top it off, had to make that heart aching decision.

Time doesn't necessarily heal all wounds—in some cases, it just dulls the pain to make living tolerable. That's what she was doing, going through the motions, living her life as best she could with the hand she'd been dealt . . . and eventually, the breakdowns had become fewer and fewer.

Kate had finished the project just in time to make it to her sister's to pick up her niece Elizabeth. On the drive over, she decided to call her good friend Becky. While she chattered away about her unexpected visitor, her friend listened intently hanging onto every word, but everything about the situation with Chris bugged her. Despite her irritation as she already judged him as a two-timing prick, Becky found herself extending an invitation.

"Kate, why don't you bring him along on Saturday?"

The sound of air deeply inhaling through Kate's teeth alarmed Becky when she answered, "I'm not sure that's a good idea."

"Why not?" she continued, condescendingly. "He's apparently hell bent on intruding into your life; you might as well let him meet us."

"We'll see. But hey, I have to go—I'm at my sister's."

"See you later, babe."

Kate closed her cell phone, threw it into her purse, and pulled into a parking spot outside of her sister's two-story apartment building. If Chris's behavior reflected anything like the night of the charity event, Becky's party would be a disaster.

❦

The front door flew wide open and Sandra was dressed in uniform – a diner's outfit. All of her other jobs, from cashiering to telemarketing, had failed—this was her most current and longest-lasting job, at a grand total of six months. Before this job, Kate's mom had pulled a few strings and gotten her sister a job at a dealership answering phones, but after two weeks, she'd been fired for sleeping with the boss. Now, running late, Sandra ran around her cluttered, tiny two-bedroom apartment, tripping over out-of-placed toys while she sloppily threw together a bag for Elizabeth.

The adorable, three-year-old sat on the worn, gray fabric couch with her feet dangling off the edge. Since her mother was too busy getting ready, she tried to finger-comb the tangles out of her long, curly brown hair, but they kept getting stuck. Kate sat down beside her, pulled a comb out of her purse, and slowly started to work out the tangles. When she was finished, Elizabeth's curls bounced in a pretty ponytail, tied with a simple silk blue bow.

"Thank you, Auntie Kate." Elizabeth smiled with her bright baby blue eyes. The sound of her niece's innocent almost angelic voice, both warmed, and saddened her heart. She would never be able to experience these moments with a child of her own.

"No problem, sweetheart." She smiled gently at her sweet niece and kissed her forehead.

"I was getting to that." Sandra smacked the sides of her thighs when she came into the living room and saw that Kate had helped Elizabeth. Sandra couldn't stand it when Kate appeared to be the perfect aunt.

"No worries. All done." Condescendingly, Kate smiled back at her sister.

In the middle of the driveway, blocking her way, was the shiny brand-new Porsche. Kate couldn't help but mumble obscenities under her breath at the sight of Chris awaiting her arrival on the porch. This was the third day in a row that he just showed up unannounced.

"What are you doing here?" she yelled as she slammed the driver's side door, and then opened the rear passenger door to get Elizabeth out of the car seat.

"You didn't tell me you had children." The sight of her with a baby in her arms was unnerving to him. Kids made him anxious; he was unsure of what to do or say around them, and having children was not something he had ever wanted—too much pressure.

"I don't have children. This is Elizabeth, my niece." After she grabbed the grocery bags and switched the baby from her left hip to her right hip, she closed the car door and whispered to Elizabeth, "Can you say hi?" Like a normal three-year-old, she squinted up her nose, shook her head in protest, and hid her face in Kate's shoulder. She was skeptical of strangers, especially men; she had watched her mom bring different men home and learned at a young age to stay clear of them. In order to comfort her niece, Kate patted her back and explained, "She's shy."

"She's cute. Here, let me help you with that." Like a gentleman, he took the plastic bags from her already full hands.

Skeptical of this new man, Elizabeth glared at him with narrow eyes over her aunt's shoulder. While they walked across the green lawn, Chris made funny faces at the little girl; self-consciously, she quickly turned in the opposite direction. Inside the house she jumped out of Kate's arms, ran to Aika, and threw herself on the poor mutt. Aika grunted in annoyance but lay still while the toddler crawled on her belly.

"So where's her mother?"

"At work," Kate replied flatly. She paused for a moment before deciding if she should divulge more details. Glancing into the living room, she caught Elizabeth dragging a large bag full of coloring paper and crayons from the play chest across the floor. Once the colorless pages sprawled out on the floor, she dumped the crayons out and ordered Aika to stay in the lines as she scribbled on the paper. A poignant smile appeared as Kate whispered, "Sandra isn't always reliable, and I don't want Elizabeth to suffer."

In a rush to get dinner done by six, she threw a frozen meat sauce lasagna in the oven, poured herself a glass of white wine, and started to chop the lettuce.

"Do you have any plans for Saturday? My friends are having a party, and I wanted to invite you. It's a pool party: lots of beer and food." As the knife sliced through the peeled cucumber, she thought to herself, *Please have plans!*

"Sounds like fun. There is something that I wanted to ask you, as well."

Damn, she cursed under her breath as she washed the ripe, red tomatoes. "Yeah, what is that?"

Chris stuck his head inside the fridge searching for a beer when he asked, "I have to go back to California in a few weeks for the premier of my new movie," he mumbled offhandedly. "And I was wondering if you wanted to go with me."

"Isn't that the new action one . . . what? You want ME to go with you?" In mid-slice, Kate froze as she gazed at him in astonishment.

The bottle cap hit the side of the off-white trash can as Chris resisted a bursting laugh at her, but sarcastically replied, "Yes. I believe that is what I asked you."

"Chris, there's something that I should have told you earlier." Calmly, she put down the knife on the wooden cutting board, took a sip of her wine, and quietly cleared her throat. "Because of your work, you live a very public life, and that's great for you. I, on the other hand, don't want to have people following me around or prying into my life. I agreed to let you in, not your irrational raging fans or the insensitive paparazzi."

Disenchanted, he said, "It wouldn't be like that."

"You know that's exactly what it would be like. The moment I show up with you, the camera will go crazy, and I don't want to end up on the cover of *Weekly Entertainment.*"

"Kate." Desperate to change her mind, he went around the corner to where she had picked up the knife and watched as she started to intensely chop away at the tomato.

She turned toward Chris with the knife blade pointed toward him, her face resolute; he stopped dead in his tracks. "No Chris. I need my life to remain private, and if you can't do that for me, then I can't do this." She flexed her wrist as the knife flickered between them.

It wasn't until that moment that Kate realized how dangerous it could be associating with Chris. There was a secret she didn't want revealed, and a past that she didn't want to relive.

"Wow." He threw his hands up in defeat. "Calm down. Sorry I asked— I didn't realize that you would threaten to end our friendship over it." Her defensive behavior clearly perturbed him.

Confused by this extreme aversion to a simple invitation to a reputable and desired event, he wondered—what could have happened to make her behave this way? Maybe there was more to Kate than the picture-perfect image she portrayed.

Much to her surprise, Chris was halfway decent with children. While she finished dinner, Chris, Elizabeth, and Aika played Flying Space Donkeys. Riding on Chris's back, Elizabeth was chasing the Space Donkeys as Aika howled excessively. It was the first time Kate had ever heard Aika howl, and even though the noise was ear-piercingly annoying, she smiled at the family unit that naturally formed in her living room. The picture that startled her eyes brought this unexpected sense of warmth and happiness to her heart. While she was pleasantly surprised to have these feelings, she was also saddened, as they were reserved for someone else. Someone she would now never be able to share it with again.

After dinner, she put Elizabeth to bed with Aika, who kept her warm in the covers. Quietly, Kate cracked the bedroom door and tiptoed down the hallway to find a pile of clean dishes on the left side of the sink. Chris was waiting patiently for her in the dimly lit living room, with two glasses of white wine.

"You didn't have to do that." Secretly, she was very glad that he had; Elizabeth had a way of draining the energy right out of her.

"No problem." Calmness surrounded them while they sat in the softly lit house; there was no need to fill the silence with chatter. Thirty minutes later, she began to twitch uncontrollably while anxiously playing with her necklace.

"Am I keeping you from something?"

"Oh no," she huffed in frustration. "It's just that Sandra is late again. I should be used to this by now."

Another long fifteen minutes passed before there was a knock; like a jackrabbit, she sprang from her seat and stomped angrily to the front door.

"Finally!" When she opened the door, Sandra fumbled to button her wrinkled, untucked, dingy off-white blouse to hide the just-been-fucked look. It was no use: Sandra's red velvet lipstick was smeared across her cheek, and the smudged mascara created black, raccoon-like circles under her eyes. When her sister left the house earlier that afternoon, her brown hair had been smooth and neat; now it was tangled and wild.

Greeted with the expected judgmental face of her younger sister, she snapped, "What? Don't give me that look. My shift ran late."

Annoyed by the same lame excuses, Kate rolled her eyes, turned away from her sister, and mumbled under her breath, *The shift may have run late, but I don't think it included shacking up with a random customer in the back of your car.* The distressed look on Kate's face had Chris concerned, and he immediately went to her.

"Where's Elizabeth?" Sandra demanded ungratefully; she wanted to leave as quickly as possible—well, until she saw Chris Cody. Intrigued and attracted, she didn't realize that her mouth had dropped open as she salivated at the gorgeousness he radiated.

In a fake, embellished Southern accent, she held out her hand, palm down, and bashfully stuttered, "Hi, I'm Kate's sister." It was apparent what she wanted—as Chris kissed her rough textured hand, chills spiraled through her entire body where his lips had touched her skin.

"Oh, my. What a gentleman." Pretending to blush, she mouthed the word *"Wow"* to Kate. The sight of her sister made Kate nauseated as she disgustedly shook her head.

Chris politely released Sandra's hand. "Hi, I'm Chris. Elizabeth is so beautiful," he complimented.

"Who . . .? Oh . . . yes . . . yes, of course." Sandra casually bypassed the topic of her daughter and diverted the conversation back to her. "What are you doing here? I don't mean to sound rude, but what could my lesbian sister offer you?"

"SANDRA!" Kate shouted angrily.

"Excuse me, Sandra, is it? Actually, I'm very satisfied spending time with Kate."

Sandra stared at him with shocked, wide-open eyes, unable to fathom what she just heard. Men were *her* forte; she knew what they wanted, how to please them, and they never turned her down.

Why does she get everything? Now she gets to spend her free time, which is all of her time, with Chris Cody. This is so unfair! Sandra complained silently to herself after she was rejected, without hesitation, from the movie star.

She bitterly placed her right hand on her hip, tilted her head, and condescendingly asked, "Oh, really? Kate, when did you jump the fence?"

It took all of Kate's energy not to smack her sister for that comment. She gritted her teeth angrily and tried to respond calmly. "Stop I'm not straight, and you know it. We met at a party a couple of weeks ago."

"Oh. OK. So you say." Patronizing her sister, Sandra continued, "It's not bad enough you take all the great women, now you have to take all the good men, too. Geez, when will you stop being so selfish?"

"Whatever, Sandra, you don't know what you're talking about. You're still intoxicated from your backseat romance." Sandra tried a rebuttal, but Kate immediately stopped her with a firm, extended hand. "Anyway, I need you to keep this to yourself. Mom and Dad know, but that's it. I don't want thousands of people swarming my house, trying to see the movie star."

"Sure, I won't tell anyone about your *platonic friendship*." Sarcastically, she did air quotes around the last two words.

"I'm serious, Sandra!" Kate was so pissed off at her sister's childish attitude that she acted out like a child herself, stomping her foot as she demanded hypocritically, just for a moment, that Sandra act like an adult.

"Fine! I won't tell anyone."

Just before she lost control and strangled her sister, she said, "I'll get Elizabeth."

The bedroom was pitch black except for the yellow hue glimmering from the hallway. Barely thirty-five pounds, the chubby toddler could easily take up the entire king-sized bed by herself. Nothing could wake this child when she slept; a twister could blaze through the middle of the house, and she wouldn't wake up until the next morning.

In the doorway she watched this precious child sleep, and thought for a moment that she'd missed out on this part of her life. The thought quickly faded as she heard Sandra laughing too loudly, trying to flirt with Chris.

When she walked around the corner with the sluggish baby in her arms, Sandra was all but throwing herself at Chris, who politely kept his distance.

Not to disturb Elizabeth, Kate carried her outside and gently placed her in the car seat. After Sandra drove away in her beat up 1992 Corolla, Kate complained to Chris, "Can you believe her?" Without hesitation, she grabbed her wineglass from the coffee table and began to chug. "How dare she say she has more to offer you than me?"

"Considering what she was offering, she isn't that far off base." Softly, he smiled at Kate, who was clearly flustered, with rosy pink cheeks.

"Please, it can't be that freaking complicated. All you have to do is be there." The next thing Kate knew the glass was empty and immediately marched to the fridge. She swung the door open, grabbed the quarter-full bottle, pulling the cork out and lifting it to her lips.

From behind she heard, "It's not that simple. When was the last time you were with a man, if ever?"

The liquid swooshed back and forth, as she dangled the bottle in the air and asked, "What does that have to do with anything?"

He tried to take the wine away from her, but she quickly moved it back to her lips.

"Everything. Sandra has been with many guys and knows her way around a dick; you, on the other hand, would probably be revolted at the idea of touching one."

"Ewe. That's gross. Why would anyone want to do that?" Disgusted at the mere thought, she made a sour face; Chris couldn't help but laugh out loud.

"See?" Red in the face from laughter, he moved toward her and gently took the white Zinfandel away. Reluctantly, she gave in.

Confused why this bothered her so much, Kate quickly laughed it off as no big deal, but deep down, she knew that Sandra could give him something she couldn't—which made her feel inferior. This really shouldn't have bothered her; these feelings were strange to her. Very strange.

The weeks seemed to pass with ease, and Chris found himself spending more and more time with Kate. When they weren't together, Chris found himself sitting on the beach enjoying the quietness of this small town. Several times his agent called, but Chris decided to ignore the calls; he didn't want anything to interrupt his time with Kate.

While having lunch one early afternoon, he noticed Kate's surfboards that leaned against the house.

"You surf?" He was taken off guard; he had assumed that she was more of a beach bunny than a surfer. Given her petite size, he didn't think she would be able to handle the waves.

"Of course, I surf; I grew up on the beach."

Chris looked perplexed. It appeared that he wanted to ask something but hesitated.

" . . . Cool."

"Want to go?"

"What?" There was a twinge in his voice. "Surfing?" It had easily jumped an octave. Even Aika looked up at him oddly.

"No, skiing. Yes—surfing." Grinning, Kate bent to give her begging child her scraps. "What's the matter with you?"

He played nervously with crust from his sandwich. "Nothing."

Concerned, she leaned back in her chair, observed his body language, and then said, "You're acting weird."

"No," he protested defensively, "I'm not!"

With a smirk on her face, she pulled her legs underneath her. "All you had to do was ask."

"Kate," he said firmly, all traces of his squeaky voice gone. "What are you talking about?"

"If you wanted to go surfing, all you had to do was ask." The awkwardness in the room began to surround them as they started to get aggravated with each other. It didn't take long for it to blow out of proportion, and when it did, Chris spoke to her in a self-righteous tone.

"I'm not accustomed to asking people for things. I tell people what I want, and they do it for me."

Kate's sweetness immediately disappeared. "Not me, you don't!" With that, she picked up her plate, called for the dog, and they both walked into the house, leaving Chris alone on the patio. The one thing she would not tolerate was rudeness.

Sitting alone, feeling like crap, he was beginning to realize the mistake he had just made. Staring at the surfboards, thinking how the conversation had gone so wrong, he suddenly noticed the surf wax sitting on the window ledge. As he touched the too-smooth surface of the surfboard, he realized it had been a while since he had waxed one.

Looking through her sliding glass door, Kate watched him sitting on the patio with a surfboard in his lap. His hand moved in a circular motion as the wax grated against the board. Aika went to investigate, and she followed shortly behind.

After she opened the door, Aika sniffed Chris, and then snorted in his face. Kate leaned in the doorway and curiously asked, "What are you doing?"

The sound of her voice distracted him as he glanced in her general direction. "Waxing your boards."

She suspiciously questioned, "Why?"

In the softest, most apologetic voice, he could manage, he replied, "Because there is something that I want to ask you."

A stern look was still upon her face as she crossed her arms and waited for him to continue.

"Kate, would you please take me surfing?"

She joined Chris on the patio while she continued to silently observe him with her narrowed eyes. The tension that surrounded the quietness made him nervous as his foot twitched anxiously, awaiting her response. Finally, a thin smile appeared on Kate's lips when she spoke. "The waves look good now."

Soaked in sea-salt water, they both trotted exhaustedly through the sand, back to the house. Pleasantly surprised by his hidden talent, Kate inquired, "Where did you learn to surf like that?"

"Kate, I grew up in California; surfing is second nature." He smiled as he pulled down his wet suit, exposing his ripped bare chest.

Chapter Six

Saturday, the day of Becky's pool party, Chris had strongly insisted that he pick up Kate. Running late, she scrambled to finish getting ready before he arrived. Three swimsuits later, she had finally decided to wear her purple halter-top bikini, covered with a white sundress and accessorized by the rings on her necklace. Given this was their first outing surrounding a large amount of alcohol, she decided to play it safe and pack an overnight bag.

Arriving promptly at one o'clock, he expected nothing less than to find Kate prepared and ready to go. When the knuckles grazed the wooden front door and the only response was barking, he became concerned. It took a moment for Aika to settle down until he heard Kate yelling *come in*.

The sight of her running from room to room with a concentrated, almost aggravated look on her face, was amusing. Instead of interrupting, he stood back and watched with his index finger covering his smirk.

Finally he had to intervene, "What are you doing?"

"I can't find my damn sunglasses!!! I hate it when I lose stuff!"

"Kate, come here." He beckoned.

"Wha . . . what?" She stammered. She stood impatiently in front of Chris while he silently but gently pulled a pair of sunglasses off her head, careful not to yank her hair.

He fought back the laughter, "Are you looking for these?"

"I swear, I would lose my head if it wasn't attached. Ready?"

"Yep."

On the way out the door with the bags loaded on her shoulder, she casually mentioned to Chris that there was a cooler on the counter. He smiled, nodded at her, went into the kitchen and lifted the cooler off the counter. The next sound was a loud grunt followed by an even louder thud.

"You OK?" She laughed to herself watching him struggle.

"What the hell did you put in here?" Still bracing himself against the cooler, his face was flushed red.

"Guess I should have waited to put the ice in. Oops." Slightly annoyed narrow eyes flashed across his face, while simultaneously, Kate happily skipped around the corner.

"You think?" he huffily managed

She peeked into the kitchen to find Chris still struggling then whispered, "It has wheels."

"Sure. Sure." He grabbed the handle and forcefully pulled the heavy cooler behind him.

Stopped at a red light, Kate glanced out the window into the bright, clear, blue sunny sky. A blue minivan pulled up next to them. The young woman inside smiled into the rearview mirror, singing to her daughter who was securely fastened in the back seat. Sadness stabbed her at the sight causing a heavy guilty sigh. That was supposed to be her. She had had a plan for her life, and it hadn't included riding in a Porsche with a famous actor.

Too painful to endure any longer, she turned her head away and glanced at Chris. "Can you explain something to me?" The tone in her voice immediately sent his nerves shivering up his back. His fingers tightly gripped around the smooth leather steering wheel. "I can try."

"Why do you like spending time with me? I mean you could be anywhere in the world right now. Why here? Why me?"

Before he could answer, the light changed green, and the engine roared as they accelerated. He thought deeply about this before answering; Kate didn't fully understand the responsibility of possessing millions.

"At the drop of a dime, I can go anywhere in the world and not think twice about it. I don't have to worry about money or entertainment. Hell, I don't even have to make the arrangements. There are people for that. Why did I choose here? For one, you're here; but mainly, because this small town is not entirely interested in me. At home, in Los Angeles, I can't walk down the street without having six bodyguards surrounding me. The screaming fans, the nagging agents, the annoying directors it's all a bit too much. I just wanted something normal, if even for a short time."

"I can understand that." Leaning back into the soft tan leather, a glimmer of a smile presented itself while she idly fidgeted with her rings, thoughts wondering back to a time when things were going according to her plan.

∞

Surrounding Becky's small suburban home were cars for the party. Almost two houses away, Chris had to drag the heavy cooler all the way to the front door, only to find a nice festive note; *come on in, party is in the back.*

The idea of walking into a stranger's house uninvited was a bit unnerving for him. "Is that really safe?" He immediately stepped to the side and faced Kate.

Perplexed with her hand on the knob, she stopped in mid-turn and slid her sunglasses on top of her head, "What?"

"This sign? Just letting people walk in."

Chuckling, she adjusted the wide black bag strap on her shoulder, "Chris, you worry too much."

Under his breath he mumbled, "In California, that's how you get shot." He followed cautiously behind Kate who walked into the house carefree.

Once he hauled the cooler all the way inside, he closed the front door, turned around, and was then face-to-face with Sheba, a snarling overprotective German Shepard. Startled, he jumped backwards, almost tripping on the cooler. *What's with people in Florida and their dogs? Does everyone own one?*

Laughing at his clumsiness, Kate stifled a laugh with her fingertips. After a few more chuckles, she finally commanded, "Sheba! Down!" The laughing smile returned once Sheba sat next to Kate. "Becky doesn't have to worry about getting robbed."

Standing up, he mumbled, "I guess dogs don't like me."

"Aika likes you."

"Only because I bribed her."

"You have to start somewhere." Beckoning Chris with a head nod, she summoned him into the guest room with her. Slowly and cautiously, he walked around Sheba, following Kate, leaving the aggravating cooler behind. She carelessly tossed the overnight bag on the bed, turned to Chris and exasperated, "Are you ready for this?"

Shaking his head at her dramatic performances he couldn't help but laugh, "Kate, you're the craziest woman I've ever met."

"Guess this is going to be more embarrassing for me than you. I can't believe I brought a guy to a lesbian party."

The kitchen was loaded with various liquors, mixers, and snacks displayed on the counter. Inside the fridge, she found that it was stacked full of her favorite beer. She smiled knowing that tonight would be one for the books. Everyone was outside engaged in random chatter until Chris stepped foot on the porch. The room went silent. Becky forgot to forewarn the group about his presence.

Behind the new couple, leaning against the house, was Becky who was more than thrilled to see Kate. A shriek filled the room. "Katie!" She screamed as the host lassoed her friend into her arms.

At a grand total of five feet two inches, everyone towered above Becky. While she may have been the shortest, she was never the smallest in weight or personality. Her rough features and spiky short hair kept most people intimidated; this was how she maintained control in her line of work – local police officer. Quite often, she was mistaken for a man, and while her friend could look past their ignorance, these comments always infuriated Kate. To her, Becky was beautiful, even if she was rough around the edges.

Delicately, she wiggled her way out of Becky's bear hug and introduced Chris. Even though they were cordial, there was an instantaneous tension between the two.

"Hey." He offered his hand. Reluctantly, Becky took it, squeezing as tightly as possible, and responded, "Hey." An awkward silence followed.

"Your home is lovely."

"Yeah. Thanks. Kate, make yourself at home." Beside herself that Kate had actually brought this guy, Becky just walked away to get another drink.

Chris leaned over and whispered into Kate's ear, "Is everyone here gay?"

"Everyone except you!"

"Even her?" He rudely pointed in the direction of a feminine blonde woman dressed in a skimpy black bikini. From behind her large dark sunglasses, Holly's full lips glowed red.

"Yes." Embarrassed by his impolite gesture, she sharply smacked his forearm with her fingertips.

"She can't be. She's too pretty."

"Lesbians can't be pretty?"

"No. It's that she's so girly . . . "

"You have a lot to learn." Underneath her breath, she chuckled and shook her head back and forth. "Lesbians can be girly, and Holly is the biggest one." She tilted her head beckoning him to follow her as she walked towards the blonde.

Not only feminine, but also extremely ostentatious, Holly carefully sipped on her strawberry daiquiri through the lipstick-tipped straw. At all times she had to look her best; her curly blonde hair carefully pulled back in a black flower hair tie as she applied another thick layer of suntan oil. At the young age of twenty-two, recently single Holly was eager to go out and play the field.

"Holly, this is my friend Chris."

The black sunglasses silently tilted down Holly's nose examining every inch of Chris while her baby blue eyes sparkled in the high-noon bright sun. A blank facial expression remained on her face while her matching red fingernail pushed the glasses back up the bridge of her nose. Snobbishly she jeered, "Girl, please tell me you haven't jumped the fence."

"Hell no!"

"Another one bites the dust."

"OK, listen here baby dyke, when you get past your infant one-pussy-eating stage, then we'll talk."

"Whatever. I'm Holly." Languidly introducing herself to Chris, she held out a limp hand for him to take. Barely paying attention, he gently took it.

"So who showed up?"

"You know, the usual crowd," sarcastically Holly continued, "Although Megan decided to let one of her followers tag along."

"Oh, that's just lovely."

"Yea. It's going to be an interesting night." Holly said snidely glaring at Chris. The reference confused Chris as he looked toward Kate for an explanation. Politely, she whispered in his ear, "Megan likes the young ones."

Gracefully, Kate escorted Chris around the yard introducing him to the girls. But the thought on everyone's mind was *why in the world did Kate bring a guy.*

In the side yard, they found Megan and Becky playing a friendly but competitive game of corn hole—a game where the players throw beanbags at wooden planks with holes in them, to get the most points.

Never having seen this game played before, Chris inquired, "What are they doing?"

"Playing corn hole." Along side the stucco house was an inch of shade and Kate stood there and watched.

"Playing what?"

While Becky had basically insisted that Kate invite Chris, she quickly began to regret her decision. Something about his persona rubbed her the wrong way. It wasn't that he had done anything wrong; she just had a gut feeling that he was bad news and wasn't shy about expressing her feelings, especially as she yelled out, "Corn hole! Wanna play, Chris? You should be really good at getting your bags into holes."

Embarrassed by her comment, Kate yelled, "Becky!" Megan couldn't help laughing under her breath.

"My beer is hot, want another, Megan?" Becky stood there pouring out her perfectly good beer while she glared at Chris standing next to Kate. When the last suds were gone, she angrily shook the bottle and walked away.

"Nah, I'm good." Megan walked over and joked with Chris, "Looks like you can turn a cold drink into a bucket of hot piss."

"Now, if I could only turn water into wine, I'd be set."

"Wouldn't we all?" Megan laughed, shaking his hand. "You'll have to excuse Becky, sometimes she gets in these funky moods. Just ignore her, that's what I do."

"Good to know." He smiled at Megan, appreciating her honesty. "Damn girl, that is one hell of a handshake." Chris playfully shook out the soreness in his right hand.

"I work out a little."

"A little?"

"Well, I have to keep the ladies happy." Megan smirked at Kate.

"Ladies, isn't that a bit of a stretch?" Kate questioned as she stole the beer from Megan's hand.

"Hmm?" Chris glanced at Kate for an explanation.

"Oh, don't let Megan fool you, these *ladies*," she teased using air quotes, "are more along the lines of children."

"It's not *that* bad."

"Really, how old is the new one?"

"This one is twenty," Megan shrugged as she smiled innocently.

"Twenty? What are you going to do? Feed her a bottle?"

With a sheepish smile of her own, she answered, "Well, I know one way she can get her milk."

"Ugh. That's gross."

"She doesn't seem to think so." Megan's eyes shifted toward her date that was talking with Holly. From a distance, Kate could see the girl had an ass to kill for and part of her understood Megan's motives.

The hot sun's blazing rays beat down on Chris's forehead as sweat profusely flowed from his pores. Desperate for some sort of relief, he fanned himself with his red T-shirt.

As he wiped the built-up residue from his brow, Megan couldn't help but ask, "Thirsty?" In agreement, he just nodded his head, stuck out his tongue, and panted like a dog.

∾

Back on the porch, Kate noticed Becky talking to Holly, who had a bored look on her face, almost as if she had heard the same conversation a hundred times already.

Underneath the protective shade from the porch, Kate and Chris both grabbed beers from their cooler and sat at the table with her friends, Charlotte and Beth.

"So have you guys found a donor?" Kate asked excitedly as she took a swig from her beer.

In her over-the-top, twangy Southern accent, Charlotte answered, "You'd never believe how much sperm there is to sort through!"

"Ew, that's gross." Disgusted at the sound of the word *sperm*, Kate's face twisted.

"Charlotte, why must you insist on calling it *sperm*?" Beth reprimanded. The hard lines on her face from years of construction made her facial expressions seem harsher than they really were.

"Well, ain't that what it is?"

"Can't you call it a *profile* like everyone else?" It embarrassed Beth when Charlotte said it like that.

"I ain't callin' it nothing it ain't."

The only reference Chris could correlate this situation to was picking up a girl at a bar. In a straight relationship, there is no choice in the child's DNA. The parents are who happened to decide to be together to have this child – no preselecting a biological parent based off a profile. When he expressed his confusion on the complexity Beth and Charlotte were experiencing, they politely explained their concerns. Relationships are tough, but gay relationships have their list of additional strains. There's a societal pressure that gay families have to be perfect in order to be accepted. Even then, there are still people who will never accept families different from their own.

As the heat index rose, so did the desire to get into the pool. Salivating at the opportunity to put Chris in his place, enthusiastically Becky suggested a game of pool volleyball. Despite the humidity, Kate wanted to take her time, slowly allowing her body to adjust to the un-heated water. Unfortunately, Chris would not allow it; like a two-year-old he jumped and splashed her until she was fully submerged.

Everyone divided into teams—Chris stuck close to Kate to ensure they were on the same team. This aggravated Becky, because she wanted Kate on her winning team.

Throughout the game, Kate was constantly putting her hand on her neck, making sure her necklace was still there. During one of the many beer breaks, she checked, and when she didn't feel the cool sterling silver under her fingertips, panic began to set in.

"Shit!! Where's my necklace? Shit, shit, shit!" Fearful that she had lost her most prized possession, she stroked her collarbone over and over, as if it would magically appear.

"What's the matter?" His first thought when she cried out was that she'd hurt herself, and when he saw the frightened look on her face, he rushed to her side without hesitation. When others noticed Kate's distress, everyone stopped the game to check on her.

"I lost my necklace; I have to find it now!" From the commotion of the game, she wasn't able to tell if it had sunk to the bottom of the pool.

"Kate, what's going on? What's wrong?" Typical take-charge Becky, immediately dashed to Kate's rescue and pulled her into her arms. "OK. Babe, look at me. What happened?"

Kate sniffled through her sobs, "My necklace."

"What about your necklace?"

"I don't know where it is." Everyone stayed on the sidelines. They knew how protective Becky could be—especially when it came to Kate. Unsure of how to comfort her, Chris stood there, and this was the confirmation Becky needed that he was useless and no good for Kate. Then, instinctively, he dove to the bottom of the pool and scanned the floor for the missing necklace.

"My necklace is gone." Frozen in place, Kate's hand rested where the necklace had been. Almost every person there knew how important the rings were; the only piece of her past that she kept. With all of her strength, she tried to stifle her sobs until Chris surfaced with the necklace. The crying stopped, but only long enough for Kate to notice that he was bent on his knees, holding them up for her. All she could think about were the memories that surrounded the rings, and his position caused her to cry again.

"Don't cry. It's OK, I found them." Dazed, she took the necklace and without a word, got out of the pool, grabbed a towel, and went inside.

He was confused and looked around at the sad faces and asked, "What did I do wrong?"

"You didn't do nothin' wrong, darlin'. I guess she hadn't told you yet, that's all." Charlotte placed a reassuring hand on his shoulder. "Kate went through a really hard time a while back, harder than you can ever imagine. But she'll tell you about it when she is ready."

"OK," Megan called, "You guys know the rules, back to the game!"

"Yes, Megan, we know you must burn as many calories as you consume," Holly snickered as she readjusted her hair.

With a sharp tone, Megan glared back at Holly. "Not that rule, the other one."

To get the game back on track, Megan shouted again, "All right, back to the game!" Everyone listened this time.

Concerned, Chris went to Kate and found her in a guest bedroom, sitting on the beige Berber carpet, staring at the wall. He gently knocked on the door. She quickly glanced over, and then turned away. Before he could completely sit down, she blurted out, "I don't want to talk about it."

"OK. You don't have to talk about it." His large protective hands were warming her cold-tipped fingers, and almost immediately, her shield began to crumble. The wall that she'd built to protect herself from the world and from people getting through wasn't working anymore. He was somehow penetrating her barrier—the harder she fought, the farther he got through. All she wanted was to live the rest of her life alone; at least, that's what she had told herself, thinking she would never love again.

"Will you tell me about it one day?" Unsure of how to comfort her, he did his best and sat there silently while he rubbed her hand.

"I don't want to be upset today." The damp fingertips pulled the tears from under her puffy eyes as she forced a smile and asked, "How do I look?"

"Beautiful." Allowing herself to be vulnerable, she fell into his surprisingly comfortable large arms; he kissed her head and whispered, "Everything will be all right."

While they were inside connecting, Becky was outside fuming.

"How dare he? Who does he think he is?"

"Becky, what the hell are you talking about?" Megan dropped the inflatable beach ball from a serve position as she heard Becky arguing with herself.

Standing against the pool wall with her arms firmly crossed and her eyes narrowed, she complained, "Him. Chris! He has the audacity to go after her like . . . like he knows her, when he doesn't even know what is going on."

"Maybe he is trying to figure out what is going on," a snotty voice called out from the other side of the pool.

"You know what, Holly? You don't know what the hell you're talking about."

"What's da matter with Chris?" the Southern belle chimed in. "He seems fine to me." Within minutes, the entire party had gathered at the shallow end to hear Becky complain about him.

"What he's doing now! *That's* what's wrong with him. Seriously, what could he have in common with her? I'm telling you, he's dangerous."

"Oh, please, I highly doubt that someone like that is dangerous; you know exactly what this is about." Megan snorted back to her.

Insulted that one of her closest friends didn't support her, Becky snapped as she threw the hand-crushed beer can. "Have you lost your sense of judgment, Megan?"

"Have *you*? Becky, you know damn well this has nothing to do with Chris." Automatically, Becky opened her mouth to make a smart comment, but stopped short when Megan shot her a warning look.

It never used to be this intense—her overprotectiveness of Kate; hanging out with her used to be fun. That had all changed four years ago when Kate had fallen on hard times. Becky had assumed the role of protector, and even when things returned to normal, she continued in her self-defined role.

While she played Kate's hero, somewhere along the line she'd ended up falling for the damsel. Unfortunately, she didn't have the courage to express her passion. Fear of rejection and of losing the friendship meant that she just buried her emotions.

It took about ten minutes, but Kate's eyes returned to normal. The red puffiness began to dissipate into a faint memory as she grabbed another beer from the fridge. Happily, almost couple-like, Kate and Chris joined the party outside.

After three shots of Patrón and six beers, she felt extremely mellow. The music was turned up, the chairs pushed to the side, and the girls began to dance. Despite Kate's lack of rhythm, she continued to sway like Drake in the Hotline Bling video.

Away from where the girls were dancing, Chris leaned back in a chair while he watched her in her element. *She is so full of life and sparkle. I never thought that I would have so much fun doing normal things.*

From across the room, Becky scowled at Chris, whose eyes were glued to Kate and who was sporting a large grin. Unable to stand his cheerfulness, she decided to give him a piece of her mind—but not before drowning herself in liquid courage.

Chris heard her sneak up behind him, as she leaned into his ear and whispered in an unwelcoming tone, "How are you enjoying the party?"

"It's great." Even though he could feel the anger in her voice, he refused to take his eyes off Kate—which just further infuriated her.

A predator circling its prey, Becky walked around his chair until she was standing in front of him, intentionally blocking his view of Kate. "Everyone here loves Kate, and no one wants to see her get hurt again."

His lips turned into a hard line and his eyes went cold as he met her threatening glare. *Give me a reason, any reason at all,* Becky thought to herself.

In an exceedingly polite tone, he responded, "I'm only her friend, I don't mean any harm."

"Well, of course you don't, darling." The sweet country voice melted the tension like butter on warm toast as Charlotte put her arm around him and shot Becky a cautionary look.

"But that doesn't mean harm can't be done," she snorted, ignoring Charlotte.

"Oh stop, Becky. Go have another drink and leave him alone." Annoyed by Charlotte's pushiness, she stomped away, growling under her breath.

"Sorry about that; Becky is very sensitive about Kate. I think she might have a thang for her." Since the sound of metal furniture grating against the patio deck rattled Charlotte's nerves, she picked up the chair and sat next to Chris.

"I couldn't tell." He smiled sarcastically, but finished sadly, "But I could hurt her, and I don't want to do that."

"Chris, whenever you get close to someone, there is the chance of them hurtin' you, and vice versa. That's life. Look at her. Do ya see how happy she is? There is something different about Kate, and I think it has to do with you."

"You know, the funny thing is that I came here because I thought *she* was going to make a difference in *my* life."

With both of their eyes locked on Kate, and without a glance in Chris's direction, Charlotte smiled. "She has; you just don't know it yet."

Returning from the dance floor, Kate was in desperate need to quench her thirst. Placed safely on the window ledge behind Chris sat her much-desired beverage and, wobbly, she unsuccessfully reached out. Taking pity, he ever so politely reached behind him and handed the bottle to her. She happily fell into his lap, taking him by surprise. The sudden display of affection made him feel slightly uneasy. He tried smoothly to remove himself from under her, but she demanded otherwise.

On the other side of the patio, Becky was watching them, ignoring Holly as she kept jabbering on about something insignificant.

You'll never love her, as much as I love her. You don't know how to love a woman the way I do.

Drowning her sorrows in the comforting fizz of a Sparks Lemon Stinger, Kate began to lose control of her proper protocol. Desiring more legroom, she shooed Chris out of his chair and swung her legs on top of the arm.

Noticing the obviously glazed look in her eyes, Chris quietly suggested that it was time to leave. Following orders, Kate slowly placed her feet on the ground, causing the room to spin. Ignoring the dizziness, she stood, but not for long. It was half a second before both Chris and Becky reached out to catch Kate.

The majority of Kate's limp body landed in Chris's arms, however, Becky still had a good grip on her wrist. Protectively, Chris said, "I got her," causing an immediate reaction. Becky's eyes narrowed while she puffed out her chest, challenging her rival. Without hesitation, Chris moved Kate further away from Becky. Determined to stand on her own, Kate maneuvered out of his grip while slurring very loudly, "I'm *fine*. Would you two stop fighting over me?" The swirling motion of the room increased causing her eyes to roll backwards and she stumbled. Luckily Chris caught her again.

The engine stopped purring when Chris turned the key. Passed out in the front seat, Kate nuzzled her head in the doorframe. The sound of the driver's door opening awakened her. Weakly, Kate's thumb tried to release the seatbelt, but she couldn't make it any further without assistance. The door opened, and Chris helped her roll out. It took a good five minutes of carefully maneuvering her through the yard and coaching her up the stairs, but they made it to the front door. Silently, Chris stared at Kate hoping she would remember that she needed keys to get inside.

"Keys?" he asked. Before the words registered, Kate stared blankly at the door swaying.

"Oh . . . yeah . . . umm . . . in my purse." The motion of looking down in search of the keys made her even dizzier. Resisting the urge to vomit, she flung the purse to Chris. Impressively quick, he was able to locate the keys and open the front door before she tumbled down the stairs.

The moment the bolt lock turned, Aika went into protective mode and barked at the potential intruders.

"Down Aika!" Chris commanded. In a drunken fog, Kate sloppily raised her right index finger to her lips, "*Shhhh . . .*" she slurred, moving her now open palm toward Chris's face to pat it indulgently, but missing it entirely.

"Time to go to sleep," Chris whispered as he led her to the bedroom.

Kate spoke sluggishly, poking her chest with her extended index finger. "Yeah, yeah. I'm in my bathing suit." She held on to the post at the edge of her bed and continued to sway back and forth until, without warning, she began to peel off the layers.

"Wait a minute!" Chris pounced toward Kate, stopping her right hand from unhooking the bikini top. Annoyed by his gentlemanly qualities, she rolled her eyes, huffed, and threw herself back onto the bed. While she lay there, rhythmically kicking her feet, Chris rummaged through her drawers and finally came across a set of pajamas, laid them beside her, and left her to change.

The screen door screeched under the weight of Chris's hands. "Come on, Aika, outside."

In the guest bathroom, he found two aspirin in the medicine cabinet and poured Kate a glass of water. He waited a few more minutes before letting Aika back in, then securely locked up.

His fingers lightly tapped on the bedroom door and slightly above a whisper, he asked, "Are you dressed?"

The door creaked as it opened and once Kate spotted him, a loud voice emerged, "Here I am!" The sight of Chris provoked so much excitement that Kate threw up her hands like scoring a touchdown.

Instead of putting on the pajamas that Chris had so neatly set out for her, she ransacked her drawers and was now dressed in a white wife beater and a pair of faded, navy blue gym shorts.

"Yes, you are," he laughingly concurred. "Come on, get into bed." A slightly sour look appeared, but Kate didn't argue. Instead, she crawled into bed and curled up, placing her head on the pale yellow goose-down pillow.

The two aspirins were tucked safely in the curve of his palm. "Take this; it will help in the morning."

The weight of her tired head made lifting it rather difficult, but after she popped the pills with a swish of water, she let her heavy head plop back on the pillow. It didn't take long for her eyelids to take on a life of their own and close. Awestruck by her beauty, Chris stood there enthralled by the sight for a moment before he quietly tried to leave.

"No!" Kate reached out sitting up too quickly. "Don't leave. Stay."

"OK." This affectionate behavior was unlike her. Happily surprised that there was more to Kate's tough exterior image, Chris watched her cling to the headrest. "Just lie back down."

Once she resettled back in bed, he slowly climbed in with her, careful not to disturb the half-unconscious beauty. Insecure about the rules of sleeping with a lesbian, Chris lay on top of the covers trying to keep his distance. Despite his best efforts, Kate pulled his arm over her waist and snuggled into him like they were long-time lovers.

Chapter Seven

The warm sunbeams streaming through the sheer curtains roused Kate. Thud. Thud. The pounding of her headache required her eyes to remain closed. Subconsciously, Kate lay there rubbing her hand up and down the arm she snuggled. *It feels good to wake up cuddling,* she thought. *The comfort of these big strongarms...big...strong arms?*

It didn't take her long to realize the arm belonged to a man. Terrified, her eyes flung wide open while her mind raced on how she got herself into this position. Scared out of her wits that something truly horrifying happened, she jumped from her bed screaming, "What the hell are you doing in my bed?"

Startled and disoriented, Chris barely croaked, "What? What's wrong?" He'd only been asleep for an hour—every time Kate moved, he awoke to ensure she was all right.

"You're in my bed! What the hell happened?" She stood defensively between the bed and the nightstand with her arms crossed. She tried to wait for the answers, but unexpectedly, the room began to spin again. It didn't take long for the nauseous feeling to bubble in her stomach and her temples to throb as she tried to rub the aching pain away.

More concerned with her well being than her ridiculous questions, Chris commanded, "Get back in bed."

"God, please tell me nothing happened."

"Oh, just relax. Nothing happened, you passed out drunk. Do you think that I would take advantage of you?"

Irritable and sleep deprived, Chris wasn't in the mood for her snide comments. For most of his adult life, he had been considered the unattainable bachelor, with a reputation for using women. But how could Kate think that of him? He had treated her with nothing less than the utmost respect.

Quietly, Kate spoke, "I want to talk to you about what happened last night." Just from the tone of her voice, he immediately began to wake himself up, sensing that this was extremely important.

Slowly, Kate's sorrowful eyes closed as she began to talk, "So, I'm sure you've figured out that something bad happened to me." A strategic pause was needed to collect her thoughts as she realized the last time she spoke about this was over a year ago. "Five years ago, my life was perfect. I had everything that I ever dreamed about. My wife, Riley, and I had been together for almost eight years, and she was the love of my life—I knew from the moment we met she was my soul mate." Another pause and now a smile appeared as a memory flickered through Kate's mind...

"Baby, are you almost done?" As she pulled her head from under the hood of her '69 Z Camaro, a grease-covered Riley looked up at an antsy Kate.

"Yeah, I'm almost done. I just have to finish this one thing."

"Riley, that's what you said two hours ago."

"Can you hand me the socket wrench?" A confused looked clouded Kate's face as she pretended to search for it.

"Which one is the socket wrench again?" Suddenly, grease-stained hands were intertwined with Kate's red-polished fingertips from behind.

"How does a girl who spends so much time in a garage not know what a socket wrench is?" Riley whispered into Kate's ear.

Shyly, Kate shrugged her shoulders. "I don't know; maybe because I don't spend as much time in here as you do."

"You know which one; it's this one." Riley rubbed Kate's hand under hers and pointed to the steel wrench.

"Ahh. That's right. Silly me, what would I do without you, my dear?"

"You were just trying to distract me."

"I have no idea what you mean." They smiled coyly at each other as Riley followed Kate out of the garage.

Placing the memory to the side, Kate continued, "Riley was the most adventurous person I've ever known. Something simple like a car ride could easily turn into a four-day road trip. The way that she cared for other people was beyond me. It didn't matter who it was, Riley was always there to lend a helping hand. I'd always suspected that's why she joined the police force."

There were times when Riley's charity caused inconveniences in their lives and Kate had complained. Today, Kate cursed herself for her ungrateful behavior because she would give anything to have one of those moments back.

"We were happy, but we wanted something more: children. After she received a promotion, we started thinking it was the right time to start our family. Countless hours of discussions and arguments about whether to adopt, use artificial insemination . . .we even toyed with the idea of having a surrogate, but we were still as confused as when we started, if not more so. After weighing the pros and cons of each option, we decided that the best route would be for me to carry the child. Trying to cut costs, Riley had this brilliant idea that I could get pregnant at home. I had never seen her so excited and nervous all at the same time." Beautiful memories of Riley began to flood Kate's mind causing a smile, but also a small tear trickled down Kate's cheek. The pauses were becoming longer and longer and Chris debated whether or not to intervene.

"January nineteenth, two thousand ten, is a day that I will never forget. We were having an ultrasound done. I remember Riley nervously holding my hand, so anxious to find out the gender. When we were told it was a girl, Riley's face lit up like fireworks. Happiness couldn't describe the joy we felt. In that moment, God granted us our every wish." Silently, Kate sat there as her facial expression sadly changed. "I say moment because that is exactly how long my happiness lasted."

Words couldn't escape through the thick sobs that consumed Kate's emotions. Her cries sounded like shrieks that roared through her throat while she shook herself back and forth. She couldn't hold back anymore, she didn't want to. The events poured out of her.

The drive home from the doctor's appointment was like any other afternoon in sunny Florida. Riley sat in the passenger's side, treasuring the image of their baby girl. The small green Honda CRV, that Riley had just purchased two weeks ago for the expected baby, was filled with smiles and excitement beyond imagination.

While stopped at a red light, Riley started throwing out possible baby names.

"I love the name Emma," she pleaded. Not completely sold, Kate looked over and smiled sweetly at her. This was a stall tactic. The light turned green and Kate pressed the accelerator.

Fifteen minutes earlier, an out-of-town businessman stopped at the local bar for an afternoon cocktail. While he had problems with alcohol in the past, he had promised his wife it was no longer an issue. A self-proclaimed functioning alcoholic, he always thought he could handle himself, until today.

Only a mile away from the intersection where Kate and Riley were, his phone slid off his seat and he reached for it, swerving around an elderly lady in the slow lane. He never saw the red light.

There were no screeching tires, just this very powerful metal on metal crunching together. His Altima slammed directly into the passenger side, and the girls folded like a piece of soft bread. His car pushed them across two lanes, until they hit a metal lamp post. Riley was pinned against the dashboard and her head slammed several times against the glass. Kate tried to call out, but the only sounds that escaped were a series of grunts, forced out by the pain of restraint. The car lurched to a hard stop, swinging her head against the window.

When she opened her eyes, the only thing she remembered seeing was smoke bursting from the hood. And that's how she knew they had just been in an accident. Kate's first thought were of Riley and to make sure she was okay, but all Kate could see was a jumble of hair and blood everywhere! She didn't know what to do. She was pinned against the dashboard; her entire seat had been slammed forward when the doors crumbled in. Riley was so squished; she wasn't moving, and the blood poured out. All Kate saw was her wife looking so broken.

Every time she tried to reach out to Riley, the seatbelt cut further into her ribs. It didn't take long for Kate to notice that Riley's seat had been jammed where the gear shifter should have been. There was no way out. Kate was trapped between a thick large metal lamppost and Riley. She screamed and screamed, but nothing, She was surrounded by broken glass and blood.

The horrific images weren't something that Kate could ever erase. By the time she finished sobbing her story, Chris had a better understanding of Kate's demeanor. Chris let her break down as he sat helplessly, frozen in place. After a few minutes, Kate collected herself. She wanted to finish the story.

For a moment, Kate's eyes fluttered shut and the next thing she knew she was at the hospital with people standing around her whispering. She could only identify a few words. "Tragic." "Recovery." "Unlikely."

Kate took a moment to break down at the memory that she tried so hard to forget.

Painfully, the swollen eyelids forced themselves open. The bright fluorescent lights caused Kate's sensitive eyes to tear up and small droplets to roll down her cheeks. Emily was the first to notice Kate's eyes were open, and the hushed whispers disappeared. Silent, the room ached with quietness, aside from the rhythmic beeping, until the doctor spoke up. Sympathetically and gently, the doctor checked Kate's blood pressure, flashed a light into her eyes, and listened to her heart. A few scribbles on the chart and the doctor flashed Kate a sad smile. Emily had the same look.

After the doctor left the room, Emily's voice cracked, "Katie, dear." The only time Emily ever called her daughter Katie was when there was something wrong.

"No." Kate didn't know what her mother was going to say, but she refused to hear it since it could only be bad.

"Baby. Please. Listen to your mom," her dad pleaded from the corner of the room. Shifting her teary eyes to him, Kate couldn't force back the tears any longer. Gently, Emily shifted Kate's swollen face to hers and as softly as she could she whispered, "We lost the baby."

"No. No!"

"Kate, please calm down." Emily desperately held Kate's arm before she pulled out her own IVs.

"There has to be a mistake!" Kate pleaded with her eyes closed—she furiously shook her head, trying to wake herself from a bad dream.

"Sweetie, there is no mistake." Tears filled her mother's eyes to see her child in so much pain.

"I want to see Riley."

"You can't see her now."

"I want to see my wife, damn it!" Uncontrollably, Kate screamed at the top of her lungs-until the nurses came in and sedated her.

"I felt as if the tears would never cease. My heart was broken beyond repair and I just fell into this sadness, where nothing mattered. My father refused to leave the room, especially on the day the doctor explained what happened to Riley. After several large words that sounded completely foreign to me, it finally boiled down to this: when her head smashed against the window, the brain became so swollen that it basically caused her to fall into a vegetative state." Then it happened again, another heartbreaking memory surfaced that Kate shared through her sobs.

In a hospital-issued wheelchair, Kate managed to push herself down to the Intensive Care Unit. Rolling past each patient made her heart tighten. She worried whether she could handle seeing Riley in that condition. Or worse, should she tell Riley about the loss of their only child? The tears streamed down her cheeks as she held back her sobs and continued to push forward.

Room two twelve had the name Riley Reynolds printed on a small plastic nametag. The wooden door was all that stood in the way of Kate coming face-to-face with reality. Forcefully, she pushed the door hard enough so she could roll in. The dark room, lit only by the dim fluorescent light, reminded Kate of a hospital room in a tacky horror movie. The monotone beeping was intimidating and once Kate's eyes adjusted to the depressing mood lighting, the sight of Riley broke her heart. Clear tubes came out of Riley in all different directions while she lay there stiffer than a corpse. Other than the faint motion of Riley's chest rising and falling, there was no sign of life.

After three hours of sitting with Riley's hand wrapped in hers, a nurse came in to usher Kate back to her room. Tired, Kate flatly refused the warden in the stiff white dress, but it wasn't long before the nurse returned again and took Kate to rest.

"Daily, after my therapy, I visited Riley until the nurses kicked me out. Once I was discharged from the hospital, I continued to go back every day. The thought of leaving her killed me; if she woke up and I wasn't there, I wouldn't have been able to live with myself. A month passed with no improvement, and the doctor pulled me aside."

"Ms. Woods, we need to sit down and discuss what you are going to do next."

"What do you mean? Is there a new treatment that we can try?"

"That's not what I meant. Given Ms. Reynolds's condition . . ."

"Her name is Riley," Kate quickly interrupted, "Riley. My wife; Riley."

"Yes. Given Riley's condition, it's very unlikely she will recover."

"I'm not going to kill my wife, if that's what you are asking me to do. I won't give up on her."

"I understand how hard this must be, but you have to think about what she would have wanted."

"I am thinking about Riley; that's why I'm fighting for her. All you people care about is opening up another bed." With that Kate stormed out of the doctor's office and down the long white hallway.

Tears blurred Kate's vision and before she could continue, she had to clear her throat. "A month turned into two; two turned into three, and my hopes of a miracle were fading quickly. I had meeting after meeting with doctors, specialists, and anyone that could offer an option that might bring my wife back to me. But each time it was the same story; *there is no cure, all we can do is keep her comfortable.* All the new technology and medical breakthroughs, and they couldn't wake someone up. I was beyond frustrated, and I turned to the only person who knew Riley better than me – Becky."

Suddenly, it became crystal clear to Chris why Becky had been so protective of Kate. With a diminutive smile she continued. "Becky reminded me of the painful truth; Riley had been stuck in a vegetative state for the past three months, and even if she did regain consciousness, there would be a severe amount of brain damage.

"This only provided further confusion; everything was spiraling out of control. I didn't know if I was prepared to see my vibrant wife unable to handle the simplest of tasks like holding up her own arm. Night after night, I tossed and turned until I made the hardest decision of my life. To let Riley go."

The tingling vibrations of the last words upon her lips made her heart feel lighter. It had been years since she spoke about Riley, and somehow retelling her story made Kate feel relieved. She had become so comfortable that by the time she finished talking, she was wrapped in Chris's embrace.

He whispered softly as he held her tight, "Kate, I had no idea. I'm so sorry."

A nod of appreciation was her only response. Peaceful moments passed until Chris thought about something. "Where was Riley's family?"

Kate's eyes sprung open—this question took her by surprise. Nervously, she answered, "Riley's parents did show up, but they didn't stay for long."

"What? Why? I can't imagine a parent losing their child and not being there."

"Riley and her parents weren't on speaking terms. Remember how I told you, sometimes a family disowns their child when the child comes out of the closet?"

"Yeah . . ."

"Well, this is the perfect example. Riley's parents are wealthy Southern Baptists and had an image to uphold. Having a lesbian daughter didn't fit into that picture."

"That's heartbreaking." Then another random question popped out of his mouth almost as if he'd been saving them up, "I know you called Riley your wife, but were you legally married?"

"At that time you couldn't in Florida."

"Then how were you able to . . ."

"I had power of attorney. Everything was left up to me. Given Riley's line of work, we needed to be prepared if anything happened. We just never thought it would happen like that."

The experience of losing a loved one is hard, which Chris understood—but his experience couldn't compare to Kate's. When his mother had passed, as hard as it was, he knew that she was dying, and had time to mentally prepare for it. But Kate, poor Kate, didn't have time—that was taken away from her. Everything that was important to her disappeared in a flash.

Enveloped in her thoughts, she stayed quiet. She had no desire for Chris to ask any further questions about Riley's parents. There was a particular part of the story that she had purposely left out. No one knew that it had happened, and if left up to Kate, not a soul would find out.

"Kate, Kate . . ."

The sound of his voice startled her back from her thoughts. Huge drops of tears made jagged, paths down her cheeks. They continued flowing, one right after another, so fast that it looked as if a river was eroding her face. Remembering that her dream life was no longer her reality, Kate could feel the absence of Riley, and it made her want to die.

Still surrounded by the softness of her sheets and the warmth of Chris's arms, she used the silky material to pat her puffy eyes dry as she mumbled, "You surprise me."

"What's that supposed to mean?" Puzzled by her comment, he lifted Kate's chin with his forefinger and thumb to get a better look.

"I just never thought in a million years you would have been this understanding. So sympathetic."

"A lot has changed in the past few weeks. I've found that being here has shifted my perspective in life. You've had a major part in that and, without knowing it, you've helped me move forward in a more positive direction."

His words were warm and sweet and somehow sensual. *How could this be?* There wasn't a sexual attraction to him, but something deep inside of her began to stir, causing all kinds of confusion. Even four years after the accident the idea of dating someone, much less falling in love, seemed like a luxury she would never be afforded again.

Why couldn't he be a beautiful woman? It would make things so much easier, she thought to herself. There were too many feelings racing through her body: compassion, guilt . . . and love? *How can I love him? He is a man.*

To stop her mind from racing, she needed to set the record straight, but before she could finish her sentence Chris placed a wisp of hair behind her ear and exhaled, "Kate you mean the world to me, but I get it; this is nothing more than a friendship."

Relieved, she just nodded her achy head, grateful that he spared her the trouble of an explanation. The truth of the matter was that Chris was changing himself for the better, and Kate was the reason. She could see it and as much as she wanted to ignore it, the signs were there day in, day out. This only caused her more guilt. The type of guilt that makes a person feel as though their lives were ripping apart at the seams with no way to escape it. If she could only tell him how the story truly ended, but no one could ever know. This only caused her more anguish, that one small decision had changed everything and still haunted her today.

Chapter Eight

Yesterday, Kate revealed more than she had ever expected to, which caused her fragile emotions to fray at the edges.

On the patio, she relaxed on a plump lawn chair with a book in her hand, thoroughly enjoying the warm sun melting into her olive skin as the cool breeze surrounded her. Unfortunately, it didn't last long enough.

A now familiar voice interrupted the peace and quiet. "I have to go back to L.A. this week, and you should come with me. Plus, I have some friends that I'd like you to meet." It had been three days since the pool party, and Chris had refused to leave her side.

Since the day he arrived in Florida, he wasn't tied to a strict schedule and with this freedom, he found himself getting lost in Kate's simple world. It wasn't long until reality came creeping back. His agent scheduled a meeting with his publicist and an interview for his upcoming film. Not to mention, there was prep work for the new film.

The dilemma—to his own bewilderment, was that he didn't want to leave her side. Over the past few weeks, an intense connection had developed; but once Chris learned about the tragic accident, he surprisingly felt more protective.

In a monotone voice Kate replied, as she turned another page in her book, "That sounds nice, but I'm not sure."

"What could you not be sure about?" Annoyed by her careless tone, Chris sat up in his lawn chair, planting his feet firmly on the hot pavement. For an extended moment he just stared at her with slightly narrowed eyes as she continued to read her book.

Her eyes never moved from the black print. "Well I'm not sure how you're going to be able to keep the media away from me out there." She lightly moistened her finger upon her lips and turned another page. Chris's patience turned paper-thin as he pressed his own lips together and impatiently waited for Kate to acknowledge him.

After a few moments, he snatched the book out of her hand, firmly placed it in her lap and exclaimed, "Damn it, Kate, you're not listening to me!"

Aggravated, she threw her book on the concrete floor. It bounced off the side of a chair and almost toppled into the pool. "What the hell? I'm listening!"

To calm his agitation, Chris took a deep breath and spoke softly, "Keeping your privacy intact is not an issue; we'll just have to put a few rules into place."

"Rules? What kind of rules?"

"Nothing you need to worry about on your end. Everything will work out." This was not the answer Kate had expected. Despite her urge to argue, she knew it was pointless. In the end, he would win. He always did.

"OK," she finally submitted, "just let me know when, and I'll get tickets." Having thought the matter settled, Kate extended her reach to regain possession of her beloved book almost falling over in the process. After finding the lost page, she readjusted herself and casually glanced at Chris who just smirked.

"Don't worry about that!" he burst with excitement, "I'll take care of all the arrangements!" From the small table he grabbed his cell phone and disappeared into the house.

Kate found it peculiar for Chris to be so excited about a simple trip home. This whole idea made her uneasy. Here, she could maintain control - but out there - on his turf, she would be subjected to his ostentatious lifestyle.

It didn't take long for Chris to return and when he did, he flashed that charming smile at her and said, "We leave tomorrow!"

"Tomorrow?" The book gave a thud as it fell out of her limp hands and hit the ground.

"Yeah. Why? What's wrong with tomorrow? Do you need me to push the date back?"

"It's just that it's so . . . soon. We just decided to go." Awakened by the stress in Kate's voice, Aika stretched her hind legs and let out a loud yawn.

"What about Aika? I can't leave her behind! She still hasn't forgiven me for the New York trip." The 80-pound fur baby grunted at the memory of the lonely kennel where she was ditched.

"Well, of course we're taking Aika! I couldn't leave my girl behind." Long tongue draping from her slobbery mouth, the mastiff ran happily to Chris throwing her whole body into his lap.

Traitor. Betrayed by my own dog.

A good, loyal dog would have helped her owner get out of this mess - - not encourage the perpetrator. Instead, Aika sat contently in Chris's lap, and though Kate couldn't prove it, she would have sworn that the furry beast and toothy swine had planned the whole thing together.

"We're only going for the weekend! Plus, you're going to have a great time."

"Sure," she mumbled, unable to fight the two adorable faces that were melting her heart. She sighed discontentedly—she knew she was outnumbered. "I'd better start packing." Disappointed by all of the interruptions, she flopped the book on the floor for the final time and pulled herself out of the chair.

"Oh, no, you don't . . . we have all day for packing; right now, you're mine." His strong arms reached out and pulled her closer, catching her off guard. Between the confusion and the sudden imbalance, both Kate and Chris fell into the pool fully clothed.

It took all day for Kate to pack. Normally, this was a quick, simple task, where she threw whatever into a bag—but this trip was different. Never before had she realized that her entire wardrobe consisted solely of jeans, shorts, and T-shirts.

A soft knock at the door caught her attention. There was Chris, with his sexy, still-damp hair, leaning against the doorframe with a beer in his hand. It was stunning how gorgeous this man could look dressed only in loose-fitting denim and a white T-shirt.

In an almost seductive voice he said, "How is it going?"

Attempting to ignore his flirting, she diverted her attention back to her plain wardrobe, "I'm just trying to figure out how to put my whole closet into my suitcase, that's all." Playfully, she threw a shirt at him, but he quickly ducked, almost spilling his beer.

"Remember, it's just a weekend. If you forget anything, we can get it there. You know," he continued cautiously, "they do have stores in California?" He waited warily for a minute, expecting a pair of jeans to come flying next.

Kate sarcastically lifted a pair of jeans above her head, but threw them down into the suitcase. "Really, they do? I've would have never guessed." she teased, wrinkling her nose.

In order to close the heavily packed suitcase, Kate crawled on top of it, applying as much pressure as possible. The sight of a tiny woman on top of a suitcase twice her size trying desperately to zip it up was hilarious. Chris found himself leaning against the doorframe for support.

"You know you could come and help me?" But, doing the complete opposite, he hurried out of the room.

Dumbfounded, Kate sat on her suitcase and yelled, "Really?" Within seconds, he staggered back into the bedroom with Aika in his arms and promptly plopped her in Kate's lap.

Barely able to breathe, she huffed out, "Ugh. That wasn't the kind of help I was looking for!"

"Yeah, well, it worked. Didn't it?" Firmly, but with a condescending smile, he pulled the zipper around the edge of the suitcase until it was completely closed. "I hope you don't need anything out of here, because I'm not opening this until we get home."

Kate shoved the dog back to Chris. "What time does the plane leave?"

"Whenever we want." Politely, he extended his hands to help her off the bed.

When her feet touched the soft carpet, she looked up at Chris with puzzled eyes, "What?" Without waiting for an answer, she passed him and made her way into the kitchen.

"We're taking a private jet." With an amused smile, he followed Kate who pulled out a cold bottle of water from the fridge.

Still bewildered, she leaned her left side against the silver, double-door refrigerator. "You're joking, right?"

Seriously, Chris responded, "No, I'm not. Kate, I hope you do realize that you're going to get spoiled rotten this weekend?"

Ignoring the uncomfortable feeling in the pit of her stomach, she twisted the cap off the water bottle, and shot him an inquisitive look. "Ugh . . . I thought I was just coming along while you got stuff done?"

"That, among other things." His lips began to curl upward in an inscrutable smile as he continued. "I just want you to relax and have a good time. Nothing to worry about."

"What do you mean by 'spoiled'?"

Out of the blue, Chris pinned her back against the marble counter as he gently placed his hands on her hips and easily lifted her up on the counter top. A small, squeaky gasp escaped her throat while she tried to reposition herself.

Slowly and seductively, his hands slid from her hips down to the edge of the counter, as he leaned in close and whispered, "I mean you can have whatever you want. No limits."

Why would he want to spoil me? Well, he said whatever I want, and I don't want anything, and you can't spoil someone who doesn't want it, she thought defiantly.

The next morning, there was an unexpected knock at the front door. Dressed in black suits with matching sunglasses stood two muscular men on Kate's porch. After opening the door without glancing through the peephole, she took an instinctive step back from the strange men. Aika, who always follows Kate to the door, aggressively barked and snarled her teeth; neither of the men flinched.

Above the barking, one man calmly spoke, "Good morning, Miss Woods."

From the top of her lungs Kate screamed, "CHRIS!" but her eyes stayed angrily focused on the men as she barricaded the front door.

Concerned about all the commotion, Chris nearly slipped on the tile as he turned the corner. Even with Chris's presence, Aika didn't release her stance until Chris commanded, "Aika, down! Good girl." Still skeptical about the situation, it took their protector a moment to finally follow orders and sit down.

"Good morning. Follow me." Squeezing his way past Kate, Chris greeted and led the men into the house. It was as if nothing was wrong. Flabbergasted at his reaction, her mouth dropped and once she picked up her jaw, she slammed the door and yelled, "Who are they, and how the hell do they know my name?"

All three men stopped in the living room, but Chris calmly explained, "They're the drivers. One is going to take us to the airport, and the other is going to drive my car back to the dealership." The two men who were now carrying her luggage smiled at Kate.

"That still doesn't explain why they know my name."

In an almost dismissive tone Chris said, "I told them! Why don't you get your stuff and then we'll be on our way." Still angered by the situation, she glared at the men as she went to the other room.

There was the faintest of nods between Chris and one of the drivers while he stacked up the suitcases. Immediately, they understood each other what men through the ages could silently communicate.

That's what I love about her.

Instead of arriving at the terminals, like most travelers would, Kate and Chris had the luxury of skipping the check-in process and shuffle through security. The Escalade parked about six feet away from a Global Express XRS corporate jet. Without delay, someone else in a black suit, almost identical to the driver's, opened the door and helped Kate out. When her flip-flop covered feet touched the ground, it wasn't the concrete she had expected, but instead a plush red carpet that led directly to the plane. Never having someone wait on her hand and foot, Kate wandered to the trunk of the car and tried to get her luggage.

"Good morning," she said chirpily to the skinny man in a suit who was opening the trunk.

"Good morning ma'am." He smiled politely back. The door lifted up, and immediately Kate reached for a suitcase. "Oh, no ma'am. I got these."

"It's no big deal, I can help." She lifted the luggage up and placed it by the tire. When she looked up, the man was nervously staring at her.

From a distance, Kate heard Chris say, "Kate, don't worry about. They will take care of it." The man's worries faded away, and he returned to his work.

Everywhere she turned, there was someone dressed in black with sweat beads on their forehead, racing to complete each new task. Several men were loading the luggage, while others were prepping the jet, but the one thing they all had in common was the nervous look on their faces.

A man dressed in a sleeker black suit walked across the tarmac towards Chris. It was apparent that he was the one in charge. After a mutual greeting between the two men, Chris beckoned for Kate as he extended his hand, "Kate, I would like you to meet the owner of Prive Jets." She slowly approached, remaining silent as Aika tagged along.

"Hello, Madame. I'm Monsieur Jacques. It's a pleasure to meet you." He kissed the top of her hand ostentatiously. Uncomfortably, she tried her hardest not to roll her eyes.

"Hi." Once Jacques released her hand, she let it fall to her side and wiped the excess slobber against her jeans. Forcing a smile, she laughed under her breath, *this man is full of crap. What is it with all the black? It looks like I'm going to a damn funeral.*

After a long, and what felt to be an inappropriate stare, Mr. Jacques redirected his attention back to Chris. "I do hope you both enjoy your trip."

"We will. Thank you for everything." Chris shook Jacques' hand and led Kate down the red carpet to board the jet, with Aika following closely behind.

The plane came equipped with what Chris called a "small staff" of seven people to wait on them hand and foot, each accessorized with a bright and cheery smile. The jet had been designed with the best luxuries: large plush reclining leather couches with three forty-inch flat screen TVs. Located at the back of the plane was a small bedroom with a queen-sized bed and each little section of the craft carrier could be divided by soft thick curtains. Aika took it upon herself to sprawl out on a couch and let her tongue droop out to the side.

With his arm around Kate, Chris smiled and pointed to the lazy mutt, "I think she's comfortable." As the drool slobbered down from Aika's tongue, onto the custom Italian leather, Kate hung her head in embarrassment.

Once the plane was up in the air, the flight attendant served an assortment of fruit and refreshments. Slowly, Kate allowed herself to become more relaxed with this special treatment, but she still felt ridiculous and uncomfortable.

"Isn't this a bit much just to fly to California?"

"It's the easiest, plus a lot more discrete than flying commercial, don't you think?"

With a gentle and warm smile, Chris handed her another enormous, juicy, red strawberry. Taking it politely, she nibbled at the tip. "Can I get some water? I'm not a fan of champagne."

"Of course, you can." A button on the wall behind Chris summoned an attendant with a cartoon smile plastered across her face.

Kate hadn't realized just how hungry she was until after she consumed a plate full of crackers, assorted cheeses, and cured meats. Now with a full belly, she couldn't keep her eyes open. It was inevitable; every time she traveled she fell asleep on the plane.

Almost to their destination, the pilot spoke courteously over the intercom: "Mr. Cody, we should be landing in approximately fifteen minutes."

"Come on, time to get up." Kate had fallen asleep on the couch with her head nuzzled comfortably in his lap.

"No . . . Ten more minutes," she grumbled.

Finally able to force herself up after a three-hour nap, she slowly rubbed the sleep from her eyes and excused herself to the restroom.

The rubber tires bounced as they connected with the LAX runway. Taken off guard, Kate quickly grabbed Chris's hand.

Curious, she found herself peeking through the window; suddenly her smile turned into a scowl when she spotted the stretch limo and another red carpet. "Are you serious?"

The agitated tone in her voice made Chris smirk, "What are you talking about?"

"Why must you insist on being so extravagant?"

"Kate, everything is for a reason. I'm not doing all this to torture you, that's just a bonus." Chris chuckled to himself. He was beginning to like Kate's reactions more and more. "Those limos are the best in the market. That's a Mercedes-Benz S600 Pullman Guard. It's the safest and the most discrete."

"There is nothing discrete about it!" Annoyed with the sight of it, she turned her back toward the window. She was starting to reach her limit of all these pretentious extravagances.

"No one will be able to see us." He smoothly patted Kate's knee, trying to pacify some of her frustration.

There was no way Kate could have prepared herself for what was about to appear.

Upon the entrance of Chris's estate stood two iron gates surrounded by a six-foot high red brick wall. The metal doors slowly lurched backwards allowing the limo to move forward on the cobblestone drive. It took about a half a mile before the magnificent structure began to emerge through the one hundred-year old oak trees. It was at this point that the 8,500 square-foot, hacienda-style, estate came alive. Built with majestic grandeur, it was surrounded by stately oaks and rolling, manicured lawns.

The moment the engine stopped, the grandiose, custom emperor-sized wooden doors opened, and yet more staff came out to service Chris. More than anxious to run free, Aika began whining and scratching at the door.

"Aika! No!" Kate scolded.

"Don't worry about it, she's fine."

The moment the door opened, the unruly beast sprang out of the limo, running around the yard with her nose dug into the green grass, sniffing. Two minutes later, she disappeared behind the house.

After completing the inspection of the backyard, the blurry pooch flew in full force from around the other side of the house, scrambling and getting tangled in the maid and butler's feet. To free herself from the chaotic confusion, she dashed directly through the open doors into the house. The freshly waxed marble floor provided no grip for her paws and her legs slipped uncontrollably from underneath her. Racing up the stairs, Aika was in search of a place to rest. The location of her choice was none other than Chris's bed. She dug furiously until she was under the covers and nestled snuggly into his pillows.

Flabbergasted at how many people rushed out of the house just to unload a few bags, Kate couldn't understand how Chris lived this way. To him, this kind of treatment was standard; he was proud of his accomplishments, and people were impressed by his expendable wealth. Well, not everyone; Kate rolled her eyes in annoyance. She was beginning to understand how he had become so deluded.

"Good morning, sir. How was your flight," asked Mr. Whittaker, head of the house staff. His sole responsibility, and an extremely important one, was to make sure that everything in the household ran smoothly and according to the specifications of Mr. Cody—no matter what. As simple as that might sound, Mr. Whittaker took great pride in his position. Dressed like an English butler, without the accent, Mr. Whittaker wore a starched, stiff, black-and-white suit, his posture just as rigid as his uniform.

"It was excellent, George. Are the rooms ready? I believe that Kate is ready for a nap." Standing next to Chris, desperately trying to keep her eyes open, Kate was observing the changes in him: a formal tone, a stiffer posture, and even though he was technically beside her for stability, she sensed a distance between them.

"Of course, sir. They are ready. Good morning, Miss Woods, I do hope you enjoyed your trip?"

In a muffled mumble, she yawned with her palm against her mouth. "I did. Thank you."

"Wonderful. Well, let's get you two settled in." Without another word, Mr. Whittaker turned stiffly around on the ball of his foot and led them into the house.

Inside, grandeur and brilliance greeted them. A Strauss crystal chandelier sparkled like diamonds as it hung delicately in the foyer setting off the marble floors and dual custom oak staircases. It was breathtaking.

Mindlessly following Mr. Whittaker upstairs, it took Kate a few moments to realize that Chris wasn't with her. Automatically, she called out to him, "Are you not coming?"

"I'm letting you get settled in."

The sarcastic reply echoed in the large space, "OK. I'm going to need a map to find you."

"Don't worry, I'll find you. I did it once before; I think I can do it again."

"Whatever," she smirked as she followed the staff up the stairs, and then joked, "What, no elevator?"

"I'm so sorry, Miss Woods, I should have taken into consideration that you had a long trip. Of course, we can take the elevator." Almost instantaneously, Mr. Whittaker changed directions.

Stunned, Kate turned to Chris and blurted, "Are you serious?" All he could do was shrug his shoulders.

"Good God, it was a joke! Mr. Whittaker, the stairs are fine; I was just kidding!" In disbelief, she shook her head while she followed the butler up the marble stairs. Chris stood at the bottom for a moment and watched as Kate rose to the top and disappeared.

Kate followed as she was led down a long hallway until finally they stopped at a pair of giant wooden doors.

The room was gorgeous; it was obviously decorated by a famous designer whose name she wouldn't even be able to pronounce. The silk sea-crest blue comforter matched the drapes over the large bay window that looked out onto the grounds. The creamy soft yellow painted walls soothed her tired eyes.

Almost in a trance, Kate slowly walked around the room, taking in every detail. The attached bathroom was equipped with dual marble sinks, a stone crafted shower with three heads pointing toward the center, and a large Jacuzzi tub.

Opening what she thought was a linen closet, she stepped back when the light flickered on. Instead of sheets and towels crammed into a small space, the room was actually a walk-in closet. The size was incredible, basically as big as her bedroom and filled with designer clothes, shoes, and accessories organized by brand and style. Nervously, she gently held out a Donna Karan sweater, wondering if it would fit her. She looked at the tag and saw the size: six. Still skeptical, she picked up a Chanel blouse and turned over the tag—and the six stared back at her.

Unable to comprehend why Chris had a closet full of women's clothes in her size, she called out to Mr. Whittaker, "Whose are these?"

In a regimented posture, with his hands placed behind his back, he promptly replied, "They are yours, ma'am."

"These are not mine; I've never seen them before."

"They are compliments of Mr. Cody. I hope you find them suitable."

It became clear why Chris didn't escort her to her room.

"Thank you, George." A forced smile appeared as Kate tried to maintain her manners—she didn't want to seem ungrateful. Besides, it wasn't Mr. Whittaker's fault that his employer didn't listen.

"Before I leave you to rest, I need to show you how to use the control panel, Miss Woods."

"Just 'Kate', no 'Miss.' you make me feel so old."

"Oh. OK." Mr. Whittaker ignored the implied humor as he walked toward the bedroom door. "Kate, here is the control panel." Carefully, he removed the remote control off the wall and continued, "With this you can adjust room temperature, light brightness, or volume of the music. The entire room has surround sound, so you can either play from the list that has already been downloaded or play the radio. You can also open and close the blinds from here as there is a switch on the side of each nightstand. Do you have any questions?"

"I think I can manage. Thanks," she lied, unsure of the instructions that were being relayed to her.

"Then I will leave you to rest Miss . . . err, Kate."

I told him that I don't like expensive things and I didn't want him to go all crazy.

Jet-lagged, Kate threw the silky, lace pillow off the bed and curled up into a little ball. It seemed like only a few minutes had passed since her eyes had closed when there was a knock at the door. Exhausted, she refused to move from the soft heaven of bliss and ignored the intrusion.

Whispering softly into Kate's ear, Chris lightly stroked her tangled brown hair. "So, how do you like everything?"

"It's too much. Especially that closet," she mumbled almost incoherently as she rolled toward him and shoved a silky-smooth pillow on top of her head.

Slightly disappointed, he meekly asked, "You don't like it, do you?" The letdown cracked in his voice.

Kate sat up with her hair wisped all around her. "It's not that I don't like it, it's just a bit too much. I appreciate it, but don't be offended if I don't wear any of it."

"I won't be; it's only there if you want it. I want you to feel comfortable here. And you're welcome." Slightly happier, he asked, "So, do you want a tour?"

"Sure. When does the bus arrive?"

"Keep it up; I'm going to put you on the short bus!" Chris grabbed the nearest pillow and clunked it on Kate's tired head.

Tickled by his silliness, she laughed, "No worse than being the driver of the short bus!"

Strolling down the hallway, Kate was captivated by the expensive décor—beautiful antiques and exquisite artwork, but nothing resembled the Chris that she knew.

"Later on," Chris said casually, "some friends are coming over to watch the game. That's OK, right?"

Distracted by her decadent surroundings she mumbled, "Sure it's your house," only half listening to him.

Pulling her from her trance, he gently faced her toward him and sincerely explained, "Kate, I want you to feel at home here, and if there's anything that I can do, just let me know." At that exact moment, her stomach growled and with a meek smile she said, "Well, you can show me where the kitchen is."

After a delightful gourmet meal prepared by the kitchen staff, Kate was beyond stuffed. Satisfied, she leaned back in her chair, rubbed her bloated belly and sighed, "That was amazing!"

Pleased with her reaction, Chris smiled, "I'm glad that you liked it. My chef, Mr. Giordano is the best."

"He sure is. He won my heart."

"Your heart? I thought your heart wasn't up for grabs. Not for a guy, anyways." Sarcastically, he leaned over the small, round, dark oak table and studied Kate.

Ignoring his stunned, mouth-dropped stare, she joked, "You know . . . the best way to a girl's heart is through her stomach."

"So, that's all it takes? Hell, I would have made you a feast had I known that."

"Geez, it takes a little more than that, but you've got the right idea." Knowing that there was a lot of truth in that joke, she nervously glanced away from him.

After lunch, Chris showed Kate the rest of the house, including the theater, workout room, and the spa, which led to the Olympic-sized pool, and of course his favorite spot, the game room. The incredible man cave had a digital screen projector for the TV along with every gaming system ever manufactured. There was an air hockey table, pool table, a fridge filled with ten different types of beer, and a liquor cabinet in the back, completely stocked.

Turning on the TV, Kate's eyes began to droop. As her head bobbed back and forth, Chris guided her into a snuggle. After ten minutes of lying on the couch, she fell asleep once again with her head in his soft, protective lap.

Chapter Nine

Barely an hour after Kate fell asleep, Mr. Whittaker entered the game room and announced that Chris's friends had arrived. Politely, Chris whispered, "Thank you, Mr. Whittaker. Let them know I'll be there shortly." After receiving his orders, Mr. Whittaker left the room and attended to the guests waiting in the foyer area.

Once alone, Chris leaned over his knee to look into Kate's sleeping eyes and softly spoke, "Kate, it's time to get up." A low grumble emerged, but her eyes didn't budge. It took the smooth rocking of his knee from side to side to wake her from her deep slumber.

"Hmmm . . . what?" Her eyelids slowly fluttered opened and after a moment she pulled herself up, rubbing the sleep from her eyes. Unaware of the time, she started and asked, "How long was I out?"

"For about an hour." Wild and untamed, Kate's hair flowed in every direction; happily, Chris placed a clump behind her ear.

"Why didn't you wake me?" Moistness in the corner of her mouth caught her attention as she wiped it clean with the back of her hand. It was then that she noticed the small puddle she left on his knee and the embarrassment set in. "And look, I drooled all on your pants. I feel like an idiot." Mortified, she hid her face in the palm of her hands. To Chris, it was adorably childish. He loved her like this.

"You're not an idiot, just tired." Soothingly, pulling her hands down, he began running his fingers through her tangled hair. "It was relaxing watching you sleep. Do you know that you talk in your sleep?"

"I do not." Kate comfortably leaned her head further back into the massaging tips of his fingers. He continued to flex for another minute until he whispered, "Our guests are here." Feeling unprepared, a sour look appeared on Kate's face. When his fingertips stopped massaging her scalp she asked, "Where's the nearest restroom?"

"Down there, third door on the left." Chris pointed to the hallway that was next to the large, blank white wall, where the projection system displayed.

"What, only the third door?"

"That's the first bathroom. There's at least six after that one." Kate half-expected laughter to follow the comment, implying some form of a joke, but there was none.

"Give me a half an hour and if you don't hear from me, send a search party."

Chris pressed his lips together making a humming noise while his index finger tapped them, "I'll think about it."

"Thanks. Ass." It was apparent he wasn't kidding; the hallway in which he sent her down seemed to go on forever.

The same time Kate returned from the restroom, Mr. Whittaker had just shown Chris's guests into the game room. There was a brief formal introduction when Mr. Whittaker presented Eric, James, and Sam. There seemed to be an awkward tension between Chris and his friends, but Kate couldn't figure out why. It was only a moment before he spotted Kate and pulled her close.

Almost overly excited he greeted his friends, "I'm really glad that you guys made it." Meekly, Eric and James smiled, but Sam's lips didn't budge. Now slightly nervous, Chris continued, "Guys, I want you to meet Kate." Outside of the awkward *Hellos* that were mumbled between them, the room fell silent again.

Angered by something, Sam spoke up, "Chris, you know I'm still angry with you."

"Oh, come on Sam, I apologized on the phone. It really wasn't my fault."

The call that needed to be made laid a heavy burden on Chris. Two days after the charity event, the same night he met Kate, Chris decided that things needed to change in his life. The first step toward that change was to make amends to the people he had wronged.

Ring after ring, Chris anxiously waited. He hadn't expected Sam to answer, but the sweet sound of confusion in her voice when she said "hello" made his nerves skyrocket. He fumbled his words, hoping she wouldn't hang up. Chris thought, at most, he would get a few minutes, but that quickly turned into hours of catching up.

Even after the phone call ended, and he felt a bit better, he knew that Sam was still upset about the historical site, and it would take time to earn her trust back.

Not interested in the pitiful look that Chris portrayed, Sam growled, "Oh, bullshit! You are so full of it. Same Chris, same tricks."

Helpless to the rage of Sam, he glanced towards Eric and James looking for some type of support – neither of them provided any. Chris had been wrong, and he needed to make amends, but Sam wasn't making this easy.

"No tricks. I'm truly sorry; can't you just forgive me?" His plan had worked out better in his mind. He hadn't planned on Sam being so damned determined to hold onto a grudge. From first hand experience, Kate knew that Chris could be a downright ass, but she wondered what exactly he had done. After a long, awkward pause, Kate interjected, "Um…is everything OK here?"

Sam's sharp eyes shifted to Kate as her voice cracked the same harsh tone, "He ruined something very important to me!" Her arms tightened around her midsection, and she lowered her voice before she continued, "I ran an organization that preserved historical landmarks. Two years ago, Chris co-produced a film that was set in the 1800s. Instead of using a studio, he shot his movie at Shirley."

Unaware of what "Shirley" was, Kate just shrugged her shoulders in confusion and let Sam continue, "Shirley is one of the oldest plantations in Virginia. It was also one of the locations I was working on at the time. He refused to budge, and the plantation was ruined from all the crew and equipment that was brought in."

Chris arrogantly strained his back, looked down his nose, and proudly spoke down to Sam as his right hand landed on his chest, "That's not fair, Sam. Besides, the entire plantation is being fully renovated, compliments of me."

As Kate looked at the man standing next to her, she was reminded of the Chris she met at that NY party. This did not please her.

"Seriously, Chris, this is your response to your friend? I may not know anything about historical buildings, but I do know that this seemed important to Sam and since she is your friend, why couldn't you have granted her this one favor?" Disappointment radiated through Kate's face when she looked up at him. Immediately his attitude changed as the look on Kate's face was more than he could bear.

"You're right, Kate. I'm sorry, Sam. I should have done more to help you." The stunned look on Sam's face was priceless; she had never seen Chris sincerely apologize to anyone before.

"Ooh, I *like* her," Sam laughed with her hand extended out to Kate. "I'm Sam by the way." Before Sam smiled, there was something very intimidating about her – an angry woman who stood five-foot-eight with short, pointy hair. But once the anger subsided and her normal, chirpy voice rang out, Sam almost seemed childlike.

"I'm Kate." No longer timid, Kate warmly smiled and took Sam's hand. The firmness of the handshake surprised Kate, but what really threw her was when Sam said, "I know who you are."

"You do?" Searching for an explanation, Kate glanced at Chris. Before he could explain, Sam redirected Kate's attention with a mischievous smile, "You're the girl Chris couldn't stop talking about."

"What?" It never occurred to Kate that Chris would have spoken to his friends about her.

"Don't listen to her, Sam dramatizes everything." While Chris's words sounded careless, his eyes screamed the truth. He wasn't prepared for the humiliating taunts from his friends.

"*Do* listen to her. For once she isn't being dramatic." Eric introduced himself with a firm handshake that took Kate by surprise. His appearance did not match the strongly gripped hand around her own. In wrinkled jeans and messy hair, Eric looked like he just rolled out of bed.

The low sexy sound of 'Hi' diverted Kate's attention toward to James, but she didn't respond.

By now, Kate had made her way back to her comfortable spot – inside of Chris's arms. Chris politely introduced Kate to James, "This Fabio wannabe here is James." Smoothly, James extended out his hand, but maintained his seductive glare at Kate while eyeing every inch of her body. It took all of Kate's efforts not to slap the inappropriate *I want you* look from James' stubbly face.

In another low tone James nodded at Kate, "Hey."

Unimpressed, she pressed her lips together before she sweetly said, "Nice to meet you." It was apparent that he was over-compensating since he was the shortest person in the room, standing at only five-foot-five. His shoulder length, thick, sandy blonde hair was tightly pulled back away from his face to accent his baby blue eyes. In a ripped skintight white shirt, James shamelessly flaunted his bulging muscles and wore ass-hugging jeans.

Still intrigued by Chris's portrayal, Kate changed the topic, "Eric, what exactly has Chris been saying?"

"Oh, you know, how much . . ." Before he could finish the sentence, Chris flung his entire body at Eric, throwing him into a headlock, and the two began to wrestle. Quickly, everyone stepped back. After a minute, Sam became annoyed and grabbed Kate's wrist, "Let's get something to drink."

"Oh, OK." She laughed and stumbled along behind her.

"OK," Sam mumbled to herself, searching through the glass liquor cabinet. "Let's see what Chris has here . . . Oh, there you are, my lover." With a happy smile, Sam pulled a bottle of Plymouth Gin from the back of the cabinet. Without hesitation, she grabbed a martini glass and shaker, and began making her drink. It wasn't until the clear liquid poured from the shaker into the glass, that she finally spoke again, "What are you drinking?"

"I'll grab a beer." Kate didn't realize how thirsty she was until the cold beverage hit her parched lips. Gulp after gulp, it took her a moment to notice that the room had fallen completely silent. Nervously, her eyes flickered around the room trying to figure out what she had done wrong.

"That sounds like a great idea." Easily distracted, Chris dropped Eric and got himself a beer.

"Hell, yeah . . . and here we thought we were going to have to behave!" Excitedly, James punched Eric in the arm and joined Chris. In the past, when they all used to hang out, Chris had been extremely particular about his friend's mannerisms around his women of interest.

"Ouch!" Eric complained, pampering his delicate arm, then made himself a dirty martini.

It wasn't long after everyone settled comfortably on the couches that a loud bark and clicking nails came running down the hall. As the sound grew closer, a terrified look appeared on Eric's face.

"When did you get a dog?" Eric stuttered fretfully as his hand began to twitch. Not a pet owner, Eric had been afraid of dogs for as long as he could remember.

"That's Aika. She's a big baby," Kate answered as she leaned forward, waiting for her girl to run into her arms.

The fear cracked in Eric's voice, "What k-kind of dog?"

"Umm . . ." Knowing how much big dog breeds freaked Eric out, Chris tried to interrupt Kate before she blurted out, "Bullmastiff."

"*What!*" Full of panic, Eric shrieked and jumped farther back into his chair.

"Oh, shit!" Chris exclaimed, knowing that this was going to be a disaster. From around the corner, Aika spotted Kate. She had every intention of jumping into her mom's lap, but the slippery tile caused her to lose control and she ended up on Eric. Screaming like a girl, Eric tried to scramble out from underneath the slobbery mouth that was now face-to-face with him. The scream unsettled Aika's nerves, causing her to fall off the couch and then bark at Eric. The loud noise and stress proved to be too much for Eric. Needing an escape, he balanced himself on the soft leather, but every time he moved Aika barked.

Trying to obtain control of the situation, Kate commanded, "Aika!" Completely infatuated with pursuing Eric, Aika ignored Kate's command. The barking did not cease until the dog heard Chris snap his fingers and yell, "Aika!" Agitated, Aika sat between Chris and Kate and licked her chops while she continued to glare at Eric. The moment she was under command, Eric dashed out of the room to safety.

"What the hell? How did you do that?" Extremely irritated at Aika, Kate couldn't believe her baby had behaved for Chris and not her.

Chris chuckled. In an attempt to make the fear-stricken Eric more comfortable, Chris rang for Mr. Whittaker to take the dog outside. Of course, she didn't leave the room without a lot of affection from Chris and Kate first.

Sam laughed as she yelled out to Eric, "The coast is clear!" Timidly, Eric poked his head around the corner. Realizing that the beast was gone, he slowly came out of his hiding spot.

Embarrassed by Aika's lack of willingness to follow her commands, Kate changed the topic. "So, why would you guys have to behave?"

"He thought that we might scare you away." Eric mocked Chris in a flamboyant voice as he answered Kate's question.

Balancing her martini glass Sam blurted, "Well, I think Aika scared you more than you scared Kate!" Everyone chuckled at the image of Eric's pale face when he heard the words *bullmastiff*.

Turning her direction toward Chris, she asked, "What, did you think the small-town girl from Florida would take one look at this place and go screaming in the other direction?"

"No, I just wanted to give you time to adjust," Chris whispered sweetly and pulled her in close. "Life out here is completely different from where you are."

Feeling the intense connection between them and the audience watching, Kate quickly distracted herself by looking at James and joked, "He thinks I'm weak."

Chris immediately protested, "I said no such thing!"

Pushing herself away from him, Kate declared, "You didn't have to!"

"You're blowing this way out of proportion." This was the first time that Sam, James, and Eric had ever witnessed one of Chris's ladies actually stand up to him. They all remained silent to see what would happen next.

"OK, I know how to settle this. You. Me. Air hockey—right now!" Kate displayed her confidence as she stood up and chugged her beer.

Annoyed at the show Kate was putting on, Chris complained, "This is childish. I'm not getting into a competition with you."

"What? Are you *chicken*?" After putting down the empty bottle, Kate started to flap her arms up and down, making clucking noises. "Bawl . . . back." The sight of Kate flapping her arms around caused James to snort his beer through his nose. Quickly, Sam smacked him across the chest to hush him up. She didn't want anything interrupting this debate.

"Kate, you look ridiculous."

Confronting him, Kate demanded that Chris step up to the challenge, "Best out of three wins!"

"All right, I'll play." A challenging smirk appeared as Chris continued, "What are the stakes?" *Checkmate, I've got her now.*

The once overly-confident attitude quickly drained from Kate's face. She didn't expect gambling. It was something she never liked, and now she had an important decision to make; would she allow Chris to back out, or make him step up to the challenge?

Firmly, Kate placed her hands on her hips. Carefully, she inspected Chris's every movement while her eyes narrowed. "Hmmm . . . OK, if I win, you have to do hard time."

He couldn't fathom what had just happened. He thought for sure that gambling would make Kate back down—but apparently not today. "What's that supposed to mean?"

"You have to volunteer your time to an organization that helps people in need – and writing a check doesn't count."

"Fine. If I win, you have to allow me to do something for you, and you're not allowed to argue."

You're not going to win this bet, Kate thought, as she determinedly glared at Chris.

Every time Chris swore he had Kate figured out, she would throw him another curve ball. The more complex she became, the more intrigued he was.

Always the instigator, Sam egged them on, "It sounds like we have a bit of a competition!"

"Shit, my money is on Kate!" James encouraged as he snatched a $20 bill from his wallet and slammed it on the coffee table.

"Well, let's go. Sure you can handle this?" Accepting Kate's challenge, Chris stood up and gave Kate a *no mercy* look.

"It's going to be like taking candy from a baby," Kate taunted following Chris to the air hockey table.

Smartly, he replied, "I don't hear any crying, do you?"

"You will once I'm done with you." Teasing, Kate put her balled-up fist under her eyes and rolled them in circles. When Chris stared at her blankly, she said, "I'll be nice and give you one last chance to back out."

Before Chris could get a word out, James punched him in the shoulder and said, "Hell, no. Chris is a real man. He doesn't back down from anything, especially a girl." Chris rolled his eyes at how ignorant James sounded.

Once they were standing on opposite sides of the air hockey table, Chris tried to intimidate Kate by forcefully sliding the puck to her side, almost knocking it into her goal. "Ladies first."

Much to Chris's surprise, Kate slammed down her mallet and caught the puck in midstride; it made a loud slap that let Chris know she meant business.

Innocently, Kate flashed her pearly whites and smiled, "Cheating won't help you, but nice try."

Very precisely, Kate placed the puck off to the right, leaned in, and waited a long minute before she nailed it with her mallet. The only sound heard was the clink of the puck as it slammed into Chris's goal.

"Uh-oh . . . girl's got *skills!*" James bragged, "She's going to slaughter him!"

"I don't know, I think he's holding back," Eric rebutted.

Pumped by the excitement of the bet, James took his aviator-style glasses off his head. "Want to bet?"

"You're on!" Eric dug into his hipster wallet. "Shit, I'm three bucks short," he complained and looked at Sam. "Help me out?"

"Sure, but I'm taking my percentage of the winnings." Sam smiled. They both put their money on top of James' twenty. Always the fun-loving, broke friend, Eric did not like to part with money, so Chris knew he'd better win.

The first game, Kate killed Chris by ten points, but on the second game Chris was able to regain his dignity, but only by a few points. The third game was intense. Both Chris and Kate began to sweat. It all came down to this game point. Nerves raced through the room. There was a loud clink . . . but no one saw whose goal the puck went into. At the same time, they looked bent down to check their goal. From under the table came a loud groan. Wildly, Chris popped up cheering, "Yes! Yes! Boom! He wins! Chris dominates the table and retains his superhero status."

"You got *so lucky*," Kate complained, as she tossed the bright yellow puck on the table.

"Maybe, but I still won!" He beamed a triumphant smile, but not over Kate's defeat—it was just that now Chris had an excuse to give Kate what he had already planned on. The idea that Kate would have to accept it graciously was the candy-coated topping to Chris's already sweet victory.

Kate fought back a laugh. She was upset that she lost, but he was funny dancing around like an idiot. In her best sore loser stance, Kate pouted and crossed her arms across her chest. "You know I'm not happy about this."

"And! ... you're not allowed to complain," he provoked as she flashed his winning smile and tapped her on the nose. "You are so cute when you pout." In protest, Kate rolled her eyes as Chris kissed her forehead. Eric performed his most prideful stride as he swayed his way over to collect his prize. Like lightening, James snatched all the money from the table with a snarl.

"Come on, pay up, James." Eric rightfully held out his hand, expectantly.

"Sorry, James." Now Kate really felt bad.

"No worries, I know he cheated." It was a feeble attempt to make Kate feel better as he slapped the wad of cash into Eric's hand. "Plus, it was only twenty bucks."

In a proud, sarcastic tone, Eric replied, "Thank you." He put the two bills neatly into his dirty wallet.

Laughing at the boys, Sam handed everyone a new beer. "Peace offering," she explained.

Everyone looked at James who paused, and then grabbed the beer with a smile. That changed the vibe and the group laughed as they teased him.

"Well, that was easy," Kate was relieved.

With beers in hand, they gathered around the projection screen to watch the football game. Just as involved as the guys, Kate yelled out when bad calls where made. This surprised Eric and James who had expected Kate to have the same level of interest as Sam – none.

More interested in Kate than the game, Sam slid over and carefully set her drink on the coffee table. The fact that Chris Cody, the most eligible bachelor, described Kate as a *gorgeous woman with a beautiful soul* had Sam very intrigued.

As the referee called a foul on the opposing team, Sam lightly slapped Kate's thigh and asked, "So, what do you do in Florida?"

Distractedly, Kate answered, "I'm a graphic designer." The idea of small talk during the fourth quarter did not thrill Kate. Politely, Kate did her best to juggle her attention between Sam's rambling questions and the pulse of the intense game—it didn't work out very well.

"That's cool. How have things been going with you and Chris?"

The question caught Kate's attention and she turned toward Sam in confusion, "Wait, what?"

"You know, how are *things?*" Encouragingly, Sam nudged Kate with her elbow and flashed a knowing smile. Kate couldn't figure out what Sam was trying to imply. *Things? What things?* When Kate glanced at Chris for clarification, he was just as baffled.

Realizing her error, Sam quickly tried to rectify it, mumbling through her hand-covered mouth, "Oh, my gosh! You two haven't hooked up. Oh! I'm so sorry."

"Not unless Chris has gone through some major transformations that I'm not aware of," Kate blurted out bluntly, as her eyes glazed at the scoreboard.

"What?" Sam arched her eyebrows at Chris in hopes of an explanation, but all she got in return was a smug grin.

Continuing the thought, Kate snorted, "You've got a better chance than he does."

Nothing was making sense. Sam couldn't figure out what Kate was trying to imply. Feeling puzzled, she shrugged her shoulders and muttered, "Huh?"

James and Eric's ears immediately perked up at Kate's intriguing comment. They glanced at Chris for confirmation; the subtle nod was all they needed. Laughing under their breath, James and Eric couldn't believe that Chris, of all people, brought home a lesbian.

Frustrated by Sam's lack of common sense, Kate blurted out, "I'm gay, Sam. I like women!"

Sympathetically, Sam gently patted Kate's jean-covered calf, which was lazily draped across her other knee. "I'm so sorry."

"Why? I'm not!"

"No. I don't mean it like that. I mean for assuming you two were together. But you have to admit, it does seem like you are." Kate and Chris just stared at Sam blankly, unsure of how to respond to her accusation. *How could these two not be together*, Sam thought. It was plainly obvious that they cared for one another. Even now Kate was curled up in Chris's arms. In order to make her point Sam needed back up, but Eric and James were focusing on the game just a little too hard. A large chunk of peanut brittle flew across the room and bounced off Eric's head, "Guys, a little help here, please!"

Very meticulously, Eric turned, folded his hands and placed them on top of his knees, and chimed in, "I hate to admit it, but she does have a point."

Taken off guard, both Chris and Kate sat up a little bit straighter, but Kate only moved a few inches away. Beginning his explanation Chris said, "Well, we are very close . . ." Then, with a smooth transition, Kate finished the sentence, "But trust me when I say we are just friends."

Suspicious of Chris and Kate's too perfect, almost rehearsed answer, the group didn't believe that their intense connection, in an extremely short period of time, was just a friendship. There had to be something more.

Unexpectedly, Sam exclaimed, "We should go to Club 8!"

"Definitely! Kate, you would like it, there's always a lot of hot girls!" James added.

In a bored tone Chris assured Kate, "It's just a nightclub out here. I'm sure you wouldn't like it."

Images from the night when Kate demanded that Chris keep her life private flashed before him. A nightclub was not the easiest place to do that, and Chris knew that if he failed there would be hell to pay.

Irritated with Chris's lack of enthusiasm, Sam jumped off the couch and feverishly protested, "Just a club? It's only the best place in L.A.!"

After three beers, Kate was feeling adventurous. "Why don't we go? It sounds like fun."

This was not the reaction Chris had hoped for. He was concerned for Kate's privacy, so he laid all the cards on the table, hoping to change her mind. Gently, he turned her head with the soft tip of his index finger and explained, "Kate, it's a very popular club. There will be a ton of photographers and media. You told me that you didn't want to be around that." The excitement instantly drained from Kate's face, as she understood Chris's intentions. Sadly, she knew that her well-being depended on the ability to keep her personal life private, but deep down, a new desire was brewing—just for a moment to be someone other than the woman who was haunted by her decisions.

A light bulb went off above Sam's scheming head as the solution to Kate's dilemma appeared. "That's not a problem! I'll take her in the back entrance, while you handle the crowd at the front. All of the cameras will be on you, and you'll take your time entertaining them, like normal; that way we'll be able to sneak in the back, and no one will ever notice." Proud and excited, Sam sat on the edge of the ottoman waiting for Chris's response.

In theory, Sam's plan sounded good, but still unconvinced, Chris demanded details. "And how are you going to get access to the second entrance?"

"The owner, Jacob, absolutely adores me. I'm sure we can work something out." Ultimately, the final decision was left to Chris, and Sam shamelessly flirted as she batted her sweet eyes at him.

Still uneasy, Chris readjusted himself when he felt Kate's petite hands intertwine with his, and the sweet sound of her whisper melted his defenses. "Chris, it'll be fun."

Face-to-face, Chris took Kate's hands, held her palms to his cheeks, and softly kissed the back of her hands as he sighed. "Kate, that's not my concern. I'm worried about you."

She glanced up through her long eyelashes to see worry written all over his face. Sincerity shined in her big brown eyes as she said, "It's just a club. I think I can manage."

"It's a straight bar."

Kate squeezed Chris's hands and threw herself into his lap. "I just want to go out and have some fun," she pleaded.

"Fine. Sam can make the arrangements." Completely against this idea, Chris wasn't happy about the predicament in which Kate had put him in. It was a double-edged sword: no matter what decision Chris made, Kate would get hurt—but despite his best efforts, he couldn't say no.

Skipping excitedly out of the room with her cell phone in hand, Sam yelled eagerly at Chris, "You're not going to regret this!"

Distressed, he shook his troubled head and complained, "I already am."

"It'll be fine. Don't worry. Plus, I'll have you and the security team to protect me." Happily, Kate wrapped her arms around Chris and flashed him a smile in the hope of cheering him up—but it didn't work.

Upon reentering the game room, Sam announced, "We have security in place. Kate and I will meet Jacob at the second entrance at ten p.m. Then we'll meet up with you at the VIP room shortly after."

Something in Sam's demeanor changed; she became frozen and unable to take her eyes off of Kate.

After several blinks, Sam's perfect pink smile returned to her face. "What are you going to wear?"

Uncomfortable, Kate avoided Sam's glare as she answered, "I don't know . . . probably jeans and a shirt."

"Oh, no! You can't just wear jeans and any old shirt to this club. Come with me, there's work to be done!" Forcefully, Sam grabbed Kate's arm and yanked her out of Chris's embrace.

In a panic, Kate resisted and reached for Chris as she cried out, "Help!" *This straight girl has lost her mind thinking that she is going to dress me up like a Barbie doll.*

"Kate! I don't understand—you were all dressed up for the fundraiser. Why is this any different?" Chris smiled evilly as he enjoyed the tormented look on Kate's face.

"Sam, are you going to put me in a ball gown?"

"Hell, no."

"See? That's how it's different. Plus, Alexa knows my limits."

Once again, succumbing to Kate's plea, Chris let her off the hook. "Fine. Fine. Fine. Sam, why don't you come over tomorrow and raid the closet?" Relief emerged from Kate's face as she quickly scurried back into the protection of his arms. It was times like this when Kate really appreciated Chris's charm, especially when it benefited her.

"Fine! You're no fun." Sam pouted and stuck her tongue out at Chris as she flopped back on the couch next to Eric. "But tomorrow," she said to Kate, "you're mine."

❦

Later that night after everyone left, Chris and Kate were on the lanai, by the pool, watching the waterfalls cascade along the six-foot slide and into the island blue water by the grotto. On a long pillow-inflated chair, Kate stretched out while Chris sat next to her with his right ankle comfortably placed on his left knee. A warm breeze brushed slowly through Kate's brown hair, and a smile appeared as she absorbed the serene beauty of the man-made paradise.

The relaxing sound of running water from the marble angel fountain reverberated in the background while Kate asked curiously, "You're not really going to let Sam torment me, are you?"

"Hey, you got yourself into this mess. I tried to save you, but you didn't want to listen." Unable to contain himself, Chris laughed at the idea of Sam forcing Kate into every piece of clothing upstairs.

"You're so evil. What's the matter with my clothes, anyways?" Annoyed, Kate huffed and re-crossed her ankles.

"Nothing, I like the way you dress. However, there is a dress code for this place . . . and I think Sam wants to bond with you and playing dress up is the only way she knows how. Isn't that the way you girls get to know each other, by having slumber parties?" Casually, Chris chuckled under his breath and ran his fingers through his soft, ungelled hair.

Teasingly, Kate smirked as she rolled her head to the side and glanced at him. "I wouldn't know. My slumber parties are your wildest fantasies."

"I'm jealous of you." Without thinking, he automatically and affectionately leaned over and squeezed her arm. In disbelief, Kate pondered why Chris would be jealous of her. The man who had everything was jealous of the woman who had lost everything?

"Why, because I sleep with women?" Suddenly needing to shift positions, Kate sat upright and Chris automatically placed his hand back on his own chair.

"Sort of. You know what you want and who you are. I wish I had that. You're an amazing woman, and you'll make someone very happy one day."

Kate noticed the warmth and depth mingling with a hint of sadness in his words. She also caught onto the fact that he used the word *someone*—not *woman* or *girl*. This was a game Kate was very familiar with—the gender game. Normally, individuals who were not *out of the closet* referred to their significant others using non-gender-specific words.

Translation: *I'm jealous that you're gay, because I don't have a chance in hell. You're the best thing that's ever come into my life, and it's unfair that I can't have all of you.*

As the sun went down, the chill in the air made Kate shiver. Unaccustomed to the colder weather, she rubbed her hands across the prickly goose bumps on her arms and curled into a ball trying to preserve her body heat. Without question, Chris squeezed behind Kate and wrapped his arms around her. The warmth of his body caused the chills to disappear. Completely relaxed, Kate's deep sigh turned into a yawn, and she sank back into him.

Gently, Chris put his head on her shoulder and whispered in a soothing voice, "Ready for bed?" Kate nodded her head in agreement. The coolness from the breeze had subsided, but Kate's goose bumps returned the moment Chris softly kissed her neck.

Chapter Ten

Awake, Kate opened her eyes, but she was confused for a moment since the room was still pitch black. The clock on the nightstand glowed in a red tone: 10:30 a.m.

I haven't slept in this long in years.

Weakly, she slung her arm to the nightstand and began to hit buttons until the blinds started to follow the track back to the side of the wall. The bright morning sun filled the room with warm honey sunshine.

Rolling over, indulging herself in the softness of the sheets, Kate realized that she was alone. Aika always slept with her. A small ting of loneliness crept into her heart; she missed her baby.

Under her white silk robe, Kate wore blue cotton, pajama bottoms with a teddy bear print and a light-blue spaghetti strap top. She roamed aimlessly around the house until she found Aika in the last place she had ever expected.

"What the hell?" What Kate found was unbelievable. "You traitor!" Aika's head popped up from the pillow when she heard Kate's voice.

"So this is where you slept last night? With *him*?" She noticed the guilty look on the traitor's furry face; she'd been caught sleeping with a man. Quickly trying to make amends, Aika nuzzled up to Kate.

"Don't try to suck up. Not after what you did!"

Still under the covers, comfortably reading the paper, Chris tried to protect his new best friend. "Don't be mad at Aika. It really wasn't her fault. It just happened."

"Ugh. Don't defend her." On the edge of the bed, her puppy sat real pretty giving Kate the saddest brown eyes. Unimpressed, Kate glared quietly at Aika until she let out a heart-wrenching cry that Kate couldn't resist.

"I still love you . . . even though you crossed to the dark side." The happy pooch wagged her tail, hopped out of bed, and trotted out of the room as if nothing had happened.

"Where is she going?"

"Probably to breakfast." Chris threw the heavy comforter back and got out of bed. His stomach growled under his silk pajamas. "Hungry?" Without letting Kate answer, he took her hand and led her down the hall to a formal dining room where breakfast awaited them.

"Did you sleep all right?" Chris liked the way Kate looked when she woke up; there was something sweet and innocent about the messy hair and sleep boogies in her eyes.

A big yawn escaped Kate as she stretched out her tired arms. "Good. I feel like I slept forever."

"You were out for about twelve hours."

Through another yawn she managed to get out, "Oh, my. Sorry." Feeling a nudge on her thigh, Kate instinctively started to pet Aika who had come to show her love.

"Yes, baby, I still love you." While scratching the fuzzy ear, Kate noticed that she was clean, and her nails were trimmed. Pleasantly surprised, Kate looked up at Chris and asked, "Did you give her a bath?"

Happily, Chris bent down from the table and started talking to Aika in his playful baby voice. "Well, she wanted a bit of pampering, too. Didn't you girl?" A single bark followed as Aika uncontrollably wagged her tail under the pleasure of Chris's rub. Kate felt a sting of jealousy about the apparent bond between Chris and Aika.

With a snide comment she quipped, "Looks like a photo shoot for *Better Homes and Gardens.*"

Slightly offended by the comment, Chris sat up slightly flushed in the face and asked, "What is that supposed to mean?"

"Perfect dog, perfect house, perfect guy."

Condescendingly Chris added, "Don't forget the perfect girl." Annoyed by his too-perfect answer, Kate threw a large piece of blueberry muffin into her mouth and mumbled under her breath, "Hardly."

In the natural quietness of the morning, Chris returned to his perfectly folded newspaper and Kate continued to pick at her food.

Bored and irritated by the silence Kate blurted, "So what are we going to do today?"

Chris didn't look up from the paper as he answered in a formal and uninviting tone, "Actually, I have to go see my agent today."

"Oh. OK." Thrown by Chris's abrupt tone, she quickly realized how much she had come to rely on him.

What the hell happened? Why am I allowing myself to depend on someone aside from myself?

Never before in her life did Kate ever depend so much on one person. For eight years, Kate had been with Riley and in that time, she was still able to maintain her independence. This was confusing. Kate tried to figure out where she went wrong; of all people to be sensitive about, why did it have to be Chris?

The unusual silence caught Chris's attention. From over the top of the newspaper Chris inquired, "Are you OK?"

Feeling a little sensitive, Kate avoided his piercing eyes and grumbled, "Yeah, I'm fine."

Perfect guy. Perfect life. Remember, Kate, you don't fit here. It was a painful reminder that she and Chris lived worlds apart.

Chris knew enough about women to know that when the words *I'm fine* came out, there was nothing fine about them. Neat and precise, Chris folded the newspaper, setting it next to his porcelain cup of coffee and gently asked, "You know that you can come with me to my agent's, right?"

"I don't want to impose," Kate answered firmly. To keep herself from looking directly into Chris's eyes, Kate quickly grabbed the crystal pitcher of orange juice and poured herself a glass.

"Don't be ridiculous. It's not a big deal." Resolute, Chris took a sip from his hot mocha coffee.

"That's what you made it seem like. I get it, you have business to do and don't want me around."

The coffee cup came down harder than expected making a loud clank, causing Kate to jump. "That's not fair, Kate. I didn't offer because I didn't think you would want to be stuck in a stuffy office all day." It annoyed Chris when Kate made a big deal out of something so simple as a misunderstanding.

Kate tapped the base of her chin with her extended index finger and contemplated, "What in the world am I going to do for fun in LA by myself?"

"Shopping?"

"Have you ever seen me shop?"

To Kate, shopping was a necessity, not something done for pleasure. In a joking manner, Kate opened her mouth and stuck her index finger inside while making a gagging noise.

"OK, true. You do hate shopping." His leg twitched anxiously. Ready to get this day started he suggested, "Well, let's get this boring business out of the way."

After the warm massaging shower, Kate ventured into the closet and came out with a pair of DK jeans and a sleeveless Chanel rose blouse. The soft material clung to Kate's legs making them look even longer.

Standing in front of the floor length mirror, Kate noticed how well everything fit. She hadn't felt this sexy in years.

It wasn't long before Mr. Whittaker interrupted Kate admiring her reflection to escort her downstairs.

Chris stood waiting patiently at the bottom of the stairs. He was dressed in a pair of Lucky brand relaxed jeans and a collared, black shirt with a few buttons undone, displaying a silver chain laying neatly against his collarbone. Once Kate reached the first floor, Mr. Whittaker quietly disappeared.

"Look who decided to raid in the closet." The smile of approval in Kate's decision was extraordinary.

Kate's cheeks flushed a light pink and she quickly diverted, "It's been forever since I was in the closet." A quiet giggle followed as she bashfully covered her lips with the tips of her fingers.

"Isn't that a good closet to be in?"

The curve of her smile slightly faded when Kate realized Chris didn't understand the reference, "That's not what I meant."

"I know what you meant, and no one can put you back in the closet."

"Just figured it would make you happy." Kate smiled timidly as she tugged on the blouse.

Firmly, Chris reminded her, "It makes you happy, too."

The rose color came through Kate's flesh-pink cheeks despite her best efforts. Before Chris could make another blushing compliment, Kate quickly piped up, "Ready to go?"

The dynamic between the two was unique; a special connection between two unlikely people. Chris had an uncanny talent for understanding what she needed without having to be asked. While this quality was beneficial at times, it also got on Kate's nerves. The only other person who'd been able to surprise Kate in this manner was Riley.

Because of their deep-rooted connection, Kate always figured that Riley was Kate's once in a lifetime soul mate…but now Chris could do the same thing. Did that mean Chris was Kate's soul mate, too?

A mischievous smile appeared as Chris turned away from her. "Hold on, one more thing. Remember our little bet?"

Oh, shit, Kate thought, as Chris walked to a small table in the corner and opened the drawer. When he returned to Kate, who stood frozen on the bottom step, he held a medium-sized black velvet box. Instantly, Kate dropped her Gucci purse when she realized what he had.

Teasingly, Chris reminded Kate, "You're not allowed to complain." The soft velvet box felt like it weighed a hundred pounds as it sat unopened in Kate's palm. When the sparkle escaped the black abyss, Kate's jaw dropped as she gazed up at him. In her shaky hand, the white-satin-trimmed jewelry box contained a beautiful, shimmering necklace. With eighteen-karat white gold and two karats of half pavé diamonds that sparkled like the sun, it was the most extravagant thing she had ever seen.

"It's for your rings," he explained, "to replace the necklace that broke at Becky's. I know how much those rings mean to you, and they shouldn't be hanging on a piece of string." Since the party, Kate had every intention of getting the clasp replaced, but just hadn't found the time. The piece of twine she now wore around her neck felt rough between her thumb and forefinger as she nervously rubbed it.

Stunned by Chris's generosity, Kate didn't know what to say. Granted, Chris was good at spending money, but this had taken time and consideration; Kate hadn't expected something so sentimental.

"Wow. I can't believe you did this for me. It's beautiful."

"I also had the original chain designed into it. You can see it here." Chris pointed to the chain that Kate knew by heart.

"You had this made?"

"Actually, it was designed for you." Taken off guard, Kate staggered as she sat down on the cool marble step.

"Here, let's put it on." Gently, Chris took the box from Kate's hands and detached the necklace, while Kate struggled to undo the knot underneath her hair.

Hands shaking, Kate couldn't get a grip on the twine, and Chris shooed her hands away. "Here, let me help you with that." The twine had been double-knotted to ensure the safety of the rings. Unable to loosen it with his fingers, Chris pulled out a pocketknife and snapped it open. Automatically, Kate jumped at the sound of the blade clicking into place.

"Sit still," Chris commanded as he began to cut the frayed, brown cord from around her neck. The rings fell into her palms, and she firmly wrapped her fingers around them.

One by one, Kate carefully strung the rings onto the necklace that Chris held out for her. It was shocking how perfect the metals matched. Once the final ring had connected with the first, Kate flipped her hair over her shoulder and Chris draped the necklace around her collarbone and clasped it shut.

"Beautiful." Chris smiled proudly at Kate who was glowing.

The ride to Chris's agent was a quiet one. Side-by-side and silent, they sat, each pondering their own thoughts; Kate continued to fidget with the necklace. Despite the heaviness, Kate needed the reassurance that her rings were safe. Slowly, Kate's fingers maneuvered on top of the engraving and she wondered, "Who designed it?"

"It was designed by Goodman." Unaware of designers by name or their works, Kate was completely oblivious about what it meant to wear jewelry by Goodman.

Charlie was madder than hell. It had been three weeks since his last conversation with Chris. This was unlike Chris and Charlie was beginning to worry that his multi-million deal was about to fall through. The director had been up Charlie's ass for the past week, screaming that Chris had failed to show for production. Every call, Charlie would have to slap on the charm and convince the director that everything was fine, while behind the scenes he was cursing Chris for causing yet another ulcer.

The office building, a bleach white building that stood thirty floors high, was guarded by minimum-wage security officers. From his one-seat, air-conditioned, white shed, the guard stepped out and requested identification. When the limo parked in front of the double glass doors, two bellmen immediately stepped out to hold the doors. Kate couldn't believe all the fuss.

It's just an office, for goodness' sake.

Instead of a fast-paced environment with people rushing to meet deadlines, the lobby was quiet except for the soft pitter-patter sound of the secretary's keystrokes. Instead of whitewashed walls, like outside, the room was painted a warm green, with live plants and throw pillows on the couch.

Behind a long black counter, the secretary sat in a rigid upright position with a small quaint headset. Even though she was on the phone, her voice never rose above a whisper. When her call was done, she gently pushed the headset against her ear and came around the counter to greet Chris. Her face appeared to be about Kate's age, however, her mannerisms suggested much older. Dressed in a freshly pressed white pleated suit, a long black-and-white necklace dangled in the center of her exposed chest.

After she politely offered the two of them beverages, she rang Charlie, Chris's agent. Immediately, Kate and Chris were sent up.

Next to the secretary's desk were two large dark wooden doors that led the way to the elevators. Once the lady pushed the button under her keyboard, the doors slowly opened, revealing a set of golden brass elevators at the end of a long bright hallway. Chris hit the thirtieth floor button, and a few moments later, the elevator dinged.

Impressed, Kate commented, "That was fast."

"Everything here is about luxury and efficiency." The doors opened, and together they stepped out into a small room with yet another set of double wooden doors, and yet another secretary.

"How many doors do we have to go through to get to this guy? I feel like I'm in a Matryoshka doll," Kate complained quietly to herself as she readjusted the purse on her shoulder.

Perplexed, Chris looked down at Kate and asked, "What kind of dolls?"

"Those Russian nesting dolls." When Chris looked at her blankly, Kate simplified even further. "Those tiny wooden dolls where each doll has a smaller doll inside of it."

"Nope. Never heard of it."

"Google it."

Behind a huge, solid oak desk, and perched in a soft leather chair, sat a tiny man with a groomed beard, manicured nails, and silver spectacles resting on the tip of his nose. Although Kate thought he would be bigger, she wasn't surprised to find he wore a sleek, tailored suit that boasted a luxury lifestyle. Next to the phone, a stream of gray smoke emerged from a rather robust cigar in a glass ashtray. Quietly watching while he finished an intense call, Kate covertly surveyed the room as though she were peeking inside of a stranger's medicine cabinet. After a few minutes, Charlie abruptly ended his call, slamming the phone onto the cradle.

Like a real pro, Kate watched the intense anger drain from Charlie's face as he quickly changed hats to greet his number one meal ticket. From around his desk, Charlie stood and with his husky voice greeted, "Good to see you again. Thank you for coming down on such short notice." Longtime friends, Charlie hugged Chris, happy to finally see him.

"Not a problem." The moment Chris's foot crossed the threshold into Charlie's office, his mannerisms changed - back to cold and impersonal.

"This must be Kate." Charlie held out his hand, but allowed his inquisitive eyes to skip over Kate. Something about Charlie made Kate hesitant – she didn't know if it was the stench odor of cigar perfuming from his clothes or the way he casually avoided direct eye contact.

"It is," Kate answered taciturnly, as she extended a tense hand.

Generously, Charlie offered them a glass of Dalmone Scotch before he sat back in the comfy, gigantic brown leather chair. Instead of immediately addressing the issue of Chris's absence, Charlie sipped on his Scotch, trying to figure out the best way to approach it.

"Charlie, what was the reason for the emergency meeting?" Chris was quickly becoming impatient.

The glass of Scotch clicked on the wooden desk as Charlie leaned forward and explained, "We got a response for that new Meyer movie. They want to start production in one week."

"One week! I can't be prepared in that short amount of time! Plus, they haven't even finalized the script!" This was going to put a real damper on Chris's plans. Beyond frustrated, Chris was pissed that Charlie had dragged him downtown for this. Everything could have easily been discussed on the phone, and the script could have been couriered. This *important* meeting was interfering with Chris's plans.

"I know it's a short turnaround, but you've done it before with shorter notice. Work with Meyers, he's talented."

"I can't believe I'm only getting a week's notice."

"That's the other reason why I called you in here today," Charlie paused for a slight moment then continued. "For the past three weeks I haven't been able to get ahold of you. There were meetings you missed. I want to make sure you're OK and that there aren't any distractions." Casually, Charlie quickly glanced in Kate's direction.

Chris spoke dismissively, "I was out of town."

"I understand, but we have agreed to do this film." Charlie smiled back at Chris and said, "I think this is the role you've been waiting for -- Oscar worthy!"

"OK," Chris agreed hesitantly.

"Thank you for coming in on such short notice," Charlie reiterated again. "Keep your phone on!"

Anxious to leave, Kate promptly stood up and Chris automatically put his arm between her and Charlie, leading her out of the office.

Before his hand reached the brass doorknob, Chris said, "See you soon, Charlie."

The moment the elevator door closed, Chris's cell phone buzzed. Without looking away from it, he said, "Well, that wasn't too bad, was it?"

"I guess not," Kate mumbled, however, all she could think about was how Charlie implied that she was distracting Chris from his work and continued, "Still don't like him."

"Fair enough, but he is the best." Click. Click. Click. The only sound in the elevator was Chris's fingers typing against the BlackBerry keys. Even when he responded to Kate his head didn't lift as he continued to type. "You are so cute when you get like this."

"Like what?"

"Feisty!"

Annoyed, Kate rolled her eyes and turned her back toward him. In the mirror-filled elevator, she watched him continue to click away intently on his BlackBerry.

Bothered by his expressionless face, she whined, "How would you know? You haven't looked up from your phone."

"Trust me, I know." The firm, thin line of his lips began to curl upward in a satisfied grin.

Chapter Eleven

Anxiously awaiting Chris and Kate's return, Sam was busy pacing back and forth in Chris's foyer, wearing a hole in the marble floor. The moment they walked in the door Sam screeched, "Where have you been? I've been waiting for almost an hour!"

Coming from someone who wasn't punctual —Sam was always late— it surprised Chris to be bombarded by her super-hyper, over-the-top screech. "Relax. We're here now. Besides, why are you here so early?"

"I'm not early! You're late! Do you know how long it's going to take me to get her ready?" Beyond aggravated, Sam rolled her eyes and poked the air in front of Kate with her index finger to prove her point.

"Geez, Sam, she isn't some homely teenager with bad acne."

With each moment that passed, Sam got more and more impatient with this pointless conversation. Left hand squeezing her hip, she started to tap the marble floor impatiently with her Manolo Blahnik stilettos. This was precious time Chris was wasting, and Sam needed every minute she could get.

"It's going to take me a couple of hours to get her ready! She is a complete mess. I mean look at that hair!"

"OK, seriously. What is it with you two and this insane desire to talk about me like I'm not here?" Suddenly, a panicked look flashed across Kate's face as she fretfully asked, "Wait, what do you mean 'a couple of hours'?" An opportunity revealed itself, and Sam jumped on it faster than a jackrabbit in heat. Quickly seizing Kate's arm, she pulled her up the stairs, but not without informing Chris, "You can't see her until tonight at the club!"

"Why?"

"You're just going to have to trust me!" A satisfied smile spread across Sam's pale cheeks as she placed a short piece of her hair strategically behind her ear.

"Whatever," Chris mumbled under his breath as he walked away.

"Sam, what the hell do you mean a couple of hours?"

Ignoring Kate, Sam continued to walk up the stairs. "Chris!" Kate yelled out again. With no response, Kate knew that she was on her own; Chris had caved and left her to fend for herself.

Opening Kate's bedroom door, Sam said, "Oh, come on, Kate, it's going to be fun!"

"Says who?" An overly excited and creepy smile appeared on Sam's face, and Kate knew instantly that she was in trouble. Dashing to the intercom, Kate stabbed the button and yelled to Chris, "I'm going to get you for this!"

A sarcastic tone transmitted back, "I'd like to see you try." Frustrated, she had a good indication that Chris was downstairs in his study, laughing hysterically.

In the middle of the room, Kate thought about making a run for it, but when her head turned toward the door, Sam quickly shouted out, "Don't even try it! I'll chase you down and drag you back screaming and crying." Something told Kate that Sam wasn't kidding.

From inside of the closet, Sam yelled out, "Kate, this is fun!"

Coolly, Kate retorted, "For whom?"

"Mostly for me, but you're going to love the way you look." When Sam emerged with more than fifty different pieces of clothing in her arms, Kate's heart stopped.

"Uh . . . Sam . . . I'm more of a casual girl." Kate shuddered picking up an extremely short black spandex dress from the bed.

Admiring the treasure trove of clothes, Sam thought about snagging a few items to add to her collection as she said, "I have to admit, Chris does have good taste."

Appalled at the idea of someone picking out her clothes, Kate argued, "He didn't buy these! Well, he *bought* them . . . I mean, he didn't pick them out. They were already here when I arrived."

In the process of organizing the mound of clothes on the bed, Sam replied, "True, but he was clever enough to get your sizes without you noticing. That has to count for something, doesn't it?"

"I guess so . . . but why would he go through the trouble?"

Surprised, Sam threw a pale green halter top back on the bed and stared intensely at Kate. "Are you really that blind? You can't see that he cares about you?" On her way back into the closet, Sam walked by Kate, who stood idly by, unsure of what to do.

"I know that he cares, but why does he always feel the need to go above and beyond, like this necklace?" With her index finger, Kate held the necklace up and then let if fall against her chest.

It stunned Sam that she didn't notice Kate wearing a new piece of jewelry; she was normally good at picking up on that kind of stuff. Sticking her head out of the closet to get a better look, Sam saw the sparkle, and the shoes fell from her arms. In a zombie-like motion, she walked toward Kate and questioned, "Is that what I think it is?"

"I don't know, what do you think it is?" Hesitant to answer, Kate took a step back.

With a crazed look in her eye, Sam demanded, "Who is the designer?"

Trying to think back, Kate looked down at her necklace, "I think it's Goodman . . .something… Yeah . . . I think that's what Chris said."

"Are you freaking kidding me?" Unable to control her reaction, Sam took a few steps closer to Kate.

Intimidated, Kate took a few more steps back, until she bumped into the nightstand. "OK, you're scaring me. It's just a necklace."

"That's not just any necklace! I know you don't understand designers, but you probably have three hundred thousand dollars on your neck right now." Kate couldn't fathom what she'd just heard; the idea that she casually had that much money in a daily piece of jewelry made her dizzy. She went to sit down on the bed, missed it completely, and fell to the floor.

"I'm guessing he didn't tell you that part," Sam said as she squatted down next to Kate, who just silently shook her head.

In all the years that Sam knew Chris, he had never once bought someone jewelry. Sitting on the hard floor, a distinct memory came to Sam. *Chris specifically told Sam that he would never buy jewelry for a woman unless he loved her. Things began to make sense. Chris reached out, not only to make amends with his friends, but also to impress the woman who didn't love him back.*

Glancing at Kate, Sam wondered why she seemed so sad. Chris would give her the world with no questions asked, and instead of joy, it only seemed to burden her.

Casually, Sam brushed Kate's hair off her shoulder and inquired, "Why can't you just be happy?"

"That's a strange question," Kate surprisingly shot back. "I *am* happy, just a bit stunned right now." Her fingers continued to idly graze the smooth, cool necklace that lay on her collarbone.

"You don't seem like it. I mean, seriously, with all that Chris has done for you just in this week alone, you'd think you would be a bit more grateful."

Grateful!

Immediately, Kate's fingers stopped, and she slowly turned an angry glare at Sam. How dare she accuse Kate of not being grateful! She knew nothing about Kate or why she didn't believe in spending money so freely.

"Really, you don't think I'm grateful?" Before Sam could even begin to answer, Kate stood up and towered over her in response, "I didn't ask for these things, and right up front, Chris knew how I felt about this topic."

It didn't take long for Sam to get up and defend her point, "You don't have to ask for them, that's the point. Chris deeply cares about you, and when men care about a woman they take care of them." Flabbergasted by what Sam was trying to imply, Kate pushed past her while mumbling under her breath. Suddenly she stopped at the end of the bed, turned to Sam, and firmly clarified, "I don't feel that way about Chris. I'm gay. Don't you get it, I don't want to be in a relationship with a man."

Righteously, with her arms firmly crossed, Sam glared at Kate with a scowl. It took a moment before Sam finally spoke, but when she did her voice was firm and direct. "You're naïve if you think that you're not already in a relationship with Chris. You need to open your heart."

"It's not like that." The uncertainty in Kate's voice left her trying to convince herself more than Sam. There was no need to further this argument; Sam already knew the truth, and it was slowly becoming clearer to Kate.

After a moment of awkward silence, Kate finally smiled and gestured to the pile of clothes. "How many do I have to try on?"

"Until we find the perfect fit."

Distracting herself Kate asked, "What about you, Sam, any love interests?"

Sam politely glanced away while Kate rolled down her jeans and exposed her purple, semi-laced full panties. "Not to toot my own horn, but I'm a very sought out photographer, and it takes up much of my time."

"I thought you restored historical buildings?"

"Oh, I used to. Shirley was my last project," Sam held up a blouse and threw it back in the pile as she continued, "Photography was a hobby of mine, until someone noticed my work and put me in an art show. Next thing I know, people are knocking down my door for my work."

"What happened with your other company?"

"Surprisingly enough, someone actually offered me a great price, and I sold it to work-full time on my photos."

"Sam, you can't spend your whole life working. You need to find happiness!" Kate grunted as she jumped up and down, squeezing herself into a miniskirt. As her stomach bulged out, Kate thought maybe Chris wasn't the best at determining her size. Oh well, she didn't want to wear the miniskirt anyway.

"Like you?" Sam snapped in spite as she walked out of the closet.

"That's not fair," Kate argued. "My situation is far more complex than you can imagine." She exhaled and threw the skirt back to Sam, who stood near the bed. "I don't think this is going to work."

"Sorry." Sam lowered her eyes guiltily, and then continued, "Besides, I have plenty of time to find the right person."

"You don't have as much time as you think. You've already spent . . . what, ten years on your career?"

"Ten years! Holy shit, Kate I graduated from college like three years ago! I'm only twenty-four!"

There was a loud crash from inside the closet when Kate stuck her head out and asked, "Twenty-four?"

"Yeah, why? You OK in there?"

"Fine." Tripping over the shoes piled on the floor, Kate stumbled out of the closet. "That's a huge age difference between you and Chris; he's thirty-five. What do you guys have in common?"

"I get asked that a lot. Most of my friends tend to be older. Chris and I just get each other, that's why it works." Given Chris and Kate's odd relationship, Sam expected her to be more open-minded.

Kate scooped up a pair of heels and delicately pried, "Has there ever been any . . . you know, feelings?"

With a twisted, face, Sam shrieked, "No! It's nothing like that! Chris is like a big brother."

With a satisfied smile, Kate pointed to a dress in the pile and suggested, "That's cool. Here, I'll try that dress on, but I'm not making any promises."

At precisely ten o'clock the doorbell chimed, notifying the house staff that the black Lincoln was parked out front and ready for the girls.

The ride to Club 8 was rather quiet, until they turned down Hollywood Boulevard. Kate was unprepared for what she saw next. Multi-colored lights flashed brightly with a line almost around the block. Women were dressed scandalously in skimpy glittery dresses and painful high heels, desperately waiting to get in.

Chris's Lincoln was directly in front of them, stopped at the entrance. Confidently, almost cocky, Chris emerged from the car, waving to his screaming fans that were held behind a red velvet rope with security. In the short distance between the limo and the door, Chris signed several autographs and was greeted by the club manager.

He was a tiny little fellow who blubbered on and on about his excitement regarding Chris Cody choosing Club 8 for his entertainment. Proudly, the manager escorted Chris to his VIP area, located on the top floor with an open view of the entire club. Three designated bottle service girls were hired to exclusively serve Chris and his guests. The VIPs also had a private bathroom area – to avoid the hassle of waiting in line.

It did not surprise Chris at all to find people already there – especially James and Eric; it was normal for James to round up strays.

Nervously, Chris waited for Kate's arrival, pacing and glancing continuously over the balcony. The constant movement of the back and forth began to drive Eric insane until finally he scolded, "She's fine! Good God, relax."

Unaware of his behavior, Chris plopped down on the couch with his friends and ordered a drink in hopes of calming his nerves.

"Who's fine?" James asked.

"He's worried about Kate," Eric sighed as he rolled his eyes at James.

Twitching his leg, Chris made the couch vibrate when he responded, "Well, she should have been here already." Once again, Chris anxiously popped up and began scanning the club—still no sign of Kate or Sam anywhere. *Where could they be? Shouldn't they be here by now?*

Sarcastically, James teased Chris, "Ooh, this girl is getting to you."

"Oh please, this is ridiculous," Eric snapped.

Infuriated by James's comment, Chris glared at them and defensively yelled, "She hasn't gotten to me!" His harsh reaction caused several people to stop their conversations to eavesdrop. The women who were standing close enough to overhear the entire conversation instantly became jealous of this mystery woman who appeared to have Chris Cody's full attention, and the envious hate spread like a wild fire.

"Whatever, man," James laughed and walked away. Chris jerked his drink off the server's tray and turned away from the crowd.

The simple idea that a woman could get under his skin was preposterous. Chris had spent a lifetime building a reputation of the unattainable bachelor, and he refused to admit otherwise. But it was too late; his actions had already told the entire story before he could even try to deny it.

A few minutes later, Eric edged up to Chris and leaned against the balcony railing with him. They exchanged a mutual glance and while Chris thought Eric was being supportive, he was about to be proven wrong.

"Chris, I know this girl means something to you, but what do you know about her?"

The words stung since Chris half-expected Eric to be the most understanding. "Are you serious?"

"Dude, I'm just saying you don't know anything about her." Eric jingled the ice in his half-melted glass of Scotch.

"I know Kate," Chris shot back, still gazing into the crowd.

"Really? What's her favorite color? Her favorite food? Her favorite flower?"

"That stuff's not important."

"What do you know about her past? Did you even run a check on her?"

The words felt like a direct attack on Kate, and angrily, Chris puffed out his chest warning Eric, "I would never invade her privacy like that!"

"Why, because you're so respectful? You didn't have a problem doing it to Hazel."

"She was only after one thing!"

"At least she was honest about it! You knew where you stood with Hazel; you're clueless with Kate!" Chris couldn't believe that Eric continued to doubt, not only Kate's intentions, but also his own judgment.

Anger raged through Chris as his fingers gripped tightly around his glass, and he poured the rum down his throat. A small droplet remained on his lips, and aggressively, Chris wiped his mouth with the back of his hand and firmly spoke, "It's not like that with Kate."

"It's always like that with women. If you're not holding all the cards, she's playing you for a fool!" It was unfathomable to Eric how naïve Chris was acting about Kate. Still scanning the crowd, Chris remained silent; he didn't have an explanation. Even though Eric's words stung, for the tiniest second Chris thought *maybe* there was some truth to it.

Somehow, after Chris disappeared into the club, fans broke through security and began to swarm the front, piling into the streets. It took fifteen minutes to get the drunken fans out of the road and safely back on the sidewalks.

Slowly maneuvering through the remaining crowd, the limo finally turned around the block toward the south side of the building. In a small alley, the Lincoln parked next to a door that was guarded by a three hundred pound, bald-headed bouncer. The loud music vibrated through the concrete walls until the owner stepped outside and extended a proper hand to Kate and Sam. Elegantly stepping out of the car, Kate looked stunning in a short, silky black cocktail dress, accessorized with her brand new Goodman necklace.

A busy man, the owner only had time for a few polite exchanges before he led the girls inside.

It wasn't even midnight yet, and there was a line at the bar and a packed dance floor. Dazed, Kate tried to take everything in, but between the strobe lights flickering, the pulsing music, and the paid half-naked dancers on the platforms, it was all too much. Without warning Sam grabbed Kate's hand and led her through the crowd to an opening she spotted at the bottom of the staircase.

Watching the crowd like a hawk, it didn't take Chris long to spot Sam's short pixie hair, slicing through the dance floor, dragging a girl behind her. Before Kate could take three steps, Chris rushed to her side and pulled her in close.

The happiness didn't last long though when Chris turned his attention to Sam. The combination of being unaccustomed to waiting and a deep sense of worry about Kate, proved to be an unpleasant mixture.

"Where have you been? Why didn't you text?"

"I'm sorry; we were a little busy trying to get through the road block your fans created," defensively, Sam shouted back.

Ignoring this logic, Chris returned his attention to Kate, "Are you OK?"

"I'm fine. Relax. Everything is OK." She looked up at him with a comforting smile. "Besides, I'm surprised we even made it here at all. Sam literally made me try on at least fifty different outfits."

"You look great."

"Thank you."

Sarcastically, Sam rolled her eyes walking past Chris and up the stairs.

"Hey Sam," Chris paused for a moment allowing Sam to turn back around. "Sorry I lost my temper."

"Don't let it happen again, or I'm going to put my heel up your ass."

"Yes, ma'am," Chris jokingly saluted Sam.

Arm in arm, Kate and Chris walked together toward the man guarding the VIP area—Kate noticed a roomful of curious eyes watching them carefully. All were inquisitive except for one pair. Full of scorn, they gave Kate chills when she saw them.

"Looks like we have an audience." Holding onto Chris's flexed bicep for support, Kate tilted her head toward the group, who gawked openly at the two of them.

"People are interested to meet you."

"I don't get it. I feel like a science experiment."

"I think you were Sam's experiment."

"Yeah, thanks for reminding me. I'm really going to get you for that, she tried putting me in a miniskirt." Each step required Kate's full concentration and when she almost twisted her ankle, she grabbed onto Chris even tighter and stuttered, "Good thing I convinced her otherwise."

"Good thing." The black cocktail dress Kate wore was revealing and drove Chris's hormones wild, but if that skirt were any shorter he didn't know if he would be able to control himself. It was hard enough to deal with the fact that a gorgeous woman like Kate would never be interested in him.

Quickly trying to prepare herself, Kate took a deep breath as they walked into the roomful of judging eyes. Uncomfortable, she nervously squeezed Chris's hand as her eyes flickered around the room.

In an aggressive tone, Chris yelled out to the gawking stares, "What?" With that, everyone turned their attention elsewhere.

Having already done his pre-game drinking, James was wired for the night. "Hey, Kate! I see you survived Sam!" Hyper, James gave Kate a big wet kiss on the cheek.

"Gross, James! UGH!" In disgust, Kate wiped the trail of saliva that was left behind. "I barely made it out of there alive."

"Pulling teeth would have been easier," Sam chimed in charmingly, until she glanced at Kate and wanted to scream. "Damn it, James. Can't you keep your sloppiness to yourself? You're going to ruin her makeup."

Kate tried to wipe the moisture off with the back of her hand. "It's fine, there's too much on, anyways." Like a six-year-old boy, James snickered at Sam, who rolled her eyes in annoyance. Ever so casually, Chris leaned into Kate's ear, "I think you look beautiful without makeup." Surprisingly, Kate blushed softly, but before anyone noticed her flushed cheeks, she quickly pushed those thoughts out of her mind.

"Well, you look marvelous," James complimented Kate while his eyes undressed her.

"Thanks. I just like the plain-Jane me." A timid smile appeared while she glanced around, trying to avoid the ogling eyes.

Spiteful looks burned into Kate as Eric accused, with two full drinks in his hands, "So you're just pretending to be someone you're not."

Able to see right through Eric's bullshit, Kate snapped, "No, Eric, I know exactly who I am; you, on the other hand, might want to figure that out for yourself." Face-to-face, Kate breathed confrontationally down Eric's throat, then without a pause, she took one of his drinks, gulped it back, handed him the empty glass, snidely said, "Thanks for the drink," and walked away.

Speechless, Eric didn't have a smart comeback, and his friends were shocked as they awkwardly glanced at their drinks. Deep down, Chris was slightly impressed with Kate's boldness. A humiliated Eric slumped his shoulders and sulked his way downstairs as he tried not to trip over his own slinky legs.

In desperate attempts not only to scope out the new arrival but also to get close to Chris, three girls bluntly started a conversation. Despite Kate's best attempts to ignore the ditzy trio, she couldn't help but see, from the corner of her eye, that one of them in particular was throwing herself at Chris. Even though, at every advance, Chris politely and subtly dodged her, she was apparently incapable of understanding the message: *Not interested.* She couldn't help but laugh at this girl's desperateness. Instantly, the girl's eyes scanned Kate, and the tension between the two was intense. With her glaring eyes fixed on Kate, the girl asked Chris in a nasty tone, "Who is she?"

Proudly, Chris slung his arm around Kate's shoulder and introduced her, "Kate, this is Susanna, Hazel, and Claire."

It was common knowledge in this circle of so-called friends that Susanna was obsessed with Chris and couldn't stand anyone getting in her way. While the conversation continued around them, Susanna's crystal-blue eyes continued to glare in Kate's direction.

Annoyed by the evil gawking, Kate lashed out, "What the hell are you staring at?"

For a moment, Susanna blinked her mascara-plumped false eyelashes, and flipped her thick, luscious blonde hair over her shoulder, as a fake smile appeared. "Someone who doesn't belong."

Instantaneously, Kate's nostrils flared. "Go fuck your mother!" Bewildered by Kate's extreme abrasiveness, Susanna was rendered speechless and stomped off sucking her teeth while her friends trailed behind hers.

After four drinks, it wasn't hard for Sam to convince Kate to get on the dance floor. Twenty minutes later, Kate stumbled her way to the private bathroom to relieve the full bladder.

The sound of cackling girls stopped Kate from unlatching the stall and she waited for a moment. It didn't take long for Kate to recognize the voices – Susanna, Hazel and Claire. They were all complaining about something…. Kate.

"I just don't understand what he's doing with her," Susanna criticized, pushing her way through Hazel and Claire to be in the center of the mirror. Snottily, she flipped her blonde extensions while she touched up her lipstick; her cheap press-on tips poked her fake nose.

"Me, either!" Hazel snorted, agreeing with Susanna. Big surprise, Hazel always agreed with Susanna – she lacked the imagination of an individual thought.

"Did you see that dress? It's way too expensive for her. She probably begged for it, and poor Chris is a sucker." Susanna figured if Chris was going to spend money it should be on her and no one else. Again she sucked her teeth and complained, "There's nothing sexy about her. She looks like some hooker he wanted to play Pretty Woman with."

While fluffing her bangs, Claire accidently slipped up, "Julia Roberts was hot in that movie." In unison, both Hazel and Susanna shot Claire a nasty look. Disappointed, Susanna sighed and shook her head. "She's practically a baby. What is he going to do, give her a pacifier to suck on?"

"It's not a pacifier she's sucking on!" Hazel blurted out. They all laughed at the image of Kate sucking Chris off.

Fed up, Kate slammed the stall door open, startling two of the girls. Hazel jumped so hard that she smeared her lipstick onto her cheek. If Susanna was surprised, it didn't show—not even a flinch. She just glared at Kate through the mirror with a malevolent look.

"Susanna, you should probably ask yourself why Chris would rather spend time with a lesbian than you. Guessing he doesn't like silicone and plastic. It's no wonder why he flew across the country to find me."

Right before Kate pushed opened the bathroom door, she turned and faced the three women who were now speechless with their lip-glossed mouths hanging open. In a circular motion Kate extended her index finger at Susanna, then allowed her hand to smoothly and sexily run down the silky material of her dress before she corrected, "Oh, by the way, this is my outfit. I don't need Chris to buy me anything."

Righteously, Kate left the bathroom leaving the girls stunned.

Once the door swung closed, Susanna growled into the mirror with her angry reflection staring back at her, "That bitch!!! I'm going to get her."

In the heat of the moment, her mind began to devise a plan to ruin Kate. No one talked to Susanna that way and got away with it. From experience, Hazel and Claire knew that when Susanna got this angry, the last place anyone wanted to be was in her path of destruction.

In the VIP area Kate found Chris lounging on a couch by himself. Naturally, Kate strolled toward him and plopped herself on his lap. Curious about the unexpected public affection Chris inquired, "Are you having a good time?"

"I am." Kate smiled while she glanced among the crowd in search of Susanna. What Kate wanted the most was for that girl to walk by and see her cuddled up with Chris. *Stupid girl! How dare she think she can intimidate me?*

Noticing that Kate was more interested in something else Chris offered, "Here, try this."

The moment the bubbles hit Kate's lips, her face twisted up in disgust as she complained, "Ewe . . . what is that?" Repeatedly, she smacked her lips to remove the taste from her mouth.

From behind Kate's shoulder an annoying voice screeched, "Not everyone is made for our lifestyle. There is a certain amount of class required, and you just don't have it."

Slowly, Kate stood from Chris's knee while she shot daggers at Susanna and retorted angrily, "How in the hell did you get in?" A small step forward with her face fire engine red, Susanna was prepared to fight, but Kate spoke first, "It doesn't matter. I don't want to be around people like you."

Kate politely handed Chris the glass and walked away. Confused, he called out to Kate, but there wasn't a response.

"You're right! You don't belong here!" Susanna hollered at Kate's back.

This was exactly why Chris didn't want to come; he knew people like Susanna could be unnecessarily cruel. Naturally, he stood up to chase after Kate, but immediately Susanna blocked him.

Passionately, her small hands groped Chris's biceps while she explained in a sexy tone, "Oh, let her go. She doesn't belong here. She isn't one of us." Chris tried to take a step back, but Susanna held him tighter with an even sexier smile.

Upset that she allowed Susanna to get under her skin, Kate shoved and bumped through the crowd until she made her way to a less-populated bar. She went to pull money from her purse but was annoyed to find that it wasn't dangling from her wrist. Pausing, she remembered that everything was placed on Chris's tab.

The bartender happily greeted Kate, "What can I get you?"

"Bud Light bottle." To release some of the pressure from her shoes, Kate divided her weight between her elbows on the counter. The bartender smiled politely but found it odd that one of Chris Cody's guests would order cheap beer. For a brief moment, Kate glanced up at the VIP and saw what appeared to be Susanna and Chris in a romantic embrace. *That is someone Chris should be with, not me. We're from two different worlds.*

While deep in thought about how she didn't belong, Kate didn't notice the guy who was next to her …staring.

"Hi, I'm Mark," a random voice offered. Startled, she took a small step away from the guy. Well dressed with tight curly brown hair and blue eyes, this man stood very confidently holding his beer.

"I'm sorry; I didn't mean to scare you," he continued when Kate didn't respond. After a quick smile, Kate hoped that if she just ignored him he would get the hint that she wasn't interested and move along.

He extended his hand to introduce himself. "My name is Mark. And you are?" Apparently, he didn't get the hint.

"I'm Kate." To send a clear signal that she wasn't interested, Kate squeezed his hand tightly.

Playfully, Mark shook out the soreness from his crippled hand and complimented, "Wow! That's quite a grip you have! You know it's not very often that a beautiful woman is alone at a bar." What he really wanted to know was if she was here with a guy or girlfriends.

"I'm not alone, I'm with friends." Unknowingly, Kate answered his question, and when a grin appeared, she quickly realized her mistake. "And the cheesy pickup lines won't work, either." Frustrated at herself, Kate took a swig of her beer and rudely smacked her lips.

Disregarding Kate's subtle hints of irritation, he said, "I'm sorry; I didn't mean to offend you. So, where are your friends?" Impressed by Kate's feisty personality, Mark was intrigued by the challenge. Normally, he would ignore a girl who gave him the cold shoulder, but not Kate; something sparked his interest.

Nonchalantly, she motioned around the club to imply that her friends could be anywhere. "Around." After she chugged her beer, Kate tipped her bottle toward the bartender.

In an embellished, concerned voice Mark preached, "Wow. You better slow down." But the truth was that if Kate got drunk, it would be easier to get her home, which Mark counted on. Unexpectedly, he put his hand on Kate's wrist. "Let me get that for you." Shocked at his forward behavior, Kate stared at him and quickly shook his hand away. Quickly realizing his mistake, he took a small step away from Kate.

"No, it's fine. Thanks, though." Kate motioned to the bartender for another beer, but unlike before, he took an extremely long time to serve the drink.

The more Mark continued to chatter in Kate's ear about pointless stuff, the more her patience wore thin. In an attempt to release some of her frustration, she tapped her fingers on the counter in an impatient rhythm.

Finally, the bartender came back with the drink, and Kate was ready to find Sam.

Politely, Kate said to Mark, "It was nice to meet you, but I've gotta go . . ."

Detecting her abandonment and attempting to keep her near, Mark observed, "Looks like your friends ditched you."

Not responding to his comment, Kate grabbed her beer and rolled her eyes.

Despite all the roadblocks Kate put in place, Mark continued, as he suggested with an implication in his smile, "Want to get out of here and go somewhere quiet?"

Appalled by his intrusiveness, Kate snapped, "No!" and turned to walk away. All of a sudden she felt his firm grip around her arm as he forcefully pulled her back toward him.

"Hey, where do you think you're going? I'm not done with you," he commanded.

"Get your hands off me!" Kate tried to pry his hands off her arm and yelled, "Yes, you're done!"

"You're not going to blue-ball me and get away with it!" Instantly, something switched; Mark was no longer the shy boy who annoyed her, but now the drunk who refused to leave without what he wanted: Kate.

"Blue balls? You asshole, I'm gay. I don't want to fuck you," Kate screamed, desperately trying to get out of his grasp. The harder she twisted, the more it hurt as he increased the pressure on her arm. Kate winced in pain.

"You're coming with me!" There was a serious and dangerous look in his eyes as he started to pull Kate toward the back door. Unable to pry her arm free, Kate took her full beer bottle and clunked Mark on the head. Unfortunately, with his adrenaline rush, the bottle didn't affect Mark; a vicious smile appeared. Instinctively, Kate started screaming for help; Mark refused to let go and pulled harder. No one heard the screams over the loud music and the back corner became even more unusually isolated.

Luckily, one of Chris's bodyguards noticed the struggle and quickly yelled a code into an earpiece which immediately notified Chris. The bodyguard closest to Chris yelled out *Kate* and pointed in the general direction. That was all Chris needed; he raced with the bodyguard down the stairs, pushing anyone in their path. The other six bodyguards on duty began maneuvering through the crowd, each from a different direction, yelling into their earpiece as they closed in on Kate.

Mark's thick biceps had both of Kate's arms pinned down, and despite her struggles, she couldn't break free. Desperate to get away, she forcefully sank her white teeth into his arm, tasting small droplets of blood. The sound of howling pain echoed in Kate's ear and when Mark's arm dropped, she took a quick step away, but it wasn't enough. He grabbed Kate with his uninjured arm and spun her around to give her what she deserved.

"Bitch!" Mark pulled back his fist to hit her. Prepared to take the blow, Kate squeezed her eyes shut and waited. The hard feeling of knuckles pressing into her cheek never came. In the same split second Mark prepared to throw his punch, Chris came in from behind and laid Mark out in a single blow.

Carefully, Kate opened her eyes only to see three large men dragging Mark out of the club. She hadn't noticed that Chris was standing next to her, and when he gently put his hand on her hip, she screamed out and prepared to strike.

"Kate. It's OK. It's me." With catlike reflexes, Chris bolted Kate's arms to her side and once she realized she was safe, her muscles stopped flexing against his restraint. Relieved, Kate happily threw her arms around Chris's neck, thankful for his protection. The mere fact that Chris came to her rescue baffled her since she was so certain that they belonged in two different worlds. She struggled to understand his motive, but at that moment she was just grateful that Chris had been extra protective.

"Come on, let's get you home," he ordered as he followed the lead of the bodyguards; not for a second did he let Kate out of his sight.

Barely able to get the words out of her mouth, Kate remembered, "My purse." Through the holes of the bodyguard wall, she could see people staring at her strangely; embarrassed, she turned away.

"I'll have Sam get it for you." Chris called to Sam who had just pushed her way through all the commotion. "Sam, can you get Kate's purse? I think she left it in the VIP room." In frustration, Sam grumbled at the thought of tackling her way through that crowd again. Sympathizing with the exhausted look on her face Chris suggested, "Take Bryan with you. I'll meet you back at the house; the car will be waiting for you."

While Kate and Chris managed their way through the massive crowd, Susanna spied from above in the VIP room, fuming with envy and jealousy. Unable to watch the happy couple any longer, she turned away and spotted the unattended purse on the couch – an evil smile appeared. Quickly, she snatched the purse, opened it, grabbed something from it, and threw it in her purse. Unexpectedly, Sam caught Susanna with Kate's purse still in her hand.

Frozen, Susanna thought of something quick, and pretended to be helpful. "Here Sam, I think Kate will need this."

Sam sneered at Susanna's fakeness and snapped, "Why do you care? This happened because of you." Pissed off, Sam snatched the purse from the troublemaker's hand. In a rush to get out of the club, Sam didn't check to make sure that everything was there.

Susanna just lightly chuckled to herself in amusement.

On the ride home, Kate didn't dare leave the safety of Chris's side, even when the limo stopped in front of the house. Chris carried Kate to her room. After Kate found her pajamas, Chris respectfully turned to give her the much-needed privacy to change.

Unable to help it, he blamed himself for what happened; he was upset that he allowed Kate to walk away. *If only I had stopped her, none of this would have happened*, Chris cursed to himself. Aika sat next to Chris like a longtime best friend; they both had the same worried expression.

After the last button was fastened, Kate gently tapped Chris on the shoulder giving him a weak and timid smile. The look of her tired eyes, surrounded by her long tangled hair, just broke his heart. No words were exchanged; Chris guided Kate to the bed and folded down the sheets for her. Exhausted, Kate felt her eyes flicker up and down as she desperately tried to fight off sleep. Once Chris saw that she had succumbed to the weight of her eyelids, a small surge of relief embraced him, as he watched her dreaming peacefully.

His mind raced with all the details from that night, and to clear his thoughts, he idly paced around downstairs so he wouldn't wake Kate. Aside from the raindrops banging against the windows, the house was dead silent. Suddenly, crashing through the front door, Sam stumbled her way inside, drenched from head to toe. Her black hair was plastered to her head as she tried to wipe her soaking bangs from her eyes. Exasperated from trying to outrun the rain in her heels, she stopped to catch her breath, creating a puddle on the floor.

The concern in Chris's eyes was apparent, and Sam reached out, "How is she?"

"Sleeping." A large sigh escaped his dry, cracked lips as he ran his hands roughly through his hair, pulling a few blonde strands out in the process.

"Good. A little help here -- I could use a towel." Finally noticing that Sam was still dripping on the freshly waxed floor, Chris shuffled to the small linen closet in the guest bathroom and came back with a warm, fluffy, olive green towel. After Sam had mopped up as much of the water as possible, she wrapped herself in the towel and kicked off her shoes. Naturally, she pulled Chris into her supportive arms and whispered, "Come on. You need a drink."

In the eerie silence of his mansion, they sank into the leather couches and distractedly peeled the labels off their beers.

The quietness began to engulf their surroundings, and it irritated Chris's nerves. "You know, I never realized how quiet this house is."

"That happens when you have a big empty house." Hesitant for a moment, she looked at the desperate expression written on Chris's face and cautiously continued. "OK. I know you're worried about Kate, but you need some advice."

The look of sadness changed to perplexity as Chris inquired, "What do you mean?"

Now with her clothes a little dryer, Sam took the green towel and rubbed her short hair. The damp cloth hung on her forehead while she sipped on her beer. "I know that you care a lot about Kate, but you need to be careful. I don't want to see you get hurt."

"Thanks, Sam. I do care about her, and for some strange reason, I feel very protective of her. I don't know why."

Sam teasingly threw the wet towel at him, "Retard, you love her."

Slow with intoxication and sleepiness, it took a moment for his brain to catch up with what his heart instantly felt when Sam mentioned love.

In a self-pitying tone, he whispered, "She doesn't love me." The words crackled in his throat.

Fed up with his wimpy, boohoo-me attitude, Sam smacked him upside his head. "She loves you. You love her. It may not be a romantic relationship, but you two have something special. You have a friendship with a love that is so intense that you're connected at a soul level. But heed my warning: Kate will never move past a friendship. So if you can handle the fact that she'll never sleep with you or commit to you the way society expects you to, then you'll have her in your life forever." Sighing in frustration, Sam continued, "I wish I was half as lucky as the two of you."

Stunned by Sam's wisdom, Chris smiled at the very idea of a long life with Kate. "You're right, sweetheart. Thank you for smacking some sense into me. Literally." Chris wrapped his arm around her shoulder and held her close.

Exhaustion overcame her, but not before a smile appeared, followed by a yawn. "What are friends for?"

Despite his extreme sleepiness, Chris couldn't sleep; there was a lot to figure out. He sat quietly in his office in the old hickory, burgundy chair and thought back on his life. This was everything he ever wanted, the fame, the fortune . . . but at the ripe age of thirty-five, he had started to believe that something was missing. He had found a woman who had all the qualities he'd never realized he wanted. Kate was someone he could spend the rest of his life with . . . however, there was one small problem. He had a hard decision to make; could Chris spend the rest of his life with the woman of his dreams, but never achieve anything more intimate than a platonic friendship?

On his way to bed, Chris stuck his head in Kate's room to check on her. For a long moment, he just stood in the doorway and watched her sleeping peacefully while her faithful companion snuggled her arm. When Aika heard the creak of the door she lifted her head, but didn't dare leave Kate's side.

"Good night, Aika," Chris whispered very softly.

In his own room, lying in the middle of his mahogany, California king-sized bed, Chris kept his eyes wide open and thought about what Sam said earlier. *So if you can handle the fact that she'll never sleep with you or commit to you the way society expects you to, then you'll have her in your life forever.*

Slowly, Kate opened her eyes and felt the soft, warm sun that radiated through the window. The sheets were different; instead of silk, she was greeted with the softness of cotton. A morning just like any other, Kate stretched out and recognized a familiar hand around her waist. It was a woman's hand, a little rough around the edges, but it rubbed Kate's stomach softly. Kate rolled into the woman's embrace to be awakened by her beautiful wife, Riley.

Despite spending most of her life as an officer, Riley had very soft features. Granted, her skin was permanently tanned from long days in the Florida sun, but her dark brown eyes glowed with love and kindness. The warmth behind her perfect smile was intoxicating and made everyone around her smile. Nothing pleased Kate more than running her lanky fingers through Riley's short medium blonde hair.

"Riley?" The hoarse and raspy sound that escaped Kate's throat surprised her. She wasn't sure if she believed what she was seeing.

"Morning, baby." Riley reached out, and took Kate's soft cheeks between her hands. She kissed her sweetly before she got out of bed and asked, "Coffee?"

A creature of habit, Riley picked up the white terrycloth robe that was always on the wicker chair in the corner of the room. Unsure of what was happening, Kate sat up in the bed and tried to gather her thoughts. The first thing she noticed was that she wasn't in some fancy guest room, but in her old home before the accident. There were pictures on the wall of the vacation they'd taken in 1998, to Vancouver, and some on the nightstand with photos of a family reunion. The soft cotton sheets smelled like her wife's shampoo, and the hamper was overflowing with dirty clothes.

When Riley walked back in, she held in her hands two familiar coffee mugs: Dallas Cowboys and New York Giants. Kate happily shook her head and said, "How ironic that I fell in love with a Cowboys' fan. I still can't believe you won my heart."

"Sweet Southern Texas charm, my dear."

After Kate took her Giants mug, Riley pulled back the goose-down comforter and slid back into bed. "How are you feeling?"

An automatic response of, "I'm fine, why?" slipped from Kate's mouth. It took Riley a moment to observe her before she let it go.

The heat from the mug felt warm against Kate's chilled hands while she sat in bed and tried to find a solution for this sweet delusion; a bitter taste appeared on her lips. Kate pulled the mug away from her mouth, and when she looked down, an almost pitch-black liquid reflected back at her.

"What is this?" Confused, Kate smacked her lips together to get the bitterness out of her mouth.

Riley sat her mug down on the green, wooden nightstand and answered, "Coffee with sugar."

"Coffee? I don't drink coffee." Dumbfounded by her wife's comment, an odd and concerned expression appeared on Riley's face. Suddenly feeling scrutinized, Kate nervously looked down at the crinkled sheets and fidgeted with the mug.

"Kate, you've been drinking coffee for as long as I can remember."

"I haven't touched the stuff in years."

"What? You had it yesterday morning." Concerned, Riley took the mug out of Kate's hand and pulled her close. "Are you feeling OK?"

With no way to answer this loaded question, Kate sat there quietly and thought, *If this is my reality, then did I dream about Chris Cody? Were the past four years a nightmare that I just woke up from and none of that bad stuff really happened? It must be so, because Riley is sitting here with me drinking coffee. I don't drink coffee, or at least I haven't since she passed away. What's going on? Nothing makes sense.*

Riley's familiar voice broke Kate's concentration. "Baby, I think you're still drunk from the tequila. We had a crazy night at the bar. How's your headache?"

Surprised by her question, Kate asked, "How did you know I had a headache?"

"You always have a headache after we go to the bar. Baby, are you sure you're OK?" Genuinely concerned about her wife, Riley gently felt the side of Kate's clammy face.

"Oh yeah, that's right. I guess I must still be tired. What did we do again?" Stalling for time, her nerves began to rattle by the uncertainty of her surroundings. In need of security, she grabbed Riley's hand, and the comfortable feeling soothed the butterflies in her stomach.

Incapable of telling which memory was real, Kate decided that since this was what she longed for, she would focus on every little detail, right down to the small, black eyelash on the corner of Riley's cheek. Because if her nightmare came true and this reality was a dream, Kate wanted to remember every bit of it.

Concerned, Riley whispered, "We went to the Tulip."

In the warm crease of Riley's arm, she lay comfortably while Riley allowed her fingertips to massage her scalp. A sense of relief embraced her as the sweet aroma of Riley's morning breath and coffee breath mixed together and filled the small space they occupied. Kate thought to herself, *This has to be real. This is my life, my wife, and everything is as it should be. It was all just a bad dream.*

When Kate opened her eyes to see Riley's concerned, warm brown eyes gazing at her, tears began to form. Then Kate whispered, "It feels like it's been a long time since I've seen you."

Everything was perfect, a dream come true. Things had worked out; this was where she belonged, not in a fantasy world with a famous actor. What a horrible dream, to have dreamt that Riley had been killed, and Kate did nothing but spend her time with Chris Cody, the actor. All of her bad memories had to be a figment of her imagination. The longer she stayed in Riley's arms, the more real her surroundings began to feel. She couldn't have been happier.

"Baby, I'm right here, and you saw me last night when we fell asleep together." Riley smiled at how silly this woman could be sometimes. Suddenly, Kate shifted in the covers, put her hands on Riley's plump cheeks, and caressed their lips together. Automatically, Riley returned the kiss and pulled Kate in by her hips. The passion continued to rise as Riley laid Kate down in the pillows, leaning her partially exposed body, and placed her warm wet lips on the corner of Kate's neck. Kate grabbed the back of Riley's neck, unable to resist her desire. Lips traveled down Kate's neck to the center of her collarbone, and she let out a moan of pleasure, automatically leaning her head back. Heeding the invitation, Riley placed her hands under the loose nightshirt, feeling her body respond as she brushed Kate's soft, plump breast. Without hesitation, Riley flung off their shirts, and continued to explore her body. Breast to breast, Kate's hips started to thrust as her hands rubbed up and down Riley's back. Unable to contain her desire to please her woman, Riley lowered her hand in between

Kate's warm legs as she ran her fingers up Kate's thighs. After moments of intense teasing, Riley finally let herself pleasure her prey, and watched as Kate's eyes rolled into the back of her head. Tangled into each other, they continued to rub and thrust in a mutual rhythm until they each reached the peak of their climax. Refusing to let go of one another, they lay there with their hot, clammy, naked bodies intertwined. Each of their hearts pounded as they felt the blood pulse through their tiny bodies.

Satisfied, Kate closed her eyes for a moment to visualize the seductiveness of their passion. When her eyelids fluttered open, she was not prepared to see Riley beginning to fade. Almost as if she were a hologram and the connection began to break up.

Fearing for the love of her life Kate screamed out, "Riley, don't go. No, No NO!!!" Frantically, Kate kept trying to reach out and grab her wife like a child trying to grab running bath water. No matter how hard they tried, the water always seemed to disappear; and so was Riley. It didn't matter how hard Kate held on, even with her arms clinging to her image, she watched helplessly as the love of her life faded away.

"RILEY!!!!!"

Now alone in her old bed, Kate grabbed a familiar worn-out pillow that emanated the scent of her wife. Heartbroken, teardrops began to soak the beige cotton as Kate cried out for her lost love.

In the middle of her tantrum, the room began to spin out of control.

The dizzy motion finally began to cease, and Kate's crumpled eyelids began to relax. Slowly, as her eyes flickered opened, she found herself clutching onto an unfamiliar sea green silk pillow. The softness of this pillow taunted Kate, reminding her of all she lost…and would never get back. In a furious rage, Kate choked the pillow and flung it across the room, knocking over a hand painted red porcelain vase that crashed into pieces falling off the dresser. Kate cried out in despair.

This can't be happening! The past four years were supposed to be the dream, not Riley! I need her!

From the edge of the bed, Aika began to howl.

The sounds of breaking glass and screams awoke Chris too soon from a deep slumber. Groggily, he managed to stumble his way to Kate's room, with the assistance of the walls, only to find her curled up in the middle of the bed, sobbing and clinging to the bedspread. In an immediate rush, he ran to her, wrapping his arms around her tiny weak body. This time, his strong supportive arms did not provide the comfort Kate needed; instead, it only caused her to lash out in anger when he tried to smoothly rub her back. The rage didn't last long as Kate collapsed back into her sobs.

No matter what words of comfort Chris provided, Kate continued to cry out, "Riley." Tears streamed down her cheeks onto Chris's lap while he rocked her back and forth.

Soothingly, Chris whispered in her ear, "It's OK. It's going to be OK. I'm here."

In agony and with achy muscles, Kate bawled, "It was so real. I miss her so much. It wasn't supposed to be like this. We were supposed to raise our children together. Grow old and sit on the porch in our rocking chairs and watch sunsets. Why did this happen? Why us? Why her? Why couldn't God have taken me? She had so much life. We had a future, and in a moment, it was all gone! I'm gone, I don't know where I am, and I can't find myself. I'm so lost."

It didn't take long for the exhaustion to set in and Kate fell asleep, but not for long. The pain she endured broke Chris's heart; he had never seen anyone so tormented by their past, and he desperately wished he could make it all better.

Only fifteen minutes after Kate's eyes fell victim to her tiredness, a throbbing headache woke her. Red and sore, Kate's eyes burned as they slowly tried to pry themselves open through the crusted lining causing a blurry view. Several blinks later, the room came into focus, and once again, Kate was disappointed with tearstained cheeks.

Still awake, Chris felt her shift slightly in his arms, so he whispered with a raspy voice, "Are you OK?"

There wasn't an honest answer she could give him. Any response would just lead to the return of her sadness, and it was more than she could bear. Only able to nod, she felt the room began to spin. Comfortably, Kate rested her head back into his muscle-padded shoulder with her eyes tightly squeezed shut; the only thought that Kate pondered was how to get back to Riley. But it was pointless; the only image Kate saw was the back of her eyelids. Silence engulfed the room until Kate whispered, "I want to go home." Between the excitement at the bar and this horrific dream, Kate could no longer stand being away from her comfort zone. It was the one place that she felt safe—nothing could hurt her there. It had taken her four years, but home was her safety net, and this pain was what she tried to protect herself from.

"Of course. Anything you want."

For some strange reason, the words stunned Kate like a slap across her face. Anger boiled up to the surface at his insensitivity and she yelled, "You can't give me what I want!"

Shocked by the one-eighty turn in Kate's behavior, Chris stared down at her. Fury and rage emanated from her normally sweet eyes as Kate threw the covers off and scrambled out of bed. Still fuming, she turned to Chris and yelled, "I want my wife back! I want to wake up next to her! I want to feel the heartbeat of my unborn child! I wanted to watch her grow up with her mothers! I want! I want! I want . . . But that doesn't mean I'm going to get it."

With each second that passed, her voice rose and rose until it started to crack. Consumed by so much pain and guilt, all of Kate's emotions boiled together into an angry rage. Every feeling about Riley that she had suppressed in the past, came to the surface in this one big explosion, and poor Chris paid the price for it.

Still furious, Kate continued her rampage, "I don't belong here!! Why did you bring me here? Everything was fine until I met you!" The moment the words left her lips, she regretted them. Frozen and appalled by her own behavior, she immediately saw the hurt in Chris's big brown eyes. Without a word, he stood up and stared at Kate. She half expected him to storm out of the room and never speak to her again, but like every other time before, he completely surprised Kate.

Embarrassed, she buried her face behind her lanky fingers. "I'm so sorry. I didn't mean it."

"If being around me is too painful, I can take you home, and you'll never hear from me again." Each word burned on the tip of his tongue. The last thing he wanted was to be out of her life, but if she needed it or wanted it, he would give it to her. It didn't matter how much it killed him.

The second the words left his mouth, Kate sobbed even harder. She protested through her cries, "No . . . no . . . no . . . That's not what I want. I'm so sorry. I never meant to say that, I want you in my life."

Gently, Chris whispered, "Kate. It's OK. I understand." He tried to lift her head up, but, too embarrassed, she resisted as she pushed down with her chin. "Look at me, sweetie." Slowly, she looked up to see he was more than understanding and supportive. Red and blotchy, Kate's face was covered with tears, but Chris just smiled at her like she was the most beautiful woman in the world.

The next morning, he took her home.

In midflight back to Florida, Kate realized that she didn't have her phone. Assuming it lost, Kate was irritated that she would have to go through the hassle of purchasing another phone, not to mention re-entering all of her numbers. To make life a bit easier for Kate, Chris called his assistant, and by the time they got home, there was a package on Kate's doorstep.

Back home in Florida, Kate's life slowly began to return to normal; however, across the continent someone was up to no good. Susanna decided that she would give a private detective a call. Desperate for revenge, she wanted dirt, and she wanted it bad.

This investigator was known for finding the deeply buried skeletons; the stuff others in his profession couldn't provide. His information was guaranteed to ruin lives, and that's exactly what Susanna wanted.

It was early on a Tuesday afternoon when she met the private dick, Eli, at his office, in a creepy abandoned complex—it was only one room with a desk, computer, two chairs, and a film-covered window. Naturally, Susanna watched every step and stayed as far away from the faded green walls as possible. She made every effort not to touch anything, especially Eli.

He was in the middle of lunch and had a grease-filled burrito in his hand, which he quickly put down when she walked in. Clumsily, he wiped his greasy hand on his wrinkled, beige, pleated slacks, leaving a large smear on his thigh, and extended his semi-clean hand. Susanna hesitated and wrinkled her nose at his hairy knuckles, but lightly touched it with the tips of her fingers. After he let go, she blatantly disinfected her hand with some sanitizer from her purse.

The room reeked of an odor that resembled rotten eggs and decomposed rodents. The smell was so foul that it was impossible to determine the source of the stench. Not concerned with the location of the smell, the only thing that Susanna cared about was her information and getting out of the gas chamber as quickly as possible.

"What can I do you for today?" It was plainly obvious that Eli didn't graduate from charm school; he took his hand and ran it through his oily hair, leaving crumbs behind. It was not an everyday occasion that a woman of Susanna's status came to visit Eli, and he attempted to charm her with a smile, but she just glared at him coldly.

Offended by his mere presence, she snapped, "I just need you to find out everything you can about this person."

"Please have a seat." The idea of touching anything in the room made her sick to her stomach. Not so politely, she shook her head and held up her hand as she declined his invitation.

Awkwardly, Eli walked behind the square wooden desk, took a seat, leaned back in his creaky chair, and put his cheap loafers up on the table top.

Pig, Susanna thought annoyingly as she rolled her eyes.

"Thanks, but I'm in a rush." Taking a package from her purse, she carefully threw it on his desk in order to prevent any additional contact. A small cloud of dust dispersed when the package landed, and while Susanna softly coughed, the dust had no effect on the lowlife.

Surprised by the large, padded white envelope on his desk, Eli asked, "What's this?" Annoyed by the stupid question, Susanna just glared at the package to imply he should open it. The confused expression on his face questioned everything about the contents.

Susanna's hands were firmly placed on her hips. "Is that going to be a problem?" she asked.

Before he answered, he picked up the cell phone and stared at the name on the small, folded sheet of paper. "Shouldn't be a problem."

"Then I should hear from you in a week?" In a demanding tone, Susanna wasn't asking a question but stating a fact.

The phone purposely slipped from Eli's fingers and dinged against the dingy desktop, his eyes flickered up at a scowling Susanna and he responded firmly, "A week is fine. And payment?" The most important thing to Eli was his money, and he needed a lot of it for his chronic gambling problem.

Irritated that she just couldn't beckon him like a dog, Susanna pulled another, smaller white envelope out of her Gucci purse and again carefully tossed it on his desk; this one was filled with cash. The heaviness from the money caused a thicker cloud of dust to appear, making Eli lightly cough.

In a sharp tone Susanna stated, "You'll get half now, and if I'm satisfied with the information, you'll get the rest next week."

Susanna didn't allow any room for objections; Eli opened the envelope and started counting as his thumb brushed the edge of the bills. "Fine."

"I'm expecting results; you better not disappoint me." And without another word, she turned on her heel and left. Eli just sat there with an envelope full of cash and a cell phone.

Chapter Thirteen

Given the episode that had occurred in California, Chris decided to extend his stay in Florida a little longer. Time and time again Kate declared that she was okay, but he refused to leave her -- making one lame excuse after another. Emotionally fragile, Kate was secretly glad to have him around, plus she knew that once the production for his movie started, he would become scarce. Granted, Kate would never admit it, but deep down the idea of Chris not being around made her sad.

The day after they returned home, the new cell phone rang, and Kate ran to her room, where it sat on the nightstand charging. The slender and keyless phone displayed a number in bright blue. Kate tried to hit the answer button, but instead of another voice, she was greeted with a piercing fax tone.

Frustrated that she couldn't figure out the device, Kate screeched, "Damn it! I can't figure this thing out."

Chris heard Kate from the patio, shook his head, and got up to find out what the problem was.

He found her in the bedroom, hovered over the nightstand, shaking the cell phone in her hand. Cautiously, he asked, "What's the matter?"

"This damn phone doesn't have any buttons! How does a phone not have any buttons?" Irate, Kate chucked the brand new cell onto the bed. She was old-fashioned in the sense that she rejected technology, and it didn't bother her one bit that it rejected her back. All Kate wanted was a simple phone that worked; she didn't need all the fancy gadgets and apps. Was that too hard?

Apparently so.

"Here, let me see." Chris picked up the phone—the same one that Kate had threatened to throw into the pool the day before—from off the bed, and tried to figure out what had gone wrong.

After he examined it, it was apparent that Kate had hit the fax button instead of "answer"; he cleared out the system and gave it back to her. "Looks like Sandra called."

At the sound of her sister's name, her eyes narrowed, and she mumbled, "Good, I hope that fax made her go deaf . . . not that she listens to anyone anyways."

Earlier that day, the phone had only been on the charger for fifteen minutes before she had gotten an irate call from her mother. Apparently, while Kate was on vacation with Chris, Sandra had met a random guy and disappeared for the weekend, leaving Elizabeth with her parents. Poor Emily and Mike were not only worried about their daughter, but they also had the daunting task of trying to explain to a three-year-old why her mother disappeared.

Sympathetic, Chris tried to be a mediator, "Don't you think you should at least call her?"

"No, I don't think I should call her! She's going to say that she needs someone to watch Elizabeth, and then she'll run off with that guy again. I know my sister; this is what she does." In a rage, Kate snapped at Chris while she stormed past him toward the patio and cursed under her breath, *I'll be damned if I'm going to help her avoid her responsibilities.*

In the corner sat a little gnome statue surrounded by springy, fresh green plants that held Kate's stash of cigarettes and accessories. Not a habitual smoker, the pack of Marlboro Lights were a month old and kept in the safety of the gnome so Elizabeth wouldn't accidently pick them up. When Chris came out on the patio, he found Kate's back facing the door in a lawn chair with a cloud of smoke lingering around her.

He was irritated that she was pouting like a two-year-old. "What are you doing?" Barely listening, Kate just flashed her best I-don't-give-a-shit look and ignored his judgmental expression as she took another puff from her cigarette.

Gently flicking the ash from the tip, she exhaled as the smoke escaped her mouth. "Look, I'm pissed off because my sister does this shit all the time. She's irresponsible, inconsiderate, and expects everyone to clean up her messes. Mom and Dad shouldn't be taking care of a three-year-old, much less have to explain to that child that her mother went missing again. This is bullshit; she needs to grow up and be a mother to that kid. But she'll never learn." Only pausing for a moment to allow the filter to brush her lips, Kate took another puff, and then continued. "I'm sorry I took it out on you, I know you're just trying to help."

In an attempt to change the subject and break the tension in the room, Chris suggested a walk on the beach. *What else could he do?* There was no solution to this problem.

∾

While Eli nervously stood outside in the shadowy side alley, he looked over his shoulder every few seconds. Even though it was warm outside, chills still ran down his back. This was a risky business. Granted the money was good, really good, but if he messed up with this particular client, his career was done.

Every time he heard the clicking sounds of high-heeled shoes, his heart would skip a beat. After about thirty minutes of small, mini heart attacks, the sound of firm heels spiking into the concrete approached him. Instantly, Eli knew that she was there, as he slowly turned to see the blonde curls that bounced in the shadows. Susanna lingered for a minute before she stepped into the light, revealing an evil smile that was outlined by her ruby-red lipstick.

Not the type to waste time, she demanded, "You better have what I want." She was repulsed by the requirement of having to meet Eli in an alley . . . but then again, the alley was much cleaner than his office. Scared by her presence, Eli nervously held out a file and prayed that she would be satisfied. Annoyed at his timidity, she snatched the file out of his hand causing Eli to flinch backwards. Scanning through the documents, Susanna rolled her eyes at the disgusting, grease-stained fingerprints on the corners. Barely glancing his way, she closed the file, threw another envelop at him, and walked away. Once again, this woman had left Eli with a large amount of cash and the sense that she had taken part of his manhood along with her.

Being a woman with many contacts, Susanna went from a dark alley to one of the most prestigious restaurants in Beverly Hills, where another man waited for her. The polar opposite of Eli, Robert was extremely clean-cut and ten times meaner than Eli could ever imagine.

The ability to attain a short, five-minute conference with Robert was extremely difficult. If one *was* able to reserve time with him, being late was not an option, as the consequences were severe. Inconsiderately, Susanna walked past the hostess and sat down across from Robert. Aside from his drink, the only item placed on top of the white tablecloth was a crystal vase with a ruby-red rose in it. Rudely, Susanna snapped her fingers at the waiter to order herself a gin and tonic.

Angrily, Robert snarled, "What took you so long? You know I don't wait around for people."

Before she responded, she nonchalantly rolled her eyes when the waiter came back with her drink. After a few gulps, the glass clunked against the table, her long, bright, red-tip fingers lingered around the crystal and tapped in an annoying rhythm. Matching his tone, Susanna answered, "Look, it's not my fault that private dick took so long."

Unimpressed by her attitude, Robert leaned in and whispered, "Your little dick is not my problem, and I don't give a shit about your excuses."

Carefully bending into her purse, she pulled out a manila envelope and dropped it on the table. The file had a medium thickness, and when it hit the table there was a light thud. Annoyed by Robert's arrogance, Susanna glared at him with an evil look. "Look, you're not the only who can get me the coverage I need. I came to you out of respect, and this is how you treat me? Like I'm a regular client that just walked in off the street? I should walk out that door with my information and take it elsewhere." Without another word, she went to snatch the envelope—and felt a firm hand slap down on hers.

In an attempt to keep Susanna interested, Robert said in a soothing voice, "Now, let's not be so hasty." At his anticipated reaction, a coy smile appeared on her face. *That's what I thought.*

Silently, Robert slid up from the table and disappeared into the commotion-filled kitchen toward the back parking lot, where his car awaited. Just like every time before, Susanna willingly followed closely behind. The steam-covered windows smudged with fingerprints were just one of the many marks Susanna had left. When her blonde, tangle-haired head popped up from the seat, she seductively wiped the reward from her chin and with a glistening mouth she smiled. "I knew you would see it my way."

With curious eyes, Robert asked, "Now tell me, what do we have here?"

Even though Kate was exhausted, her eyes popped open at seven a.m. Within thirty minutes, she and Chris were both up, fully dressed, and almost ready to start their day. The only thing missing was the morning caffeine. While Kate started brewing coffee and put the teakettle on the stove, Chris plopped down on the couch to flip through the channels. The TV turned on to a dull commercial about hair removal cream, before he switched the channel and landed on the *Today Show*. The scroll at the bottom caught his attention as he noticed his name before it disappeared from the screen. Sitting upright, Chris quickly turned up the sound on the program and watched with horror as the last thing he ever expected to see was being broadcasted. Immediately, his stomach began to flip-flop, with sailor-sized knots.

"Breaking news: Senator Herbert Reynolds caught in a scandal? Anonymous sources reveal that Senator Herbert Reynolds's daughter is a lesbian. The most conservative Southern Baptist Republican who voted against gay marriage has a gay daughter. The worse part is that when he was running for election there was never any mention of a daughter. To make matters worse, his daughter, Riley Reynolds, was in a horrific accident with her ex-lover Katherine Woods, who has recently been spotted in L.A. with the famous Chris Cody."

When Kate noticed something was off, she called out, "What's wrong?" Chris waved his hand to shush her, and continued to give his full attention to the news. At that moment, the teakettle began to whistle loudly, distracting Kate from the broadcast. Carefully, she made her tea with two sugars and a little cream, then poured Chris's coffee and served it black.

When she turned the corner, Kate froze in place, unable to believe what she saw on the screen. Pictures of Kate dressed in that skimpy, tight black dress, drunk on Chris's lap from the night at the club. Her heart froze at the sight of herself on national television. "Oh, shit!"

Neither Kate nor Chris dared to take their eyes off the HD plasma screen. Police photos from the accident appeared along with Riley in the hospital hooked to a ventilation system. The sight of Riley mangled and torn like a rag doll broke Kate's heart. Tears silently streamed down her cheeks. Harder and harder, she continued to grip the mugs as the boiling rage started to fester in the deep pit of her stomach.

The show's host came back on and continued, *"Interestingly enough, after Riley Reynolds passed away there was an unexplained wire transfer into Katherine Woods's bank account in the amount of $1.2 million dollars. Where did this money come from? Better yet, what was this money for?"* In a smooth transition, the show moved to the next story in their lineup.

Carefully, Chris clicked the off button on the remote and let the black clicker slide from his limp hand onto the wooden coffee table. Hesitantly, he looked up to find Kate still staring angrily at the blank screen. Consumed by so much rage and fury that had built up inside of her, she couldn't hold it back any longer. Without hesitation, the porcelain mugs were slammed from her white knuckled fingertips onto the tile floor, and pieces of glass and hot liquid scattered everywhere. In a motion of panic, Aika ran into the safety of the bedroom.

Surrounded by glass, Kate screamed at Chris, "You son of a BITCH!!!!" Naturally, Chris's first instincts were to explain that he didn't know how this had happened, that it was a huge misunderstanding.

Still irate, Kate continued to scream, as her face turned bright red. She pointed her finger accusingly at him. "Don't you dare come near me! How could you do this to me? I trusted you!!!" Attempting to remain calm, Chris walked around the coffee table and reached out for Kate.

From the corner of her eye, she caught a glimpse of him, and in the heat of the moment the next sound surprised them both. The large, sharp crack that echoed in the room was the sound of Kate's open palm, powerfully making contact with Chris's cheek. Bewildered, he just stood there – never in his life had a woman hit him the way Kate just did. The feeling of betrayal and hurt stung harder than the pink handprint against his face, but despite this, Chris did what he still believed was right and once again reached out to the woman he loved.

She started screaming, "Don't touch me! Get away from me! I hate you! I fucking hate you!!" The vehemence continued to build and build while Kate aimlessly and repeatedly swung at Chris.

A quick dive to the right and Chris was able to bypass Kate's wild punches. Immediately, he tamed her by pinning her arms to her side, shaking her and yelling, "Kate! Kate! KATE!" When her eyes met his, she instantly stopped fighting. Her poor emotions, frayed like tethered yarn, couldn't handle any more stress. The fight at the bar, the heart-shattering dream of Riley, the argument with her sister – it all proved to be too much. Kate stopped fighting as she went limp in Chris's arms and passed out.

Naturally, Chris laid her down in her room. Not even twenty minutes later there was a loud, fist-pounding knock at the door. Before Chris could answer, Mike and Emily, who eagerly used the spare key, stumbled through the door trying desperately to get away from the large crowd of cameras and invasive questions.

Typical parasites, the gossip-column reporters had no concern or compassion about the people they interviewed; they shoved microphones in Mike's and Emily's faces and yelled out questions:

"What is your relation to Kate, did you know about the money?"

"Is Kate really a lesbian?"

"Was Kate the lover of Senator Reynoldss' daughter?"

The moment Emily made it in the house, she turned towards the blood-sucking reporters and happily slammed the door in their faces. Locking the dead bolt, Emily's pretentious smile instantly disappeared, and she directed her focus on Chris.

Accusingly, she pointed her index finger at him. "What the hell is going on? How did this happen?" In her beige flats, Emily began to charge Chris, each step becoming more powerful than the one before – the sound of her hard souls slamming against the tile made Chris's heart jump. While Mike was just as angry as Emily, he unexpectedly stepped forward, blocking her from reaching Chris.

"Emily," Mike spoke slowly and softly. "I know you're upset, but it's not going to do any good to start attacking everyone." Emily glared at her husband, wanting to challenge him, but years of marriage told her this was not the time. Her posture relaxed, and her angry tone only subsided slightly when she demanded from Chris, "Where is she?"

Tilting his head to the side, he cautiously answered, "She's in bed."

It suddenly became very clear to him where Kate got her temper.

Chris was at a loss; he didn't know which way to turn. Everyone blamed him, and he didn't know how to fix it. Luckily, Mike extended some support, "Don't worry about Emily, she's in mother mode." With his hand on Chris's shoulder like a son, Mike continued. "How are you hanging in there? I see Kate got a hold of you." Mike motioned to the fading pink outline on Chris's cheek. Carefully, he brushed the side of his cheek, feeling not only residual throbbing from the blow, but the sting of his guilt, knowing he caused Kate so much pain. Too ashamed to speak, he nodded at Mike as they sat down at the dining room table.

In a feeble attempt to ease Chris's worries, Mike offered, "I know you're concerned about Kate, but she'll be fine. She's tougher than people give her credit for." His words didn't provide the comfort he wanted, but they would have to do.

Disappointed, Chris put his head in his hands, muffling his voice. "I know she's strong. After everything she's been through, I'm shocked that she's not bitter at the world."

Mike's eyes focused on Chris and away from the painting he was blankly staring to clarify, "Oh, don't let her fool you; she *is* bitter, but she's good at concealing it."

Not only does my daughter have this man fooled, but she also has him wrapped around her pinkie, Mike thought silently.

Idly, Mike twiddled with his thumbs; a forced smile appeared as he hoped that things would start to pan out for Kate. "I know one day she'll pull her life together and make her dreams come true."

From across the table, it was clear that Chris genuinely cared about Kate. Fatherly instincts told Mike that this was the type of person Kate needed, someone that was able to connect with her and bring her out of her shell. Heartfully, Mike prayed that the media frenzy would end quickly and life would return to normal. It had to; he couldn't watch his daughter torment herself again.

The cell phone buzzed on the dining room table, blinking Charlie's name like a strobe light. Politely, Chris picked up the phone and walked into another room as he answered, "Hey, Charlie."

"Have you seen the news this morning?"

"I have."

"Is there anything I need to worry about? Are you connected to this in any way?"

"I didn't know. I barely knew about Riley."

"If you know anything, tell me, we need to get ahead of this. I don't want anything coming back to bite us."

"Charlie, I know how the media works. We are in the clear."

"Ok. Good luck with Kate. Talk to you soon."

"Yea. Thanks."

Chris needed to find out who did this, and then he remembered that Eric had a few contacts in the newspaper industry. There was no hesitation when Chris dialed Eric's number.

"Hey, Eric. I need a huge favor."

"Sure. Does this have anything to do with Kate?" Eric had already seen the news and knew what Chris needed.

"Yea. I need to know who leaked this information to the press."

"I'll have to make a few calls. Get back with you later?"

"That would be great man, thanks."

"No problem." The call was quick and short, and he knew that Eric would come through.

Walking back into the living room, he found Emily on the couch, staring mindlessly at the TV as she flipped through the stations. With each change of channel, her facial expression grew angrier and angrier.

"Can you believe these lies they're telling about Kate? This is bullshit!" For a moment, he stood there and listened to what one reporter said, and his jaw dropped.

Ever so tactfully, Mike put his fist over his mouth and pretended to cough; he looked at Emily with an expectation. Annoyed by the request, Emily mumbled, "Fine" under her breath.

"Chris, look, I'm . . . " Trying her best to maintain some composure, she cringed as the bitter words barely escaped her mouth. "I'm sorry that I yelled at you earlier." When a weak smile appeared upon Chris's lips, she looked away and mumbled just loud enough for him to hear, "Even though you deserved it."

"I understand." This half-attempt at an apology was all that he would ever receive from Emily.

A sudden, loud, banging noise made Aika growl loudly from the bedroom. Blinded by the hundreds of flashes, Emily was not surprised to see her other daughter on the porch, posing for the photographers while she waited for someone to answer the door.

Without hesitation, Emily grabbed Sandra by the collar and dragged her into the house, growling, "What the hell are you doing?"

In her perfected fake innocent voice, Sandra asked, "What?"

"Get in this damn house!" Emily furiously slammed the door shut. Like any other day, Sandra ignored her mother. Staring down at the ground in shock, Emily's head popped up even angrier than before, "Where is my granddaughter?"

Dismissing her mother, Sandra waived her hand, "She's at a friend's house," in a tone that described dropping off a broken car. Predictably disappointed, Emily just shook her head sadly, turning away.

In her three-inch platform heels, Sandra smoothed out her black, tight mini-skirt feeling sexy for a brief moment. It was blatantly obvious Sandra had mad an appearance for the cameras and not for the concern of her sister.

It had been almost two hours since Kate fell asleep and every time Chris checked to make sure she was ok, she was out stone cold. Bored, and pretty much stuck in the house, the family just sat around the television waiting for Kate to wake up. The local news stations continued to repeat the same

Reynolds scandal story over and over again – until new information was released.

"This just in – an update on the Reynolds scandal. Our sources reveal that Senator Herbert Reynolds secretly paid Katherine Woods $1.2 million dollars from a shell corporation he owns located in Switzerland. This was all in an attempt to conceal the fact that he had a gay daughter because, let's face it, she didn't fit in his political agenda. It was easier to get rid of Riley, despite treatments in China with high success rates, but his daughter's life wasn't worth saving. And Katherine Woods, who tried to play the victim in all of this, accepted the money knowing what was going to happen. How dare she claim to love her wife when she signed Riley's life away for blood money paid by the same people who detested her? Apparently, love does have a price and it's $1.2 million. Since Kate has been spotted with Chris Cody, we now have to ask what is his involvement?"

Before the first commercial ended, Charlie was ringing Chris's phone again – this time Chris knew it would be bad. In the other room, Chris clicked the answer button and Charlie began to loudly scream a line of obscenities.

Once Charlie was exhausted from his tantrum, he took a deep breath, composed himself, and barked out orders. "Look, this is what you are going to do. You're to come back to California immediately and start work. I've booked you to appear on *The Mary Show* in two weeks. Rehearsals are getting ready to start for the movie, and I'll take care of the rest."

The mere idea of returning to California and leaving Kate behind broke Chris's heart. "I'll be back as soon as I can. I have some things I have to make sure are taken care of here before I leave." Without waiting for a reply, Chris hung up the phone. There was no way he would leave Kate here, unprotected, with the paparazzi.

One final call had to be made to his personal assistant. While he explained what he needed, Carmen quickly jotted down all the information on a legal pad. Within fifteen minutes, she had a private jet prepped for his return, a car in transit to Kate's house, and a security team of nine bodyguards en route to assist. Four of them would escort Chris to the airport, and the other five would remain with Kate.

The sounds of cell phones and different muffled conversations woke Kate. Questions like *"What should we do?" "How is she going to handle this?" "These accusations can't be true, but what if they are?"* were asked, but no answers had been provided. Still foggy, Kate didn't have a clue as to what they were referring. Even with the smallest movement, her stiff body ached as she slowly tried to roll herself out of bed. Using the nightstand for support, she stood up with shaky knees and started to make her way to the living room. Despite the spinning room, Kate staggered through the dizzy maze of her hallways into the lamp-lit living room. Without a word from anyone, she felt death upon her, and the tension in the room was excruciating.

Everyone froze when they noticed her leaning weakly against the corner for support; her wobbly legs had a difficult time holding her up. Chris immediately whispered, "I have to go," hung up his cell phone, and pulled Kate into his arms.

Her limp body crouched into his like an old rag doll. Chris's heart became guilt- stricken as he whispered, "Kate, I'm so sorry. I never meant for this to happen."

Unable to respond, she felt like a puppet with no strings. Barely able to look at Chris, she glanced at his shoulder and saw the sadness in everyone else's eyes. It was the same look when Riley passed away, and instantly, her world began to crumble. Gently, Chris took her chin between his index finger and thumb and lifted her head in the hopes of finding a glimmer of reassurance that she would make it through. There was nothing; she had nothing left to give as she stared back at him with empty eyes. Four years ago, with the sudden loss of her wife and child, Kate's heart had been ripped to shreds . . . and now, after so many years of protecting herself, her heart was about to be torn wide open again.

At this moment, the only thing Kate wanted was to crawl into a deep black hole and disappear forever.

Slowly things came into perspective, and for Kate it felt like the fog over her eyes had been lifted. When the haziness disappeared, there was clarity, and everything hit her like a ton of bricks. Her mind quickly raced at the events that had occurred in the past six hours, as she remembered everything: the news report, the pictures of Riley and the accident, and what she had done to Chris.

Oh, my God! I slapped Chris across the face, how could I have done that? Shocked by her actions, Kate stepped away from the concerned group. Seconds later, her mind began to stumble over different questions.

How did everything fall apart? I've spent years putting my life together, and now here I am again, at rock bottom. The moment I opened myself up, it all shattered. I guess I'm not destined for happiness.

Sadden by her thoughts, she tried to take a step back, but Chris wouldn't allow it; he held her tight in his embrace then led her towards the couch.

Weakly, she collapsed into the soft cushions of the beige couch while Chris exhaled in turmoil and asked an extremely difficult question. "Is it true?"

Confused, Kate's head tilted and she inquired, "Is what true?"

The thin lines around Chris's lips tightened as he glared down at her, "Kate, this isn't the time to play stupid."

For a split second, Kate thought the unthinkable, and her heart stopped and sank into her stomach; there was no way that he could know that. Anxiety pulsed through her body as she sat further back on the couch and pretended to play ignorant, hoping that it wasn't what she thought it was. "I have no idea what you're talking about."

"Damn it, Kate! I'm not fucking around!"

Shocked by his temper, Kate tried to slide further away from him, but he had already leaned into the couch with his arms extended around her. Upset at the sight of his daughter, who was obviously frightened, Mike interjected, "Chris. Back off."

It took a moment, but Chris pushed himself away from Kate and allowed her room to breathe. In an attempt to air out the tension, Chris stepped back and paced in short steps in front of her as he ran his fingers through his hair.

Timidly, Kate whispered, "Chris, is what true?" Furious, he stopped dead in his tracks and snapped, "Did you kill your wife for a million dollars?" The room fell silent as they waited for Kate's response. Fear-stricken, she nervously continued to rub her palms together in an attempt to defend herself, she joked, "That's absurd. Where in the hell would you hear something like that?"

Shocked that Kate would even try to lie about this, Chris snatched the clicker off the coffee table and turned on the TV. The first station's news ticker read: "Wife was dying, so lover Kate profited." Pissed, Chris flipped the channel, another news ticker provided the same effect. The next channel, then the next, and the next all said the same thing: "Kate killed her wife for a million dollars!" Beyond furious, Chris turned the TV off, looked at Kate and said, "How do you explain this?"

Kate stood up defensively and yelled, "Explain what? There's nothing to explain! That's trash and rumors." Unable to control his rage, Chris took the clicker that had been held tightly in his hand and threw it clear across the room.

The black remote shattered into pieces against the wall and he screamed, "God damn it, Kate, they have statements from Herbert and Gloria Reynolds!" Speechless, Kate's eyes flickered around the room in desperate search of a diversion – there was none to be found.

When there was no response, Chris demanded answers. "Kate, did you do this?" Unable to escape the disappointment in his eyes, Kate sighed. "It's not what you think."

Irate, Chris screamed, "Not what I think? Not what I think? It is exactly what I think. Kate, you took money and agreed to end her life. How could that be any different?"

Furiously, Kate shook her nerve-rattled hand at Chris and yelled, "Jesus, would you let me explain before you start accusing me of murder!"

"Explain, Kate. I'm sure we would all love to hear about how you murdered your wife!"

"Boy, I know you're upset, but you're about to get your ass whooped!" Mike hollered at Chris, flashing him a warning glare. Chris nodded and took another step away from Kate.

Sick and tired of not only Chris's accusations, but also his attitude, Kate lashed back, "Christopher!" Her eyes glared angrily at Chris until he backed down slightly. Letting out a sigh, Kate continued, "In private."

"No, you're going to face this head on."

Every set of eyes in the room demanded an explanation; with no leeway, Kate was going to have to face her past.

As a last resort, Kate found herself in the hospital chapel; even though she wasn't a religious person, she needed guidance more than she had ever imagined. Sitting in silence with maybe one other person, Kate was unsure of how this was done. It had been three months since Riley had fallen into her coma, and Kate had begun to lose her faith about recovery. Her eyes closed and her hands folded in a prayer pose; she didn't pay any attention when someone sat down in her pew, but continued to pray. A soft, drawling voice spoke to her and rattled her nerves. Kate had prepared herself for this moment; it was only going to be a matter of time before they showed up.

She opened her eyes, but continued to stare at the front of the church as she whispered, "What are you doing here?"

It took a long moment for a response, but when it did it sounded like nails on a chalkboard. "I'm here to see ma daughter. But I could ask ya the same thing. Ya know, darling, God doesn't really approve of homosexuality." Irate, Kate turned her head and stared into the eyes of Gloria Reynolds. Dressed in her light pink, pressed Chanel skirt suit with satin low heels to match, Gloria was the only woman Kate knew who would wear nylon stockings in Florida. The short, auburn hair was sprayed together with a can of hairspray, and her makeup was perfectly thick enough to cover the years of bigotry and hate that she supported while her husband preached it to the masses. The "click, click" sound of her perfect manicured nails on the set of pearls that she wore every day of her life drove Kate mad.

Without a word, Kate got up and walked out of the church. If there was one thing she'd learned in the past eight years, it was not to feed into Gloria's snide comments.

Later in the day, after Kate had spent four hours next to Riley, she went outside and sat on a bench around a small flowerbed. Once again, Gloria reared her ugly face.

Knowing that this woman wouldn't stop, Kate rolled her eyes and sighed. "Where is your bigot husband?"

"My husband, Riley's father, is at home," she replied as she stiffened her chest and smoothed out her skirt. "I'm here to talk to you."

Taken off guard, Kate turned to her and asked, "Why? In the eight years I have known you, you've barely spoken two words to me. What could you possibly say to me now?"

"This isn't fair to her, or to you, for that matter."

In the past eight years, Gloria had never spoken a kind word to Kate; she'd barely acknowledged her existence. Alarmed by the comment, Kate rubbed her hand across her greasy forehead, closed her eyes, and tried to make sense of everything. It had been two days since she had been home, and it showed. The tired, baggy eyes with purple rings under them, plus the paleness of her face from barely eating enough in the past month, were the greatest indicators that she was under a lot of stress. Kate had lost about twenty pounds, and had it not been for her street clothes, most people would have mistaken her for a patient. People stared at her like she had one foot in the grave, and sometimes that's exactly how she felt.

Lately, patience had not been a luxury Kate had been blessed with, and at this moment, the only thing she wanted to say to the woman, who in so many ways had disowned her own daughter, was "Fuck off."

Even though Kate already knew the answer to the question, she asked it anyway. "Have you seen her?"

Ashamed, Gloria barely mumbled, "No."

Not surprised, Kate shook her head in disgust. "You didn't come here to see your daughter. Why would you? You could never accept the fact that she's gay. To be honest, I'm shocked you even showed up."

Insulted, Gloria snapped, "Now listen here, missy, my daughter is not gay, she's confused!"

Unable to help herself Kate interjected, "For thirty-two years?"

"It's people like you who've brainwashed her, confused her with promises of worldly pleasures."

"Says the woman wearing a three-thousand-dollar outfit."

In a self-righteous voice, Gloria proclaimed, "I have been blessed by the hand of God."

"So was she. Riley knew who she was and had found the love of her life."

Angrily, Gloria stood up to stomp away, but not without one last comment. "As the end approaches for Riley, I pray that she begged God to forgive her for her sin so she may walk in the heavens with her Creator, unlike you, who will spend an eternity in damnation."

Not fazed by her grand performance, Kate simply replied, "Will God forgive you for turning your back on your child in her desperate time of need?"

The next day, like every other day since Riley fell into her coma, Kate sat next to the hospital bed, hand-in-hand with her beloved wife. The nurses said it was good for her to talk to Riley like she would with anyone else – and that's exactly what she did, talked to her wife.

"So your mother stopped by the other day. She's still as annoying as ever. God this, God that—I really wanted to shove a Bible down her throat." While Kate brushed Riley's hair, she continued, "She wants something, I just haven't figured out what she's up to. Any ideas?" The room was silent, and Kate playfully answered the question. "I know, but she can't convert everyone to Southern Baptist, can she?" She smiled at Riley, and for a brief moment, she thought she saw Riley smile back.

"Ughm." The Southern voice interrupted a personal moment and Kate looked up annoyed. "Really lady, don't you ever go away?"

Dressed in a very similar outfit as the day before, pastel blue this time, Gloria stood at the edge of the doorframe, but didn't dare enter the room. "Can I speak with you?"

Condescendingly Kate asked, "Don't you want to come see your daughter?" Fear consumed Gloria's face as she looked at her child, who was hooked up to a ventilator. Immediately, she shook her emotions aside and spoke firmly. "I need to speak with you privately."

Quietly, Kate whispered to Riley, "I'll be right back." Instantly, Kate's eyes went cold when she looked back up at Gloria.

After they walked down the still-white hallway, Gloria pulled her into an empty office. Annoyed that Gloria had interrupted her time with Riley, Kate huffed as she put her hands on her hips. "What do you want?"

Gloria clasped her hands together, placed them in front of her small mouth, and sighed sympathetically. "I've talked to the doctors. They say there's no hope for her to recover."

"There is a new experimental treatment being done in China, but the doctors won't do it because my insurance doesn't cover it."

"Well, I'm not paying some astronomical cost only to be told nothing can be done. Hasn't she suffered enough?"

Outraged, Kate lashed back, "You don't want her to suffer? Are you kidding me, Gloria? You wouldn't even go into the room to see your own child!"

"Despite what you may think of me, I love my child very much. I may not accept certain aspects of her life, but I love her nonetheless."

Before Kate responded, she plopped down in the office chair and crossed her arms. "So, were you loving your child when you went on national TV and said that all homosexuals are demons and that they need to either be converted or destroyed?"

Once her round bottom hit the black fabric of the office chair, Gloria smirked. "I gave her the option of conversion, didn't I?"

Angrily, Kate slammed her fist on the table. "You people are unbelievable! Gloria, what is this about? Spare me the 'I love my child' bullshit act you're badly performing."

In a second, Gloria's demeanor completely changed as she leaned forward and intertwined her fingers, and spoke as if she was in an executive board meeting, "Fine. George is running for office, and we don't want those damn *liberals finding out we have a gay daughter. It would ruin everything." Gloria rolled her eyes in disgust at the idea of her good name being tainted by her daughter's bad decisions.*

Coldly, Kate asked, "How is that my problem?"

"Well, at the moment it's not, but it could easily become yours. The medical expenses are high, and you don't make a lot of money. And a lot of the household income came from Riley."

"So what? Money is tight, nothing I can't work through."

"How are you going to work through it without a job?" Gloria leaned back happily and pretended to fix her hair.

Kate knew how this game was played; carelessly, she put her fist up to her cheek and asked, "Are you threatening me?"

"I know a lot of people in high places that would make it very hard for you to find work," Gloria answered smoothly. This was not a threat but a promise, and Kate knew it. She had heard the stories from Riley, about how her mother got whatever she wanted and went to any means necessary. Calmly, Gloria sat there as she tapped her nails on the oak table and waited for an answer.

The chair creaked as Kate leaned in close and angrily spat the words out, "I'm not going to sell out your daughter for your political gain."

Without batting an eyelash, Gloria smiled, "Yes, you will."

*O**ver the next few days, Gloria's words repeatedly rang in Kate's head. The day that they were the most prominent was when she had a private discussion with the doctor on staff. In the tiny boardroom, she sat and listened to the doctor in the starch-pressed, white coat continue to explain the unlikeliness of Riley's recovery and the cost to prolong her life. At a loss, the rambling sound of numbers and statistics had begun to muffle into a fog. Glancing up, she looked through the small window and saw Gloria, who glared back while idly twirling her pearls. It was at that moment that Kate knew Gloria was right.*

The arrangement was simple; Kate had to revoke her rights to the living will, which would grant Gloria parental rights to pull the plug. In exchange, Kate would be gifted a special donation from an anonymous company in cash for one million dollasr. The Reynoldss would take care of Riley's medical expenses, and it would appear as if Kate had never existed in Riley's life.

Kate couldn't believe what she was doing; not in a thousand years did she ever think she would agree to such a vile thing. During the negotiation of the details, Kate demanded one thing before she agreed to sign anything.

"I'll take care of the funeral."

Carelessly, Gloria had replied as she touched up her pink lipstick, "Do whatever you want, Riley made her choice a long time ago." Kate gripped the clipboard harder and harder, fighting back the urge to slap Gloria across the face with it.

Irritated, Kate mumbled, "What a wonderful mother you turned out to be." Then she began to sign.

Snidely, Gloria glared down at Kate while she struggled to get this over with. Her pointed nose judged everything about Kate, and she smirked, "I told you, you would sell out."

Firmly, Kate gripped the pen and stopped in mid stroke as she thought about whether or not to shove the forms back in this disgusting woman's face, but instead she let the clipboard brush the side of her jeans. After she pushed herself away from the cold, undecorated hospital wall, Kate angrily replied, "Don't stand there and judge me. You turned your back on your child and then on her deathbed used her for your personal gain." Spitefully, Kate flipped another form and began to sign on the dotted lines.

When Kate reached the end of the stack, Gloria commented, "Kate you are so naïve; you and I are one and the same."

Kate lifted the pen from the form and scratched her head, "Not even close."

"Everyone has a price, and I found yours. You were willing to trade your ethics for money."

"The difference between me and you is that I never turned my back on Riley. We spent eight loving years together, and if it hadn't been for this tragic accident, we would have spent the rest of our lives together. You, on the other hand, condemned your daughter a long time ago, and the only reason you're here is not out of compassion or even to seek forgiveness, but to simply use your own flesh and blood for your personal gain. You are a heartless person." Fed up, Kate signed the last form and shoved the clipboard at Gloria, who for the first time since she arrived, was silent. "I want nothing else to do with you. I want you completely out of my life."

It had taken Kate twenty minutes to wander back into Riley's room to say her goodbyes.

Hunched over the hospital bed using the railing for support, Kate sobbed her last words, "Riley, you must know I never wanted it to come to this. You are the love of my life, and I can't bear to see you suffer any longer. I'm sorry. I hope one day you can forgive me."

In the midst of Kate's teary final departure, she gently rubbed Riley's soft cheek trying to remember every little detail. Almost against her better judgment, Kate's pale hand dropped to her side. It was there, in that tiniest moment, that Kate's entire universe regained hope. Before Kate stepped away the muscles in Riley's fingers tightened around her hand refusing to let go. Excitedly Kate returned the squeeze and kneeled down beside Riley, whispering to her, encouraging her to come home. It was silent for a moment, then Kate heard the gasp that sounded like, "Kate." That was all she needed to scream out for the doctors. There was improvement; there was hope that Riley would get through this.

The doctors walked through the door, but not how Kate anticipated –Gloria was with them, along with two other men in suits who appeared to be lawyers. Kate pleaded with the doctor to check Riley, but by that time Riley's hand had gone limp, and the only movement was the slow rise of her chest.

"Miss Woods, I'm going to have to ask you to leave," the doctor said firmly.

"What? I'm not leaving my wife. She just said my name."

"She didn't say your name, sweetie, now it's time for you to go." The doctor said as she motioned toward the security guards, who arrived seconds after Gloria appeared.

"No! You can't do this! What about the experimental treatment in China." Kate tried to put as much distance between herself and the guards.

The sound of Gloria's voice rang like shattered glass, "I can do this. You gave up your rights. Officers, escort Miss Woods out of the hospital." There was only the tiniest hint of a smirk upon Gloria's lips, but her eyes evilly glowed, reminding Kate that she had lost.

Detained by the officers Kate screamed and kicked, "I made a mistake. She said my name. Don't kill my wife," as she was dragged away.

The room was eerily silent, with stunned faces, as no one had even the slightest indication that this happened. For the past five years, Kate carried the burden of her decision along with a lifetime sentence of guilt. Tears barely absorbed created a small puddle in her lap. No longer angrily hovering over her, Chris found himself on the couch consoling Kate.

Rhythmically, Chris rubbed her back and asked, breaking the silence, "Why didn't you tell anyone?"

Sadly, Kate's swollen eyes looked up at Chris, "I couldn't. Who would believe me? He was a senator; I can't compete with that. Besides there was a privacy clause." Feeling Kate's hopelessness, Chris just hugged her tighter.

"This is just unbelievable! She basically murders her wife for money, and you people feel sorry for her!" Sandra lashed out sucking her teeth in the process.

"SANDRA!" The sound of Emily's voice shocked everyone. In the Woods' home it was Mike who did most of the scolding, while Emily agreed with her husband's decisions.

"How dare you! You could never comprehend the pain Kate endured watching her love die." Emily lashed out again.

"Then why take the money? Why didn't you just end it and try to move on with your life?"

"Because I wouldn't give up on my wife. You wouldn't understand a commitment past a weekend."

"You did give up on your wife, the moment you signed those papers and accepted the money." Kate opened her mouth to respond, but nothing came out. It was expected of Sandra to be self-absorbed, but to actually make a valid point was shocking to everyone.

"You know what Sandra, you're right." Sandra couldn't believe the words her sister had said. *I'm right,* Sandra never thought she would see the day, but then Kate continued, "But let's not forget something. I had stopped working six months ago to have a baby, and the only income was Riley's. My wife was dying and all my savings vanished trying to save her. The scariest part was that I didn't have any rights to her life insurance, pension, or any other benefit that a married woman would have received. I was afraid and alone and couldn't support myself, so at that moment, I had to do what I thought was necessary."

There it was, in just a few well-structured sentences, Kate managed to turn the room back on her side. Instead of feeling compassion for her sister, Sandra only felt the sting of jealousy.

While Chris sympathized with Kate's heartache, there was another matter that needed to be handled.

"Kate," Chris said drawing her attention toward him. "Do you realize the media nightmare this secret of yours has caused?" The sternness in his voice caused her eyes to narrow in surprise.

"You're blaming me?" Kate couldn't believe this. First, the media publicly slandered her name, then her own sister accused her of selling out, and now Chris was complaining about how this would affect him.

"You should've told me. Now there is a huge mess to clean up."

"Are you serious? Is that the only thing you care about, how this is going to make *you* look?" Insulted, Kate scooted away from him.

In a slightly softer tone he said, "That's not how I meant it," he reached out for her hand, which she allowed to be taken.

Gently, Kate reminded him of their initial agreement, "None of this would have happened if you'd kept your promise."

Kept your promise. These words rung clear and true in Chris's mind as he vividly remembered promising Kate that he would be able to keep her life private, while at the same time, wondered why in the world she got so upset. Now it was clear why, but the damage had already been done. Undeniably, he failed, and he knew now that Kate would keep her word. *If you can't keep my life private, we can't be friends.* The anticipation became agonizing as he waited for Kate's next words –his heart began to tear at the edges.

The ache began to set in as her words started to crackle, "You knew how important this was to me." The words were almost unbearable just to think, much less say; however, she knew that they had to be spoken. In a tiny, breath barely above a whisper, Kate mumbled, "You need to go."

The silence engulfed them, and for the longest moment, Chris remained at Kate's side hoping that she would change her mind. Sadly, she did not, avoiding his gaze. His grip held tight until defeat set in and quietly he nodded. "You're right," his voice cracked gently. Silently, he stood, not releasing her hand until the last second possible, but when they parted, tears rolled down Kate's cheeks. This was the worse pain Chris had ever felt in his entire life, and before he left the room, he turned toward Kate and promised, "I'll fix this."

The empty promise was more than Kate could bear, "Haven't you learned not to make promises that you can't keep?" Heartbroken, Kate turned away from him trying to stifle her tears. Chris desperately wanted to comfort her, but he knew it would only cause more pain and quietly, he grabbed his black duffle bag from the bedroom.

Before Chris turned the front door knob, Mike approached him semi-sympathetically with a heavy hand on his shoulder.

"I'm sorry for any hardship that this might have caused. I'll do everything I can to fix this," Chris whispered apologetically.

"Son, that's not something you need to tell me; that's something that you need to show her." With a supportive nod and a pat on the shoulder, Mike led Chris out of the house.

Once the front door opened, the scummy photographers began ferociously clicking away, desperately trying to get any shot possible. Fortunately for Chris, two large bodyguards blocked most of them. In addition to the rampage of photographers, reporters instantly screamed out insensitive questions about the newest details. There was nothing but sadness in his heart; all he could think about was Kate and the pain he caused her.

The two large bodyguards who were instructed to escort Chris to his limo, which was only ten feet away, stood defensively dressed in tight black suits that stretched at the seams. Finally behind the human barricade, Chris stood on the wooden porch while reporters desperately tried to get around the security, but proved to be unsuccessful.

Once inside the safety of the dark tinted glass of the limo, for the first time in a long time, Chris felt relieved to be away from the obsessive attention. In the past it provided him a sense of entitlement, now he found it rude and annoying. Immediately, Chris dialed his assistant's number to ensure everything was taken care of, but before Chris could even say hello into the speaker Carmen began rambling off details. "The jet is prepped and waiting for you at the Executive Airport, and you're scheduled to land at eight fifty-seven p.m. The house is fully staffed, and I forwarded your updated weekly schedule from Charlie to your phone - you should receive it shortly." The phone buzzed in Chris's hand two seconds later. "Also, I know you didn't ask, but I hired a few extra security personnel to stay at Mr. and Mrs. Woods's home. I hope that's all right?"

When Carmen took a second to catch her breath, Chris interjected, "Thank you, Carmen. That's perfect."

"Anytime, sir," she chirped happily.

On the ride to the airport, Chris felt his cell vibrate on the soft leather seat next to him; the screen displayed Eric's number.

"Hey did you find out anything?" Chris asked answering the phone.

"Yea. You're never going to believe this. The information came from Robert Reeves. You or Kate must have really pissed someone off."

"I can't imagine whom," Chris said more to himself.

"Is there anything I can do?" On the other end of the line, Eric shook his head as he thought, *I told you so.* "So I have to know, is there any truth to this?"

"I'm not sure; I didn't know Kate five years ago." Normally, Chris would have been upset by this question, but he figured it was coming, and there were more important things to worry about.

"Fair enough."

While Robert was known for his high-end contacts in the media, which was mainly used to filter career-damaging information to the public, he very rarely used it for personal attacks. This filtration was not cheap; clients would approach him with the specific information and regardless of the results, the client always paid upfront.

Quickly, Chris's sadness turned into rage as he began to realize that this wasn't something the media had just stumbled upon. Angrily, he held the phone so tight that his knuckles began to turn white, and his nostrils flared while he tried to think of who would have sought out information on Kate.

There was only one way to find out who did this, and the only person that knew the answer was Robert. Seems simple enough, but Robert had an impeccable record of keeping his clients' identity confidential. No one had ever been able to make Robert crack; however, Robert had never dealt with Chris Cody.

It had been years, but for the strangest reason Chris began to think about his mother, and someone that provided a lot of influence in his younger years...

The owner of the nightclub where Julia worked took a fond interest in her and her son Chris. One year, when Chris was about ten, Mr. M. took Chris to a baseball game. Behind third base, enjoying their cold hot dogs and stale popcorn, Mr. M. started up an important conversation at the end of the fifth inning.

It took a moment of maneuvering, but Mr. M. twisted his large beer belly toward Chris and spoke in a husky almost wheezy voice, "Listen up, kid. Chris, you're becoming a man, but that doesn't come without responsibility." Chris gazed up at Mr. M. feeling extremely manly, shoving half a hot dog into his small mouth. "The number one rule of being a man is treating women with respect, even if you only know her for a night. Understand?" A blank expression appeared on Chris's face as his baby peach fuzz-covered face stared back at the dark, fat, Italian man. Unknowingly, Chris just nodded his head in agreement. Having thought the lecture complete, Chris turned his attention back to the game, but then Mr. M. started again, "You're going to do great things kid, but remember everyone needs help once in a while." Grunting sounds escaped Mr. M. as he tried to lean to the right to pry something out of his pocket. It was a simple piece of paper with a number written on it. "You take this, and if you ever need anything . . . anything at all, call that number. I don't care if it's thirty years from now you call that number. *Capiche?*"

"Sure." Carelessly, Chris tossed the paper in the cup holder next to his Pepsi.

The tone of Mr. M.'s voice changed instantly. "No. Listen up, kid. This is extremely important. It's a one time deal, so keep that number safe and only use it when you *really* need to." Chris's young eyes began to comprehend the magnitude of Mr. M.'s message, and he carefully placed the number in his jeans pocket.

A sudden fear jumped into Chris's heart when he realized that for most of his adult life he had been able to buy his way out of messes – but not this time. To Kate and her family, money didn't matter; relationships were important. Guilt was an emotion that Chris rarely experienced, and naturally the only thing he wanted to do was make it go away.

From the plane, Chris spotted the aggressive reporters surrounded by the obsessive fans, all awaiting his arrival. No amount of money could keep him hidden from this scandal. Walking on the tarmac from the plane to the rented Escalade, he realized how cruel the reporters truly were.

Why are you seeing her?

Are you trying to convert lesbians?

Did you help kill Senator Reynolds's daughter?

Each question stung harder than the last and for the first time, Chris couldn't understand why he'd always craved this attention.

The arrival of home was less than welcoming. Mr. Whittaker acted as if nothing happened and continued with his daily duties. Not even a whisper or a murmur about the situation, or even a concerned question about Kate's welfare.

How pathetic is my life? After all my success, I only have awards to show for it – not a single relationship.

Groggy from the jetlag, Chris sluggishly dragged himself up the stairs to his master suite. Alone in bed and depressed, he just lay there fully clothed, too tired to change. Happy thoughts of Kate strolled through his mind, as he remembered how joyful it was to have her here. The emptiness surrounded him as his eyes closed, and he drifted into a deep slumber.

Instead of being awakened by the gentle sounds of a buzzing alarm clock, or even the overly polite knock of Mr. Whittaker to inform Chris that guests had arrived, the loud annoying sound of a banging fist on his bedroom door shot him up. In the next second, Eric and James busted through without concern of Chris's current state and gave him the proper fraternity wake-up call.

The next thing he knew, his body slowly began to drag toward the edge as James yelled out, "Get your lazy ass out of bed. It's three o'clock!"

Eric and James each had one of Chris's legs and didn't have any intentions of letting go.

Despite the cripplingly headache Chris hollered, "Fine. I'm up, I'm up," as he wiped the crusted sleep from his eyes.

"Get dressed. We'll be downstairs," James said as he pulled silver aviator glasses from his gray shirt pocket, and popped them on. Then both Eric and James left, leaving the door open.

Trying to block the sunlight with his forearm plastered across his face, Chris mumbled, "You guys are a real pain in the ass," loud enough for them to hear. Perfectly timed, Eric popped his head in the doorframe and snidely commented, "That's not us. It's your pity stick you shoved up there." Condescendingly, Eric smirked at Chris, and then closed the door.

Chris stunk to high heavens—he was in desperate need of a shower. The warm water pulsating on his back seemed to restore his sense of reality, somewhere he didn't want to return. A half hour later, he made his way downstairs, where he found Eric and James in the game room. When he walked in, James put the game on "pause," and Eric put down the white Xbox controller, and they both glanced sadly at Chris.

The sentimental moment for which he was not prepared made him extremely uncomfortable. "It's not as bad as it seems," he lied.

"Yeah, it's worse!" Angrily, James tossed his controller on the table and got himself a drink from the fridge.

"What the hell is your problem?" Chris lashed out.

"You!" The fridge door slammed shut. "Kate is the first woman who was worth your time, and this is how you treat her?"

"Come on, James, you don't know the details around their situation. I'm sure Chris has a perfectly logical explanation as to why he left Kate in the middle of a media scandal," Eric spoke softly from the couch watching his two good friends yell at each other.

"Bullshit! Don't defend him!" The beer cap gave a hiss as James angrily twisted the top off—and the pointed edge of the cap pierced the inside of his hand. Unable to hold back his frustration, he chucked the beer top at Chris, who ducked to avoid being hit. "So, do you? *Do* you have a good excuse?" Silence rang true; he could no longer deny the hurt as a slump appeared in his shoulders.

"She didn't give me a choice," Chris whispered softly.

"You're pathetic! That's all you ever do -- runaway when things get hard." James words were spiteful but true.

In one swift motion, Chris stood inches away from James's face with his index finger pointed and yelled, "*Fuck you, James!* You have no idea what you're talking about!"

The brown bottle in James's hand began to rattle from anger. "You're full of shit! Kate was the best thing for you and worth the fight, but you're just too damn scared."

"She also killed her wife for a million dollars and lied about it!" Before the words evaporated from Chris's tongue, the guilt began to set in. He didn't mean it, he was just angry, but he couldn't take it back now, and the awkward silence set in.

Still in his original spot, Eric remained on the couch watching his two friends duke it out. While he agreed with James, none of this would have happened if Chris had just heeded his advice and ran a background check on Kate in the beginning.

"You're a fucking idiot! I don't even know the details behind that story, but I have a hard time believing that someone went to Kate and said, *Here's a million dollars if you shoot your wife.* Don't be so stupid; her wife was in a coma and wasn't waking up. What would you have done?"

Exhausted, Chris shook his head in his hands as he mumbled, "I don't know."

For the next few minutes there was nothing left to be said – until James mumbled a little too loudly to himself, "I can't believe you just left her."

"*Left* her? It's her house, and she kicked me out! Even after that, I still provided her with full protection."

"At least she is OK, we were worried about her," James said.

Chris slammed his empty beer bottle on the coffee table. "Thanks for your concern for me."

"Dude, I warned you about this! So don't act like this is a big shock." Eric didn't want to say I told you so, but Chris's self-pity was annoying him more than he had expected.

The hard expressions of anger quickly turned to intrigue as James glanced toward Eric. "You warned him how?"

"He told me to run a background check on Kate," Chris yelled out.

This was outside of Eric's norm, and it shocked James as he stammered, "You didn't! Why?"

"Of course, I did!" Cockily, Eric stood by his decision. "And apparently, it was good advice not taken. Had you done it, none of this would have happened!" Self-righteously, Eric sat up taller on the couch.

"Even knowing what I know now, I still wouldn't run a background check on her. You may not care about dragging other people's skeletons out of the closet, but I never meant for Kate to relive hers."

The cocky, self-righteous expression quickly faded from Eric's face as Chris continued, "Remember one thing, Eric—everyone has secrets, so don't judge unless you want to be judged." Embarrassed by Chris's wise words, Eric just sat on the couch speechless, fidgeting with his black Rolex.

After too long of a silence, James finally asked, "How did all of this happen?"

"I have no idea. After the night at Club 8 she had a really bad dream and convinced me to take her home early. Two days later, the scandal was plastered on every channel."

Images of the horror Chris saw in Kate's eyes when she saw pictures of Riley on the TV, continued to flash in his mind. It was depressing; Chris felt horrible about everything as he slumped into the couch, nursing his second beer, and trying to avoid eye contact with his friends. In all the time they had known Chris, they had never seen him so tormented.

It was becoming clearer and clearer how miserable Chris really was, and Eric extended a sympathetic apology, "I'm really sorry."

"Yeah. Me too," James mumbled, feeling guilty for the way he overreacted.

Half-heartedly, Chris smiled, "Thanks, guys." But his smile was forced and filled with heartache.

"I want to know who did this and beat the ever-loving crap out of them." James angrily punched his fist into his own hand, twisting it upon contact.

"Me too," Eric added.

"What? You haven't been in a fight since middle school when you got beat up for wearing pink."

"I can't help it if I have great style. You're probably still the last guy to pop his collar," Eric smirked. Happily, James smoothed out his extended white polo collar.

Punishing the person responsible for Kate's pain would indeed make Chris feel better, but what about Kate and her feelings?

"What's going to happen to Kate?" Eric worried that Chris had a narrow vision of what was necessary. The question took Chris by surprise. How was he supposed to know what was going to happen to Kate? She made it very clear that she never wanted to see him again.

Tired, sagging eyes glazed up at Eric from the half-empty beer bottle Chris had been focusing on, "What do you mean?"

"I mean, who is going to help her through this? She has just been thrown into the middle of a huge scandal and accused of killing her wife – those are some big pieces that fell apart. Who is going to help her put it back together?" Eric leaned over the coffee table glaring intently at him waiting for the *correct* answer.

"How am I supposed to know what happens to her, I'm not there?! I can't pick up the pieces of her shattered heart because she won't let me." Sadly, Eric's head shook in disappointment. This was not the Chris he knew; the Chris he remembered wouldn't let anything stand in his way. Chris sighed heavily with his shoulders slumped even lower as he continued, "I'm not sure there is anything I can do to change her mind. She made it very clear that I was never to return." The notion of never seeing

Kate's smile or listening to her dorky jokes again was utterly devastating to him.

James had heard enough, "This is bullshit! If you really care about Kate, then man up and fight for her."

Motivated by James's aggression Chris yelled out, "You're right, I'm not going to be dismissed because of some scumbag!" For this brief moment Chris felt confident that Kate would forgive him. But it didn't take long for the doubt to set in when he had the painful thought, *What if she doesn't?*

Later that night, after Eric and James left and the staff had finished for the evening, Chris found himself alone in his room, pacing. In the closet behind the long row of neatly hung pants, was a secret door with a vault that held all of his most prized possessions. Among the few personal effects from his childhood there was only one thing he searched for - the old, faded, delicate piece of paper that Mr. M. gave him so many years ago.

The flimsy paper felt like it weighed a ton in his left hand with his cell in his right, dialing the number. His thumb twitched as he nervously pressed the numbers, unsure that this would even work.

Ring.

Ring.

Ring.

Assuming it hopeless, Chris was ready to give up, when suddenly someone with a heavy Italian accent picked up the phone, "Yeah?"

The sound of a strange man's voice startled him as he stumbled over himself, "Umm."

It was clear that the man lacked patience as he annoyingly yelled out, "Who the hell is this?"

"Err...my name is Chris. Mr. M. gave me... " It didn't take long for the man to figure out who Chris was and why he was calling. Once the connection was made, the tone in the Italian man's voice changed to warm and friendly, "Hey, kid! How the hell are ya?" Like they were life long friends, the man's hand slapped down against the red-checked table next to his plate of pasta.

"I'm . . . good." Chris paused wondering why all of a sudden this man was so happy to hear from him. "Who is this?"

"I'm Antonio, a friend of Luca Manticho."

"Huh?"

A husky laugh rang through the phone line and Antonio said, "You probably remember him as Mr. M." Silently, Chris nodded his head in agreement. Happy memories of Chris and Mr. M floated through his mind and he regretted losing touch throughout the years.

"How is Mr. M.?" The line fell silent and Chris knew the answer wouldn't be good.

"I'm sorry, kid; he passed a few years ago. Luca spoke of you often. After the fiasco on TV, I knew it wouldn't be long before you called."

Twirling his pasta, Antonio sat quietly and listened while Chris explained the whole story to him. When he finished, Antonio's response was simple, "We'll take care of it. Family sticks together. Luca thought of you as one of his own."

"Thanks." Saddened by the loss of the only decent male figure in his life, Chris found his eyes beginning to tear up.

"No problem. You'll get a call in a couple of days with what you need. Until then, keep your nose clean, kid." There was no chance to say goodbye or even a thank you; Antonio ended the call just as abruptly as he started it. Chris was alone in his closet with a tinge of hope that everything would be okay.

The next morning, Chris found himself stuck in a stuffy conference room for rehearsal of a new movie, *Love of Loves*. He argued with Charlie that he was tired of cliché love movies and wanted an action film, but like always, Charlie convinced Chris, using his weakness – money.

Every time Chris missed his line it was politely ignored, the entire cast seemed supportive, but he swore under the fake laughs, they were cursing him. Chris couldn't care less. Every other thought was about Kate and how to reverse the wrong that was done to her.

Several times, Chris's co-star, Rachel Summers, politely nudged him back to reality. There wasn't anything special about Rachel, nothing to make Chris take notice. To him, she appeared like all the other women; a round face, short brown hair and a perky boob job. Just an actress he had co-starred with a few times before. Rachel was considered the female counterpart of Chris Cody.

The cast had been cooped up in the room for almost two hours since the last break, and they were itching to get out. When they finally broke for lunch, the room quickly dispersed leaving only Rachel and Chris the latter slumped in his chair pouting like a three-year-old and tearing up an eraser.

Rachel approached with a smile, hoping for a positive response, "It will pass. Soon people will start gossiping about something else."

Annoyed, Chris sucked his teeth and without looking at Rachel he mumbled, "I hope so." The only thing Chris wanted was to be left alone; he did not need to hear the ramblings of an actress, who only knew him on set. Irritated that she hadn't left yet, Chris shoved back his chair to silently walk past her. It was in that moment that Rachel over-extended her reach and her boundaries as she whispered, "You seem like you could use a friend, and if you ever want to talk, you know my number."

Further annoyed by her audacious act of kindness, Chris glared up at Rachel's warm, honey eyes that appeared to offer more than a friend. He brushed his arm from underneath her hand and stood there staring.

While Chris didn't accept the invitation, he also didn't move past her. They looked at each other for a moment, trying to read the other, until Chris finally huffed in frustration, "Rachel, you're a really nice girl, but I'm not interested in seeing anyone right now."

"You think I want to sleep with *you*? Yeah right. I was trying to be nice because everyone else is tiptoeing around you, but never mind – I'll leave you alone."

It was happening again, someone wasn't willing to put up with his crap, and Chris was beginning to learn the lesson Kate had been trying to teach him all along.

Frustrated that she even allowed herself to care, Rachel turned to leave and without realizing it, Chris reached out and whispered, "Wait." When she turned around, her facial expression scowled angrily at Chris; it wasn't a pretty site. Intimidated, Chris took a tiny step back; unlike Kate, there was nothing cute about Rachel when she was mad.

"I'm sorry; I didn't mean to imply, " Chris spoke timidly hoping this would make amends.

It took a moment, but Rachel's angry scowl faded into a soft smile, "It's obvious you really care about her." Chris just nodded his head as he pressed his lips tightly together. "Then why are you here instead of there with her?"

"You know why I'm here, I'm under contract."

Rachel nodded her head in agreement, but still countered, "So it's about money?"

"It's *a lot* of money."

"I get it. How are you going to fix it?"

"Fix it? I didn't break it."

"So? You care about Kate right?" Once again Chris silently nodded. "Then you fix it."

"How am I supposed to fix it?"

Rachel crossed her arms and with narrowed eyes said, "I don't know. You know her, I don't. What would make her happy?"

There it was. The undeniable truth - Chris really didn't know what would make Kate happy. He followed her request and left, leaving security in place for her safety and, in the meantime, he leaned on his old rules to impress women – gifts and flowers, but he still couldn't understand why she didn't return his calls.

Parked on Sixth Avenue, two lugs, Joey and Tony, waited semi-patiently in a beat up, green 1979 Dodge Charger; they hated this part of the job.

Since they were the best of the best, Antonio wouldn't trust anyone but these two to get the work done.

Completely oblivious to his surroundings, Robert strolled down Vassar Street as he did on any other day. Tony spotted him in the rearview mirror, nodded at Joey and said, "Right on time."

Carefully, Joey watched Robert in the passenger-side mirror. Dressed in a hand-stitched, white Armani suit, Robert walked down the dirty alley like he was on top of the world.

"Look at this guy. He really thinks he's something," Joey sneered as he ran his forefinger along the stubble under his nose.

"Not for long." Tony chuckled lightly at the thought of his fist against this guy's baby-soft face.

The moment Robert turned down another street, the two thugs quietly slipped out of the car and began to follow him. With each step taken, they closed the gap between them and their target. It happened all too quickly, the moment Joey saw the opening of the back alley, he took his opportunity and shoved Robert into the shadows, away from the wondering eyes on the busy main street.

Stupidly, Robert tried to run past the two men, who each stood over six feet tall and easily weighed two hundred pounds. Without much effort, Tony threw out his arm, which knocked Robert in the throat and caused him to stumble backwards even further into the alley.

"So this is the big and powerful Robert Reeves?" Joey mocked to Tony.

"He doesn't look so tough." Tony scratched his baldhead as he watched Robert scramble to his feet. Dark, dirty, smudge splattered the white suit, destroying it.

A smile of satisfaction appeared as Joey said, "Tony, I think he needs help getting up."

"Sure, no problem." Tony grabbed the snitch by the base of his neck with his gigantic hands and pinned him against the brick wall. It didn't take long for the oxygen to subside from Robert's lungs, but somehow, through his red face, he managed to cough out, "What the hell is your problem?"

"Problem? Do you have a problem, Joey?" Instead of a verbal answer, Joey just nodded his head. Immediately, Tony reared his head back and lunged forward. The bones under Robert's sensitive skin crushed, while he screamed out in agony. Blood dribbled out of his nose and down his face.

Slightly dizzy from the head bunt, Tony rubbed the center of his forehead and let his victim fall to the ground as he joked, "Oops—lost my balance."

While Robert curled over and moaned in pain, Joey spit on him and demanded, "I want to know the name of the person who gave you the information about Katherine Woods!"

After a moment, Robert spit out a mouth full of blood and groaned, "Man, I don't know what you're talking about." Joey kicked him in the stomach, and he howled even louder.

Annoyed at the length of time that it was taking to get this information, Tony decided to knock it up a level. "Listen, asshole, we can do this the easy way or the hard way. The choice is yours." Once again, Tony lifted his prey up with one hand and threw him back into the brick wall as Robert's head bounced off it. "I'm going to ask you one more time, who gave you the info?"

In a panic, with his head throbbing and face covered in blood, he pleaded, "I swear to God, I have no idea who gave me that info. It just showed up."

Furious at the lie, Tony squeezed his hand tighter and tighter around Robert's neck. "Then, how did you get paid?"

"I got a package. It was on my doorstep one morning." Robert's face turned a chalky white as he looked at Joey with fear-stricken eyes and begged for mercy. Joey was by no means a fool. He stopped, thought about what Robert had said, and then spit in his face. "You're a fuckin' liar! You don't run that kinda operation! Hell would freeze over before you would release anything without being paid first. I don't like liars, they make me sick. Tony, take care of this animal."

Suddenly, Tony's grip loosened a bit as he reached behind him with his left hand and pulled out a stub-nose .38 with a rubber-band grip. Robert began to fight harder to escape the grasp. It was no use.

"OK…looks like we are going to do this the hard way." There was a smile on Tony's face as he flaunted the gun and watched the fear consume him. The loud click rang in Robert's ears as Tony cocked the gun, and ever so gently, placed the barrel under his delicate chin. The cool metal felt red hot against Robert's skin, and images of his life began to flash before him.

Inches away from the sweaty and bloody face, Joey breathed, "Does this jog your memory?" Trapped between Tony's massive grip and Joey's sticky hot breath, with the smell of pastrami on his tongue, there was no way out. The realization that he was about to be murdered in this abandoned alley was something that he could no longer deny, causing his body to tremor as he lost control of his bowels.

Desperate to save his own life, Robert folded like a bad hand at poker. "Look, all I know is her name was Susanna, and she was in a hurry to get it out, so much so that she paid double the normal price."

"Susanna what?" Tony yelled as he shoved Robert against the wall. In agony, he grunted out as pain shot through his ribs, stealing his oxygen.

"I don't know. She didn't tell me."

"*Really?* The man that knows everything about everyone doesn't know this bitch's last name." Tired of being jerked around, Joey decided enough was enough. "I don't believe you. You are a dirty piece of shit, and you deserve to be taken out. Tony, put this idiot out of his misery!" The gun reappeared in Robert's line of sight, and this time the barrel was forced into his mouth.

"Hillman! Her last name is Hillman!" he gagged.

"You better not be lying. Because next time we won't be so nice," Joey promised as he smoothed out the dark brown fuzz under his nose.

When Tony leaned back and pulled the gun away, something in Robert's attitude changed as a smirk appeared.

"I saw the pictures of Kate; she's hot. Maybe I should pay her a little visit and see if she'll switch teams for me."

Astonished, Tony and Joey looked at each other, unable to believe that this guy had the audacity to threaten Kate. Given the importance of Mr. M. and Antonio, disrespecting the family was the stupidest thing this guy could have said.

Fury raged between the Italians as they turned back toward Robert, who was about to quickly regret his words. Joey jerked the gun from Tony's hand, forced opened Robert's mouth and shoved the gun in so deep that the barrel tickled Robert's tonsils.

"If you ever go near her, if you even *think* about going near her, it will be the last thing you ever do." With the gun still loaded, Joey sucker-punched Robert so hard that he doubled over, choking even harder on the silver barrel in his throat.

The tears welled up in Robert's eyes, and his face turned purple; he knew this was the end. Slowly, Joey pulled the gun from his mouth but, before he could catch his breath, Tony threw him to the ground like a piece of trash. Content with their efforts, the goons walked away, leaving Robert bruised and beaten.

Tony and Joey hadn't even taken two steps away before Robert pulled himself up from the hard gritty concrete. Instantly, Joey stopped, turned around, and pointed the gun right between Robert's eyes and promised, "Don't even think about it."

Frozen in his tracks, Robert was so scared of Joey that he soiled himself again.

∾

When the anticipated information returned, Chris was blindsided to learn that the culprit was a woman—Susanna Hillman. This changed everything. All his plans had revolved around the assumption that the perpetrator was male.

Chapter Fifteen

The next day, Chris had his exclusive interview on the national daytime talk show, *The Mary Show*. The host started her career in journalism and eventually moved up to her own show, which had become the most-watched daytime talk show for six years running. In her time on the air, Mary had interviewed some of the most prestigious idols of her time. A tiny woman, not afraid to ask the hard questions, she won the heart of the American public with her warm, brown eyes and her deep honey-mocha skin.

The entire purpose of this interview was to relieve some of the pressure on Chris's involvement in the Reynolds scandal. Otherwise, he would never have agreed to it.

Upon arrival at the studio, Chris was greeted by a production assistant who motioned to someone -- a petite girl who was barely seventeen -- to escort him to his dressing room. Her skin was as pale and smooth as a porcelain doll, and she wore a bulky headset over her jet-black hair. Escorting Chris down the hall, she hovered the clipboard with a list of several things that had to be done in the next thirty minutes—she didn't have time to be gracious. He was sure that this poor little girl would eventually run into a wall, since she barely glimpsed up from her precious clipboard, but amazingly enough she made it through the maze and delivered him to his green room. In fact, she stopped so suddenly that Chris almost ran over her as she opened the door and closed it behind him in the same movement, to race off to her next assignment.

The room was equipped with a makeup table flanked by twelve bright round bulbs and a tall directors chair. Across the room was a plush couch and a coffee table filled with gift baskets and white calla lilies surrounding the sofa. These were all the things Chris had demanded in the past, outlandish, extravagant gifts that meant nothing to him. He also knew that backstage there would be a table, just for him, filled with his favorite dishes just because of all the times he had complained. Today, it bothered him more than it ever had. Today, he realized how petty these items were and pondered why they used to make him so happy.

Barely five minutes had passed before there was a knock on the door. The makeup artist, Steve, a beautiful six-foot-two stud, entered the room. Setting up his kit, he began painting his canvas and Chris felt the uncanny comfort to suddenly discuss his predicament. Steve's feedback hit him like a ton of bricks. The solution was simple. So simple that Chris kicked himself for not thinking of it.

"All Susanna wants is to date you, why not allow her to think she has achieved her goal. Once she's completely smitten and thinks her fantasy has become a reality, then hit her with it."

"Hit her with what?"

"Everyone in L.A. has a secret to hide. I'm sure you can find something." Together they both smiled, knowing it could work. If Susanna refused to publicly apologize, Chris would ruin her reputation the same way she had ruined Kate's.

A few moments later there was a knock, and a meek voice called through the door that Mr. Cody was wanted backstage. It was the same girl who had escorted Chris to his room—however she now had tiny beads of sweat forming around the edge of her hairline. After the door closed behind him, the girl began to speed walk down the corridor, and Chris had to double his steps to keep up.

Once they reached the backstage area, he realized that Mary was already on stage. Casually, Chris waited in a director's chair, with his name printed on it, for Mary to come say hello. Instead, the host stayed on stage and began to introduce him. It was at this time that a production assistant advise him that it was time.

"But Mary normally…" Chris mumbled and while the assistant was pulling him out of the chair she replied, "Yes. Yes. I know. But we are ready for you." The next thing he knew he was on stage with Mary in front of a live audience without personally having reviewed the questions. Quickly, Chris shrugged it off, assuming that Charlie pre-approved everything prior to the taping.

When he appeared on stage the audience began to insatiably cheer for him. Despite the standing ovation, Chris spotted a few women who didn't seem too thrilled to see him, but none-the-less he continued. After a performance hug, he sat down on the white couch and faced Mary. There was something different in her eyes, less friendly than in the past, and once the crowd quieted down, she began her planned out interrogation.

"Are you dating Katherine Woods?" Bam! First question out of the gate, and Mary blindsided Chris with the scandal.

"No." Chris remained calm, but his tone was firm.

"Sure does look like it here." On the large projection screen behind them, photos of Chris and Kate snuggled together at the club flashed.

"We are not a couple..." Chris stuttered trying to correct Mary's accusations, but it didn't work – she just talked over him. The questions continued to ricochet, so quickly that Chris couldn't retort. This was unbelievable – Chris Cody being ambushed by the media.

"How can you date someone like her? I mean a woman who kills her wife for money, that's low even for your standards." This was the final straw. Chris picked up his ego from the floor and answered, "Now hold on a damn minute! Kate did everything she could for her wife. It was the Reynolds's who sought out Kate with the sole intention of personal gain. For Christ's sake, there was an experimental treatment in China that the insurance would cover, and Senator Reynolds flat out refused to save his own daughter's life. They were more concerned with their public image than their own daughter. So, Mary, don't you dare sit there and badger me about Katherine Woods's character, because by any means, her morals are a hell of a lot more intact than most."

The audience was speechless, and Mary's jaw dangled from her mouth. She assumed she had backed him into a corner to make a fool of him, and it had backfired on her. Angrily, Chris tugged off the microphone and proudly stomped off stage.

The long eighteen-hour flight from Indonesia landed, and Sam was exhausted from her excursion. After trudging through Customs and shuffling through the masses to get her bags, Sam was relieved to sit in the quietness of her car, which had been parked in the garage for the past three weeks. Habitually, Sam flipped through her cell phone and saw all the Facebook posts about Kate's scandal. Slack-jawed, Sam couldn't believe what she was reading...*Kate killed her wife for a million dollars...* that just seemed so unlike her.

There was no answer when Sam called Kate, so naturally, she called Chris, and the moment he answered she began to holler at the dashboard, "What the hell happened? I leave the country for a few weeks and you screw up everything?"

Still in his limo on the way home from the horrifying interview at *The Mary Show*, Chris was not amused. "Well, it's nice to hear from you, too."

Ignoring his sarcasm, she demanded, "Where are you?"

"On my way home." The sound of exhaustion dampened his voice, and Sam mistakenly took it for depression and felt it necessary to help. When it came to matters involving Kate, she knew how fragile Chris could be. She had seen first-hand the instinctive desire he felt to protect Kate.

"I'll be there soon; don't do anything stupid." The right blinker turned on and barely looking, Sam crossed three lanes of traffic to make a U-turn.

"But . . .!" A feeble attempt to stop Sam was proved to be useless as she snapped back, "No buts, I'm coming over, and that's final!"

Forty-five minutes after Chris got home, Sam rapidly banged on the front door. Politely, Mr. Whittaker greeted her and led her out to the back terrace where Chris was sprawled out in a comfortable lawn chair, with a cigar in one hand, and a bottle of Jim Beam in the other.

The sight of him basically incapacitated irritated Sam's nerves as she screeched out, "CHRIS!" Happily, he smiled at Sam, then lifted the bottle to his lips and guzzled a large mouthful of whiskey down his throat.

She angrily stomped over to Chris, who was still intently focused on the brown liquid pressed against his mouth. Almost instantly, she snatched the bottle from his grasp and with her free hand slapped him across the face, "You pathetic son of a bitch! What are you doing?"

The force from Sam's slap knocked him slightly off balance, causing him to scramble to stay in his chair. Stunned with the sting upon his cheek, Chris demanded, "What the hell was that for?" Sam just stood there with that angry look that upset women give, the one that Chris was becoming more and more accustomed to. Sloppily, Chris motioned his hand back and forth, "Now give it back to me!"

"What? You want this bottle?"

Annoyed, Chris leaned forward and tried to reach for it, but Sam took a step back. "Sam, this shit isn't funny! Just give me the bottle!"

In a patronizing voice, she teased Chris with the bottle as she let it dangle above him just slightly out of reach. "This one right here? This one? Well, you can't have it!" Silently, she backed away from him towards the pool and chucked the bottle in the clear water. The brown liquid disappeared.

"What the hell is your problem?" Upset and confused, he couldn't figure out why she had walked into his house and started yelling at him. It seemed that lately Chris was constantly being yelled at and he didn't have a clue why.

"I got a call from my office that you called to get Susanna's number! What is that about?" The mere idea of Chris even contemplating going out with Susanna made Sam's blood boil.

"It's no big deal, I was just going to ask her out." His nonchalant tone just continued to infuse her anger.

"No big deal? You know as well as I do that girl is nothing but trouble. You can't go out with Susanna!" While Sam stood before Chris, furiously stomping her sparkly pink Steve Madden flats trying not to pull out her hair, he just reclined in the chair secretly enjoying her tantrum.

"Last time I checked, I can do what I want." Chris pulled himself up sloppily, slurring his words, as a cheap smirk appeared at Sam's anger.

"Oh, my god. You have completely lost your mind."

"I've lost my mind because you threw my drink into the pool! What did that bottle ever do to you?" Chris pointed drunkenly to the bottom of the pool, where his bottle of Jim Beam was laid to rest. He was annoyed that he now had to go inside to get another bottle.

Jet-lagged, and still aggravated, Sam sat down in the adjacent chair. "I got a call from my office, and my assistant told me what you did. She said that you sounded depressed and desperate to get Susanna's number. This shit has to stop! Why in the hell would you ask that skank out?"

The buzz that he delightfully enjoyed was now slowly being replaced by a pounding headache, thanks to Sam's tantrum.

"I can't believe you're doing this! Kate wouldn't want to see you like this!" Disapprovingly, she shook her head.

In a condescending tone, Chris answered as he drunkenly pulled himself up and walked crookedly inside the house. "Well, Kate's not here, is she?"

The moment he returned with his new bottle of Jim Bean, she immediately continued her interrogation. "By asking out Susanna, you're becoming the person that Kate hates! And how can you do this right after what happened?"

Sick and tired of being badgered, Chris yelled, "Oh for the love of all things holy, if I tell you why I'm asking Susanna out would you drop it?"

Still skeptical, she asked more quietly, "OK, then—why are you asking her out?"

Settling back in his chair, he took a large gulp of his whiskey before beginning his explanation. "When everything happened, I called a contact of mine and found out that Robert Reeves was the person who leaked all the info."

Of all things, Sam was not expecting to hear Robert's name. Her nose crinkled with confusion. "But why would he do something like that? Did you do something to him?"

"I didn't do anything to him. He was just doing his job. Robert was paid by someone to release that information to the public."

"Who in the world would want to hurt Kate? She's the sweetest person I've ever met. She hasn't done anything to anyone, has she?"

"No, she hasn't done anything, not intentionally, anyway." Tired, he leaned his head against the cushion and inhaled the fresh smell of pine.

"What does that mean?" Her pale pink lips pursed up, then twisted to the right side of her cheek.

"The person who gave Robert the information was Susanna."

"What?" Sam's mouth dropped open and hung there for a few moments, until Chris pointed with his bent index finger toward his own open mouth.

He shook the bottle around, and inhaled the aroma of the whiskey before taking another large swig. "I can't believe it either. I just can't figure out how Susanna found out about Kate's past. She didn't even know Kate's last name."

Something clicked, and Sam realized that she might have overlooked an extremely important detail. Becoming nervous, she fidgeted in her chair shifting her eyes away from Chris. The sound of Sam's watch clicking tick… tick… tick… caused concern for him, "What's wrong?"

Guilt-consumed, Sam felt like she should have known better. She remembered her gut telling her something was off, but she didn't pay any attention–her only concern at that moment was getting home, and now Kate was paying the price for her carelessness. Rehashing the details to Chris, she would have sworn that he would be furious with her, but surprisingly, he harbored no judgment or ill will towards Sam.

A peaceful and calming moment of silence engulfed them until a thought crossed her mind. "But you haven't explained why you're asking Susanna out."

No matter how hard Chris tried to distract her, she always managed to stay focused on her question.

"I'm going to give her everything she's ever wanted, including a date with Chris Cody."

"That doesn't make any sense. How is that going to do any good?"

"Susanna isn't the only one who can pull out old skeletons." A ting of satisfaction flowed through his veins.

Intrigued by the prospect of juicy tidbits, Sam wiggled in her chair excitedly. "But what if she doesn't cooperate?"

"Oh, she will, especially with what I know."

Interested, she leaned over her Indian-style crossed legs. "Do tell."

"Sorry, no can do. But if she doesn't play ball, you'll find out just like the rest of America." An evil grin appeared as his thought about the humiliation he was going to put this girl through – just like she did to Kate.

"I'm glad that Susanna is going to get what she deserves—but what about Kate?" A soft sadness crossed Chris's face when he thought about the pain Kate was enduring and small tears began to form in his drunken eyes. When he didn't answer her question, she asked again, "What are you going to do to get her back?"

Timidly he mumbled, "I just don't know what to do."

"You have to think like Kate; what would make her happy?"

What would Kate want? he pondered. The only thing she had ever mentioned wanting was Riley. How was he going to compete with that? Desperately, he tried to think of something, anything; all he needed was a tiny little speck of hope, but he kept coming up blank. This was the woman that he had spent every day with for the past couple of months, the woman that he loved, and now he couldn't think of a single thing to prove his loyalty. Unable to perform this simple task, doubt entered his mind. *Maybe I don't deserve to have her in my life. She's probably better off and safer without me in the picture.* Misery penetrated his body.

"You know what I really liked about Kate? Her feistiness. I loved how she always challenged you."

"She's a pistol!" Slurping the last of his drink, he remembered how Kate and Aika brought so much energy into his home.

Swinging her feet back and forth on the chair Sam thought out loud, "I loved the fact that when she made that bet with you, what she wanted was something selfless."

Chris narrowed his eyes trying to re-conjure the memory but the details were fuzzy. "What did she ask for?" There was nothing that Chris would ever deny her, especially if she asked for it.

"The air hockey bet. How can you not remember this? Had she won, you would have had to donate your time and money to a local charity."

Simultaneously, Sam and Chris had the exact same thought – volunteer at a charity to win Kate's heart.

The excitement quickly subsided when Chris realized he didn't have a clue where to provide his services. The drunken fog was beginning to cloud his thoughts, until there was a small spark. A far distant conversation, he remembered Kate complaining about her community center falling apart. That was it; he would rebuild Kate's community center!

Chapter Sixteen

The white cell phone on Chris's cherry wood desk taunted him as he paced back and forth in front of it, wearing out the rug, trying to find the courage to call Susanna. *What am I going to say to her? How am I going to make her believe that I really want to date her? I have to think like the old me, the guy who gets whatever and whoever he wants.*

Before he could hit the send button on his phone, he took a deep breath and regained his composure.

Ring.

Ring.

Ring.

Ring.

Impatient, Chris huffed that it was taking so long for either Susanna to pick up the phone or the voicemail to turn on. After another never-ending minute, the high-pitched voice of her pre-recorded message annoyingly greeted him.

"Hey, guys . . . It's Susanna. I'm away from my phone, probably doing something fun! Leave your number, and I might call you back . . . *Ciao!*"

"Hi Susanna. This is Chris Cody, call me when you get this." His voice was resounding, confident, but most importantly sexy. In order for this to work Susanna had to truly believe that Chris wanted her. Now came the hard part – waiting for the return call.

Steam from the hour-long shower filled the bathroom turning it into a spa. Susanna emerged from the pink porcelain tub, carefully wrapping her wet body in a princess-pattern towel. She opened the bathroom door opened and the fog escaped into the cooler air of the lavish one-bedroom apartment. Sauntering into the living room, Susanna noticed her cell phone flashed a missed call from Chris Cody, which she had labeled *Sexy Beast.*

Collagen-filled lips turned upward in excitement; everything was going according to Susanna's plan. Once she had removed Kate, it was only a matter of time before Chris came crawling to her - that's what she thought at least.

Hastily, Susanna dialed Chris's number making sure not to let this opportunity slip away.

Gazing through the window upon the freshly manicured lawns, the sound of a purring vibration on the desk caught Chris's attention. The number wasn't registered in his phone, but he knew it was Susanna. Nerves spiked, and without preparation Chris wildly answered, fumbling with the phone.

Even though the voice was sultry it was still unattractive, "Hey, Chris. Sorry I missed your call . . . I was in the shower."

The thought of Susanna in the shower made him cringe, but he mustered the strength to reply smoothly, "How have you been?"

"I've been good," she giggled nervously like a schoolgirl. There was a pause, and then in a fake tone she continued, "How is Kate doing? I heard about what happened. I'm so sorry."

This pissed Chris off —Susanna didn't care about anyone other than herself. It was just the motivation he needed.

Disinterested, Chris spoke confidently, "Yeah, thanks. You know how these things work; here today, gone tomorrow. It was never going to work out." These awful words gnawed at his stomach. It never crossed his mind that he would have to discuss Kate with Susanna. Every syllable tasted like vinegar on his tongue, especially what he said next. "That's why I was calling you. I wanted to know if you would be interested in going to dinner with me."

Bursting with excitement and entitlement, she attempted to act casual. "Of course, I think that would be a great idea." Pleased with herself, Susanna pulled her thick blonde hair out of the towel, gently rubbed her scalp, and smiled at how well everything was playing out.

"When are you free?" Bored and disinterested in what she had to say, Chris pulled down the white blinds and turned away from the window. He already knew that she was available; Susanna was always available, and for everyone. She never turned down a date, especially with a rich man.

There was a pause as she glanced at her empty calendar. "Tomorrow night?" For any other guy, she would have gone at the drop of a hat that night, but she wanted to play hard to get—no need for Chris Cody to think she was easy.

"I'll see you at eight." Still bored with her, he began to flip through a dusty *National Geographic* that hadn't been moved from the side table in probably more than a year.

"See you then," she flirted seductively. When the call ended, she stood in front of a full-length mirror with a grin from ear to ear, as she admired herself. *Pretty soon, I'll have everything that I want.*

Disgusted with what had to be done, Chris continued to flip through the magazine trying to get the guilty knots out of his stomach. The idea of going on a date with Susanna, listening to her ear piercing valley girl voice, and pretending to be interested in her idiotic ideas, well, Chris couldn't think of anything worse.

This is for Kate. This is for Kate. I can do this for her. I just have to slap on some charm, and then the rest will fall into place. Just think of it as the most important role of my life. Chris continuously replayed these thoughts to remind himself of what was necessary.

It was time for the next step. Reservations needed to be made, and like every time before, Carmen cheerfully answered on the first ring.

"Hey, Carmen, I need you to do something for me."

"OK." There was hesitation in her; she had never heard Chris be so informal. Usually when he called he barked out the orders and she complied efficiently and willingly.

"I need two reservations to La Crêpe."

Carmen quickly pulled out a pencil that held her curly red hair in a bun and made a note in her organizer. "Aw, that's great you and Kate made up. I'm so happy for you. I'll get right on it."

"No, Carmen, Kate and I didn't make up; I'm taking someone else."

"Oh. OK." Disappointed, she thought to herself that the asshole had returned, and waited with pencil in hand for Chris to start barking orders.

"Also, have the limo ready by seven thirty."

"No problem, sir." Carmen scribbled the time and place of this date in tiny letters around the rest of his appointments and other various events. This small organizer was her whole life, which in turn was Chris's entire life.

"Thank you, Carmen."

Outside of her expensive condo, waiting in his tieless, dark gray, Armani suit, Chris was more nervous than he had been in years. Every time he thought he had enough courage to go through with it, something inside of him made him turn around. The back and forth pacing on the street became noticeable, especially when the driver rolled down the tinted window. An older man in a standard black suit with a matching black cap, leaned his elbow out and offered some simple advice: "It's like pulling off a Band-Aid—do it fast and don't look back."

Appreciative, Chris smiled at the man and went inside.

Tucked away in his inside pocket was a small, stiff envelope that continued to poke his side, but would also prove to be useful if Susanna refused his demands tonight.

The elevator dinged, and Chris stepped out into a small, beautifully decorated hallway with vases of flowers on either side of the doors. It quickly dawned on him that he arrived empty handed, and smoothly, he pulled out a red rose, shook off the water, and wandered down the hall to suite 703.

Presumptuously, the door swung open revealing Susanna, who was readily exposing too much skin in a cheap, tight red dress. This display of overt sexiness was not surprising to Chris – in fact, not only had he expected it, he had counted on it. Pleased at the sight at her front door, Susanna's lips curled upwards while her eyes undressed him before she whispered, "Hello. Please come in." Strategically, Susanna stepped to the side allowing Chris enough room to pass by, giving her the opportunity to ogle his backside.

"Thank you." Much to his surprise, when he caught Susanna gawking at him it made him feel cheap, an emotion he had not anticipated. "This is a nice place you have here." Awkwardly, Chris shoved the rose at Susanna.

"Aww." Taking the flower from his hand, she lingered, gently caressing his fingertips. "It's a little place that gets me by." She coyly brushed his arm, and batted her fake eyelashes.

Abruptly, Chris asked, "Are you ready?" He extended out his hand allowing Susanna to pass, and when she did, he rolled his eyes at the thought of the long night ahead of him.

At some point during the ride to the restaurant, Chris mentioned where they had reservations and Susanna squealed like a pig from excitement, causing the driver to swerve.

"Oh, my god! I have been dying to go there! There's a waiting list three months long! How did you get reservations on such short notice?" Overly excited, Susanna twirled her blonde hair around her index finger and inched closer.

"I have my ways. Besides, what's the point of being famous if you can't use your status to get what you want?"

Before she could agree, the limo stopped in front of La Crêpe. When a person like Chris Cody goes out to dinner, it's common for the paparazzi to be in full force. The driver opened the door, and a lighting storm of flashes appeared when his face emerged from the darkened shadow. Susanna wanted to date the famous Chris Cody; well, now she got her wish, and he was going to show her exactly what that meant. A quiet, romantic dinner – no such thing, everywhere you go, everything you do, the media is there watching and commenting.

Chris held out his hand for his date, when his faced turned away from the cameras his eyes narrowed intensely at Susanna. Instantly, her heart jumped.

Does he know? He couldn't. That's ridiculous, Susanna, he just smiled. Pull yourself together or you're going to lose everything that you want.

Her bare leg extended above the threshold as she seductively maneuvered herself out of the limo, smiling for the audience. Unexpectedly the flashes stopped – no one wanted her picture. The glamorous smile she provided went sour. Instead of the hundreds of pictures from paparazzi adoring her, she was bombarded with interrogating questions, and all about Kate.

This was not part of the plan, she sulked.

Situated in a small private booth, Chris waited until after the waiter left with their drink order before he inquired, "I'm curious Susanna, why did you say yes?" The dark lighting in the restaurant concealed the thick layer of make-up, making Susanna appear almost normal, instead of the Barbie doll look she created.

"I don't know . . . we've known each other for a while, and it seemed like a good idea." Conceitedly, she shrugged her exposed shoulders, played with the tips of her long, curled hair, then looked down at her cleavage and adjusted herself. When her eyes returned to Chris, she happily expected to find him staring at her breasts. Unfortunately for her, he wasn't into silicone.

An awkward silence lingered at the table until the waiter returned with their drinks. After another moment of unintentional silence, Susanna slurped on her Pinot Noir and leaned across the table flashing her cleavage in his face. "I have a confession to make."

"Oh, really?" For a moment he hoped that Susanna was going to be a descent human being and confess. Then he could stop worrying about the annoying envelope poking him in his jacket pocket.

Fidgeting with her napkin, Susanna tried to play nervous. "You're going to think it's silly."

Pretending to be interested, Chris coaxed her further as he leaned over the table asking, "You can tell me."

"Well, I have liked you for a while . . . quite a while, actually . . . and when you asked me, I was beyond thrilled."

"Really? I didn't know that." Disappointed, he leaned back in his chair. Of course, he knew that she liked him; all of California knew that. There was nothing discreet or subtle about Susanna. It appeared he was going to have to fish out the envelope.

The waiter, a ridged, thin French man, approached the table and focused all of his attention toward Chris, ignoring Susanna completely. Chris ordered himself a boeuf bourguignon and without regard to his date, he instructed the waiter to bring her a house salad. Promptly the waiter took his cue and left, leaving Susanna stammering.

"What was that?" she seethed.

"What was what? All you eat is salad anyways."

Keeping the peace, she rationalized, "I guess you're right—besides, it's healthier," but under her breath, she cursed him. *This is La Crêpe! No one orders a fucking salad here!*

A glimpse of that serious look he gave her in the limo reappeared as he asked, "So—you weren't expecting me to ask you out?"

The Botox-filled lines in her forehead tried to crinkle in confusion as she seductively took a sip of her wine and responded, "No. Why would you ask such an odd question?" Inwardly, Susanna's suspicions increased along with her heart rate, as incriminating thoughts crossed her mind. *Why is he asking me these questions? He couldn't know that I was the one who got the information about Kate into the media. Could he?*

"Because I know what you did." Nerves got the best of Chris, as his left leg began to shake uncontrollably. Luckily, he was the only one that noticed.

The tips of her red fingernails grazed the rim of the wine glass as she innocently asked in a nonchalant tone, "Did what?"

This was more than Chris could handle. Throughout the entire process he fought to maintain his cool, but now his tone turned low and vicious, "I know you're the one who set out to ruin Kate." Full of hate, Chris glared at Susanna with ice-cold eyes. The pretentious, bleach-white smile faded into a thin line as she tossed her napkin at him, offended and prepared to leave.

"I'm not going to sit here and be accused of something I didn't do!"

Halfway out of her chair, she was shocked to feel Chris clench her wrist and force her back down in her seat.

In a low growl to prevent any unwarranted attention, he commanded, "You sit down now! You are going to listen to what I have to say."

"Chris, you better get your facts straight before you go around accusing people of stuff they didn't do!" Irate that Chris still controlled her wrist, Susanna tried to free herself, but he wouldn't release his grip until she remained seated.

So this is why he asked me out. He wanted to see if he could get me to confess to releasing the info about Kate. What an asshole!

Once Susanna was seated properly at the table, Chris laid out all his chips, "I guess it wasn't you who stole Kate's phone then? And I guess it wasn't you who gave all of Kate's dirty secrets to Robert Reeves and paid him double to expedite the process?"

"Nope. That's quite the imagination you have." Bored with these petty threats, Susanna leaned back against the booth, pretending to stifle a yawn.

"I guess that *is* a pretty crazy story."

Conversation eluded them while they gazed at each other. When Susanna thought the argument to have passed, she broke the silence with the return of her fake smile, "See. There's no reason to argue about Kate."

Having forgiven Chris for his mildly bad behavior, Susanna wanted to continue with the date–and their future.

"It's not really a crazy story when you have witnesses. Robert gave you up." For the first time that evening, Chris had a satisfied smirk upon his lips. Thoroughly enjoying the view, he leaned back and watched Susanna's confidence fade.

The once broad smile transformed, now all that remained were tension lines as Susanna snapped, "He's lying."

"Maybe, maybe not? But that's not the important part."

From inside his coat pocket, Chris reached for the envelope that had poked him all night. This frightened Susanna, her plan was slowly beginning to unravel, and she was not prepared for a battle.

The crinkling sound of the papers unfolding seemed to echo loudly in the small booth as Chris calmly continued, "Here is some interesting news: it seems your name isn't Susanna Hillman, but actually Barbara Jean." It had been twenty years since someone called her Barbara Jean, and the sound alone caused her heavily painted face to turn a chalky pale white.

Silently, Susanna sat there too stunned to speak while Chris continued to relay her history. "Let's see here . . . born and raised in Asher, Oklahoma. Now I understand why you changed your name; Barbara Jean had quite the arrest record, everything from petty theft to arson. Quite the little deviant, weren't you? Your mother was a whore, and at 16, you moved out to L.A. and expanded the family business. It must have been really hard living in L.A. without any money, but eventually, Edward took care of that for you. Remember him, your ex-husband? You didn't love Edward; you loved the lifestyle he provided and when he started pulling back, you divorced him."

Parched, Chris paused for a moment to casually take a drink from his glass and smirk.

"You had everything you ever dreamed about: the house, the car, and most importantly, the money. Life was perfect. Then you met Daniel."

Chris didn't think she could get any whiter, but she went from alabaster to a transparent Casper the Friendly Ghost. She felt sick, and both her mind and her heart were racing.

How in the world did he find out about Daniel? I made sure to bury that so deep that no one would ever be able to find out. Oh no, what am I going to do?

Unable to help himself, he chuckled as he continued, "But Daniel was smarter than poor Edward! He convinced you that this was true love and not to sign a prenuptial. You should have signed it. He knew you were a cheater—he caught you in bed with another man. He, of course, divorced you because he was so heartbroken, and he took everything of yours. I wonder how your so-called friends would treat you if they knew that not only are you flat-ass broke, but that you're just some poor honky from

Oklahoma. What do you think, Barbara Jean?" he finished the last sentence in a practiced mid-western twang and flashed a smile that went on for days.

It had taken Susanna almost twenty years to get where she was today, and she would do anything to ensure her stability. If people caught wind of her financial situation, her reputation would be ruined; she wouldn't allow it. The brief moment of humility quickly passed and in a threatened tone she asked, "What do you want?"

"I want you to publicly apologize for what you did to Kate."

"*What? This is still about that dumb slut?*"

Chris slammed his fist on the table, causing the glasses to rattle, and forgetting himself he roared, "Kate is not a slut!" Other patrons nearby startled and gazed at the outburst before returning to their meal, but Chris didn't notice.

Enraged at her nerve, he fought the urge to slap her across the face; manners and being in a public place changed his mind. A quick chug of his drink calmed his twitching fists, "I'm done being nice. The deal is, either you go public and apologize for what you did, or I expose you for the fraud that you are. It's that simple."

A sad expression appeared along with tears bubbling in the corner of Susanna's eyes, but there was no sympathy for her.

"Please . . . isn't there another way we can resolve this?"

"Save your fake tears for the camera crew. You're going to need them."

The tears disappeared and tense lines formed around her lips. Agitated at how wrong everything turned out, Susanna crossed her arms letting her fingers idly tap on her biceps, but remained silent.

Patience was a luxury Chris was running out of and demanded an answer, "Have you made a decision?"

Unhappy with her choices, she rolled her eyes and mumbled, "Fine, I'll apologize."

Awkwardly, they silently sat there with empty plates before them. Horrified and defeated, Susanna glanced around the restaurant in an attempt to avoid eye contact with Chris. It became clear that very soon she would no longer be part of this community. Slowly, she became resentful toward the restaurant, the people in it, but mostly she resented Chris, who sat across from her glowing like a man who had just won the lottery.

After the check was paid, Susanna whispered, "I want to go home."

"Of course." Still a gentleman, Chris rose, offering his arm to his date. With a slight hesitation, she placed her arm in his, and they strolled out of La Crêpe.

Once inside the limo, he handed her a small card. "Here," he said seriously. "Tomorrow morning, call this number and someone will give you instructions. If you don't call that number by noon tomorrow, I'll know about it, and within twenty-four hours, your past will be broadcasted."

Susanna just nodded her head.

The next morning, after Susanna had enjoyed a beautiful breakfast out on her terrace, she nervously dialed the number Chris had given her. The phone only rang once before an enthusiastic young voice answered, "Good morning, Miss Hillman."

"Hi. Who is this?"

"Miss Hillman, my name is Carmen, and I have been assigned to help you through the process today."

"OK." Annoyed, Susanna took her sausage and drenched it in syrup.

"Good. There is going to be a delivery made to your home today at 12:30 p.m.; you are to wear the contents of the package. A driver will then pick you up at 2:30 p.m. sharp—you must be ready to go."

"Wait a damn minute!" Susanna yelled, irate. "I didn't agree for that asshole to dress me! I'll wear my own clothes! I only agreed to make the stupid announcement!"

"Miss Hillman, I have been instructed to let you know that if you do not act in accordance with all aspects of this announcement, then I am to inform Mr. Cody that you are not in agreement, and he will be forced to use his alternative method, which you are aware of."

Not only had Chris blackmailed her the previous night to agree to apologize, but now he had some secretary doing the same thing. Beyond livid, Susanna gritted her teeth and agreed in a nasty tone, "Whatever!"

Regardless of Susanna's attitude, Carmen remained in a chipper mood. "Very good, Miss Hillman. When you arrive at the studio, a woman named Connie will meet with you and go over your lines. You are to follow her instructions explicitly. Again, I want to make clear that if at any time during this announcement you decide not to follow the instructions given to you; Mr. Cody will be notified immediately. Do you understand everything that I have explained here today?"

"Yes."

"Good. Do you have any questions?"

"No."

"Have a nice day!" The line went dead. Susanna hung up and screamed at the top of her lungs in frustration. Thirty minutes later, her doorbell rang. She looked at the clock—it was 12:30 p.m.

A large, off-white, rectangular box with a red bow was delivered to her. After she'd signed for it and crumbled the bow into the trash, she complained, "A red bow? Really? It's not a Christmas gift." Inside was a three-piece green pantsuit, along with matching closed-toe pumps. A short sleeve jacket and a white high-collared shirt completed the outfit. Once dressed, she surveyed the damage and instantly hated the older professional appearance; she much preferred her too-tight, tramp-style clothing.

Uncomfortable, Susanna fidgeted with her outfit the entire day. The stiff cotton irritated her delicate skin, and the fabric continued to bunch in the wrong places. When she arrived at the studio, a young woman approached her and with a bright smile, introduced herself as Connie. Like most professionals, she wore a suit similar to Susanna's, and her jet-black hair was pulled back into a neat ponytail.

Aggravated, Susanna smacked her gums and rolled her eyes at Connie as she mumbled, "Hey."

"Please follow me." Connie turned promptly on her heels and began to walk through the studio, not slowing her pace for her shadow to catch up. Women like Susanna rubbed Connie the wrong way, but nevertheless she remained professional. To her satisfaction, she had been instructed not to give Susanna any special treatment.

"Connie, why aren't there any reporters here?"

"You're not telling your story to the reporters; you're going to apologize live on-air."

Unable to believe what she had just heard, Susanna choked as they entered the recording room, where a single chair was set up in front of a green screen. The entire studio was completely empty, aside from the single cameraman and the student makeup artist.

In the wobbly folding chair, Susanna sat, extremely nervous, the bright lights and heavy suit causing her to perspire even more than usual. While the makeup artist attempted, badly, to fix the imperfections on her face, Connie explained the procedure. She pointed her index finger at the small camera screen directly in front of Susanna. "That screen is going to light up when we are on the air, and you only read the message that pops up. Nothing else. If you stray in any way, Mr. Cody will be informed, and other actions will be taken. Understand?"

Barely able to get the words out, Susanna coughed, "I understand."

"Good." Without another word, Connie turned and walked behind the camera, and got ready to enjoy this public humiliation. No one offered Susanna a glass of water, even though she had pit stains the size of Lake Michigan.

The little red light turned on, and the cameraman began, "And we are on in five, four, three, two, and . . . one." The screen below the lens lit up and the words started to appear. Quickly, Susanna took a deep breath and told herself that she could do this.

"Good afternoon, America. My name is Susanna Hillman, and there's something that I need to get off my chest." The screen went blank, and Susanna tried with no success to look comfortable while she waited for the next part of the script to appear.

"A few weeks back I did something terrible. While everyone is familiar with the Reynolds scandal, what they don't know is that I brought light on the situation. In a jealous rage, I stole Katherine Woods's cell phone in order to destroy her reputation and her relationship with Chris Cody. I spent thousands of dollars and hired an investigator to find anything I could to disturb their friendship. Despite my best efforts, not only did I fail, but also I hurt innocent people in the process. From the bottom of my heart, I would like to apologize to Katherine, and sincerely ask for her forgiveness."

That was it, no more words. Immediately, Connie informed her that she was no longer needed and asked her to leave. It didn't take the studio long to have the video edited and posted on social media. Being a Marketing Director, Connie knew exactly how to increase the visibility of her post, and twenty minutes after being released, there was a large following. People who had banned together, creating support groups for Kate, latched on and bashed Susanna Hillman, the overprivileged liar.

Busy in his office, Chris was on the phone with a contractor, trying to figure out the plans for the new community center, when a beep interrupted them. He placed the contractor on hold and switched to the other caller, "Hello, Carmen. Did everything go well?"

"Yes, sir. She showed up and read the script as directed."

Pleased with the outcome, he smiled. "Good. I'm glad to hear it." The last thing he wanted was for the situation to get any more complicated than it already was. Before he hung up the phone, he politely expressed, "Thank you for all your help."

"You're welcome." For the first time in the five years Carmen had worked for Chris, she felt that he sincerely appreciated the work she did.

Once Chris hung up, he clicked the line back over and continued his conversation with the contractor. This would be the way to win Kate's heart. It had to be; he was out of other options.

Chapter Seventeen

The door slammed shut, and the loud bang caused Kate to crumple. Heavy and uncontrollable tears burst from her eyes. For the second time in her life, she felt completely abandoned by someone who had promised to always be there.

It didn't take long for the neighbors to complain about the crowded streets and noisy reporters walking through their yards. Becky had been on patrol on the other side of town when she heard the dispatcher requesting backup at Kate's address. Without hesitation, she flipped on her sirens and made a sharp U-turn, cutting off three cars in the process. The small street was packed with news channel vans, making it very difficult to maneuver around. Becky found a small area to squeeze the patrol car in about a half-mile away. After letting Sheba out, maneuvering through the crowd became incredibly easy.

From the front bay window, Mike had been watching his daughter's yard begin to resemble Woodstock more than a front lawn. In the midst of the crowd, something caught his attention – a part was occurring, and from it appeared Becky and Sheba. The reporters that hovered around the front door quickly dispersed at the sight of the large German Shepard, but still remained in shouting distance.

Mike opened the door for Becky, but the loudly yelling reporters aggravated Kate's dog as she aggressively tried to force her way outside. In an instant, Aika darted passed Mike and lunged toward the intruders, snarling her teeth at them. Becky was able to grab her before she leaped off the porch – it took both Becky and Mike to drag Aika into the house.

The chaos outside had rattled Mike's nerves long enough. Quietly, he snuck out the backdoor and managed to reach the sprinkler control without being spotted and happily flipped the switch. The cold city water popped out of the ground and the reporters fled to the safety of their vans on the street.

Once the yard was clear, Becky noticed Sheriff Danes and two other officers pulling up. She yelled to Mike to turn off the sprinklers, and once the streams diminished into puddles, Sheriff Dane crossed the yard with a trail of reporters following him. Once on the porch, he turned toward the newly appeared crowd and spoke into his bullhorn, "Anyone on this private property after sixty seconds will be detained for trespassing."

Sheriff Frank Danes had been a friend of Emily's family since childhood and, being very fond of the Woods's family, Frank always did what he could to help out. It didn't feel so long ago that he was here, providing them with emotional support when Kate lost her wife and child.

"Hey, Em, how is she doing?"

Still in the hallway out of earshot, Emily's whisper crackled, "As well as can be expected."

It broke Frank's heart to see them all in so much pain. He just gave Emily a sympathetic smile and nodded his head. "I'm going to leave a deputy here for you, so if there's any trouble, he'll be able to take care of it."

"Thanks, Frank, we really appreciate it." Mike extended his hand and gave Frank a manly hug full of warmth and gratitude.

It had been longer than an hour and Kate still refused to move from her spot on the couch. The sight of her tired and hunched over with swollen eyes broke Becky's heart, and she unprofessionally pulled her friend into a tight embrace. Kate barely responded. On her knees funneling her fingers through Kate's tangled hair Becky mumbled, "I'm so sorry, sweetie. Are you OK?"

"Becky . . . " Instead of being soothing, Becky's voice was full of anxiety, making Kate's headache even worse.

"I should have trusted my instincts. I knew he was no good."

"Becky!"

"I'll make this up to you, I promise."

"BECKY!" The sound of Kate's voice above a meek whisper startled everyone in the room. Achingly, she pinched her nose with her thumb and index finger trying to stop the pulsing beat in her head. She inhaled a deep breath, "Sweetie, I'm OK."

The last thing she wanted to discuss was Chris, and Becky couldn't see past her own narcissistic need to express how right she had been about him.

Finally alone after all the commotion, Kate thought the house felt like a large voided space, much like her heart; when thoughts of Chris appeared, so did the tears. The only thing that lingered in the empty house was the tension from her devastating heartbreak.

It took Kate a moment to notice that the house was completely spotless. Not a woman who could sit still, her mother had kept herself busy as she cleaned the house, entertained the semi-guests, and made dinner. Despite the warm aroma of the chicken casserole that sat on the stovetop, and the grumble in Kate's stomach, she didn't have the energy to eat.

Beyond exhausted, she stumbled to the couch, flopped down, pulled the quilt off the back, and passed out the moment her head hit the small, tan, decorated pillow. Aika licked her hand, which hung over the edge, made two circles, and lay down next to her.

It had been a little longer than a week, and Kate had only maneuvered off the couch for the basic necessities. Startled from a deep slumber, she heard a loud knock on the door at 3:00 a.m. Concerned that there was an intruder, her eyes flew open, but she didn't budge from the couch, too scared to approach the door. Groggily, she stared at the clock. *Who the hell is here at this freaking hour?*

The lock hatch started to turn; Kate quickly grabbed the closest blunt object and braced herself for whatever was about to come through the door.

Suddenly, Alexa walked in with one of the bodyguards, who carried her luggage, all seven pieces. Alexa ordered the man around like a bellboy, and with a seductive smile, she gazed at him like a piece of meat. "Hmm. What a sweet ass," she murmured to herself. When he returned from the spare bedroom, Alexa slipped him a small piece of paper with a warm smile. "Thanks, Dan."

Returning an even friendlier smile, Dan replied, "You're welcome. Any friend of Kate's is a friend of mine." Immediately, he returned to his station on the front porch.

The ragged sight of her friend was shocking, and Alexa exclaimed, "Oh, my god! What the hell happened to you?"

"What are you doing here?" Kate protested weakly, the brass candlestick still firmly in her grip. "I thought you were a burglar! I could have killed you!"

"Yeah right, like someone is going to rob this place." Disgusted with the mess, Alexa's expression didn't hide her distaste, while she tried to find a clean spot to place her purse. "If someone got through the reporters and the bodyguards on steroids, do you think that your candlestick would really scare them away? Well, if the candlestick didn't, your hair would send anyone running in the opposite direction." All Alexa could do was laugh at her best friend. Kate began to feel extremely silly; she put the candlestick down and quickly tried to tame her wild mane, but her fingers got stuck in the large fuzzy tangles, causing a few more strands than expected to pull out as Kate muttered, "Ouch."

There were a few bright orange crumbs lodged into Kate's hair that sprinkled like dandruff. Repulsed, Alexa pulled up her purple sleeves. "That is disgusting," she complained. "It looks like I have my work cut out for me."

"What are you talking about?" This is exactly why Kate refused to have any visitors; she didn't want to face the judging look in people's eyes. Embarrassed, Kate turned away from the truth she didn't want to face and threw herself under the blue cotton comforter that had become her fort on the well-worn couch.

"Your mother called and told me you were becoming the night of the living dead. It looks like I might be too late."

She had hoped that her friend would allow her to continue in her wallow, but she knew that wasn't Alexa. Seconds later, Alexa jerked Kate by the wrist and dragged her into the bathroom. The florescent light made her eyes painfully squint as Alexa placed her directly in front of the mirror. It took her a minute to understand the purpose of this exercise. Then she realized that she didn't recognize the person staring back at her. This was not Kate. Slowly, her fingers grazed her face and she wondered how she let this happen. Pale skin, sunken cheeks, and dark purple circles under her eyes had consumed her.

Alexa is right; I'm becoming a monster.

The sound of the warm running water broke Kate's concentration to find Alexa smiling at her best friend, "OK, in you go!"

From outside the bathroom door, she heard, "I'll try to find you a clean towel."

Kate mumbled while the hot water engulfed her body, "Good luck."

While Alexa waited for Kate, she observed that the home had become a hazardous mess. Junk had expanded all throughout the house, the dishes had accumulated in the sink and emitted a vague foul odor from the food encrusted on them, and the trash had piled up to three large bags that lingered in the garage. This tornado was too big for Alexa alone; immediately, she called a cleaning service.

The hot shower felt great on Kate's skin as she washed away the grime that had built up over the past week. Slowly, life began to creep back into her body, even though she was full of mixed emotions. After the accident, she had become numb to any feelings, and she used that to protect herself, but deep down inside she knew that it wouldn't last forever. In a clean towel, she stepped out of the bathroom and walked to her room finding a clean outfit laid out on the bed. Exhausted, she dressed slowly, using the bedpost for support.

Just after Kate had made her damp tangles disappear, Alexa commanded, "Let's go."

"Go? Where are we going to go at four in the morning?"

"Four in the morning? What are you talking about?"

"It's four o'clock in the morning." To prove her point, Kate pointed toward the digital clock on the stove. It blinked as it changed from 4:04 to 4:05.

"Really?" In a sassy attitude, Alexa placed her manicured hand on her hip and responded in disbelief, "Have you lost all concept of time?"

It was obvious Kate was confused; her irritating guest walked to a window and yanked the curtain to the side. The bright sunlight stabbed her eyes; she squinted and blinked several times to adjust. A few moments later, Alexa let the curtain fall back into place - Kate and her eyes were thankful.

"We're going to your mother's," Alexa declared, walking into Kate's bedroom. "Where the hell is your purse?" she yelled out.

The small amount of energy that the shower provided had already begun to trickle away. Kate found herself back on the couch, exhausted with her eyes closed as she mumbled, "I don't know. It's in there somewhere."

It took a bit of searching, but Alexa found the dark purple purse hidden under the dusty bed, along with a pair of sunglasses and other random stuff.

"Here, you're going to need these." She threw the purse and sunglasses at Kate, forcing her to open her eyes.

Kate pulled herself from the couch, put on the glasses, and yawned as she cautiously followed her warden. The distance between the front door and the edge of her property, where the reporters still remained, was not that far. The moment the door opened, camera flashes began clicking away, and the sound of Kate's name seemed to howl.

The sight of people hounding her down was exactly what she didn't want. "Look at these fucking parasites! Can't I just go back to bed?"

"Are you nuts? Get your ass in that car!" The next thing Kate knew, Alexa had manhandled her right into the vehicle.

"Is this really necessary? Can't we just take my car?" Kate complained, but by the time the Town Car reached the end of the driveway, reporters began to bang fiercely on the hood, and a few even tried to open the door, scaring Kate in the process.

"Get it now? You need the damn car. Stop complaining," Alexa firmly clarified.

It had been longer than a week, yet the scandal surrounding Kate and Senator Reynolds was still the hottest topic. Every radio and TV station was trying their damnedest to get an exclusive interview with her. The cell phone under her dusty couch was filled with these types of messages.

Out on the open road Kate noticed, through the black tinted window, that not only had the reporters followed her, but also that the number of them increased. "This is insane! I didn't do anything to deserve all this attention! I just want my life to go back to normal."

Supportively, Alexa hugged her neck and whispered, "I think that it's a little too late for that."

Only a few houses away from Kate's parents, the garage door began to open. The sight of her personal garage door opener in a stranger's car made Kate irate. "How did you get one of those?" With no response from the driver, she banged on the glass window and demanded answers, "Did you go into my car?"

Alexa had never seen Kate act so irrationally before and without hesitation, she grabbed her by the back of her shirt, pulling Kate into the seat. "Seriously, did you think that he just left you with a bunch of morons to stand at your door?"

"Well, I didn't know," Kate, murmured. "How was I supposed to know?"

"By getting over your H.I.A.D." Both the driver and Dan laughed to themselves.

Unsure of what the acronym stood for, Kate glanced curiously, "My *what?*"

"Head In Ass Disease." Playfully, Alexa smiled at her friend while shaking her head.

Not amused by the teasing, Kate protested while fidgeting with a strand of her damp hair. "My head is not up my ass. After everything that has happened, I have a right to feel this way."

"You do have every right to feel how you feel, but you don't have the right to attack everyone who is trying to help you. Seriously, Chris has done everything humanly possible for you. There is protection not only at your house, but also at your parents'. The entire family has been given his and his personal assistant's number with an open invitation to call for anything at all. Then to top it off, he found the person who did this and made her publicly apologize." There was a pause and a heavy sigh from Alexa before she continued, "Do you think Chris is a complete idiot? Or do you think he knows a thing or two about being bombarded by strangers? You need to give him some credit and a phone call."

"Wait. What? Chris figured out who did this?" Kate couldn't believe her ears.

"Yea," Alexa nodded her head and continued, "You might want to turn on your TV or at least check Facebook." On the phone that Alexa handed Kate, she flipped to the article and read about how Susanna apologized and explained why she did it.

Despite this new information it was easier for Kate to stay mad at Chris. The car pulled into the garage and once the grinding sound of the large door closed, Kate dashed from the Town Car.

She didn't know why, but she expected her family to still be grieving as much as she was. They weren't. In the kitchen, Kate stood frozen, observing her family having a barbeque without her.

"See," Alexa whispered as she walked past her. "Life goes on with or without you, so you better get your shit in gear and get on board." Leaving Kate behind, Alexa walked out onto the patio to join the Woods family.

A warm, sunny Saturday afternoon, Mike was outside grilling hamburgers and hot dogs, while Emily was giving Elizabeth swimming lessons. Sandra had chosen her normal spot in the corner and chain-smoked her cigarettes.

The moment Elizabeth saw her aunt, she screamed in excitement. "Aunt Kate!" As fast as her little legs would take her, Elizabeth swam away from Emily, climbed out of the pool, and gave her favorite aunt a big wet hug.

Stunned by Kate's outfit, Emily couldn't help but blurt out, "What in the world are you wearing?"

After Alexa kissed Mike on the cheek, she made herself comfortable with a soda from the cooler, sat next to Sandra, and replied, "The only thing she had left in her closet. Literally." Casually, she leaned over and took a drag off Sandra's cigarette while she rolled her eyes at Kate.

Rooted in her cut-off, stonewashed shorts and her faded *Air Supply* T-shirt, Kate stood speechless until Mike hollered, "Are you going to come in or stand there like a bump on a log?"

Elizabeth waddled back to the pool with her floaters on, stopped at the edge, bent her knees, and prepared to jump. "Catch me, Grandma!"

Unsure of herself, she looked at Alexa for support, who just motioned her hand in the air for Kate to move forward.

Before she said hi to her father, she grabbed a towel off the outdoor rack and dried off the wet imprint of Elizabeth. She then walked shyly towards Mike, "Hey, Dad."

After he flipped the last burger and put down the spatula, he said, "How are you doing, kiddo?"

Out of sorts, she shook her head and mumbled, "I'll be OK."

"Of course, you will. You're the strongest woman I know." He turned to his daughter and gave her a big bear hug, like he used to do when she was younger. Those hugs always made Kate feel better.

"*Daaad.*" Embarrassed, she blushed and leaned into her father's comforting arms.

"Plus, he isn't really that bad of a guy." Before she could protest, her dad smiled at her, kissed her forehead, grabbed his drink, and walked toward Emily and Elizabeth. One of Mike's special gifts was the ability to give Kate the advice she needed without direct confrontation.

After she took another gulp from her third Coors Light, Sandra blurted out, "We watched you guys drive here." Kate just stared at her sister with a blank expression. "You know," Sandra continued, "On the news?" The TV attached to the stucco wall still flashed the reports, but the volume had been set on mute.

In need of a beverage, Kate went to the outdoor mini fridge and got herself a beer as she mumbled, "OK. Cool." The lack of a response from her sister frustrated Sandra, and she wasn't shy about it either.

Right before she could make another snide comment, Mike intervened. "It was kind of surreal. You would have thought that there was a high speed chase headed down Main Street the way the news described it."

"Grandpa, look at me!" Elizabeth shouted in Emily's arms, kicking her legs and splashing water in every direction as she tried to swim. On the white bench near the pool, Mike smiled, not only at his granddaughter, but his entire family.

Once Elizabeth paused her leg spasms for a second, Emily said, "It's been a bit hectic around here, with all of the media. Our daughter Kate, famous!"

"Can we please not talk about this?" Stressed, Kate didn't want to discuss the media spotlight that was ruining her life. "I just want one normal day without all the hype." She guzzled her beer.

Heeding her daughter's request, Emily pulled Elizabeth out of the pool inquiring, "So, tell me, Alexa, how is New York treating you?" Envious, Sandra rolled her eyes and focused her attention on the burning cigarette.

"It's going really well. I actually have a new job as an assistant editor."

Pleasantly surprised, Kate said, "I didn't know you changed jobs! When did this happen?"

"Three weeks ago. I met some great contacts at that charity event, and one thing led to another and here I am, editing for a fashion magazine."

"That is so cool. I'm happy for you." Kate smiled and hugged her best friend.

Wrapping Elizabeth in a humongous blue towel, Emily asked, "I'm so proud of you, sweetie. How does your father feel about it?"

"He says that I work too hard, which isn't far from the truth. I tend to work about eighty hours a week, but it will be worth it in the long run."

"Good for you, a bit of hard work never killed anyone." As the words rolled off her lips, Emily glanced at Sandra.

"What?" Sandra snapped at her mother as she finished off another beer.

"Did I say anything?" Emily defensively threw her hands in the air.

Annoyed, Sandra pulled out another pack of cigarettes, lit one up, and mumbled, "You gave me that look."

Close to dinner time, Emily took Elizabeth into her arms and went inside to change, but not before she commented, "I'm your mother; I'm supposed to give you looks."

When Kate and Alexa arrived back at Kate's house, the place was completely spotless. The cleaning crew had washed the dirty dishes, dusted, swept, and sanitized the house, they even washed her clothes and sheets. They'd made her bed and laid her clean clothes on it. It felt good to have her place return to normal. On the kitchen counter was a bill for four hundred dollars from Dora's Cleaning Service, made out to Kate Woods.

When she saw this, her heart skipped a beat; she looked at Alexa and said, "What did you do? Four fucking hundred dollars!"

With a smirk on her face, Alexa said, "Hey, you needed it—and I'm not paying to clean up your messes."

Chapter Eighteen

For the next couple of days, Alexa helped Kate get her life reorganized. The first and most important thing that had to be done was grocery shopping, since Kate had bone-bare cupboards. Three hours, two shopping carts, and three stock boys later, the girls finally finished their list and got everything back to the house and put away.

The second thing that needed to be done was sort through the excessive amount of voicemails. When Kate turned on her cell phone, it politely told her that she had 117 new messages.

"Damn Chris for getting me that extra storage." Kate cursed him under her breath. Every voicemail seemed to be from the same arrogant man who wanted to make her a star or wanted to tell her story, let the world see 'the real Kate'. The real Kate was going to punch these scumbags in their faces before they even got the chance to say *Hello*.

Every few messages, there would be one from Chris, who apologized again and again, desperate for a call back. The further along in the voicemails, the more pathetic his voice sounded, and for a brief moment, Kate felt bad and almost called him; but she talked herself out of it. Chris had broken a promise, and not just any promise—this was the promise that, if broken, would destroy her; and, it had.

It was Saturday night, and once again, Kate had no plans. Finally, her friends had had enough, and wanted her to come out with them. An intervention was needed, and Becky was the ringleader. They knew better than to call because Kate would have talked her way out of it—instead, they just showed up on her doorstep, prepared for an abduction.

"Who the hell could be here this late?" Kate mumbled to herself as she pulled her hair into a messy bun and walked to the door in her pink yoga pants.

Alexa had been wondering why they were home on a Saturday night. "It's not that late, it's only ten o'clock!" she mocked. "Geez, Kate, you're turning into an old woman."

Kate opened the door to find Becky, dressed in a dark blue, short-sleeved, collared shirt and dark denim jeans, with her hair spiked and smelling of freshly sprayed cologne, Kate knew immediately what she wanted.

"The answer is no!"

Without another word, she walked back into the house, leaving the door open.

"Come on, Kate!" Naturally, Becky followed her; she refused to return to the car empty-handed. "You need to get out of this house!"

"I second that," Alexa agreed, walking in from the other room.

"I don't feel like going."

"Hey Alexa. How have you been?" Becky nodded to Alexa who was flipping through channels on the couch. Alexa knew exactly what Kate needed. She floated to the couch where Kate sat pouting, put her skinny white arm around her shoulder, and whispered, "Babe—it's been two weeks, you need to move on." Still, Kate refused to listen. "OK," Alexa continued, "It's really simple, either get your ass up and go to the damn bar, or I'm going to de-friend you for life."

That caught Kate's attention. "You wouldn't?" she challenged.

Happy to see a passionate response, Alexa replied, "Try me." Without another word, Kate got up and slammed the bedroom door. Pleased with herself, Alexa smiled at Becky and said, "She'll be ready in a few minutes."

Impressed, Becky asked, "What about you?" That was all the invitation Alexa needed—in half a second, she was off the couch and in the spare room getting dressed.

The only gay bar in the area was a hole-in-the-wall and, despite Kate's warning, Alexa still decided to wear her pleated white pants, a silky purple blouse and three inch beige heels.

Kate came out of her bedroom dressed in her standard bar attire, a lacy black tank, and skinny jeans with her flip-flops. Neatly, Kate had pulled her hair into a simple ponytail.

Back in the living room, running the brush through her hair one last time, Kate questioned, "How are we going to get out there? I mean, get away from the reporters? It's been two weeks, and I still feel like I'm being stalked."

The media had begun to slow down, however, there were still stragglers that continued to incessantly follow her looking for any new angle possible. Rockledge was a small town, and a few of the regular visitors at the gay bar were not out-of-the-closet; the last thing Kate wanted was the media exposing their lives as well.

"Don't worry about that, I have an idea." When that smile appeared on Alexa's face, Kate began to worry—she knew they were bound to get into trouble.

Parked in the dirt lot of the Rainbow Room, Kate felt a new unexpected sense of excitement. This only led her mind to wanders to thoughts of Chris, wishing that he were with her causing her smile to briefly fade. With the clicking sound of a car door and Alexa chirping, *"Let's go,"* brought Kate back to her temporary happiness.

A few rows away from the entrance, Becky and a group of girls patiently waited for Kate and Alexa. There was someone new that she didn't recognize standing next to Becky. She was skinny, but there was something seductive about the way her jeans hugged her hips and a thin line of mid-drift revealed itself when she moved her arm. Not even a word was spoken between the two, and Kate already felt an attraction – almost unbecoming.

The sight of Kate without Chris brought sparkles to Becky's eyes. Eagerly, Becky wrapped her chubby arms around Kate's waist and whispered, "I've missed you."

Meekly, Kate smiled back, "I've missed you, too."

Happiness warmed her heart as she hugged and kissed each of her good friends: Holly, Megan, Charlotte and Beth. When she turned toward the new girl, awkwardness surrounded her as she suddenly became speechless.

Their eyes met, and butterflies began to stir in Kate's stomach. Her deep brown eyes were captivating, but she refused to be caught staring. "Hi," Kate said, trying to be casual. "I'm Kate. Nice to meet you."

Ashley gripped Kate's delicate hands firmly, "I know. We've already met."

Her smile disappeared into a thin line and, while she tried to pull back her hand, she could feel Ashley's fingers caressing hers. "I think you're confused, we've never met." This time Kate pulled her hand back to the safety of her side.

"Your name is Katherine Woods, correct?" Ashley's confident smirk lingered as she put the tips of her fingers into her tight jeans.

"Anyone who watches the news knows my name." If she had met Ashley before she would have remembered it, especially the way her stomach was doing somersaults. That's a feeling one doesn't forget.

Ashley flirted smoothly, biting her lower lip. "My name is Ashley Morris. *Officer* Morris." Despite the temptation in Ashley's eyes, there was an underlining tone that implied that Kate should know who she was.

"And, is that supposed to mean something?"

"Kate!" Becky couldn't believe her best friend's rudeness.

"Hmm?" Shifting her eyes from Ashley, Kate casually glanced at Becky, wondering why she was so upset.

"Officer Morris was at the house with me . . . you know . . . that day."

"Oh . . . " The memories quickly returned—flushed, Kate turned back toward Ashley and maintained her composure, "Well, it's nice to meet you again, Ashley."

The girl just smiled and continued to captivate Kate with her smoldering dark eyes.

The bar didn't take long to fill up on a Saturday night. By eleven, the girls had to squeeze shoulder-to-shoulder through the crowd to snatch a wobbly table in the back. The place hadn't changed in years. The single bar to the right surrounded by lesbians on the hunt for beer, the old faded red-velvet pool tables in the back, and the cheap worn-out linoleum dance floor that served as a stage for the performers.

"I've got the first round. Coors Light?" Kate eagerly suggested.

"Not a chance. Tonight we are celebrating your escape. All drinks on us." Becky smiled, taking Kate's debit card away.

"Aren't you just a barrel of laughs; I wasn't in prison," she smirked, tossing her hair and glancing in the opposite direction, which landed directly on Ashley. Quietly, Becky and Charlotte made their way to the bar and wrestled for a pitcher of beer and mugs.

Slamming her palms down on the unsecure table, Beth teasingly yelled, "Yeah, just on house arrest!"

Too busy scoping out the potentials for the night, Megan hadn't really participated in the conversation. Her attention became directed at Kate when she said, "Babe—we love you, but in all seriousness, it's been too damn long."

Charlotte and Becky returned, setting down two pitchers of Coors Light and frosted mugs.

"I'll drink to that!" Beth cheered, picking up her empty mug to fill.

"To Kate," the group said in unison, clinking their full glasses together.

For the first time in two weeks, Kate was beginning to feel normal again. Hanging out at a bar with her friends and drinking beer with no one questioning every detail of her life felt like a huge relief. Sadly, this feeling wouldn't last long.

Later in the evening, while the girls were laughing and reminiscing about their trip to the Grand Canyon, an unknown drunken woman approached the table glaring at Kate and slurred, "You're, that girl right? You're Kate Woods?"

Aside from the pulsing beat of the techno version of Rhianna's *Umbrella*, the table fell silent, everyone defensively stared at this woman.

"I'm sorry. You're mistaken...you have me confused with someone else," Kate politely replied.

The drunken woman, who now needed the table to maintain her balance, intrudingly squeezed between Kate and Alexa, hovering over Kate with her foul beer drenched breath, "No, I'm not mistaken."

No one at the table spoke, hoping that she would get the hint and leave. Instead she turned toward everyone else, looking for validation. "Oh, come on! Doesn't she look like Kate Woods?"

Not a word was spoken, but nasty glares shot at her like daggers, trying to encourage her to leave.

"Why are you guys so quiet? You're sitting next to a celebrity!"

Stumbling, the woman called out to one of her friends. In that instant Ashley jumped out of her chair, catching the woman off guard, and protectively growled, "She said that's not her, so leave it alone."

Staggering back toward her friends, the woman waved her hands in defeat, spilling her beer in the process. Impressed smiles appeared around the table. No one expected Ashley to speak up; usually it was Becky that was overly protective, especially when it came to Kate.

There was a twinge of self-disappointment that Becky hadn't stepped up to the plate sooner.

"Where did *that* come from?" Becky inquired. There was a mixture of confusion and curiosity, since at work Ashley was very quiet and seemed docile.

"I just know how to deal with annoying people." There was a notable confident tone in Ashley's voice, almost as if she was speaking down to Becky.

Allowing Ashley to enjoy her moment of glory, Becky ignored the tone. "You're so quiet at work; I didn't think that you had a mean bone in your body."

"Not mean, just protective." Proudly, Ashley smiled in Kate's direction, implying that she would be willing protect her anytime she wanted.

Meekly, Kate smiled back. "Well, whatever it was, thanks for getting rid of her."

Becky quietly watched the interaction between Kate and Ashley and didn't like what she saw.

It didn't take long for Beth to notice the sulky look on Becky's face and dragged her outside to smoke. The second Becky lit her cigarette, she opened her mouth to complain, but Beth cut her off, "What the hell is going on with you?"

The puff of smog surrounded Becky's lips as she exhaled, and she inserted her pack of cigarettes back into her shirt pocket. "I don't know," she mumbled. Beth knew what this was about. It was always about this.

"You need to woman up and tell Kate how you feel, and if you can't do that, then you need to let it go. Be happy for her, even if that means accepting the fact that she cares about Chris."

Just the sound of his name infuriated Becky as she lashed out, "Don't even bring him up! That guy has been nothing but bad news since day one. Look at what he did to her!"

The sleek Virginia Slim flicked an ash underneath Beth's index finger while she argued, "Don't you watch the news? It wasn't his fault, and as much as you hate to admit it, he might actually be good for her."

"How can you say that?" Was betrayal everywhere? Becky couldn't believe her own friends were turning against her. The vein in her forehead pulsed violently as she yelled out, "And since when did you start believing the crap on TV?" The mere thought of Kate falling for Chris was incomprehensible to Becky. Just thinking about his name made her blood boil.

"Look at how happy she is. I haven't seen her smile like that since Riley. Don't you want her to be happy?"

"I do want her to be happy." A long pause followed that sentence as she thought to herself that she wanted Kate to be happy with *her*. Not Ashley or Chris.

The internal debate inside of Becky was strong. Simply put, she feared that Kate didn't feel the same way and the rejection would crumble the friendship. This would be more than she could bear and instead of facing her emotional dilemma, she continued to put a wall around her heart.

"Besides, why are you getting so upset with Ashley? They just met! They aren't running off to get married."

In an attempt to make light of the situation, Becky threw her cigarette on the gravel and put it out under her Doc Marten. "You never know; lesbians and their U-Hauls . . . " Knowing that there was too much truth to that statement, they both laughed.

Beth took one long last puff. "You know Kate better than I do, but I've never pegged her to be the U-Haul type."

The club door opened and with it so did the blaring music, causing Becky to basically yell, "I guess." Through the crowded bar, Kate smiled at her, and instantly Becky's heart fluttered.

It didn't surprise Kate that halfway through the night, she and Ashley were left alone at the table. For a few moments they sat silently drinking their beers and gazing out into the crowd, unintentionally trying to avoid eye contact. The quietness that lingered between them made Kate's nerves jitter more, until she finally spoke up, "So, what brought you to Rockledge?"

"Needed a change…so I pulled out a map, threw my finger down, and here I am." Side by side, Ashley shifted her position more toward Kate, trying to capture her every detail.

"That's a bit risky, isn't it?" Idly, Kate let her index finger twirl along the rim of her mug.

"Life is all about the risk." Propping her elbow on the table, Ashley was able to lean closer, her knee brushing against Kate's.

The contact stimulated Kate's senses giving her heart a little jolt. She nervously stuttered, "Why did you need a change?"

The flirting smile that Ashley had enticed her with quickly faded away along with the welcoming body language. This was not something she wanted to discuss, but the sweet curiosity in Kate's eyes was irresistible.

"My girlfriend of six years and I broke up."

"Geez, I'm sorry." She was sympathetic but it wasn't what she had expected from Ashley. "If you don't mind, what happened?"

"She broke a promise." Ashley's words were flat and to the point. It was obvious that Ashley didn't want to discuss her past relationship, but unfortunately Kate's intoxication urged her to pry.

"Seriously, you ended a six year relationship over a small promise?" The bewilderment in her voice was painfully obvious. Judging Ashley for her decision, she instantly began to think about Chris. *Did I do the same thing? End a relationship over a petty promise?* Kate quickly dismissed the comparison. There was none to be had; Chris had allowed something to happen that basically destroyed Kate's life.

"Depends on the promise," Ashley replied sadly, "Sometimes a broken promise is irreparable."

"What was the promise?"

Ashley made a loud coughing sound, stood up from her stool, and almost angrily asked, "Do you need another beer?" Quietly, Kate shook her head.

Chris crept back into her thoughts again while she swirled the last swallow of beer in her mug. There was a gnawing feeling in her stomach that she might have overreacted, but the feeling quickly subsided when the group returned, sweaty from the dance floor.

After another week, most of the media had moved onto new stories, and Kate's life was slowly beginning to return to normal. Alexa had gone home, and without her, Kate found herself alone, forced to deal with things she'd rather not, like Chris, or if she should return Ashley's three phone calls.

Chapter Nineteen

During this complicated time, Kate had finally admitted to herself that she might have become hysterical toward Chris. Deep down, she knew all along that he never meant her harm and only wanted to provide her with happiness. But the simple task of calling and verbally admitting her error was easier said than done.

At home, she enjoyed a quiet quick lunch on the patio before she headed to the local community center to sign up for after-school classes. The summer was ending, and the center required all volunteers to have their documents prepared in advance. Kate found it hilarious that she had to *apply* to volunteer, but in the end all she cared about were the kids.

The community center building was old and in desperate need of an upgrade. Unfortunately, the entire place ran off the good deeds of volunteers and charitable donations from businesses, individuals, and of course, a few government grants. Even with all of that, it still barely held on by a thread. The paint, both inside and out, had started to fade and chip away. All of the toys and sporting equipment had either been bought secondhand or donated through fundraising events. The facility used to have a pool, but due to extreme cutbacks from the government, they had to drain it and cancel swim classes.

The manager, Carlos, had worked for months to get the government officials to extend their grant. Endless letters had been written, several phone calls had been made, and even after a few trips to the state capital, each and every time he'd been told the same thing: *Nothing can be done; there is no more money; the center will have to wait until next year's budget.*

While Kate was filling out the same forms that she had the previous year, she noticed that Carlos had a visitor in his office. Their conversation seemed to be pleasant; they were laughing and carrying on. Even though she couldn't see who was in there with him, she was happy to see Carlos smile as, most of the time, he was stressed and worried about how he would be able to keep the doors open for another week.

Still writing her information, a familiar voice rang in the background. Kate's pen stopped immediately as her head surveyed the room looking for this particular person –the only one there was a receptionist. Feeling as though she had lost her mind, she shook it off and continued with the form. A few minutes later there was a loud laugh that sent a wave of mixed emotions through her. Sticking her head into the manager's office, Kate's jaw dropped when she found Chris sitting across from Carlos. Both men stopped mid-conversation and stared at her.

Despite the scowl on Kate's face, Carlos happily greeted her, "Kate, what a surprise! It's so nice to see you again."

Glaring at Chris, she completely ignored Carlos. "What are you doing here?" she demanded.

Before Chris could respond, Carlos answered in a pleasant but confused tone, "He's here to rebuild the facility!" Even though she heard Carlos, her eyes never once glanced in his direction.

"You think you can waltz in here and throw your money around, like it's going to make everything better?" she accused bitterly. Wisely, Carlos decided to remain silent as he tried to figure out what was going on. Until now Chris remained quiet, sitting calmly with a relaxed facial expression, patiently waiting for Kate to finish.

"You're the one that told me I should do something good with my money." The one thing Chris knew how to do was get under Kate's skin. Smugly, he just smiled at her, watching the anger grow on her face.

"Ugh! You're impossible!" Irate, she stomped her way out of the office and didn't slow down until she reached her car. Keys in her hand, she was about to unlock the door and drive away . . . but something made her hesitate.

Chris had politely excused himself from Carlos's office and followed her to the bare parking lot.

"What's the matter with you?" he yelled furiously. "And what the *hell* is your problem?" Firmly, he grabbed Kate's shoulders, spinning her around so they were face-to-face. He had reached his breaking point; no longer was he going to let Kate bully him when he did nothing wrong.

"You're the one that said that I had a responsibility to do something good with my money!" he continued, when she didn't respond. "You're the one that inspired me to become a better person! You're the one that has completely changed my world, and for the better—you're the one that showed me that the world doesn't revolve around me! Well, guess what— it doesn't revolve around you, either! Yes, I made a mistake by making you a promise that I couldn't keep, but guess what? I'm human, and part of having a relationship is the ability to forgive and move on. But no, you can't do that. Can you?"

The harshness of his words left Kate feeling paralyzed while tears began to well in her eyes. It had been years since someone was that painfully honest with her, and when she looked into his deep brown eyes and saw the hurt she'd caused, her tears began to steadily fall.

Silence engulfed them for what felt like an eternity until Chris finally softened his expression and loosened his grip.

Kate had to work through the lump in her throat, but once she did the sincere words of, "You're right, I'm sorry," came out in between the sobs.

There was nothing else for Chris to hear so he embraced her tightly and whispered, "I missed you, too."

Without warning, Chris cupped Kate's hand into his and led her through the parking lot, across the two-lane street, and over to the beach. Arm in arm, they walked in the sand and talked about everything that had happened during the past few weeks.

Kate slipped off her sandals, carried them in one hand while she asked, "How did you figure out it was Susanna that was behind it all?"

With a proud smile, Chris looked at her. "I have my ways," he replied, kissing her on the forehead. There was no possible way he could ever reveal everything he did to right the wrong that was done. Those secrets he would take to the grave.

Kate's lips twisted up knowing better, "You're not going to tell me what really happened, are you?"

"Nope."

Her eyes narrowed into a playful gaze, "You know I don't like secrets."

Happily, he squeezed her hand and changed the subject. "This is one you can live with. So—what have you been up to while I was away?"

"Not much. Alexa came into town for a little bit. She pulled me out of my funk." Embarrassed, her cheeks became flushed, and she lowered her eyes toward the sand under her feet.

"I heard about that."

"I'm sure you heard about a lot of things, since you were keeping tabs on me." Kate playfully pulled on Chris's arm implying that it was not necessary.

"Of course, I was keeping tabs on you!" he responded teasingly. "What did you expect? Did you think I was going to leave you completely unprotected? What kind of guy do you take me for?"

Unsure of how to answer that question, she just shrugged her shoulders. Chris smiled at how adorable she looked. "So I hear you snuck by my guards one night?"

Busted! Her face turned bright red; she should have known that he would find out about it. It was frustrating how he never missed anything, even when he was away it was almost like he was still there. *Almost.*

"Nothing ever gets past you, does it?"

"Well, I haven't figured out where you went that night. No one seems to know, not even Dan." Chris chuckled to himself at how bad of a liar Dan was.

"Oh, really?" Kate grinned. "Your best bodyguard couldn't figure out where we went? I bet he was surprised that we snuck out."

"It's strange he has no idea. Personally, I think he was trying to impress a girl, but I could be wrong. So, how did you get out?"

Badly, Kate tried to bat her eyelashes and smirked, "A girl never reveals her secrets."

"Fair enough. But seriously, where did you guys go?"

"Alexa and some friends dragged me out to the local gay bar." Particular moments of the night flashed through her mind, and a semi-seductive smile curled upward with thoughts of Ashley.

In an attempt to pry some gossip out of her, Chris asked, "So . . . tell me about it. Did you meet anyone?"

"Wait." Confusion struck Kate. "Just a minute ago, you were being overprotective, and now you want details?" A huge gust of wind from the ocean swirled Kate's hair covering her face, and her fluttering her skirt rapidly around her legs causing her to stumble, right into Chris's arms.

Once she was back on steady ground, he gently wiped the hair from her face and clarified, "I was protecting you from the media, not from yourself. You could have gone out and taken the guards with you for all I cared. I never wanted you to be stuck inside your house, miserable."

Unsuccessfully, Kate wrestled with her hair trying to remove the strands from whipping against her cheeks. "Well, I was miserable," she uttered.

The sight of Kate's pouty lips tugged at his heartstrings, and then politely he stepped into the breeze whispering, "I'm sorry."

Chris being near, the feeling of his hand in hers, was giving her relief. The fight left her feeling empty and hollow; it was the same feeling when Riley passed away.

She hoped that she had distracted Chris long enough to forget what he originally asked, but he quickly reminded her of it. "So you didn't tell me, did you meet anyone the other night?"

Damn it, Kate thought. She wasn't ready to divulge her heart-palpitating details of Ashley, especially to Chris, so she decided to play casual, "Yeah, I met a girl."

The sudden shyness surprised him and he continued to pry, "Well? Give me the details. Don't hold back now."

"There isn't much to tell. We met, she seems really nice, we exchanged numbers, and that's it. Really not much at all."

"She didn't call you?"

"No, she called; I just haven't returned any of them." Meekly avoiding Chris's stares of bewilderment, she lowered her head, digging her freshly manicured toes into the sand.

The evasiveness was beginning to annoy him. "Why not? Don't you like her?"

"No ... she's fine. We had a connection, just not sure if I want anything serious." A small, seductive smirk appeared while she slowly bit her lower lip and dwelled on the instant spark between her and Ashley. Then Kate's mind wandered towards Riley and the guilt stung, causing her eyes to shift back to the sand. The idea of allowing herself to be vulnerable scared her half to death.

Immediately, she dropped Chris's hand and walked away toward the dunes. On the soft sand, she stared out into the ocean and watched the waves crash onto the shore; with the pale blue sky and cotton white clouds above, she remembered the long days she and Riley had spent at the beach.

Chris could always tell when Riley was on her mind – she'd idly fidget with her rings with a dazed look upon her face. The pain she felt when she lost her wife of eight years was agonizing, but the seeping black hole Riley left in Kate's heart was torturous. Only left with memories, comforting at times, but memories of Riley were the chains holding her back from moving forward.

Chris didn't give Kate long by herself, sitting down next to her, and leaning against her shoulder, he asked, "All right, girl, what's going on?"

Kate sighed, releasing the rings from her motioning fingers, "I'm not sure. I feel like I can't date Ashley; I made a promise that Riley was the only woman I loved."

"I get why you think that, but honestly you need to start moving on with your life."

"I know ... but ... "

"But nothing. You have a right to be happy." His voice was firm and full of resolve.

"I wasn't given a handbook at the funeral. What is the proper amount of time to grieve the love of your life?"

"You mean the handbook at your coming out party doesn't cover this?" The smirk on his face was priceless, and Kate couldn't resist. Her lips turned upwards as she chuckled out loud, shaking her head at his silly sense of humor.

Happy to see Kate smile, he held her tightly and continued, "There is no right or wrong decision. You just have to follow your heart."

"Well then, I'm screwed, because I don't know what my heart says." The smile turned back upside down in a twisted manner. Feeling hopeless, she threw her head in between her knees, wanting nothing more than to forever disappear.

"You're going to be fine. You're just too stubborn for your own good." Chris leaned forward allowing his elbow to fall on his bent knee while resting his head on his balled up fist, waiting for Kate to come up for air.

Just like clockwork, Kate popped up and spouted, *"Am not."* She threw her hair back behind her shoulders, pulled it up in a messy bun, turned toward Chris, and stuck her tongue out at him. It rattled on her nerves that he knew her so well.

"See, you're going to be just fine."

"I can't believe I'm taking love advice from you!" The irritation rang in her voice as she stood up brushing the sand from her black skirt. Unfortunately, she was not conscious enough to move away from Chris, and the sand blew directly in his mouth. The gritty feeling was impossible to get out, no matter how many times he spit and wiped his tongue with his shirt. "Ugh, thanks."

She smiled proudly and giggled at his sour look while she began to walk toward the water. When she glanced over her shoulder, there was Chris chasing after her – a cute squeak and a hop, and Kate quickly picked up her pace.

From across the street she gazed into the parking lot and noticed a newly parked royal blue Mercedes. There was Sam, leaning against the driver's side door with her head down, buried in a cell phone.

Eager to cross the street, Kate quipped, "What's she doing here?" More out of habit than actual concern, Chris tugged on her wrist, preventing her from crossing the small street until he deemed it safe.

"She's helping me with a project." There it was - the tiny smirk in the corners of his mouth that told her something big was about to happen.

Prestigiously dressed in her red heels and a plaid mini-skirt, Sam excitedly pushed away from the car and darted towards Kate. Overly excited, her spunky friend animatedly squeaked out, "Oh. My. I've missed you so much!" It didn't take long for Kate's lungs to gasp for air under her death grip hug. Barely able to speak, she managed to cough out, *"I. Can't. Breathe."*

After a long moment and an extra squeeze, Sam released her grip, and Kate deeply inhaled a fresh breath of air.

"Sorry. I've just missed you," she apologized, laughing.

Kate smiled. "I'm OK." In between her large gasps of air she asked, "So—what are you doing here?"

"I'm helping with the rebuild of the community center!"

A project – Now it made sense why they were in town, but Kate was happy nonetheless.

"I had to let her come along," Chris mumbled, as he casually slung his arm around Kate's shoulder.

In a sassy tone, Sam pointed her index finger at him in a circular motion and exclaimed, "You let me *come along*. All of this would never have happened if it weren't for me! Face it, Chris, you need me more than you can admit."

Amused by Sam's attitude, Kate held back her laugh as she inquired, "So, what are you guys doing tonight?"

Red in the face from the blazing sun, Chris shrugged his shoulders and said, "No plans. The project doesn't start until Monday, so we were just going to hang out."

Slyly, Sam glanced at him as she admitted to Kate, "We didn't really know if we were going to see you or not."

"Oh, please! You planned it so we would run into each other!" She squinted from Chris to Sam and then back to Chris, and immediately their guilty faces showed her she was right. Firmly, Kate continued, "Anyways, I'm having a party tonight, and you guys should come, and I'm not taking no for an answer."

In sync, they eagerly accepted, "Of course."

Kate's head began to swivel around the parking lot looking for Chris's car, but it was nowhere to be found. He clarified the confusion on her face as he explained that he and Sam arrived in town together.

Kate followed the blue Mercedes to Chris's Azteca style house he recently purchased. They quickly dropped off the car, the staff gathered the luggage, and everyone scrambled into Kate's blue Honda.

The first stop on Kate's list was a grocery store, and Sam stayed in the car to make a call. Behind the deli's large glass counter, an older gentleman, dressed in a white chef's uniform, greeted Kate. A few moments later, he returned from the back with two large trays filled with an array of subs. With a smile, he placed the trays on the counter and spun around for a second time. This time, he returned with a veggie platter.

Chris picked up the trays causing Kate to yell nervously, "Don't drop those!"

"Oh relax, I got them." *She worries too much,* he thought to himself. *One of these days she's going to rupture an artery from all her worrying.*

In the checkout line, Kate waited patiently while she rattled her keys and blankly stared at the tabloids – she was relieved to notice her face had disappeared from the covers.

Kate carefully placed the trays into the trunk of her car and got behind the wheel. Before the key even went into the ignition, Kate buckled her seat belt and readjusted her mirrors. She turned toward Chris and noticed that his seat belt wasn't fastened.

"Put your seat belt on," Kate directed. He gave her an odd look, but complied.

The tires turned out of the parking lot and onto the almost deserted street, but Kate's speed barely increased. Kate noticed the dashboard clock displaying 2:00 p.m. and cursed, "Shit. I have to get back to the house by 2:30."

"Then you might want to drive a *little* faster," Chris teased. "This is worse than *Driving Miss Daisy.*"

"Cut me some slack. Today is my first day driving since…you know."
Chris hadn't considered that her hardship revolved around a car accident,
and a ting of guilt hit him.

"You're right. Take all the time you need," Chris smiled, and then
laughed. "We'll just be eighty when we get there." Both Sam and Chris
chuckled out loud.

"Bite me!" Kate smirked.

Sam got a great idea for the party. Immediately, she texted someone,
and a nanosecond later she had an incoming text message with information
on where she could find it: Gelada's Party Store.

Without looking up from the screen, Sam called, "Hey, Kate, I need to
go to Gelada's Party Store!"

Surprised by her request, she glanced up at Sam through the rearview
mirror. "What do you need there?"

"Just stuff." A simple response was all Kate got.

"OK, but you have to be quick; I'm running late enough as it is."

"Not a problem. It'll be quick."

This is going to be awesome, Sam thought smiling.

It didn't take long to get to Gelada's Party Store, in fact, it didn't take
long to get anywhere in the Rockledge area. In a rush, Kate simultaneously
turned off the engine, unlatched her seatbelt, and began to pull herself out
of the car until Sam stopped her, "No. You wait here. I'll get the stuff."
Quickly, she jumped out and hurried in the store. Kate thought about
following her, but when she looked in the mirror Sam was already opening
the green painted door labeled *Gelada's Party Store,* so instead, she leaned
back in her seat and whispered to herself sarcastically, "Oh, OK."

On the passenger side, Chris leaned back with his eyes closed.

It only took him a moment to feel Kate, who was watching him
closely. With only their eyes, they fell deeper into a spiritual connection,
surprising them both.

The intense moment was interrupted by Sam's abrupt entrance,
startling them both back to their own fabric seat. Carelessly, Sam tossed in
the bags and slammed the door behind her.

"Jumpy, aren't we? What were *you* doing?"

Like two teenagers caught with their hands in the liquor cabinet,
quickly they glanced at each other and nervously answered in sync,
"Nothing!"

Not believing a word, Sam looked from one to the other as she
mumbled, "*Sure.*"

This time, Kate didn't speed out of the parking lot like a bat out of
hell, she slowly put her seat belt on and asked Sam as she put the car in
drive, "So—what did you get?"

"You'll see." A cunning smile appeared as Sam playfully pulled the large bags closer so Kate couldn't peek through the rearview mirror. Kate shot Chris a concerned look.

"Don't look at me!" he laughed. "I have nothing to do with this one."

Politely, she offered, "Well, at least let me know how much it is, so I can pay you back."

"No."

"You're my guest," Kate argued, gripping the steering wheel firmly. "You don't have to pay for anything."

"I know. Just think of it as a gift."

Aggravated, she just growled to herself. Confused as to what the big deal was, Sam leaned forward and whispered to Chris, "Is she always this difficult with you?"

With a smirk on his face, he shook his head and patted Sam's hand on his shoulder. "Welcome to my world," he whispered. "She has an issue with letting people buy her things."

"Why?"

"I don't know. But she nearly ripped my head off when I tried to buy her dinner the first night I came into town."

"Oh, my . . . "

"Hey . . . I'm still sitting right here, and I can hear you!" Kate interrupted. "And I didn't rip your head off!"

Amused by her selective memory, Chris laughed. "Oh, yes, you did! Don't you remember I had to yank the bill out of your hand?"

"In my defense," she snapped sassily, "I didn't know you, and I didn't want you to expect anything."

Sam just sat in the backseat and giggled while the two of them bickered like an old married couple.

Turning the corner onto her street, Kate's nerves started to twinge as she remembered that Becky would be there. After the whole fiasco with Chris, Becky had made it perfectly clear how she felt about him and was ecstatic he had left.

What is she going to think when she sees him? Or worse, what is she going to say?

From down the street, Kate could see the bright, candyapple red Ford F-150 pickup truck parked in her driveway. Caddy-cornered to the truck, Kate pulled the Honda up and placed the gear shift into park. Becky slid out of the pickup and stretched out her short legs.

Kate sighed with a concerned look and said to Chris, "Give me a minute."

Supportively, with a gentle hand on Kate's shoulder to let her know that everything would be okay, he whispered back, "I'll be here if you need me."

"Thanks."

"What's going on?" Sam asked as the driver's door slammed shut.

"Becky and I don't necessarily see eye-to-eye on things. She thinks that I'm bad for Kate."

Sam stared angrily at Becky through the windshield. "Did she say that?"

"She doesn't have to; it's written all over her face."

"Well, that's just crazy!" Sam lashed out, all riled up. "You want me to go beat that bitch up?" Seconds away from dashing out the door, Sam was prepared to go slap some sense into this girl, but before she could grab the handle, Chris interjected.

In his most serious tone, he demanded, "Sam, sit down! You are not going to do anything." The last thing he needed was for her to make things worse. Unhappy about his decision, Sam just threw herself back into the seat and intently watched Kate talk to her friend.

Becky's smile glowed when she saw Kate walking towards, her but it quickly faded when she spotted Chris. Nervously, Kate continued smiling, "You weren't waiting long, were you?"

"Nah, I just got here." Becky hugged her and tried to maintain her composure, but the sight of Chris in the front seat sent her into a tizzy. Furious that he had the nerve to show up, she growled through her teeth, "What is he doing here?"

In a calm soothing voice Kate tried to explain, "Becky, we worked things out."

"He has no right to be here!" The sound of her voice rose the longer she stared at him sitting in there. "How could you work things out after what he did to you? You can't work that out!"

Softly, Kate spoke, "It was a misunderstanding." Stunned that Kate would defend *him* after everything was an insult to Becky, and she took it as such.

"A misunderstanding? A misunderstanding? Because of him your private life was plastered all over the news. How can you forgive that?"

The soft tone of Kate's voice had been replaced with a sharper, firm one. "*He* didn't plaster my business on the news, Susanna Hillman did. He's the one that found out about it and kept me protected from the media." Each excuse she made for him drove Becky mad. At that moment, it took all of her strength not to drag him out of the car.

"I don't care who did it! The only reason this happened is because of him! Why can't you see he's no good for you?" The rage slowly began to dissipate into a begging plea. She desperately wanted Kate to see that Chris would never love her the way she did.

She'd had enough. Kate had made her decision, and Becky would have to come to terms with it. In a tone that her friend wasn't accustomed to hearing Kate snapped, "Becky, you're going to have to accept the fact that he is a part of my life! Why is that so bad?"

Instead of surprise, she returned the attitude and barked, "Because he is trying to *convert* you!"

There was a silent moment of shock where Kate couldn't comprehend what she had just heard. "Seriously? That has to be the stupidest thing you've ever said. No one can convert me; I am who I am."

"Yes, I'm serious. Men don't do the stuff he has done for you without expecting something in return. How can you be that naïve?"

The minor dispute quickly turned into a loud brawl, and when Kate became flustered, Chris was ready to intervene. She heard the car door creak open, and even though her face was red hot she held her hand up to Chris, silently demanding more time. Unwillingly, Chris remained in the car.

Taken off guard, Kate grabbed Becky by the soft flesh of her underarm and dragged her into the house. The door slammed loudly behind them.

No sooner had the latch clicked into place did Kate begin to attack. "Have you lost your fucking mind? Is that what you *really* think of me? That a guy can do a few simple nice gestures and I'm going to fall head over heels right into his bed?" Each intense step she took closer, Becky stumbled one backwards fearing the blood rage look in Kate's eyes.

Quickly, she tried to backpedal, "That's not what I meant!"

Another step forward and Kate growled, "Then, what? What did you mean?"

Terrified to say the wrong thing, she stuttered, "I don't know . . ."

With one last step, Kate had her completely backed into a corner. With nowhere to go, Becky's head hit the wall, and Kate yelled, "I'm not that kind of person, and you know that! I would never be with anyone because of money! I don't need anyone's money . . . Remember, I have more than enough of my own . . . and at a deep cost."

Before Becky could stop herself the words flew out of her mouth, "You're not being rational. It's been a long time since someone has been interested in you, and you're latching on to him like a lost puppy."

The spiteful words were insults slung at a cheap attempt to imply doubt in Kate's sexuality, which felt like a betrayal. With Becky still hovered in a defensive position, Kate's rage released thoughts of beating her to a bloody pulp. Even Becky began to believe that she would strike, but to both of their surprises, Kate stepped away from her now timid friend. Her eyes were still narrowed in hate, and her fists shook like a seizure, and after the longest deep breath Becky had ever witnessed, Kate clarified, "There is nothing between Chris and me. There will never be anything between Chris and me! So get it through your head that he is JUST a friend!"

Now that there was distance between them, Becky began to feel her self-righteousness return, "Friends? You two act more like lovers than *just* friends."

"Jesus Fucking Christ! There *isn't*, and you need to stop being so cynical and overbearing!" The frustration exploded as Kate pounded her tight fists together, trying to keep them from making contact with Becky. "If you took a moment to stop bitching about him and talk to him, hell, you might actually like the guy."

Becky wanted to rebut, but mostly she wanted to reach out to Kate. The window of opportunity disappeared when there was a knock on the door. Naturally, Kate's head turned toward the entry as Chris poked his head around the corner and whispered, "Is it safe to enter?" Kate's scowl smoothed into an appreciative smile.

The happiness that lit up Kate's face by the simple appearance of Chris did nothing but enrage Becky. All she could do was stand there; silently, nastily glaring at Chris behind Kate's back. The argument subsided when Sam entered the room, demanding all the attention as she struggled with large awkward bags. Dragging them she panted, "Is anyone going to help me?"

Politely, Chris removed the burden of the bags and placed them in the corner of the kitchen. The sound of high heels clicking toward Becky sent shivers down his back as he feared what Sam would say.

"Hi! I'm Sam. I don't believe we've met." Her radiating smile brightened the whole room. Chris exhaled his tightly held deep breath in relief by her exaggerated sweetness toward the hateful girl.

However, the pleasantness wasn't reciprocated as she grumbled back, "I'm Becky." Despite the rude response Sam held her hand up in mid-air, patiently waiting for Becky to shake it. Once their hands connected Sam continued, "It's nice to finally meet you; Kate has said so much about you. All good things, of course."

"Hmp...wish I could say the same." In spite of the nasty tone, Sam's smile didn't falter. Secretly, it pleased Becky tremendously to hear Kate was talking about her. *Maybe there was still hope?*

Smoothly, Sam gently placed her hand on Becky's shoulder and sweetly said, "That's OK; we'll have plenty of time to get to know each other."

While Kate and Sam unpacked the bags that were brought in, which was full of lesbian-themed party supplies, Chris returned with party trays from the car. Embarrassed, Kate blushed at the sight of the napkins with tacky pictures of women on it. Becky on the other hand couldn't have been more thrilled with the idea.

"Becky, were you able to get firewood and the ring?" Kate asked.

Proudly, she boasted, "Of course; it's in my truck."

It had been months since the last beach bonfire, and Kate was excited that the weather was finally cooling down at night. "Sweet. You're the best! Love ya." Kate threw her arms around Becky and gave her a quick peck on the cheek. The flush of Becky's cheeks turned bright pink at the sound of those words. From across the room, when Kate turned away, Becky glared at Chris, reminding him that he doesn't belong. *She loves me, not you, so just leave!*

"Let's get it set up before everyone gets here," Kate said.

Smugly, Becky strolled toward the door with a chip on her shoulder, that was until Chris chimed in, "I'll help." Frozen with her hand on the brass doorknob, she couldn't believe his nerve. The last person she ever wanted help from was Chris Cody, and while she wanted to tell him such, she couldn't resist when she turned around and spotted Kate silently pleading for them to get along. In snotty tone, Becky summoned Chris like a Border collie, "Come on!"

Passing Becky in the hallway, Chris heard her mumble something to the effect of, *I don't need a man to help me unload a truck.* Politely, Chris ignored the comment and waited outside for Becky to unlock the pickup.

One log flew at his Chris's head, then another, and another; while Becky agreed to let him help she never said that she would be nice about it. Instead of chucking one of the logs back at her head, Chris tried to redirect her attention. "How long have you know Kate?"

Becky paused, gripping the base of a log in the palm of her hand. Chris half-expected her to chuck it even harder at him, but surprisingly, she condescendingly answered the question, "It's been years." This time Becky handed him the log.

"She doesn't talk about you much."

"Of course, she doesn't. Privacy is extremely important to her, but I guess you learned that the hard way, didn't you?" Another log went flying at his head.

"Hey! You know damn well that wasn't my fault, so cut the bullshit."

"Seriously, why are you here? You two have nothing in common."

"I'm here because she wants me to be here, and you better get it through your thick skull that as long as she does, I will be here, regardless of your pathetic looks." Chris paused for a moment to cool his tone and continued, "I know what you think of me, and in your mind you're just protecting Kate, but I just want what's best for her."

These too-perfect answers drove Becky mrad, but she knew as long as he remained on Kate's good side there was nothing she could do. In the meantime, she would watch Chris carefully, looking for anything to use against him.

∞

There was only an hour left before guests would arrive, and Kate still needed to get ready. After a quick hot shower, she raced to her bedroom, wrapped in a white towel, hoping no one saw her dripping wet with tangles galore. A pair of jeans and a purple shirt were all she needed before she dried her hair and dabbed makeup on her small blemishes.

Fifteen minutes to spare! —or so Kate thought, until there was a knock at the door. When she ran to get it, she noticed that Chris and Sam were sitting quietly on the couch, while Becky had isolated herself outside on the patio with a cigarette, in the hopes that the nicotine would calm her anger.

On the porch, Megan was dressed in khaki shorts with a blue popped-collar shirt, rolling a cooler on wheels behind her. In their hug, it didn't take Megan long to notice Chris in the living room. An almost I-told-you-so smirk appeared as she said, "So, I see you guys kissed and made up."

"Just made up. No kissing." It was a relief to know that at least one of her friends didn't have a problem with Chris.

Walking by, Megan mumbled loud enough so that only Kate could hear, "Not yet." Purposely, Kate ignored that comment and returned to the kitchen.

"Hey, Chris. Good to see you again," Megan cheerfully greeted while she dragged her heavy cooler to the patio. At the sliding glass door she continued, "Thought you were going to be in exile forever." It didn't take her long to prop her cooler against the side of the house, grab a cold one, and return inside.

Happy to see a friendly face, Chris hugged her, "Good to see you, too."

"It's a good thing Kate came to her senses, or we would have never seen you again."

From the kitchen, Kate yelled across the room, "I heard that!"

"We meant you to!" Megan hollered back.

Until now, Sam remained quiet on the couch. Chris turned to her for an introduction, and Megan's jaw dropped. Sam slowly rose and smiled at Megan, who smiled back like a giddy teenager. Smoothly, Megan took Sam's hand, kissing the back of it and whispered softly, "Nice to meet you."

"Oh, my. . ." Sam's porcelain cheeks started to flush pink like rose petals as Megan's lips touched her skin. "It's been years since a someone has done that."

"I'm glad I could be that someone." Sam's eyes opened wide with intense curiosity, and without another word, Megan politely excused herself happily, noticing the shocked look on Chris's face.

"Stop staring at me like that," Sam angrily whispered to him.

Scratching his head like a confused monkey he asked, "When did you start liking girls?" Chris's words muffled in the background while Sam gazed out the patio door sneaking another peek at Megan.

"Can't a girl just have fun?"

"Yes, she can." Kate came up behind Sam, wrapped her arms around her, kissed her softly on the cheek, and whispered in her ear, "Have fun."

"All right then. You girls do what you do. I'm just going to stay out of the way." Defeated, Chris threw his hands in the air and sought out the safety of Aika, who was on her bed in the corner.

After Megan twisted the top off her second beer, she found a pissed-off Becky sitting in a dark corner of the patio with a lit cigarette.

"Hey, girl. How are you?"

The smoke escaped from Becky's lips as she snapped, "Peachy. Just peachy!"

The unnecessary attitude took Megan by surprise but she returned the sentiment, "What crawled up your ass and died?"

"How can you be so nice to him after everything that happened?" There was no way around it; Becky was annoyed that everyone was happy to see Chris. In her opinion, they should hate him for what he did—but no one was listening.

"Oh, stop, Becky. Can't you be happy for Kate just this once and stop being so damn selfish?" Irritated with Becky's unjustified, whiny behavior Megan just walked away.

Once inside, she walked over to Sam. It didn't take her long to notice that Sam was without a drink, so she seductively offered her one. Once again, Sam's cheeks flushed pink with anticipation as she lightly bit her bottom lip.

Suspicious of Megan's intentions, Kate joined her behind the bar and handed her a glass with inquisitive eyes, "What are you doing?"

"Nothing. I'm just being nice."

"You're getting a girl a drink." There it was -- the player's smile that Kate knew so well. Megan was famous for wining a girl and then scooping her up for the evening.

"Yeah. Where's the harm in that?" She knew the motherly stare that was coming next so, trying to dodge it, she maneuvered to the other side of the kitchen to mix the liquors. It was no use, the glare caught up with Megan as Kate reminded her, "You know she's straight."

After she had poured the gin and tonic into the mixer, she looked up at Kate, shook it really hard, and retorted, "So is a noodle until you get it wet."

With a sigh, Kate rolled her eyes, knowing better than to try to convince Megan not to do something stupid. "Be careful."

"Yeah, yeah." With the full martini glass in her hand, she shrugged off Kate's advice. Back in the company of the woman who sparked her interest, Megan handed Sam her drink and led her out onto the patio for a more private conversation.

Chris spotted Kate alone in the kitchen and decided to join her. Behind her shoulder she heard a warm friendly voice whisper, "Is everything OK?"

"Yeah, why?" Washing her hands under the warm water, she glanced back at him.

Concerned, he gently placed a loose strand of hair behind her ear. "You just seemed a bit frazzled about Becky."

"She'll get over herself. Becky tends to be melodramatic."

Humbly, Chris wrapped his arms around her and, in an almost natural reaction, Kate snuggled her head into his chest as he whispered, "I'm not worried about her. I'm worried about you."

After a moment of peace, Kate popped her head up and smiled. "Well, you don't have to worry about me, I'm great."

Assuming they were alone, the fake cough that came from behind, scared her half to death. There, in the middle of the archway, stood Becky with her arms crossed and an annoyed look on her face as she listened to their conversation. She was not pleased.

"Don't mean to interrupt, but I'm just going to go."

"Why?" Upset, Kate took a step away from Chris, but when Becky didn't answer, she gazed up at Chris, silently asking for a moment alone.

His smile faded into a thin line as he nodded at Kate and spoke softly, "I'll give you guys a minute." Before he left he gave Kate a supportive squeeze of the shoulder, letting her know he wouldn't be far away. Still in the archway, Becky refused to step to the side and for an awkward moment, they glared angrily at each other. Finally, Becky tilted her shoulder, and Chris brushed passed her.

Once they were alone, Kate dried her hands and asked, "Why are you leaving?"

"I'm still mad about earlier, and I don't want to be around him, so I'm going home. You have a great night, though." The cynicism still rang in Becky's voice, and it hurt Kate that she was acting like this.

"Becky, there is no reason for you to go."

"Yes, there is. And the sad part is that you can't see it."

Fed up, Becky snatched her keys off the counter and stormed out the front door. In a rush to get as far away as possible, Becky didn't even notice Beth and Charlotte as she bumped into them without even the slightest mumble of an apology. At the doorstep, Kate gazed out after Becky, worried, but thankfully, Chris and Aika were right behind her.

"What was that about?" Beth asked when she reached the front door.

Kate's only response was, "Long story." Silently, Charlotte and Beth nodded, knowing that Becky was pissed off about Chris.

Apathetically, Charlotte moved on, "Good thing we brought lots of beer."

"Good thing. Come on in." Kate stepped to the side to let her friends in, still looking down the empty street in hopes that Becky would turn around.

The inside of the house was decorated in adult décor and Beth complimented, "Cool get up!"

"Who did all of this?" Charlotte inquired.

"It was my friend, Sam," Chris said. The eccentric decorations had Chris blushing like a teenager. He enjoyed the visual imagery as much as the next man, but with Kate next to him he felt uneasy. Walking through the house, he tried not to stare and just when he thought he was safe outside, he found Sam in a dark corner making out with Megan. When he glanced at Kate for her reaction, she appeared to be unfazed by the whole thing.

"Sam!" Embarrassed by her suddenly increased and apparently uncontrollable sexual desires, Chris called Sam away from the temptation - Megan. "This is Charlotte and Beth." Unhappily, but with grins, Sam and Megan left the exclusion of the corner to join the party.

Before Sam reached the group, she quickly struggled to readjust her tangled shirt, and once it was back in place, she introduced herself to Beth and Charlotte. Beth shot Megan an *aren't-you-too-old-for-this* look, but Megan ignored it like she always had.

"So, where is Becky?" Megan asked to divert the attention away from herself and Sam. In the midst of their passionate throes, neither of them noticed that Becky was gone.

"She left," Kate replied sourly.

The room fell awkwardly silent; everyone understood Becky's my-way-or-the-highway policy. The problem was that they were at Kate's house, and Becky was forced to take the highway option – all because she couldn't play nice.

Gathered around the outside patio table, everyone had drinks and the conversation easily turned friendlier.

"Sam started telling me about your project, but I got distracted by her luscious lips and…" Megan got lost gazing into Sam's eyes, and when she heard a distant cough she continued, "Yea…so what is it for?"

"It's a poker tournament to raise money for the community center. Sam came up with the idea."

"I didn't know you played poker," Kate said.

"Yep. Love it." A loving smile appeared on Chris's lips at the adorable confused look on Kate's face; he took a sip of his beer, and then placed his arm around her shoulder.

Kate thought back to the conversation she'd overheard in the community center office and continued to pry. "I thought you were just donating money? That's what you said to Carlos."

"For someone who is so keen on her privacy, you sure don't have a problem eavesdropping. I'm doing that, too. But you told me I had to donate my time as well."

"Huh?" Her eyes narrowed and her lips crinkled as she tried to figure out what in the world he was talking about.

Sloppily, Sam playfully slapped Kate's shoulder and slurred, "The bet you and Chris made while playing air hockey." She said it a bit too loudly. "Don't you remember?"

"I remember. But I lost that bet."

A warm, seductive voice whispered in Kate's ear as Chris clarified, "Sometimes when you lose, you win." Thoughts of that day brought a bright smile to Kate's face while she idly played with her rings.

Before the room could turn too sappy Beth asked, "So, when is the tournament?"

The only detail of the event Chris knew was when to show up, so he let Sam answer. "We haven't decided yet. Planning starts on Monday."

"Let me know. I'm ready to play."

Gently, Charlotte rubbed Beth's leg as she sweetly said, "Honey, you're always ready to play."

"Absolutely."

Megan cleared her throat happily, stood up, and made a toast. "To Kate, for finally coming to her senses!"

Kate crossed her arms defensively. "Senses about what?"

"We all knew that you couldn't stay mad at Chris forever," Megan smiled cheerfully at him.

With her beer bottle lifted in the air, Beth smiled. "And we're glad that you forgave him."

Charlotte raised her rum and coke, and toasted, "We all noticed the positive changes since he's been around, and we're thankful."

Sam followed suit, her hand extended, and her martini glass in the air. "I'm glad that you forgave him, too, because I've missed you."

"Not only is having Kate in my life a blessing, but I'm thankful for the new friendship building here tonight." With deep, warm eyes, Chris looked at Kate, and then lifted his glass with everyone else. In agreement, Aika happily howled and excitedly wagged her tail at his feet.

The table was filled with Kate's closest friends, and she couldn't help but feel extremely blessed to have each one of them in her life. Everyone here had touched her heart in some way or another. She raised her glass and said, "To the friends that make a family. I love all you guys." Everyone exclaimed "Cheers!" simultaneously and clinked their glasses.

But everyone Kate loved was not at this table. She felt guilty about how things ended with Becky, and silently, she made a promise to herself that she would fix it – one way or another.

Chapter Twenty-One

Over the next several weeks, Chris and Sam worked diligently to put together the poker tournament and on the night of the event, Kate was completely blown away. The community center had been transformed into a Vegas casino and the place was packed, not only with local supporters, but also with a few professional poker players Chris was able to convince to show up.

The front of the building was decorated like the entrance to the Grammys. The photographers and fans jostled on each side of the red velvet rope as they waited to see who the next guest would be.

Inside of their limo, Kate's leg began to nervously twitch causing the sequins in her black dress to jingle.

"You look fine! Stop worrying." Chris smiled calmly at her and placed his hand on top of hers.

The fidgeting stopped momentarily. "I'm not worried. I just don't understand why Sam insisted on putting me in something that requires a bottle of Crisco and a fishing line."

Chris smirked and shook his head while he readjusted the collar on his black-and-white tux. "You look amazing, and you let her do it because you love her."

Trying not to blush, Kate brushed off his comment and gazed through the tinted limo window at the overwhelming crowd. "Yeah, yeah, whatever."

There were still three limos in front of theirs; generously, Chris provided some of the staff and Kate's friends with car services for the evening.

Each turn of the tire that brought Kate closer to the large crowd only increased her anxiety. The twitching returned. "I'm not a fan of big crowds."

Proudly, Chris smiled. "I know . . . but remember, it's for a good cause. You started all of this."

"No sir, this is all you." Kate twirled the rings around her index finger, dreading the arrival as the limo inched forward.

"No, this is because of you. If I hadn't met you, none of this would have happened. Give yourself some credit."

The limo stopped for the final time in front of the center, and Kate's heart began to race. A second later, the door closest to Chris flung open and the cheers began to swallow Kate whole. Once Chris was out, he turned toward Kate extending his hand, and helped her to gracefully glide out of the limo.

The night was a roaring success. During one of the breaks, Kate was able to have a conversation with Amy Peterson, a two-time World Poker Tournament champion. A small commotion caught Kate's attention, and she politely had to excuse herself.

At the front door, the staff member who took the invitation had to call over Dan as a guest was causing a problem. When Kate arrived she got Dan's attention by placing her hand on his shoulder. "What's the problem, Dan?"

Taking Kate's distraction as an opportunity, Becky tried to take a step forward, but Dan blocked her again and she yelled, "This asshole won't let me through!"

In defense of his decision, Dan explained to Kate, "She is not in appropriate attire, Ms. Woods." Every invitation was clearly inscribed with *Formal Attire Required,* and there stood Becky with the invitation in her right hand. The sight of Becky was shocking in itself as she refused to return any of Kate's phone calls since the day she stormed out of her house.

"I don't have to follow a dress code; I'm the police!" Becky assertively barked, demanding for Dan to back down.

"It's OK, Dan," Kate said with a smile. "I can handle this." He nodded, stepped aside, and then quietly disappeared into the crowd to look for Alexa.

"Handle this? So now I'm something to *handle?*" Pissed off, Becky tried to storm past her, but Kate stepped in her way and answered, "The way you're acting right now, yes, you are something to handle."

"I can't believe you! I came here to support you, and this is how you're treating me?"

"Support me? You haven't returned a single phone call. I'd swear you're only here to start trouble." It angered her that Becky had the audacity to insinuate that she was a poor friend.

"Sorry," Becky mumbled. "I wanted to see you. Make sure everything's OK." Becky knew she was out of line, but it didn't matter, she was desperate to make Kate see things her way.

"Everything is fine -- no thanks to you," Kate snapped with her arms firmly crossed against her chest.

Desperation rattled through Becky's voice as she gripped Kate's shoulders tightly and proclaimed, "Can't you see that he's changing you? You're not the same Kate I once loved!"

The skin on Kate's arm began to turn red from the indent of Becky's angry fingers. As the hold became tighter and tighter, tears suddenly began to form in Kate's eyes as she cried out, "Becky, you're ..."

"Kate, you need to get away from him! He is turning you into something you're not! You're better than this!"

Kate's cries became louder as she tried to pry Becky's hands off. "Becky! Stop! You're hurting me!" But Becky continued to shake her; she wasn't going to let go until Kate came to her senses. From down the hall, Chris heard Kate's cry and hurried to her side.

When he turned the corner and saw Becky's hands on Kate, he was furious. "What's going on here?" Becky quickly dropped her hands, and Chris instantly pulled Kate out of the way.

Enraged, Becky stated, "You're interrupting a personal conversation!"

"A conversation doesn't include you physically putting your hands on her!" He glared down at Becky, and she took a small step back. This was the last straw; he could put up with her annoying comments and childish behavior toward him, but the moment she put her hands on Kate, all bets were off.

"This is none of your business, so butt out!" Becky's fist began to tighten in preparation for a fight.

"It is my business when you put your unwanted hands on Kate!" Silent, Kate stood behind Chris as he continued to defend her.

"Who says they're unwanted?"

Furious, Chris stepped closer to Becky. "When a woman says 'stop,' that's normally an indication that your hands are unwanted," he snarled, threateningly.

Ever so gently Kate tried to pull Chris away from Becky, placing herself in between them. It took a moment, but Chris's muscles finally relaxed, and he took a small step back.

Glancing between Chris and Becky, Kate's burden was heavy. "You two need to stop this. I can't handle all of this fighting."

Gently Chris placed a stray strand of hair behind her ear. "Kate, maybe you should go get yourself a drink," he suggested softly.

"No! Don't try to pacify me." Aggravated, she shooed his hand away. "I'm not a puppy you can pet, and everything will be better!" Ecstatic to hear Kate speak to Chris in that manner, Becky chuckled under her breath. *Maybe there was still hope for her yet.*

Calmly, Chris spoke, "Sweetie, I was just suggesting ... "

"I know exactly what you were suggesting! I don't need you treating me like a child."

The sight of them arguing was a blissful image to Becky, and when the laughter erupted from her lungs, both Kate and Chris glared at her as if she lost her mind.

A forceful step in Becky's direction from Kate was all that was needed to silence her giggles. "And you! Becky, I love you, but this is completely unacceptable. You came here looking for a fight. You're going to have to get over your issues with Chris. I want him here, and you're going to have to accept that if you want to be my friend. Everyone else has accepted him, so why can't you?"

"Because I know you better than everyone else! I refuse to give up," Becky pleaded. Quickly, Becky swooped Kate into her arms, kissing her passionately. Chris stood there speechless, watching the two women intertwine.

When the kiss was finished, Kate remained frozen, unsure how to react. Becky waited patiently for a sign . . . but it never arrived. When Kate looked at Chris and she saw his sadness, guilt consumed her, and she requested, "Can you give us a minute?"

Chris nodded and slowly walked away, then Kate turned toward a radiant Becky and began, "Becky . . . "

"I knew you would pick me over him," Becky glowed, feeling victorious. It had finally happened; Kate picked her, and Chris would disappear a broken, defeated man. It quickly dawned on Becky that Kate didn't have the same glowing look that she felt. In fact, she looked disappointed.

"Becky. I'm not picking anyone. I don't love you like you love me." Every hopeful, exultant expression of Becky's faded. In her eyes it was clear that Kate had shattered her heart. Given Kate's good-hearted nature she wanted to comfort her friend, but when she moved toward her, Becky instantly shied away.

"I don't mean to be cruel, you should know."

"You're wrong! You're confused. You'll see one day, I'm the one that you are meant to be with. Not him," Becky passionately argued.

"Becky, I'm not confused. Please stop saying that I'm choosing him. You're making me choose, and I can't choose between the two of you."

"I can't stand here and watch you do this. You're destroying yourself, and you can't even see what's happening."

Becky turned her back, and instantly, Kate grabbed her arms pleading, "Becky! Please don't do this to me!"

"Then tell him to leave!"

Insulted by the mere idea, Kate's mouth slightly parted, and her eyes glanced down to the tile floor as she embarrassingly mumbled, "I can't do that."

"Kate, you made your choice." Disappointed, Becky shook her hand free from Kate and angrily stormed out the door. Tears streaming down her cheeks, Kate turned to run to the restroom and ran right into Chris's arms.

"I'm so sorry Kate," he whispered softly. "I understand if you want me to leave." Unable to speak, she just shook her head as he gently kissed the tears away. After she was secure in his embrace, Chris whispered, "She'll come around."

The last hand of the tournament was nail-biting and nerve-racking as the final two players, Amy Peterson and Beth, were both all in. The entire ballroom held its breath as the dealer turned over the river: a queen. Beth jumped from her seat, ecstatic that she beat Amy Peterson with two queens.

After the game, it didn't take long for the guests to be ushered into another room where Beth would be presented with her winnings and other speeches would be made. Chris was assigned the honor of presenting the winner of the tournament with a larger-than-life-size check, but before he could do that there was something he needed to say.

Lightly, Chris tapped on the microphone, and the echo told him to start.

"Good evening, everyone. I'm honored that each and every one of you were able to join us in the re-opening of the community center. Before I present the award to our poker tournament winner, I want to take a moment to thank the person responsible for tonight. An active volunteer for the past three years, she has inspired many children, including myself." A small chuckle erupted from the crowd. "Through example she has shown me how to live a more fulfilling life as she is the type of person that people look up to. This amazing woman is Katherine Woods."

The spotlight swiveled through the crowd in search of Kate, and once it shined on her, people turned smiling and clapped for her. Politely, she thanked a few nearby people and prayed that the excessive attention would disappear quickly. When the spotlight returned to the stage, her smile quickly faded away. *I'm going to kill him,* she thought as she snuck out of the room.

When Chris finished his speech, he presented a giant check to Beth, made out to the Woods Charity Foundation in the amount of three hundred thousand dollars. Happily, Beth and Chris posed for the photographers.

After the presentation, it didn't take long for the crowd to mingle amongst themselves. Still on stage, Chris gazed through the crowd looking for Kate, but he turned up empty. He managed to make his way outside and found her leaning against a swing set. In the moonlight, he watched the silver hue glimmer on her dress. Quietly, his eyes glazed across the softness of her curves until his hand could no longer resist, and he gently wrapped them around her tiny waist. The feel of large hands startled her, until she realized it was just Chris.

"So, are you mad?" he cautiously whispered.

Without so much of a glance toward him, Kate twirled her fingers around her rings and mumbled, "Why would I be mad at you?"

"I put you in the spotlight." It wasn't even a second thought for his arms to tighten around her midsection.

"Hmmm . . . " she said, with a playful smile. "Nope . . . I'm not mad. Your intentions were good. But I'll get you back for it." Comfortably, her fingertips idly stroked his forearm.

"I wouldn't expect anything less." Staring up at the stars, Chris continued, "This reminds me of the night we met."

"What? This isn't anything like the night we met."

"Not the part you remember . . . " There was no need to look down; Chris already knew the weird look Kate had given him. "Before you decided to take my head off . . . "

"You deserved it."

"Of course. But before you decided to take my head off, I had seen you standing out on the veranda, staring out into the garden. Your hair glistened in the moonlight. It was obvious that you were not in your element, but somehow you found peace staring out into the stillness. It was astounding."

"Then why did you say those things?"

"I knew it would get a rise out of you. I wanted to make an impression."

"That was the first impression you wanted me to have of you?"

"Yes. When I showed up at your door, you knew exactly who I was. You couldn't forget me even if you tried." In sweet frustration, Kate growled under her breath and narrowed her eyes as she fell back into his warm arms. Quietly, Chris whispered into Kate's ear, "You love me."

"Yeah. Yeah. Whatever."

Together they smiled and gazed up at the stars.

About the Author

Tabitha grew up in Virginia, outside of Washington D.C., but moved to Orlando to attend UCF (Go Knights!) where she received a Bachelor of Science in Business Management. It was five years ago when she met her husband, who is a graduate from Deland High; two years ago, they moved back to Deland. During this time, she has fallen in love with the town and community.

Currently, she is an active alumna of Kappa Alpha Theta and serves on the Advisory Board as the Facility Management Advisor for the Epsilon Theta Chapter at Stetson University. During her free time, she loves being with her family (although they are usually working on their small family farm), traveling, and of course, watching college football.

Connect with Tabitha:
www.tabithayoung.com
Facebook: https://www.facebook.com/Tabitha-Young-297885047491814/
Instagram: @TabithaYoungAuthor
Twitter: @TabithaAuthor